C000069002

y.t. and his holiness

y.t. and
his holiness

Jennifer Rhead

Best wishes,
Jennifer Rhead.

HONNO MODERN FICTION

Published by Honno
'Ailsa Craig', Heol y Cawl, Dinas Powys
Bro Morgannwg CF6 4AH

First impression 1998
© Jennifer Rhead

ISBN 1 870206 33 9

All rights reserved. No part of this book may be reproduced,
stored in a retrieval system, or transmitted, in any form or
by any means, electronic, mechanical, photocopying,
recording or otherwise, without clearance
from the publishers.

British Library Cataloguing in Publication Data
A catalogue record for this book is available from the British Library

**Published with the financial support of the
Arts Council of Wales**

Cover design by Jo Hughes

Printed in Wales by Dinefwr Press, Llandybïe

For Laura,
From one heartache to another.

ACKNOWLEDGEMENTS

Without the years of unremitting love, patience and support of my heroically uncomplaining husband, Don, Laura's story might never have been completed.

Ni all geiriau gyfleu fy niolch a'm cariad, f'anwylyd.
Boed ddoe yn atgof, ac yfory'n fore newydd.

Special thanks to Jean M Jones who, by combining acupuncture with an unfailingly sympathetic ear, has so graciously put up with my periodic bouts of whingeing.

Laura awoke as from a dream
Laughed in the innocent old way.

(C Rossetti: *Goblin Market*)

We all come home to our own selves – always in the end.
There is no greater folly than the talk of a new life
that is about to start. We are what we are and thus remain.

(Hans Fallada: *Who Once Eats Out of the Tin Bowl*)

PROLOGUE

Lumbering and unseeing, she stumbled across the landing in the direction of the bathroom. It was night time but she didn't know. Therefore, the darkness of the unlit landing made no difference, did not impede in any way, her erratic progress. In terms of awareness she might have been a giant, ambulant amoeba and yet, within the darkness that filled her head, a small part of her brain resolutely retained its link with the screaming bladder. Thus, like some blind, Pavlovian reject, she instinctively tried to obey the silent command, striving to reach the bladder-emptying place, trying so hard to be a good little girl.

She fell many times and, after each fall, took varying lengths of time to regain her feet. Because of these frequent interruptions, long before she reached the lavatory, the poor bladder began to give up the ghost and, in an attempt to save itself from the effects of explosion or implosion or whatever, began to relinquish some of its contents. In other words, she began to piss herself.

Poor, blind, programmed bladder. Even with the exquisiteness of release so near it desperately tried to comply with the instruction snapping across the synapses, refusing to completely empty itself until its mindless shambles of an owner had reached the bathroom and somehow managed to position her swaying buttocks over the edge of the lavatory pan.

No matter that, after a feeble attempt at pulling them down, her jeans were concertina-ed round the tops of her thighs; or that the crotch of her knickers has moved no more than a few centimetres thus acting as a crude sieve for the piss as it sprayed in all directions, soaking the jeans, running down her thighs and over the seat and sides of the pan; no matter, because the long suffering bladder could rest easy once again. A small mystery was why she hadn't just pissed in the bed. She'd done so many times in the past. Even when less drunk and/or stoned than at present. Feebly, her hands flapped in an attempt to pull the wet jeans up over her buttocks. She fell many times. Once, on her knees and with her head resting on the side of the grubby pan, she vomited fitfully. Even then her hands continued their useless flittering as she tried to cover her nakedness.

1

Eventually giving up, she crawled to the door and, leaning heavily against the frame, dragged herself into a semi-upright position. A life-sized marionette, manipulated by either a clown or a psycho, she clung with picking, plucking fingers to the door jamb. After a few more crumpled falls (as though the invisible puppeteer, growing bored, had flung the wires to the floor in disgust) she seemed to forget about the need to cling to anything. Head lolling, knees buckling, she stood for brief moments between either meeting the floor in a strange almost wor-shipping embrace, or threatening to. It would have been so simple just to have staggered across the short landing to the safety of her room but instead she lurched to the left so that she was positioned, swaying violently, at the top of the stairs.

The brain, though able to communicate so well with the bladder, failed miserably when it was required to send even the most tenuous of warnings to her lower limbs. So because they had received nothing by way of an alarm to persuade them otherwise, her hapless size eights precipitated her into mid-air where she remained, a lumpy, rubbery projectile, for a micro-second or so before slamming into the facing wall of the stairwell. Stabbing needles of pain tried to convey a message of sorts as, making no attempt to stand, she began to crawl up the few steps back to the landing. By doing so she made reasonable progress and there was the advantage of being able to rest her head, for as long as she wanted, on each tread.

At last she reached the comparative safety of the landing but had no knowledge of it. The only thing that moved in the thick, black swamp in her head was a tiny threadworm of instinct that somehow conveyed to her the fact that she no longer needed to continue crawling upwards. Encouraged, perhaps, by these faint waverings, she made the error of trying to stand up. It took her a good while but she managed it and stood swaying so much that it seemed she was bouncing. She could have turned right and ultimately reached her bedroom; she could have turned left and made for the bathroom where, in time, she would have sobered up. She chose neither – if choice, as such, had any say in the matter. Instead, she began to weave and stagger around in a stumbling semblance of a circle before putting her left – or was it her right? – foot into the void once more. Plummeting down the short flight, she hit the wall more heavily this time and lay motionless in a whimpering heap. A dark, yellowish liquid seeped from one corner of her mouth and her eyes flickered as though in response to very small electric pulses. Unseeing, her eyes appeared as black as the darkness inside her head. Unmoving, she lay for some time. Maybe half an hour, maybe longer. Now and then her eyelids would flicker rapidly and her mouth give a slight twitch.

When she came to, using the wall as a support, she inched herself upright. Still there was no sense of awareness. Nothing in the darkness but a blind reaching out in response to an atavistic urge to reach a place of safety.

Out of countless errors committed and wrong decisions taken throughout her life, she now made the most disastrous, as, instead of repeating her previous action of crawling up the stairs to the landing, she turned to face the lower and much longer flight. Once again she took a step into nothingness. Relaxed she may have been in her advanced state of drunkenness but it made no difference. This time there were three times as many steps and the ancient, cast-iron radiator attached to the wall at the foot of the stairs silently accepted her arrival as though it were the sole reason for its existence these past sixty-odd years.

Unwilling sacrifice, she tried to call out but was not able to manage more than a gurgling sound in the back of her throat. Because her head had suffered the full force of the impact she quickly lost all consciousness. Brightly and eagerly, her fresh blood paid homage to the thuggish, corrugated contraption, revitalising flaking patches of rust and grime in its desire to please. But, because most of the haematoblasts had formed a thick, dark pool at the side of her head, the radiator was left looking more ugly and sinister than before as though someone had thought to do a paint job, then lost interest after the first few crimson daubs.

Lying face down on the filthy, gapped and gaping floor she breathed, and her breath disturbed layers of old cigarette butts and ash carpeted among a scattering of deformed and discoloured polystyrene containers, empty beer cans and things too far gone to be identifiable.

Some time – hours – later, she stirred. There was no lessening of the darkness inside her head but it wasn't quite the same as before. It was, but it wasn't. It was different. Different because it was no longer solely the darkness of the blind drunk. There was an added dimension and, within that dimension, there had begun to form a nucleus of fear. The beginnings of a knowledge that something was wrong; that she was in some sort of danger.

By conquering one, sometimes two, steps at a time and resting for varying periods – a few minutes here, half-an-hour or so there – she managed to crawl up the two flights of stairs. Often, it seemed she might lose consciousness where she lay. Maybe she did. But then, small amounts of bilious vomit would erupt from her mouth to lie glistening amid delicate tendrils of vapour. Perhaps because of the proclivity to her nostrils, these rancid little heaps seems to act as a spur, prodding her once again into sluggish, erratic action.

3

The shattered skull gave no sensation of pain. Only a heavy numbness. On the injured side, her head looked curiously concave, so that her features appeared distorted. Both her face and neck were wet. She was crying. How strange. Why should she cry? Amoebae don't cry – do they? Heavy perspiration added to the wetness. Nothing to do with the heroic effort of mastering the stairs but the clamminess of deep shock.

Much later, still crawling, she reached her bedroom. The fact that it was her bedroom she arrived at must be put down to chance. For a long time, she lay on the floor at the side of the bed. The bare floorboards were as dirty as the stairs and reeking of stale urine. After many failed attempts she managed to drag herself onto the soiled and malodorous mattress, falling heavily at the side of the man whose name she hadn't bothered to ask. All she'd needed to know was that he'd wanted a blow job, was willing to pay well over the odds for it and needed a place to sleep for the night.

Because she needed the money she'd obliged with the blow job and because she'd been too out of it to care, had allowed him to share her mattress. Did she know what she was doing as she struggled, like some huge damaged insect, to get on to the bed? Impossible to tell.

He didn't even stir, the unnamed punter, when she landed like an oversized sack of King Edwards at his side. But later on, when he began to surface and recent memories began to stir, he tried to wake the silent, unmoving mound to see if she'd oblige him with – well, a little something or other. By way of bonus, you might say. A hand job would do, though Christ knew he'd laid out enough for the bitch. What a night! Gave amazing head. Give her that. Getting no response from his elbowing and nudging he raised himself semi-upright, muttering that a hand job would be ace, man, if she didn't feel like giving head. Then he found himself being given head like he'd never ever dreamt of having. It took a few seconds for him to register what he was seeing and, even then, he had difficulty in believing the fragments of bone winking up at him through the crushed skull. He did come to believe it though and when he did he was off the bed and out of both the room and the squat in as short a time as it takes to exhale a breath. As he hadn't removed any of his clothing the previous night, his flight was unimpeded by the need to stop and replace any.

She didn't know that she was alone. The man who had departed with such alacrity, whose name she hadn't bothered to ask, was only one of the number of nameless punters whom she serviced, in one way or another, as a means of financing her little habits. There was no regular clientele as such. When she needed the money for a fix or a smoke or just a few cans of Special, she found herself a punter. Simple as that. Like any commodity. She had it, they wanted it and were prepared to pay for it. Economics of the market place. Nicely rounded equation.

Blood was still seeping, though much more slowly now, through the matted mess of hair. Short, spiky dark hair that looked as though she'd taken the scissors to it whilst on a bender. Because her body was so bloated she looked shorter than her probable height of a metre three-quarters. Under the booze-induced oedema, the oval structure of her face was discernible, though only at certain angles. The cheekbones were high and would have been pronounced. The lashes, long, thick and black, rested on the puffy cheeks and the lips showed, even in their flaccidity, traces of sensuality. In three months time she would be thirty years old but looked, irrespective of the effects of the accident, at least forty-five.

Her breathing had become shallower. Strangely, the expression on her mottled face was one of serenity. Swollen and dirty, the long, tapering fingers were curved upwards, giving the hands a cupped position, like grubby lilies thoughtfully placed at either side of her.

It was late evening. She didn't know. She knew nothing. There was nothing. Except the darkness. Inside and out.

There were several other people living in the squat. People like herself. Druggies, alkies, psychos or just drop-outs. Take your pick. They were all there in one of a terrace of condemned houses. Sheets of plywood and corrugated metal blocked the windows and door though an occasional pane of cracked and grimy glass glinted hopefully. Nobody missed her. They were all out of it. On another planet. Maybe one of the less stoned/drunk/freaked out might have said something along the lines of – 'have any o' yous seen ol' Blojo aroun' or what?'

Assuming anyone of the residents had made such an observation, nobody made any attempt to act on it. No one came to her room to see if she was there or not. Those still capable of thought may have remembered that she'd had a punter the previous night and assume that she might still be turning a trick. If not with the same punter, then with another. In other words, no one gave a shit.

There was no furniture in the room. And why have curtains when there were no windows, apart from a single, cracked pane that was so dirt encrusted it was difficult to distinguish it from the haphazard nailing together of bits of ply and hardboard and rusty sheeting? No rug on the floor. Not even any lino. Not as much as a chair alleviated the starkness. Only the bed and what few articles of clothing she possessed scattered around its precincts. Unconcerned that they were part of a clutter of litter and filth, they lay among crumpled vile-smelling papers that had once held fish and chips or pie and chips or just chips; countless specimens of the ubiquitous polystyrene take-aways; crushed rosettes of toilet tissue containing every sort of bodily excretion (dehydrated); used condoms welded by their contents to the floor and even a used sanitary pad, wasp-waisted and feebly sporting the jaded colours of its none too recent whereabouts, peering dejectedly from the debris.

A number of flying insects buzzed happily and busily around the room. There were rich pickings to be had for the airborne carnivores as they were soon to discover. Several were already showing an interest in the drying jelly of the wound, settling industriously for a while before buzzing angrily off into another high-pitched quarrel with their fellows. Excitement was mounting. The news was spreading fast. Also of interest were the odours and moisture surrounding the areas immediate to the damp jeans and knickers. Indeed, a few of the more enterprising were already crawling contentedly around her lower belly and groin.

Contrasting rhythms of rock, rap and other soon began to blast through the building as the residents began to emerge from the fog of the previous night's excesses and embark on a repeat. The already fragile structure seemed to shudder with alarm while the corrugated sheeting rattled wildly as though trying to find an accompanying beat of its own. The solitary, naked light bulb skeetered and jittered, sending out distress flares of frayed and dusty cobweb strands.

Much later, when the music had died and the building stood quiet, something – a mouse? – appeared from one of the corners of the room and began to sift twitchily through the cornucopia spread all over the floor and filling its mouse eyes and mouse brain. If it was a mouse.

There was no discernible movement from the body lying on the bed.

DAY ONE

August 17th

Je–e–sus did yours truly have a mother of a head – the mother of all mothers, man. Gotta cut down on the voddies. Must've been a real blinder. An' what the fuck's with the frigging cold – like middle of bleeding winter – where's that rag of a poxy blanket? Grab it for Chrissake an' cover up freezing bod – could be marinating in bath full of ice-cubes it's so fucking cold.

Just stretch the old pins a tad – waking up time easing of the bones reach out an' get hold of the pigging blanket. Gently does it so's not to let off klaxon in already shrieking noddle.

Can't move. Can't fucking move. Not a digit. One hundred per cent undiluted zilch.

Stay cool, y.t. For Chrissake stay cool. Work it out – think back – what the fuck happened last night? Some fucking shit must've been shifted to send y.t. into total seize-up. Too much shit? Bad shit? There'd been an awful lot o' voddies on the go. Voddies not to blame though. Been mates for far too long ha ha. Did some speed. Bad move. With a punter. Which – what punter? Blowjob. Musta been the blowjob. Been so fucking grateful. Cringe-making arsehole. Christ knows how many joints. Not that they counted. Like voddies. Old pals. Been any E on offer? Can't fucking remember. Wouldn't put it past. Not keen but . . . trouble with E a wee tab slips down before you know it.

Christ, what a bitch being so frigging cold – and where in the fuck are all these poxy crawlies coming from? Creeping all over phizog as though they had a frigging franchise – fuck off, vermin!

Shouldn't'ta done that. Bad move, y.t. Not only no one at home when dickhead arm told to put frighteners on creepy-crawlies; no verbal frighteners coming outta gob. Lips moving – tongue flapping – tonsils stretching like elastic band. Might as well not've bothered. Big fucking zero in the sound stakes. Come an' shack up with y.t., Jonesy, an' pick up a few pointers about panic, man! Bastard's got a real hard on.

Chill out bitch, for Chrissake. Oh nice one, y.t. O level English (*thought* about taking it – good enough, ain't it?) coming in useful

7

at last – like middle of frigging winter an' chill out's the best y.t. can soddin' come up with – why in the fuck is it so cold, middle of August, for Chrissake. C'mon babe, stop bitching an' try an' get it together – work things out, man. Done a trick; done some shit; too much shit; wrong shit; whatever. What's it matter. Ended up with real bad trip. Worst trip ever. What day today? Not Giro day. Definitely not Giro day. For what it's poxy worth. Coupla bottles o' voddie, few cans o' Special, coupla packs o' ciggies an' y.t. well an' truly cleaned out. An' how does y.t. know it ain't Giro day? 'Cos pals woulda been knocking shit outta the door to get y.t. on the move. Must be Monday. Done the blowjob on the Sunday night. Just nipped out for a pack o' Menthol an' this dude'd come up an' asked straight out, no messing, for a blowjob, man! Produced wad o' notes, said to name price an' whatever shit y.t. fancied – name it an' he'd deliver. Couldn't believe poxy luck – not every day babe gets asked to name price, eh? (What *was* price? Couldn't remember any dosh pressing sweaty little mitt – must've, for fuck's sake! Y.t. not the sort o' babe to suck off any old unwashed dick for a few voddies an' a coupla joints! No way, man!)

Monday it is, dudes. An' Monday's effin' visitin' day, innit? Holy shit!

Shout for help. No good. No dulcits. Anyway, even if pins decided to function all of a sudden, far too late for friggin' visit. *Was* it visitin' day? Every fortnight, innit. Been last week. Clear as piss. Coulda been yesterday. Had it been yesterday? The visit? 'Course it hadn't been yesterday, stupid fuck. Yesterday Sunday. Today Monday. Even if day for poxy visit (which it ain't, retard) forget it.

Big bag full o' floppy fear flumping around under ribs. Dodgy. Give a lot for a good spew – chuck bastard outta cosy little nest it's made – an' where the fuck're those mothers of so-called pals? Archie, Mo, Lennie even, at a pinch, bastard Clunie? Loada wankers, man. They'd be queuing at the door if they thought there was a chance of a hand-out. Not that y.t. minded helpin' out a pal in need. Not every friggin' week, though. They'd do the same, wouldn' they? 'Ceptin' they never had any dosh. Other than their poxy Giros. An' then only for as long as it took them to cash 'em an' cross the road to the bleedin' Offie. Just as well y.t. never in shit street, man. One o' the lucky dudes. Able to earn a bit on the side, ha ha. Friggin' amazing what a john was willing to come across with. Even for a miserable hand job.

So y.t. had missed out on a visit? First time in living memory, ha ha. Could always try to go tomorrow. How come, bitch? Visiting day is visiting day. End of story. If missed it, will have to wait fortnight till next one. Just as well. Even if poxy lock-jaw only lasted rest of day (at max) y.t.'d feel like a used bog-wipe. Ace excuse for a cop out – ha ha ha. Not every day yours truly woke up one hundred per cent functionally challenged! Definitely gotta lay off the coke and the poppers. No dosh anyway. Not unless turn couple of tricks p.d.q. Can't manage without voddies. And few joints. Lifelines. In for a right bollocking for not visiting. Dysfunction, even on such a scale, wouldn't wash as much as a g-string with his holiness. Perhaps had better go. How? Such a bloody long way. Where the fuck was it? Frigging Oxford or something. Y.t. could handle it. Wherever it was. Could handle him. Call frigging tune. No one else could. Only y.t. Big fucking deal. Only y.t. left. Y.t. and his holiness. Just the two of them. No need for any other fucker.

Stay cool, babe. Already worked this one out. No visit this week. Been last week – braindead! Couldn't handle a visit. Couldn't cope with being shagged. Truckers weren't too bad – quick in coming to the point ha ha and free and easy with the readies. Usually. One bastard had kicked y.t. out of the cab – after he'd started the effing truck! Lucky to have got away with a few bruises. Sometimes even that was better than what BMW arseholes and the like wanted. Mostly blowjobs. Mostly without a rubber. Tenner difference. Gotta think of it. Jerking off whilst staring up snatch. Pathetic. Boring. And fucking cold if they had a job getting their act together. Much worse though, were the sick fucks who wanted to shove something other than their dick up. But what was a babe to do? No dosh – no nosh. Savvy? By the time arrived at nick, all y.t. wanted was a kip. Had to go through poxy motions. Especially with cloth-head screws. Bunch of losers. Always cracking pathetic two-liners. Sometimes, y.t. couldn't get gist. Put it down to a state of noddle at the time. If bollocks of a hangover, understandable not able to tune into poxy chestnut cracked by arsehole failure. Didn't like slimy looks that passed to and fro, either. If noddle was OK y.t.'d laugh like a drain whether or not caught drift of poxy un-funny spouting outta gob of frigging deadbeat screw. Made bastards snigger all the more. Arseholes.

Hey man – y.t.'s prob'ly in same shit as whole lotta other cool dudes – couldn't get more cool than Hendrix an' Morrison. Nice one, y.t. Cool is fucking dead-on fucking right. Whatta sick bitch retard picking on a coupla long-gone stiffs! Must be loads o' famous dudes still strutting their stuff – wouldn't exactly blab about uncool shit like y.t.'s little prob, would they?

Sick o' this cold, man. Chill out any more an' y.t.'ll end up on a slab ha ha. What is it with these sick-fuck funnies, bitch? Stiffs're uncool enough without bringing in fucking slabs. For Chrissake get few remaining brain cells onto something – something with a bit o' frigging warmth to it. Anything – anything to get away from this freezing fucking cold.

Cold or warm, it didn't really matter because the eyes, like the pale eggs of a hedgerow bird, were being covered by the sliding lids and the mouth hung slack, allowing a thread of viscous saliva to glisten out of one corner. As it began to leave its snail-y trail down one side of her chin, the eyelids went broody, tucking the eggs well under as she drifted into the darkness.

Warmth. Way out, off the fucking planet warmth. Doused, from noddle to tootsies, with heat. Must've died an' gone to heaven – or hell ha ha. Trembling around tonsils. Nix verbals. Here comes that enterprising old fuck panic, trying to get a grip on y.t.'s guts. No way dickhead, no way. Piss off an' jerk off someplace else. Y.t. having dream to end all dreams. Would rub peepers but can't. *Must* be a dream, man. What else, for Chrissake?

There was y.t. Baby y.t. Baby yours truly sitting like a little buddha in a minty-green number wriggling fat little buddha tootsies in the gritty, toasty warmth of crunchy, cornflake-coloured sand. Y.t. sitting on the beach. A tiny tot of a buddha. No more than two – can't be two – birthday in October – middle of heatwave – must be summer – not more than two so must be about eighteen months – whatever, y.t. sitting patting fat little mitts onto the sand, flattening it then lifting podgy handfuls and letting it run through dumpy digits whilst gawping at it like a right little retard. Whaddya know, dudes, the radioactive cornflake sand pressing its geiger counter mitts onto baby buddhas fat little buddha-bum – 's nearly enough to make the totty wee thing have a totty wee come, man!

Really need to rub peepers, man. This cannot be happening. How was it possible? There was Mum. There she was, sitting on

10

the crushed cornflakes, reading a book an' looking all yummy and golden-summery. Just like a Mum should.

Bexhill-on-Sea. Fucking Bexhill-on-Sea would you believe! Mum an' baby y.t. sitting on poxy Bexhill-on-Sea beach. Must be summer of '65. Why? Donno. Just 'cos. That's why. There'd been a frigging heatwave in the May of '65. There *was* a heatwave – there *is* a fucking heatwave, man, an' Mum an' y.t. are sat right in the frigging middle of it! Mum'd got sunburnt, stupid bitch. Bad enough to have to stay indoors for a few days wearing a huge, tenty thing an' clarting her charred flesh with dollops of calamine. Y.t.'d been OK 'cos of surplus of sun cream an' sun-hats. Daft bitch, Mum. Always overdid the beach thingy when the currant bun put in an appearance. Suffered far more from missing out on all the relentless infra-red or ultra-violet or whatever than by the raw meat simmering under the calamine. Not that she only went for walkies an' sitting on the beach in Gobi desert weather. Oh no. Mum'd be striding out in all poxy weather fronts, legging it along the promenade trundling y.t. ahead of her in a second-hand pushchair. Loved the sea did Mum. Almost say she was addicted to it. If such a thing was poss. Outdoors sort, wasn't she. Always had been. Spent most of her time running to the sea when she was a wee bairn ha ha.

Y.t. at the other end of the spectrum. Could not put up with all that ozone-y crap. Christ – the come-factor of the hot sand squeezing through tootsies!

Bexhill was where Mum an' Dad had first met an' then set up flat. An' where y.t. had popped the pod. Not Bexhill as such. Near as dammit. Mince pies had first come unglued in St. Helen's hossy. Just down the road.

Wonder what piece o' crappy prose Mum's got her hooter buried in. Something deep an' meaningful, eh Mum? Been doing a bit o' studying before Dad shoved his oar in. Trying to make up for leaving school at fifteen. Or something. Never works Mum. Took her one an' only O level through a correspondence course. Only just scraped through. Sad.

University entrance. That'd been the idea. Heap o' shite. Still at it aren't you, you daft bitch. The self-fucking-education shit. Wonder why she looks so yummy? Fat lotta good it did her, all that poxy reading. C'mon Mum, let's have a butchers – must be one of the heavies – no it ain't – yes it is, can just make out the big D – no, it ain't, it's dorky *Creative Dressmaking* for Chrissake!

Full o' friggin' surprises, is Mum. Must be in heaven, man. Yours truly must've popped clogs an' ended up (surely some mistake?) on the other side of pearly gates. (Less o' the graveyard funnies, retard bitch – OK?) Must be heaven for Mum too 'cos, wot a surprise, y.t.'s digits ain't glued to roof of gob! Sudden ripple of bad vibes disturbing idyll. Mum's slapping Dork Manual down on sand and her mush has gone into Aberdeen granite mode. Y.t. not to blame, though, for sudden warp in heaven's cloth 'cos Mum's staring right over buddha-bum's noddle.

Christ – this sodding heat's unbearable – why doesn't the stupid bitch show a bit o' motherly concern an' find a shady nook for buddha-bum? Or take it down to the poxy sea for a dip before it shrivels into a crisp in this microwaving hell?

There's the sea for Chrissake, only a waddle or two away, playing the King of the Wankers as usual, with an army of micro-dot magicians hidden in its gob all mouthing endless curlicues of silver lurex ribbon onto the rasping sand.

Why the fuck ain't baby buddha in final stages of heatstroke, man? Sitting on fat little arse showing no sign at all of fainting/sizzling/melting/frying. And the sand! All this white-hot grit drying gob out something chronic – look at the retard for Chrissake! Shoving its sandy mitt into its cakehole – taking it out again pretty sharpish but leaving gob filled with burning grit. Think about something, babe, anything to get little grey cells off death by dehydration scene. Not possible. Baby buddha *is* y.t. Y.t. *is* baby buddha. And yet isn't. Else baby y.t. would be frying alive. Frying to death. Whatever. Losing it, man. Y.t. must be losing it. Part of bad trip, man. Must've taken acid. No. Never, never take acid. Fucked up once. Never again. E. Could've had a tab. Don't usually. But could've.

Have a butchers at Mum, buddha-bum. Picked up Dork Manual but mind's not on masterly prose 'cos she keeps peering across the beach in a nor' westerly direction. Something/someone's winding her up. Should've twigged. Who else but the Fag lady. Prototype for Cruella. Dad's arseholing apology of a mother. Ma McPhee. Enough to wipe the grin right off anyone's mush, never mind poor ol' Mum's. An' if that wasn't enough of a downer, she had her brood of drones parked around the picnic spread, grinning witlessly like a bunch of Evangelicals stoned out of their skulls on whatever it was Evangelicals got stoned on. Visions of the Second Coming? Whatever that might be. A First Coming would see y.t. all right, man – ha ha ha.

Debbie, must be about sixteen. Big lumpy tits, gobful of metal glittering ominously as the broiling buggering sun smacked into it. Tits not big, or good, enough to take everyone's peepers off all the ironmongery keeping her gnashers under control. David. Eleven or twelve and a prize arsehole. Martin, a precious little seven year old mincing fart. Far more of a babe than the hefty, steel-reinforced Deb, man.

All three drones half-siblings of Dad's an' all looking more like him that he did. Ha ha. Even though they'd been spawned as a result of the Fag lady's fucking with the butcher whose shop, as well as whose dick, she'd served whilst hubby away fighting in war. Came home unexpectedly to find butcher and Fag lady in mid-hump. Walked out there and then, leaving two year old Dad and three an' a half year old Uncle Simon to be butcher's boys. Nice little dollop of useless fucking info – managed to keep brain cells on the go for a few mos – get them to work on something other that the fact that THERE'S SOME POOR BITCH LYING HELPLESS ABOUT TO FRY IN THIS GOD AWFUL FUCKING FURNACE!!

Look at the old witch – leaning across the picnic cloth, dolloping nosh on to the plates held out by the arse-licking groupies – still managing to have her inseparable pal hanging outta the side of her gob. Dangling like some wagging little extension of her dental equipment, it never got in the way of her speech; her inability to sneer, jeer, leer, hiss, spit vitriol, vomit venom etc. Or her being able to carry out her role as a special edition, hall-marked Cunt. Always making one of her fucking 'funnies'. Euphemism for humiliating, belittling, emasculating and eviscerating whatever poor, unsuspecting twat happened to be in her sights at the time.

There they sat, vacuous grins plastered across their mugs, within a few metres and fully aware of Mum an' the barbecuing baby buddha. Impossible not to be. Aware. So close must they have passed by. Something must've been said during the course of the traipse across the beach. Instructions must've been issued by the animated ashtray. She must've located the pair of lepers with her laser vision an' primed the Evangelicals to behave accordingly. How else could the traipse have ended with them stuffing their cake'oles within spitting distance of the pariahs? Could hear the nicotine-freak instructing the hellish brood, with a dimpled chuckle (good on dimpled chuckles; one of her specialities). 'Let's play "embarrass the lepers" dears. Time it. See how long it takes

Mummy Leper to admit defeat and slink off with baby leper back to their leper lair.'

(Getting a tad carried away there y.t., ain'tcha? So fucking what – anything, anything to get brain cells away from the fact that y.t. CAN'T FUCKING MOVE.)

Didn't work, did it, you old witch. Mum wouldn't get up an' leave – she wouldn't give the bastards (and they *were* bastards! The butcher's missus, being a good Catholic, refused to give him a divorce, so, though the Fag lady called herself by his moniker, wife was she not! Mum didn't know. Not even Dad knew – not for years after. After what? After this – this whadyacallit. [Ain't a dream, man. That's for sure.]) the come of knowing they'd got so far up her snitch. So she suffered the looks and the laughter.

Sand or no fucking sand, let's have a quick suck of the ol' digits whilst Mum's still in the middle distance. Poor Mum. Hated by the Fag lady from the word go when she twigged that Mum was going to wean Dad away from her nicotine-stained clutches. OK. So she hated Mum an' wanted to ruin her day. But what about y.t.? The dishy little minty-green baby buddha? The Fag lady's one an' only grandchild? Ah well, there goes the essence of that particular Grannydom. Funny looking bitch. Obvious where the brood had got their swarthy boat-races. Boasted about her Grandmother having been a quadroon. The old tarbrush had fairly licked through the lot of them (inc. Dad an' his proper bruv) making them look like a bunch of frigging Arabs.

A small, thin, flat-featured bitch with a squashed dog turd of a hooter (only feature the brood hadn't got; all of them, but especially Dad, had big, hooked conks) and short, wiry black hair which, when it felt like it, took to falling out in lemon-sized clumps. They hadn't all got short, wiry hair either. None of them had. Dad's was dark-brown, but lank. Bruv Simon's was fairish an' he had hazel-y peepers 'cos, colouring-wise, he took after his Dad, the cuckolded Capt. FitzHugh. So what did they have, retard? Black hair, tarbrush skin, big date-stone peepers . . . Christ, what the fuck does it matter? What's with all this wittering on about fuck-all – getting right pissed off with this bunch o' dead-beats – what the fuck is going on down here, man? If y.t. on a trip, could at least have a half decent sort of trip instead of all this pathetic shite.

Shame, all the same, that Mum's day pissed on by a bunch of Evangelical Arabs happy-familying their way through a yummy picnic whilst scum-Mum fiddled with a Marmite sanny an' tried to lock the little grey cells on to *Creative* fucking *Dressmaking*.

An' all y.t. could do was jiggle buddha-bum in the hot sand, patting it (sand) with one starfish mitt as the middle and fourth digits of the other podgy paw tried to grab hold of Mr Epiglottis. The sensation of digits crammed almost down the throat was as near come-mode as poss.

Suddenly, the ego-tripping bastard of a sun was no longer drilling its uranium rods through skull; nor was there any hot, toasty sand sifting grittily through tootsies. The blinding pain above the left peeper screamed as through a knife was fucking the flesh whilst grabbing at whatever it could, squeezing ribs, humping noddle, clutching at throat with bony, greedy fingers.

What the fuck's going on, man? Want to puke – going to throw up – Jesus what's happening? Can't – can't get anything outta gob – can't puke – can't scream – peepers bursting outta skull – something stuck through peeper – above peeper – please God let the pain stop – please . . . Sweet Jesus. Must've done acid. Fucking freaking out on real bad trip. Must've been acid. Yours truly. Flapping an' flailing about on the floor like a dwarf bit-player in a Robin Hood movie. Or a large, dysfunctional, green an' mustard beetle.

Throw up – gotta throw up – puke up the pain – never known such hurt – can see it – can see the hurt – winking wetly an' redly – winking, winking – how the fuck can pain wink, man? The glistening red column of the reel holder of an old sewing machine. On the floor. Without a cover. Not far from the Sherwood Forest dwarf. Can't fucking see – what's going on – don't make y.t. blind for Chrissake! Can't see a fucking thing – black – everything's black – sweet Jesus – sweet Jesus . . . !

Being lifted up from floor and clutched vice-like against someone. Le Train Bleu. Mum. And hair. Long hair. Tickling phizog. Awful lot o' trembling. Mum? Y.t.? Or both in unison? A strange, uncoordinated, trembling togetherness. Must be Mum. Can't breathe – ease off Mum, for Chrissake! Back being patted; noddle being stroked. It seemed that Mum was having a bit of a blub.

'Dear God, I didn't mean it – I didn't see the sodding sewing machine – why hasn't it got its sodding cover on – I didn't see it – I didn't mean to – we'll have to go to the hospital – she'll have to go to the hospital – there's blood everywhere – she'll have to have stitches – Oh God Oh God Oh God I didn't mean it – I didn't mean it . . .'

Whilst Mum wittering on about how sorry she was and she'd never forgive herself etc., sound of dude's voice making meaningless, soothing-type noises. That'll be Dad. Very good at making meaningless noises, was Dad.

In between witterings, Mum was saying, 'Why does she keep doing it – why does she never stop? Day or night, she never stops. It doesn't matter what happens – what I do – she never stops.' Now y.t. knew how scar had come to be above left peeper. Don't remember Mum ever saying why. Don't remember ever asking. Must have done. Why must have? Knew what Mum was going on about. Why does y.t. keep sucking digits. Quite simple, Mum. Sucking lovely juicy fingers gives y.t. lovely, warm, juicy feeling deep inside. Inside and outside. Warm and juicy. Juicy and warm. All over. Brill for y.t. But, for some reason, drove Mum witless.

The pain was so intense that she was sobbing. Though, of course, there was no sound. All she could do was swallow and move her tongue and the muscles in her throat. The tear ducts seemed to be working, as a weak, but steady, emission apathetically meandered down the waxy cheeks.

What the fuck was happening? What the fuck was all this weird shit and where the fuck was it coming from? Not just memories – no way just memories – y.t. *was* that snivelling little ratbag – seeing and hearing and feeling everything it saw and felt and heard. Christ – it seemed as though the spike from the old Singer was still embedded above peeper! Shivering now – what's with the shivering? Give anything – anything for a swig o' Special – never mind Special, any old piss would do – throat and gob on fire. But neck and phizog like bleeding ice, man. Could do with wiping phizog. Itching like hell – feels as though army of fucking ants crawling all over. Skin feels as though it's creeping around – shifting and settling, gathering in sociable little clumps behind ears before creeping off again in all bloody directions dragging sackloads of fucking ice-cubes along with it. Shit man, when was y.t. going to be able to move? Pain now dull, sick throbbing. Never mind the poxy Special – like nothing better than to shove fingers in gob. Funny way of doing it. Trust yours truly to go for something other than a straight suck – ha ha ha! Nothing as boring as just shoving finger or thumb into gob. Jesus only knew where method had come from but it was the left mitt, with palm facing outwards, and fourth and middle digits shoved up and in as far as it was poss to go without bursting a blood vessel. Lovely – lovely – lovely.

What the fuck's happened to the rap, dudes? Couldn't remember the house ever being so hushed – always shaking fit to fall into a heap of rubble (wouldn't take much – ha ha) with every dude's mix trying to get on top of everyone else's.

Must have had the pigs round. Happened every so often. Complaints from vinegar-faced old shites with stitched-up arseholes neighbours. Been told to stop playing loud rap after eleven o'clock. Eleven fucking o'clock! No dude ever got started much before eleven fucking o'clock, man! What effing planet did some of these dorks come from?

They'll be here soon. Fucking useless bastard mates. Prob'ly been in already an' made out that y.t. 'aving a bit o' kip. Be here soon. Bastards. No big deal, man.

Strange. Lust for a swig of something – anything – had split. Iceman still here tho'. What y.t.'d really go down on was a nice, hot cup o' coffee for Chrissake!

Suddenly, as though some fucking genie had sprung out of a bottle or a lamp or whatever, the smell of fresh coffee pumped its way right up hooter and into centre of noddle. How the fuck could a smell be so orgasmic, man? It was like sunshine. Proper sunshine, not the fucking Sinai Desert of Bexhill-on-fucking-Sea. All warm and safe and comforting. It was a dream. A fucking dream. Surely? Couldn't remember last time smelt real coffee. Christ almighty – what the fuck did it matter when? Or what? *Where* was the million dollar question. Where the fuck was it coming from? The thought of any of that load of wanker so-called mates making as much as a cup o' instant . . .

Everything was bright and warm and pig-sicking home-y.

Twilight Zone time again, dudes. There was yours truly. Still a fat little buddha sort of an apology – must be the same summer – only a coupla months older – wearing another of Mum's *Creative Dressmaking* efforts. And there's Mum. Also by courtesy of Dork Manual. Quite a neat little number. Sort of off-white lineny thing with big, splashy flowers all over. Could've been total dorksville. Wasn't. Lookin' finger lickin' good, Mum.

Source of all yummy smells revealed. Percolator perking merrily on top of Aga, filling every hole with swooningly scrummy pong of Kenya Mountain Blend. How come y.t. got such effing know-how? 'Cos the scene being the Fag lady's pile, all the percolator was permitted to perk was Kenya effing Mountain Blend. What the fuck were they doing here, Mum an' y.t.? Mum never *ever* visited the Fag lady without Dad. Only because of him she ever set foot in the crummy pile at all. Bit of a knock on the kitchen door – door opening, Dad's bonce, followed by most of the bod, appearing round the door. Flustered, mush darker-than-usual yellow, hair clinging sweatily to his sticking-out forehead. (Was it his forehead, or was it the top of his noddle that receded a tad sharpish? Funny, never noticed it before. Yet it stood out – nearly as much as yer 'ooter, Dad! Ha ha. Perhaps 'cos the wet hair exposed the geography of his skull. Funny, all the same.)

What in the fuck is y.t. wittering on about the shape of Dad's skull for? 'Cos he looked so weird, man. Standing in the doorway, flushed dark yellow instead of red, wearing his really nerdy chef's gear – even the way out nerdy titfer stuck on the back of his bonce – maybe that's what was making his forehead look so Neanderthal, man! The prat's hat! And the gobs of sweat dripping and dangling (when not dripping) from the end of his e-e-e-normous hooter!

Daddy – Daddy – Daddy . . . (Christ! was y.t. really that bowed in the pins even then? It's not 'cos of a lifetime of shagging, after all!) . . . and the baby buddha's waddling across the room to be scooped up in the starched chef's whites that held the funny, nerdy Dad. Dad's not hanging about – the dude means business – dumps y.t. back on to bandy pins. Good ol' Dad, just by opening his gob and uttering 'chops' he's managed to nuke the grin off the Fag lady's phizog. Standing her ground, though. Not letting him off the hook that easily. Simpering and moue-ing, wagging a digit so fag-stained it looked as though she'd just pulled it outta her arse, telling Dad, in a little-girly falsetto, that there was no way he was going to get his naughty old chops until he'd come into the kitchen and said hello properly to HIS MOTHER.

Typical Dad. Wimp of the century when it came to dealing with the Fag lady. Just standing. Looking like the Chief Nerd of the Entire Universe. Burbling an' stuttering on about these poxy lamb chops. What lamp chops, for fuck's sake?

Mum's had enough of staying shtoom. About time, too.

Aberdeen granite par excellence, zipping over to the fridge, taking out polythene bag heavy with pink nakedness and practically throwing it across at Dad. What's she saying? Dad's gone all shifty. 'If these are supposed to be for today's lunch, Desmond, you'd better get back to the hotel with them as quickly as possible, hadn't you?'

Dad's mush gone slack with relief that dominant female no. 2 had made decision for him. Left wearing sheepish (ha ha) grin, shouting 'See you later' as he got on his bike. Still granite-cast, Mum turned back to find the Fag lady leaning against the Aga, arms dangling, peepers glazed and gob hanging slack, the moist, fleshy lower lip quivering like a browny-pink slug on the look-out for a crumb or two of nosh.

'My God, she's had a stroke,' Mum said. But made no move towards the stricken Cruella. Just stood as though mesmerised, as a huge glob formed in the corner of each heavy-lidded, almond shaped peeper and began to roll turgidly down the rouged cheeks. (Sweet Jesus – she had no brows over her peepers! The Fag lady had no brows, only dark, thickly pencilled lines where the peeper protectors should be! Had Mum noticed?)

Poor Mum. 'Cos she didn't know what was wrong with the hag, she hadn't a clue what to do. Could see it dawning on the dissolving granite that, whatever it was, it sure as hell wasn't a stroke or a heart attack. Warily advancing on the browless Fag lady, gob twitching as though on the verge of suggesting they make free with the manically perking Kenya Mountain, Mum was out-verballed by the sudden animation of Cruella. A cattle prod shoved up her arse couldn't have done better. Peepers no longer glazed but staring wildly; hair staring just as wildly (been like it all the time), standing ramrod stiff (no choice with a cattle prod stuck up her arse ha ha), she began a deranged sort of litany.

'My son – my son – how could he do this to me – to his mother – my son – after all I've done for him – my son – my son . . .'

And on and on and on.

After what seemed like a frigging lifetime, the litany ceased, a fag was lit, the chinky (browless) peepers turned cold and steely, the top lip narrowed until it almost disappeared and the gasteropodous lower swelling was stuck with being a browny-pink slug. Mum seemed to have got the message that the best thing to do was keep her gob shut because her Ma-in-law had gone completely off her trolley.

19

With icy enunciation, the Fag lady recommenced denouncing the thankless, no-good Dad as though he were the most recent incarnation of the Anti-Christ.

Spit flew and the syllables of the words seemed to form out of the globules of flying spit and then hang, momentarily, in mid-air as though invisibly suspended in bubbles of saliva. When at last the Fag lady's motor ran out of fuel, daft bitch Mum opened her cake'ole. Surely, she wittered, you realised that Desmond only called to pick up the chops and hadn't been able to stop and chat 'cos he had to get back to cook lunch? Surely you wouldn't have wanted him to jeopardise his job for the sake of a cup of coffee, would you?

Words no sooner outta Mum's gob than extra hard thrust applied to cattle prod. Work – love – sacrifice – (spit spit spit) life devoted – waking moment – heartless – (spit spit) self-sacrifice – devotion – turning back on – (spraying of spit) few precious minutes civil – penny-pinching – selfish – mother – mother – mother (spit spit spit and more spit). Yours truly more than a tad pissed off with the endless dirge of reiterated crap. Bit of a whinge an' snivel in order, just to make presence felt a smegma in excess of nil. A little light-bulb of relief lit up Mum's phizog as she latched on to y.t.'s gurning, blurting that they really must get home as it was past Lou-Lou's lunchtime and she needed a change of Paddies. (So *that*'s what the effing great bulge round the arse area is! Dirty nappy, thank Christ! Bit old to be wearing Paddies, y.t. – thought for a few mos bulge might be something to do with bandy pins, man!) And a nap, etc. etc. The old bat hasn't finished, for fuck's sake. Head for the effing door, Mum. Never mind about catching poxy bus – just get the fuck out of shithole Manor an' Fag lady Macbeth.

There was a blanking out. Not darkness, but a sort of nothingness. As though time had stopped just for a few seconds. During that brief hiatus, she thought that she had become blind. Then she noticed the narrow, orange shafts coming from the street lights and filtering shakily through the gaps in the corrugated sheeting. Unable to penetrate the thickly grimed half-pane of glass, they had to make do with creating a fitfully orange ghost of a glow. The light bulb, hanging motionless, appeared to have died. Allowing her heart time to regain its normal rhythm, she watched the wavering, petulant rays and decided that it must be quite late. It could well be the middle of the night. The squat was as silent as if she were the sole occupant.

The Fag lady lying on a small settee. Mum standing, gazing down at her and y.t. sitting on floor, sucking digits. Makes a change, dudes. Not in kitchen. Living room of sorts. Scottie's made a cock-up! Beamed Mum an' y.t. up, then fucking beamed back down. Warp factor five when Jim finds out ha ha ha.

Hang on a mo. Things are different; Mum's got same wild Dork Manual number on, but y.t.'s wearing naff gingham. Must be a different day. Same summer but another day. Wonder why? Twat-face David reading a comic. Poof-in-the-making Martin fidgeting with a model train set. Must be late afternoon. Or a weekend. Otherwise prat bros 'd be at school. Could be hols o' course. Most likely is.

What the fuck's going down, Scottie? Why back at the Fag lady's stately pile? Mum's asking prat D if Fag lady ill. D shrugging puny shoulders whilst wimp M sniggering into his shuntings. Why the fuck is Mum wasting time with such a bunch o' deadbeats? Gently shaking Fag lady by the shoulder, prat bros darting sneaky looks across. Fag lady's peepers doing lambada under lids. Lids raising, letting dark, pebbly things stare blankly and blearily up at Mum. Mum looking a tad green around the gills. No bleeding wonder. Dead mince pies more than enough to give skitters.

Something beginning to stir in the murk; surfacing, in a few mos, hand in hand with best pals gnash an' wail.

All of it a big heap of pure shite.

In the background, prat bros stood, huddled and sniggering witlessly.

Mum hasn't moved, hasn't said a word, but having sick bag of Fag lady's true confessions emptied all over her. She's on the move, Mum! The old witch is on the move! Getting physical, for Chrissake! Clutching Mum's arms an' using her as a prop to do a Lazarus! Caressing her phizog an' hair, squeezing her like a sponge, holding her in a boa-constrictor grip against the ashtray bod – Christ, if you could see your phizog, Mum! On the point of total freak out. Glancing helplessly across at prat bros. Can't suss out all the whispering when Fag lady in such deep shit. Shouting at D to go and phone for a Doc – couldn't he see that his mother was ill? Poor Mum. Trying to convey sense of urgency to prat bros an' all she got in return was an extra burst of giggling before the pair of pansies ran outta the room. As he reached the door, D turned and shouted, 'You're fucking thicker than you look – hasn't anyone ever told you?' Mum almost throwing a wobbly herself at this display of what she saw as pathological neglect so busied herself by patting and soothing the Fag lady.

Lazarus not only regained use of pins once more but also ability to loud mouth again. And wouldn't you know it? Sad bitch still using poor ol' Dad as arsewipe supremo! Treacherous – flinthearted – destroyer of family life as we know it – bla bla bla bla . . .

Suddenly, as though new CD inserted, arsewipe Dad chucked to one side. Vomitously maudlin, she crooned into Mum's ear'ole. 'You, Maggie, you – you are far more a daughter to me than Desmond was ever a son – I love you – I love you – I love you far more than I ever loved him. Truly, Maggie, truly. Please say that you believe me – please.' Can't blame Mum. Head really being done in. Didn't know what the fuck was going on. Though not taking any of the vomit seriously, she went an' shoved her tootsies right in it by offering a crumb or two of advice. Bad move, Mum. Real bad move.

Didn't say much. Didn't have to. First coupla words an' the hounds from hell were loosed. 'Don't you think,' says dickhead Mum, 'that you ought to give Desmond a bit of credit – you know, with regards to his work-decisions, etc. . . .'

Should've come right out with it Mum. Wouldn't've been any worse if you had. Should've told the old hag straight to let Dad off the leash; undo his collar – let him run free. He's not a Son anymore. He's a Dad. Wouldn't've made any difference.

Lazarus up and off the settee as though jerked by unseen strings. Wordlessly, with a mush like a fat little African statue thingy, puffed an' shiny, pointing with yellowy digit towards the door. Looked a fucking nightmare. Totally minus any marbles. Sparse little clumps of hair sticking out – like noddle of long-abused doll where someone's tried to glue some scraps of nylon 'hair' back on – phizog swollen and mottled like one of these weird fish things – what're they called? Puffer fish, for Chrissake – she looked like a fucking Puffer fish! Hey Granny, give y.t. a smile, you old Puffer, you! Last thing the Puffer felt like doing was smiling, man. Not a happy Puffer. A poisonous Puffer. Fag lady's dulcits, though. Steel-tipped; acid-dipped, each syllable an ice-wrapped bomblet clustering round the pointing, been-up-an-arse (could've been – who's to know?) finger.

'Get out. Get out of my house, you cow!'

Phizog the colour of recycled bog paper an' shaking as though doing cold turkey, Mum looked about to pass out. The whole scene like a Victorian bleedin' melodrama. Unreal. Nasty though. That was real enough.

Y.t. starting to gurn an' no effin' wonder. What with all this flak an' no hope of any nosh – not even a poxy biccy hovering on the horizon. Gurning gave lifeline to pole-axed Mum. Voice shaking so much it kept leaping an octave, she asks Fag lady did she realise that she was ordering her grandchild out of the house as well? Her only grandchild. Is that what she really wanted?

'Out.' Syllable settled on end of shit-stained digit and gave V-sign.

Y.t. waiting to hear 'cursed spot' tagged on end. Missed your chance there, you vile old bitch.

They'd left Bexhill and gone to London because of the Fag lady. She'd been the main reason. Not the only one. Not only the Fag lady that had been driving Mum nearly witless. Don't want to think about that. Won't think about it. All in the dim an' distant, anyway. Like everything else. Except y.t. an' his holiness. The Fag lady had turned up once, about six years later, when they were living in Wimbledon. Ask Mum quite openly to take her to the nearest Offie to replace empty half-bottle of Courvoisier she had stashed in her handbag. All out in the open, then. Had to be once the Fag lady, as a result of being a tad careless as to the where-abouts of her ignited darlings once they'd left her gob, had set fire to the country pile. Bottles hidden everywhere. Hard to believe no one, not even the Butcher, had ever as much as suspected. The immaculate enunciation might've provided a clue. But, because she always had a skinful, she always had perfect paraphrasing.

Sometimes, apropos of zilch, a card would arrive, bearing a muddled message often of a religious nature. Only whilst they were living in Wimbledon. Mum had never replied. Dad had pretended not to care. Something he was very good at. Pretending.

What the fuck was happening now? A steady downward pressure forcing y.t. onto knees. Something coarse textured biting into flesh. Nasty little uppity ridges making comfy in poor, naked knees.

Through the darkness, diluted orange-juice emissions wavering

23

through corrugated sheets and pale orange jellyfish pulsing faintly against muddy pane.

What the fuck's happened to the light bulb? Died a death, and no frigging wonder. Been there, same poxy bulb, months – maybe years. At least it was night time. Good night's kip and all this shit would seem no more than a bad dream man.

For Chrissake – knees feel as though being cut into slices like fucking salami! Some really weird shit going down here, man.

There was a dude in the room. Could make out breathing. Two lots of breathing. Two dudes. Two dudes in the room. Bastards hadn't forgotten Blojo after all! Knew it. All along. Knew mates wouldn't forget. Keeping a bleeding midnight vigil by bedside ha ha ha. Which of the no-hopers playing Flo Nightingale, then? How the fuck can y.t. get them to zoom in? One lot o' breathing right inside shell-like. Rapid and hissy, yet laboured. What fucking dickheads – why don't they say something – stoned out of their effing skulls and y.t. needed a Doc p.d.q. Arseholes. Why don't they change the fucking bulb . . . Sweet Jesus – why couldn't y.t. see anything – what in the fuck was happening?

Arms being manipulated like levers being pressed down, thereby pulling forcibly on shoulders. Nowhere further to go. Knees already halfway through fucking rustic tintawn. Sharp, searing pain. How the fuck did y.t. know about the tintawn? In the pitch dark? Without even thinking, knew it was the tintawn carpet Mum and Dad had bought for the new flat when they'd moved to Blackheath. They'd been there a few weeks before being able to afford it. Until Mum had got a job and y.t. a place at local nursery. Now the poxy tintawn was eating y.t. From the knees up.

The hissing, as though jetted through a hose, fizzed and bubbled right inside shell-like.

'You little bitch – you filthy lying rotten little bitch. I know you're lying – why can't you admit it – admit you're lying you filthy rotten little bitch . . .'

Suddenly the pressurised hissing veered away, the words becoming floaty and distant.

'She's lying isn't she – any fool can see that she's lying through her rotten teeth – why does she do it – why does she keep doing it? Any fool can see that they've been bitten – she knows that – so why does she keep on lying?'

The hissing, now on a roll and well on the way to becoming a shriek, was back inside y.t.'s shell-like, making it draw back as a hermit-crab might, from the verbal vomit.

'Why won't you admit it then – why – why – why – why don't you just come out and admit that you've bitten them, you rotten, disgusting, lying little bitch?'

The shock of the thin, reedy pathetic piping was like a slosh of cold water.

'I never bit them – I never – I never – it was the lady at the nursery – the lady cut them – it wasn't me I never bit them – I never!'

The hissing at last conceded defeat to the shrieking and fiery licks of pain fingered and thumbed their way up and down y.t.'s arms and shoulders.

Then came a different voice; a low voice; a man's voice, its tone wheedling and craven in its pleading. The voice that belonged to the second lot of breathing. Dad's voice.

'Why don't you be a good little girl, Lou-Lou and tell Mummy the truth, and then this business will be over for good, eh?'

Wheedle, wheedle and more unctuous wheedle. Typical Dad. Anything, but anything, for the promise of a quiet life.

Now Mum was weeping. Like she always did afterwards.

'Get her out of my sight – just get her out of my bloody sodding sight before I do something – something . . .'

Flat and shagged out, the voice trailed off into the darkness and, for a moment, it seemed that the return of the hissing and shrieking would be preferable to the dark and empty nothingness it left in its wake.

Did yours truly think that then, as that scrawny little scrag, or was yours truly thinking it now – in the here and now? Here and now – here and now – thank the fuck – y.t. back in the land of the living! Jesus – what a mother of a head! Otherwise, all feelings of pain had disappeared. Arms no longer burned nor felt at snapping point and knees no longer fused to the rustic tintawn. And no breathing to be heard. Neither the rasping hiss or crescendo-ing shriek of Mum nor the fearful and stealthy exhalations of Dad. Stealthy! What a funny word to use! Well o' course the horrible little scrag had bitten her effing nails – and right down to the quick! No way was the kiddo going to own up to it – and quite fucking right, too! Stick up for your rights, Lou-Lou – if you don't, no other fucker will!

Sweet Jesus – was y.t. knackered or was y.t. knackered? Why wouldn't poxy peepers close? Could well do with a spell in the land o' nod. Feeling a tad weepy. Can't have that. No effing way. Only a bad trip, man. No need to feel sorry for bleeding self. Daft bitch. His holiness'll be wondering why he hadn't had a visit. Good to let him stew a bit. Make a bleeding change.

Christ – how many effing times, you stupid bitch! Not due to visit till next week – thought that one had been sorted out. For the tenth time – retard! Will have to write the old tosser, though. Else y.t.'ll be in deep shit. Can't manage without y.t. can you, you old fucker-face? There'll be plenty to write this time round – what a fucking unbelievable load o' shite! All his effing fault, anyway. Never had more than the occasional joint till Amsterdam.

Hey man – what the fuck is going on? Mother of a bed's come alive and trying to split y.t. in two – right down the effing middle! Arse on fire – pins spreads so far apart almost touching shell-likes – rubbing – something rubbing; something wide, hard and not unlike the frigging Tintawn, only less ridged and uppity. Pain unbearable! Something pressing itself in – not penetrating, but feeling as though pins are being wrenched apart, crotch and arse crevice about to be extended upwards so that y.t.'ll be cleaved in two; red-hot rubbing on thighs; the killer bed heaving up and down – bringing y.t. onto what feels like ridge of fucking granite. Going to fall off – be thrown off – this arsehole of a living bed!

Holy shit! – if it ain't yours truly herself – yours truly sitting on a little black gee-gee with Mum, as big as an elephant in a hideous carmine and tangerine tent thing, running at the side of the trotting hay-bag! No wonder y.t.'s pins and nethers giving such effing gip! Just take a dekko at the boat-race! Hey Lou-Lou – don't look so shit scared! Jesus, did y.t. look scared shitless or what? Hey kid – chill out some, for Chrissake!

But y.t. was scared. Bowels felt at melting point. Why was scrawny y.t. such a gibbering wreck? Two counts: 1) Scared of being split up the middle and ending up as two halves; 2) Scared of falling off poxy nag and breaking every bone in scrawny bod.

Was that ribby little bag o' bones really y.t.? The phizog on it, for fuck's sake! Looks as though it's done a dump in its drawers! Maybe it had. What a freaky looking effort it was – dead straight, shoulder length, dark brown hair. About the only item y.t. had inherited from Mum. Different colour, but same dead straight, dead fine, pissy awful hair. Between the rickety pins of y.t. was one fuckingly fat New Forest which, thank Christ, had slowed down to an amble. Probably 'cos Mum was about to pass out. What a fucking head case! Weighing in at thirteen stone, at least, and only a matter of weeks before due to whelp and running like an Amazon on acid in a psychedelic tent and red Scholls! Someone striding along the other side of fat nag. Wearing manly gear and striding manly stride. None other than dykey old Hester. C'mon y.t. – be fair. Old was OK as the old bird was around the three score and ten mark, but dykey, in spite of the blokes gear, was not. Mustn't be so gross to the old bird. Been bit of all right to y.t. in dim and distant. Shame y.t. had to fuck up. Only dude other than Dad who'd visited Mum in hossy after she'd whelped with y.t.

Weird though, that she and Mum were such buddies. Fifty years difference and they spent most of their time together, when not around a bleeding gee-gee, giggling and nudging and whispering like they were sharing a joint.

Dyke had said to Mum in hossy, 'Is it meant to look like a little prune, Maggie darling?' Bloody nerve! Typical wanking remark from an old dyke spinster! Funny though, the sodding name had stuck. Only for a couple o' years. But it had stuck. Little Prune. Pathetic. Thank Christ they were getting y.t. off the back of candidate for knackers yard. Jesus – did butt hurt! And the little scrawny pins – would they every be able to unbow themselves? Had they? Didn't y.t. still have bowed pins? Always used to think that it was result of constant shagging. And all the time it could have been because of that mad fuschia/carmine/tangerine/whatever-clad grotesque forcing y.t. to mould weedy green bones round gross girth of equally grotesque Chippy. Chippy! What a crass fucking name! How come y.t. remembered? Chippy!

Dyke/Hester unsaddling and just look at Mum. In her sodding element. Freaked out. Acting like an acid-head. Rubbing and nuzzling her phizog against the nags whiskery muzzle – won't do the acne any good, Mum! Bet she wished more than anything she could just swing a leg over and ride off into the big blue yonder. Different bitch when round a gee-gee. Or a moggie. Gee-gees first, though.

Must be on a visit to Dykeland. Moved to Blackheath when y.t. was coming up to the big 2 and Ginnybitch (reason for at least three of Mum's thirteen stone) had first spawned in Blackheath flat.

27

Dyke an' Mum had first met when Mum had answered advert in *Horse & Hound* for girl to help in small Riding School. Just what Mum'd needed at the time. Low profile. Peace an' quiet. Had been working in Riding School in Essex. Had serious fella. Engaged. Marriage on cards. Living with his family though his sister hated sight of her. No monkey business. Tried, but couldn't let him touch the outside of her knickers never mind her actual cunt. Every time she felt the juices start to flow, she prised herself out from under him, rushed to the lav, scrubbing the offending snatch before coating every cranny with Johnson's baby talc.

The poor dude died, impaled on the steering wheel of a second-hand Jag his Mum an' Dad had got him for his twenty first birthday. Brakes locked as he and his Dad were trying it out. Died without having had a fuck. Thanks to Mum. She had to leave. Too much grief. The Dad had died on the way to E.R. Didn't freak out. Would've done if she hadn't discovered Dykeland. Only stayed a few months 'cos, apart from being bored shitless trying to drum into snotty-nosed bratskis difference between front and rear end of gee-gees, couldn't be pissed with she-who-liked-to-wear-blokey-gear getting into a bate every time Mum wanted to go out with a real dick. (Sure Dyke ain't a dyke?) Yet couple years later, with marbles shrieking for their freedom, 'twas Dyke Bungalow Mum zoomed in on. Turned up in the pitch dark and pissing rain of a February night carrying a plastic bag with few bits o' gear an' a mog in a fucking mog basket. Forever after, the Dyke had referred to Mum's arrival as 'The Night of the Dripping Apparition'. Guaranteed to have them in pleats. Pair of dildos. Never told the old bat what happened in the Big City. Mightn't have let her over the threshold if she'd opened gob an' spilled beans.

Hey man, this is real – the old dyke's bringing in a big dish with a roast chook plonked in the middle an' all the yummy extras crowding round – roast taties, sprouts – or was it runner beans? – who gives a fuck – the pong is something else – can't wait to get a gobful, dudes! Mum's off; can't even wait for the plate to be plonked in front of y.t. Flinging little, needley darts of: 'Don't eat too much; don't eat too quickly; don't stuff gob too full (fat chance!) but, most of all, don't look at Mum whilst shovelling in forkfuls of Dyke delicacy.'

Why ever not, Mum? Don't put mockers on y.t.'s bit o' fun. If its OK for you to stick y.t. on back of fat, four-legged lawnmower so's crotch feels as though splitting up to chest level, why shouldn't y.t. get rocks off in return? Not real reason, but what the fuck. Casting peepers your way whilst filling cake'ole – where's the harm in that, Mum? Eh? Yummy, yummy – nosh too scrummy to be arsing about trying to get one over Mum.

Why the fuck doesn't grade-A retard y.t. shove some of mind-blowingly juicy nosh into face instead of pissing around with poxy peepers? Pong alone from crispy chook enough to make y.t. pass out never mind gobful of the juicy ooze! For Chrissake – grab a forkful, moron!

Chook's gone – vanished – before y.t.'s had a chance to taste even a smidgen of crispy skin. Scottie's into beaming up mode again. Bastard.

Cool breeze for a few mos. Then what the poor chook must have felt like in the bleeding oven. Or under a grill – or on a spit. Fucking broiling scorching no-fucking-let-up heat. The sun trying to do its Sinai desert thingy again; sending flames of heat down in crashing great searing waves. Only this time not onto Bexhill, but the heath, as in Blackheath. Y.t. and Mum walking on heath. Even more vast-bellied Mum. What the fuck was the stupid bitch doing out in such a killer heat? Still wearing the gobsmackingly violent cerise and fuschia, or whatever, tenty thing – though, come to think of it, dudes, this warp being the late sixties an' all, Mum was prob'ly the coolest pregnant bitch in the whole of SE 13 in her psychedelic little frock! Ha ha ha.

An ice-cream. They each had a fucking ice-cream. A ginormous cone, filled to melting overflow with swirly, creamy whiteness. Mum licking and lapping tongue round rapidly disappearing pile of pigfat. What the J. Arthur was y.t. up to? Cone plus mindbog-glingly scrumptious heap of fat stuck out in front of phizog as though infected by flesh-eating bug! Get it into gob – fucking moron! Sweet Jesus – the desire to wrap tongue round glistening, melting creaminess; to feel cool, smooth fattiness sliding over gnashers and gums, clinging for a sec to roof of gob, before slithering sweetly down throat.

Ice-cream's gone. Vanished. Like roast chook. No more ice-cream.

Y.t. ambling behind like a retard bent on keeping single brain cell intact inside skull. Showing not slightest sign of ever having had ice-cream within light year of scrawny phizog. This sick-fuck stuff's way outta line. Doing y.t.'s head right in, man.

Mum's slowing down; come to a halt. Scooping skirt of carmine etc. creation round fat, tanned thighs and lowering bulk onto grass. Safely beached, leaning back gently stroking vast dome ballooning from under psychedelic tent.

Mum's mush looking almost as crimson as said tent, and sweat trickled steadily from her scalp where pissy-fine hair was clinging. Bare, tanned arms glistened, as though first oiled then brushed with fine gold dust. Peering closely, braindead y.t. could see that gold was really very fine hairs bleached to baby blondeness by poxy desert-creating sun.

'God – this awful heat is killing me,' says Mum, and pats the grass for y.t. to come and sit next to her. 'O my God, Lou-Lou – just look – just look at it will you – just look!'

Y.t., ever obedient, looked as and where instructed and got fright of scrawny life. For there, violently pushing at the restricting garishness of Mum's frock as though hellbent on poking a bloody great hole in it, was a fucking great Alien-type lump! Yellowing round gills and Mum's grabbing y.t.'s mitt and shoving it on top of heaving alien! For Chrissake – look out, Lou-Lou – fucking alien might pop out and gobble-gobble at any mo! Ha ha ha.

'That,' blithered Mum, 'that is part of your little brother or sister, Lou-Lou.'

'What part, Mummy?' asks the retard.

'Well, it could be a foot, or a knee, or an arm, or an elbow. I don't think it's a head – it's not big enough for a head. It's most likely part of a leg and a foot – a kicky little foot – or it could just as easily be a little punchy hand and part of an arm.'

A head – how many heads were there, for fuck's sake? Y.t. shit scared at thought of what was living and feeding off Mum's innards. She was so huge, for Chrissake! There was no telling how many X-files creatures were likely to thrust their alien noddles out, when the time came, from the enormous swelling belly.

'Feel it Lou-Lou, feel it . . .' warbled Mum, oblivious to the frozen terror etched on y.t.'s phizog. Sweet relief! The hyperactive growth's decided against doing an Alien and began to subside back into Mum's guts.

Now, like a huge whale, she's lying back on the grass totally knackered, legs spread, hands wandering compulsively all over the carmine/fuschia mountain looming before her.

'Mummy-Mummy – look at the funny doggies, Mummy!'

Never mind the funny doggies, take a butchers at y.t.'s boat-race! Peaky phizog all lit up, skinny finger pointing across the heath, bum an' pins wriggling as though trying to contain a dump. Mum, puffing and gasping as though still hooked on the tar-stick Gauloises she used to suck until the thing in her belly took root, pushing her bulk into a semi-sitting position, resting on elbows and peering across at target of y.t.'s skinny digit. 'Oh, they're beautiful, they're so beautiful . . .' gasps Mum and, right on cue, delicate crystal drops appear in each corner of the blue peepers.

For Chrissake Mum, didn't think you'd be that freaked out by a pair of dumbo Afghan doggies belting across the heath with red-faced owners in fat pursuit. Funny, yes. Tear-jerking, no. Looked pretty neat, though. One was dark-chocolate with silvery bits on noddle an' pins and the other was pale blonde. As they ran, in great leaps and bounds, their coats floated around them like unravelling bolts of silk.

Totally ignoring increasingly harsh shouts of deadbeat owners, they gained speed until, with a doggie nod an' wink, they broke into a headlong gallop towards Greenwich Park. Mum wasn't finding it in the least amusing. Peepers had turned decidedly bloodshot from all the sloshing acid tears. Lowering herself back on to the grass, she snuffled for a few mos before closing her peepers an' seeming to doze off. Nice one, y.t. Don't just sit there, dork-features – have a bit of a toddle round while Mum's in land of nod – see if any goodies lying about. Lay mitts on some tasty morsel to shove into gob. Waste bin over there. Go an' have a rummage round, Lou-Lou.

Pins've given up the ghost. Turned to jelly. Like poxy brain cells. Stand up y.t. for Chrissake! Can't. Can't straighten frigging knees, man – can't even get poxy arse off the ground never mind stand up. Coupla inches an' that's yer lot. C'mon babe, get it together – plant mitts on floor an' push up from behind. Babe is right, man. Same fat little buddha-bum, though a tad longer in the tooth than the beach-baby buddha-bum. Why the fuck does it keep crashing onto the carpet? Wearing its Robin Hood gear again. Green jersey, brown cord tunic-y thing an' green tights. Must be winter. Holy shit, it looks like a mangy splodge of the poxy carpet, trying to free itself and take on human life! At any mo, there'll be a fucking great 'plop' an' the carpet'll have produced its first clone!

Steady on y.t. Getta grip, girl.

C'mon buddha-bum – what the fuck's with the dodgy pins? Why only the rise (to podgy knees), flop, sprawl; ditto; ditto routine? Well shit a brick, buddha-bum is making its first attempt to enter the world of the bipeds! There's Mum. Standing with waiting, outstretched arms. Huge grin splitting phizog. Like one of these long doughnuts waiting for the cream to be squidged in. Eyes all sparkly – hair all shiny – like a fucking halo, man. Now baby buddha's planted its fat green bum back onto the green carpet – mummy carpet not ready to say ta-ta to her clone yet – and patting the floor and making gurgly noises like a total moron. Mum's laughing. Laughing and patting her thighs.

'C'mon, Lou-Lou – you can do it – try again – just for Mummy.'

And the baby buddha, with one heroic heave, lurches more or less upright on the bandy pins, stands swaying fatly for a few mos before tottering wildly towards the laughing, sparkling, halo-ed Mum. Both laughing now. Together. Mum an' baby buddha. What a moron – chortling and crowing with single-brain-cell pride as it's swept up into the woolly jersey warmth and has the breath squeezed and kissed out of it.

'Wait till we tell Daddy – just wait till we tell him – won't he be proud of our little Lou-Lou . . .' Witter, witter, witter goes Mum. Way over the top, man.

Where was Dad, anyway? At work, s'pose. What time o' day? Can't tell. All hazy. Swimmy green 'n' brown carpet-clone buddha-bum. Swimmy, sparkly, golden-y Mum.

Fourteen months old when first tottered. February. Still at little fourth-third?-floor flat in mouldy old Bexhill. Dad working in hotels. Not a lot doing at this time o' year. Didn't the dude have a job in a girls' school? Funny business. Suddenly got the order of the boot. Wouldn't say why. Mum got in a right bate. Injustice of it an' all that shit. Rang Headmistress an' demanded to know why she'd sacked Daddy-O. Wished she hadn't. Frozen old trout refused to tell her. Said it'd be better if she didn't know. Mum an' Dad rowing for days. Could get zilch outta the dude. Where did he go then? To work? Where was he now? Always in an' outta jobs. Not always his fault. Sometimes. No money. Often. Mum had to get cleaning job. Landlady kept a peeper on baby buddha. Quite the thingy lying in cot all morning sucking delicious digits. Before entered tottering phase. Never crawled. Funny. Missed the amoeba stage. Buddha-bum back with once-mummy carpet.

Mummy no more. Plopped right out. Warmth, warmth, warmth. An' digits stuffed right up into top o' gob where they belonged.

Must be wank-features Dr Who running this side-show, dudes! Hurling y.t. in and outta time whenever and wherever the old fart feels like it!

His holiness'll be doing his head in without a visit. Chill out, y.t. No visit this week. Slipped through the old sieve-like again, ha ha. Will have to send a few scrawls though. Else y.t.'ll be in shit street. What's happened to poxy warmth? Fucking ice-cubes time again. Think of warm thingies for Chrissake – snuggly, cuddly, flowing through tubes like a good shoot thingies. Don't care how. Want same buzz as toasted sand on Bexhill beach. What a naff thought, man! Of all the effing places – Bexhill! Can't help it. To feel the hot sand squidge grittily through baby buddha tootsies; to be able to glance up at a golden Mum leafing through *Creative Dressmaking Made Easy*; to be able to freeze-frame it and re-run it before the Fag lady and bunch of born-agains arrived and spoiled it all. Losin' it, y.t. Losin' it babe.

*   *   *

On the beach. Not. But cold no longer. Still winter, though y.t. cocooned in choccy-brown M&S quilt an' hooded gear. Sitting on Mum's lap like a mini Michelin Man. A grinning old tosser in a white coat sitting on the other side of desk. Not taking any notice of Mum's blethering. Old dried-up cunt sat twiddling pencil, smiling a thin, I've heard it all before, smile.

None of spilled beans news to y.t. All in that sad, pathetic whinge a.k.a. Mum's book. Not that y.t. remembers. Heap o' shite. Not easy listening, all the same. Y.t. been slapped about a bit when six months old. Fair do's. One slap. Only the one. Wouldn't have been a big deal if Mum's ring hadn't made bright red mark on y.t.'s peachy baby cheek. Scared Mum shitless enough to send her time warping down to kiosk to ring Surgery. Blubbing and blabbing to GP who asked if y.t. all right.

Mum said 'Yes', so he told her to come to the evening surgery and they'd have a chat. Fat lot of good that did the blubbing, baby-bashing Mum at eleven in the bleeding a.m. Dragged herself back to flat, with chilled-out-with-digit-sucking y.t.

It was the sucking that got her down, she told cunt-features. Not *per se*, but the fact that it was the most important thingy in y.t.'s baby life. As long as fingers in gob nothing else seemed to matter. Y.t. perfectly happy lying in cot, up to neck in piss and shit, as long as able to suck–suck–suck on digits.

Old c–face looking at Mum with expression of boredom on dried up mush. Poor Mum! Telling smirking old arsehole all this shitty stuff, stripping soul bare to his bony stare. And what did he offer in return? Other than saying, in a thin, smarmy, patronising monotone, that didn't she think she might be over-reacting somewhat? – sweet FA. But what about the incident with the sewing machine, burbled Mum, impressing upon the grinning skull that y.t. had had to have three stitches inserted above peeper-brow – the scar was clearly visible and still livid.

'An accident, my dear,' purred the cadaver, 'You didn't *mean* to impale your little girl to the reel holder, now did you?'

'N–no,' stammered Mum, 'but I *did* mean to push her.'

No way was the old bastard going to make things easy for Mum. Anything but. Leaning back in his nerdy swively chair and grinning a thin, oily grin, the old wanker told Mum that she was, wouldn't she agree, making a little bit of a mountain out of a fairly small and quite normal – quite normal – molehill? Eh? Why, the little girl was responding to her mother in a perfectly natural fashion – making eye-contact, touching and being touched, not drawing back, even slightly, in any way. In other words as far as he could see, participating in a perfectly normal and healthy one-to-one mother/child relationship.

'Yes, but . . .' cried Mum, phizog going all red and tears sprouting as though a wee watering-can had suddenly sprung a leak behind the scenes, 'you don't understand – you just don't understand!'

And so, gulping, squirming and snivelling with shame and embarrassment, she told old fuck-face, in detail, about the shoulder shaking, the pressing down in the cot, the leaving of y.t. in the cot, lying in a midden of piss and shit – waiting, waiting for her baby to cry out for its Mum. Which, alas, y.t. never ever did. If Mum had left it long enough, then y.t. might have got peckish and start to whinge. But ten in the morning was the latest Mum was prepared to go, and then she kept popping her phizog round the bedroom door to see if y.t. still OK. Every time poor Mum came into room she found y.t. lying, quite the thingy, waving fat, bandy, shit-covered pins in the air and sucking, sucking, sucking.

Might as well not have bothered, Mum. Didn't she realise it was just a phase the child was going through? And didn't she think she ought to try and get out of the flat more – find herself a bit of an outside interest?

Didn't bat an eyelid when, still snivelling, Mum told him that she had a morning job as a cleaner whilst the landlady kept a peeper on y.t.

'Well, my dear, all I can do is give you something to calm you down during this somewhat difficult phase you're going through.'

And he gave her a prescription for two of her old pals; Largactil to accomplish said calming, and Seconal to send her to sleep. He was no stranger to Mum. Introduced her to Larg. and Sec. when she was in foal with y.t. Tried to top herself with Sec. once. About three weeks before y.t. split pod. Cry for help. Did it all the same. Uncool.

'If tablets don't do the trick, or if you feel like another little chat, just ring my secretary and make an appointment. You won't need to go through your GP again.'

And he leaned back in his naff chair and leered. Was it meant to be a leer? Or was it an attempt at a smile gone wrong?

What the fuck is Mum up to now? Instead of getting up and leaving, she's clutching on to the back of the M&S choccy number and blurting out something about Dad and . . . oh no – oh no – back off, Mum! No one wants to listen to that shit! Luckily, least of all wank-features. There you go! He's off on his mountain and molehill jerk-off theories again! (True, in this instance, though. Definitely true.) Grinning at Mum and reminding her to be sure and take the medication as prescribed.

C'mon Mum, for Chrissake get your carcass together and get outta this shithole! Chill out some an' stop blubbering and clutching, can't you? Take a pill, for fuck's sake!

Can't breathe – gob an' hooter blocked – Gawdawful stink seeping through pores, creeping up through air 'oles and squatting in brainbox.

Peepers glued together with sticky goo. Can't see. Only feel.

Ol' pal panic having a quick go on bongoes under frigging ribcage-bastard!

Something – someone pressing down hard on back of neck. Noddle being pushed something chronic from side to side. Thick goo moving as well, sliding slimily further an' further up snitch and into cake'ole. Retch-making stench-puke time, dudes! Only can't, 'cos of fistful of clobber grabbed at back an' y.t. flying in air before landing arse over tit in what felt like bath of freezing water.

Can see now. See as well as hear. Prob'ly 'cos of flailing about in back on bottom of bath. Water splashing over phizog and loosening wodges of thick shite mask covering both said phizog and noddle.

Sweet Jesus – glue peepers together again – please – please! Y.t.'ll do anything – promise anything – take vows – become a nun – sell life – soul anything, if only unable to see. But there it was. And there y.t. was. And there was the Hissing Woman. Not Mum. Or Mummy. But an ugly Hissing Woman. Hissing and spitting. Spitting and hissing. Then a lot of shouting. Before or after immersion in bath? Donno. Hoarse at times. Then high and shrieking. All of it a tad muffled 'cos of shell-likes being plugged with dollops of shite. Where was it? Bathroom looked weird. What a totty y.t.! Still a baby buddha, for Chrissake! Must be first flat. The one they'd come to straight after y.t. popping the pod. How old was y.t. for Chrissake?

No hissing now. Or shouting. Only sobbing. And words flying jerkily around the room. Not letting themselves be caught. The Hissing Woman, no longer hissing, looked like Mum. A demented Mum as, leaning across the edge of the bath, she scooped up the flapping, wailing, still shitty turtle into her arms and pressed the stinking, wet little bod violently against her chest, shit an' all, as though fusing them into one flesh once more might erase what had just happened.

Clutching y.t. under one arm and blubbing enough to wash out the poxy bath, Mum let the diluted shit swirl down the plughole before swishing fresh water round it until clean. Then ran a warm bath into which, mingled with her tears and a gob or two of snot from her blubbing, she gently placed the naked, but unspeakable sticky and stinky turtle. In a low, trembly voice, she let low, trembly words flitter fitfully into the steamy air. Y.t. didn't give a toss what Mum was wittering on about. All that mattered was the yummy warmth, no more bongoes under the ol' ribcage an' the come factor of digits stuffed right up into top of gob. Where they belonged.

Breath gone again – suffocating – pungent prickling stinging peepers, tightening throat – closing it for Chrissake – puke surging up gullet – hooter blocked – going to lose it, man. Puke or pass out. Or both. Can't be re-run of shitty-babe-in-the-bath scene – can't be. Don't let it be that. Please, please don't let it be that. Isn't. Pong's nothing to do with shit. Or anything nasty. No way nasty. Just nukingly strong. Ferocious olfactory assault on y.t.'s tubes. Old Spice. Old fucking Spice having a shag (ha ha) with Old effing Holborn! Only one dude in the entire Universe could deliver such a nasal nuking – Dad! Must be some ways back – not graduated to Tabac yet, Dad? Ha ha ha.

What the fuck is the dickhead doing to y.t.? There he is! And there's y.t.! No effing wonder y.t. unable to draw breath. Rammed up against Dad's chest, phizog buried in weird black an' white tweedy thingy. Sweet Jesus – ease off a tad, Dad! Get a loada those skinny cranefly pins in white ankle socks an' red StartRite sandals dangling against lower half of vomitously nerdy black an' white checked tweed, three piece suit. No. Not just a three piece suit. A Burton three piece suit. A woollen, Burton three piece, black an' white checked tweed frigging suit, for Chrissake. Was he mad? He'd had it made to measure, chosen the tweed himself. It was summer, for Chrissake! Apart from white socks an' StartRites, the dangling cranefly had on a sleeveless, flowery, Mum-made frock. What a total nerd he was. Wearing naff gear like that an' thinking himself a cool dude, man! Admit it Dad. You're a complete wanker – the original – the prototype – the Daddy of all wankers. Light years from present day Mr Cool. Present day – present day – what the fuck *is* the present day? Where the fuck is y.t. now and what the fuck is all this time-hopping crap about, man? Who the fuck's running the show – not y.t., that's for sure. Must be somebody out there – IS THERE ANYBODY OUT THERE? Dr fucking Who an' his poxy kiosk s'pose. Not funny. Getting way beyond a joke. For Chrissake, chill out some, Dad. No need to squeeze cranefly quite so hard. Can't breathe in, can't breathe out 'cos of your frigging woolly waistcoat. A waistcoat, for fuck's sake! Small cranefly crushed to death by Killer Burton Checked Waistcoat ha ha ha. Ain't half got smelly breath, Dad. Gnashers ain't gotta lot going for them either.

Thank Christ he's easing off the old ribcage – oxygen shifting a tad through tubes! What's the daft tosser warbling on about – words like wriggly little pond creatures, whispering raspily and moistly in y.t.'s ear'ole.

'Don't worry Lou-Lou, you'll always be Daddy's special little girl. No matter what happens. Daddy promises you that you'll always be special.'

Tosser! Burton Check relinquishing hold on the cranefly and lowering it onto StartRite tootsies. Dad sure is one big dude, man!

Saying something – whispering raspily again – fuck, but it was far out seeing young Dad! Funny. No probs with young Aberdeen Granite features. Aberdeen Granite's Aberdeen Granite, s'pose. Hadn't changed much. Older, natch, but hair still the same long(ish) straight disaster and phizog same chunk of acne-d tundra. But Dad was another matter. What the fuck is he whispering.

They were walking along a carpeted corridor. Hand in hand. Yours truly an' Dad. Christ, but he must be the tallest, lankiest, dorkiest looking dude in the entire galaxy an' y.t.'s wee mitt felt like a toasted teacake nestling in the huge Dad's paw. Always a bit of a mumbler, Dad. Weird scene going down, man. Slow motion. Or something. Dad an' y.t. walking along corridor but had covered no distance at all. Still in same frigging spot. Moving, though. Moving forwards. Don't look, bitch. Making noddle all swimmy.

'You've got a little baby sister, Lou-Lou. Mummy's fine and so's the baby. Daddy wants you to be a very good girl and try not to upset Mummy. She's very tired and needs to have a nice, long rest. OK?'

Whelping time, is it? Data received an' processed O Twilight Zone-y One. Must've just come from stuffy pair o' wrinklies next door – no, few doors along. Lotsa scrummy biccies an' gooey cakes to keep y.t. busy while Mum whelping. Anything better than near seizure of brain cell when thought Mum had wanted y.t. to be in on moment of Alien emergence. Dad had been there. Natch. Mum had phoned him at work when midwife had shown up an' he'd fetched y.t. from playschool on his way home.

Y.t. had nearly done a runner at sight and sound of the madwoman panting an' squealing like an injured beast as she did her waddling run round an' round the flat, belly looking as though ready to explode at any mo and splatter mangled Alien all over walls, ceiling, herself and y.t. Why the fuck couldn't y.t. have stayed at playschool until gruesome business completed? Y.t. had been scared shitless as to what might come out of that huge, swelling belly and what it might do to Mum. Could see it in there, for Chrissake! Flexing muscles – doing friggin' push-ups, getting ready to commit murder! OK for Nerd-of-the-Universe Dad. What a pair of sickos they'd been – going to antenatal classes, practising special breathing (psycho-something-axis . . . psycho was dead right, man!) leg-spreading on the poor ol' tintawn; she'd even had a friggin' tune to sing during the final mos of spawning for Chrissake. Dickheads or what?

Something bugging Dad. Y.t. could tell, as they made their slow-motion-y, no progress way along the corridor, that something was eating him.

Like a Burton-checked Count Drac he's swooping down on y.t. an' pond-life syllables once again wiggling into y.t's shell-like. Has he got a sore throat? Doesn't usually sound like Kermit.

'It's another girl, Lou-Lou, another girl. I can't believe it – it just won't sink in – can't take it in at all. We were so sure it was going to be a boy. Got all the boys' names. They said it might be twins, or a boy, because Mummy was so big. So sure it was going to be a boy. Haven't even thought of a single name for a girl. Never would've believed it.'

Poor fuck almost sounds as though he's having a bit of a blub.

Suddenly the whingeing stopped and they were inside 31 The Hollies, the door closing behind them. Funny how the ethnic-y look's cool again. Rustic weave tintawn looking real good. Not the psycho purple coffee table, though. Far out, all this memory lane shit. Dad'd made the coffee table when they'd first moved to the flat. Mum'd had major probs getting hold of purple paint. Dark-green Aztec-y swirl curtains Mum'd made and the scrummy old carved chair she'd upholstered in wine brocade just to let the mogs lie on it. Wonder what happened to it? Could've been a family heirloom. Who knows? Rugs she'd made, shaggy an' unshaggy, scattered all over the tintawn an' hanging on the walls. Cushions to match. During last weeks in life cycle of the Alien, y.t. had thought Mum an' Dad right off their trolleys. Dad was the worst. Only just. 'Cos Mum had always been into making things. Only difference was hugely increased variety an' output. Like one-woman cottage industry. But Dad had suddenly shown signs of the most sicko nesting tendencies, reaching rock bottom when he made a wooden rocking cradle with effing hearts cut out at either end for Chrissake! Mum not far behind with a tree made outta chicken wire – where the fuck had she got hold of chicken wire in SE 13? – and swabs of coloured tissue paper.

Funny how they were doing all those nerdy nesting thingies

together and yet Mum couldn't stand being fucked by Dad. How many times y.t. had lain awake, late at night, listening to Dad trying, in vain, to hump Mum. Didn't know that at the time, o' course. Just knew that Dad was doing something horrible to Mum. Something that made her cry out, 'Don't – don't, please don't,' sometimes. And, other times, 'it's hurting – it's hurting – please stop.' Then there would be the weeping. For hours on end. Or so it seemed.

Sometimes Dad would slam and shout out of the bedroom and into the bathroom where he'd jerk off into the wash hand basin. Once, y.t.'d listened as Mum caught him in mid-wank. Screaming, screaming. No matter what he said she just would not believe that he was only giving his dick a good wash. Y.t. shit scared she might throw herself out of window. Third floor. Running up and down. Screaming.

All Mum's fault for being a frigid bitch. Only good thing about few shags she'd had with Rog. Found out that frigid she was not.

Funny, though. Mum hadn't always hated it. Being humped by Dad. Y.t. had cutglass memory of being plonked on floor (digits in gob o' course) behind armchair screen whilst Mum and Dad groaned their way through screwing the settee. In the living room! In broad daylight! Must've had the hots something rotten if they couldn't even make it to the bedroom, man. Wonder how it all got fucked up – or unfucked ha ha.

Lotta decibels coming from Mum's bedroom. Lotta braying an' cackling. Toasty, nutty, smoky pong prickling inside of snitch. Need to sneeze man! – can't. Nice, spicy pong, like Dad's Old Holborn. But spicier and much nice-ier.

Dad an' y.t. in the bedroom and, over by the big window, was source of yummy pong. Anything less yummy hard to imagine. On a scale of nice-iness he would register a big minus. Unc dickhead Simon (Dad's older and shorter – by at least twenty cms – bolshie little prick of a bruv) puffing, like a real grown-up, on a cigar almost as big as his shortarse self. Though full bruvs, they hadn't as much as a spit in common. Apart from acquiring dwarf status when within range of Giant Dad, Unc was fair-skinned, with light-brown hair an' hazely peepers. (All been said already, y.t. Losing it, babe.) Nicest thing about him. His peepers. Only concession to orange-grove ancestry was fleshy gob an' big 'ooter. Same gob as the Fag lady. And same li'l red rooster strut. As dickheads do, he fancied himself a real cool dude. The best

40

actor, dancer, choreographer, comedian, cameraman, boom boy (or was it bum-boy ha ha) in the entire frigging industry. In the real world, Unc was a zit-brained loudmouth who got on everyone's tits as soon as he opened his gob.

Blacklisted by his own agent, for fuck's sake! Like most short-arses, Unc was mega-conscious of his lack of vertical cms, blaming it on his failure to hit the big time as a ballet dancer. Wonder what you'd make o' that Ruski dude, Unc? Not to mention li'l ol' Wayne Sleep.

Got his bit part actress bitch with him. Beaker of booze sloshing about. Braying on an' on. And there was Mum. Sitting up in bed; bright pink phizog an' hair a disaster zone. Glass of booze in the one mitt whilst cradling, in the crook of her booze-free arm, a not-so-small bundle wrapped in one of her hand-knitted cobwebby efforts. No bleedin' wonder y.t.'d had the shits about what exactly was growing inside that great belly-pod! Could've been a nest of sodding great spiders, man. Couldn't it?

Everyone smiling/grinning different sorts of smiles/grins. No need to waste space on dickhead dwarf an' his braying bitch. Mum had a mega-soppy crinkly sort of smile playing silly buggers with her gob and, though she looked totally shagged, there was a soft glowiness all around her edges. As though lit from within by a wee lamp. Close to it, but never looked *quite* that way when round a gee-gee.

Wish same could be said for Burton Man. Holy shit – come outta the murky depths, man – Dad's middle name really is Burton! Fag lady's moniker prior to wedlock. Weird or what? Jesus – why the fuck can't y.t. laugh – throat wobbling like fucking frog-spawn but no effing sound coming out. Fucking hurting, man. Don't need this shit. No way.

Wish same what could be said for Burton Man? Oh yeah. That he had a glowy thingy hanging round his yellow gob instead of that 'orrible twisted grin. Forcing his mush into what he thinks is a jolly smile an' all it comes out as is a hideous rictus. Can't suss it, dudes. Can's suss what's wrong with the daft tosser.

Action, for Chrissake – y.t. being summoned to Mum's side to say 'hello' to the Alien. Bloody great enormous Alien with red, wrinkled phizog all screwed up with peepers scrunched shut – *something*'s scrunched shut, maybe not peepers at all! *Anything* could be curled up under the red, dried-up lids! Two little, scaly reptiles – one under each lid, maybe – anything, could be anything!

Fucking nasty piece of Alien, to tell the unvarnished!

Suddenly, great weight crashing down on to y.t.'s scrawny shoulders. Awesome in its hugeness, it sat squatly, sniggering in y.t.'s shell-like.

Mum's asking y.t. what she thinks would be a nice name for the baby; for y.t.'s baby sister. For fuck's sake, Mum – just 'cos you an' Dad hadn't the wit to think of any girl's monikers, no need to foist shit on to y.t.!

Should've known Mum, that the little red StartRite couldn't wait to shove itself firmly in the shit. Pathetic. Here comes the reedy piping for Chrissake.

'Peter. I want to call the baby Peter.'

Peter, for fuck's sake! Get a life, y.t. – Alien it might be – but a fucking *female* Alien! As blabbed *ad nauseam* by Dad in the corridor. Uttered like a true retard, y.t. Everyone laughed. Dickhead Simon thought it a real hoot. Correction. Everyone didn't laugh. Everyone, except Mum, laughed. Instead of going into amused mode her phizog darkened as Ugly Irritation winged across it, nuking the soft, blurry glowy thingy right out the frigging third floor window. In spite of the nuking, she managed to stay in control.

'Why, Lou-Lou? Why have you chosen Peter? You know it's a little sister you've got, not a brother, so why did you choose a boy's name? Why not a girl's name?'

C'mon y.t. – for fuck's sake think before opening retard gob an' dropping StartRite in shit again – think, y.t. – think!

'Because, because I want it to be a little brother. That's why, Mummy.'

Nice one, y.t. Even at age of four and three-quarters destiny being fulfilled as bringer of bum note. Not only y.t. though. Bum notes, though silent ones, coming in their droves from direction of Burton Man. As soon as y.t.'d said about wanting little bruv something sly had slithered under his sallow skin. Wasn't there for long. Now ya see it now ya don't. Now? Now? what the fuck is it with now? Christ, why don't they all just fuck off an' let y.t. have a bit o' shut-eye. Feel as though haven't had a decent kip in days. Weeks. Some help dickhead Unc had turned out to be in y.t.'s hour of need. That was later, though. Whaddya mean, bitch? Later now or later then? Bastards the lot of them.

No chance of a sodding kip with icicles having a meet round extremities. Going beyond poxy joke, man. Shit should be wearing off now – even if E. Been in this shit hole bed for fucking hours man – where the fuck were those poxy so-called pals? No better than shortarse Unc – turn backs on y.t. in hour of need.

Fair do's, y.t. Must be middle of fucking night. Squat dead quiet and dead dark. 'Cept for feeble winking from street light or some sort of light. Moonlight? What the fuck'd happened to the poxy light bulb? Christalmighty, entire universe ganging up on y.t. including effing lightbulb. If could only grab, hold a blanket to drag across bod an' keep off gawdawful chill, man. Feels like some dude's rubbing blocks of ice all over skin. Right through to the bone.

Sweet Jesus – sweet fucking Jesus – noddle snapping off with force of swinging great swipe. Room reverberating, shutters clattering their corrugated applause – not ended, then? Why – why – why in the fuck's name why is it so fucking cold? Ear'oles buzzing from bloody fat slap. What the fuck's y.t. done to fuck up now, man? No rest for the fucking wicked. Wearing a thin flowery nightdress Mum, well into hissing mode, towering over y.t. like – like – like Mum well into hissing mode. Can't get a lot worse. Peepers trying like fuck to pop outta sockets and bounce round room; gnashers struggling to get free from casing of flesh an' bone; Mum doing her best to keep them there, where they belonged.

'You idiot – you stupid, brainless little idiot – who told you that – who? – who?'

Dear God, is there to be no end to this catalogue of drear? No more shit – not even a joint, OK? Is it a deal? Y.t.'ll even try an' believe in you, you sick fuck, if you'll put an end to all this Twilight Zone-y shit. Please, God. Please.

Standing at the foot of the bed wearing one of pretty, flowered dresses courtesy of good ol' Dork Manual and Mum's nifty needle work, the same dark-haired, scrawny, peaky-faced y.t. as dropped StartRite in shit. Nausea doing a bit of a jig an' one of arms being shaken so hard it feels it's going to ripped from mooring of shoulder. Here comes that thin, reedy piping piercing its way out of the skinny-ribby, shit-scared wee bod.

'The nurse told me – it was the nurse that told me – she told me it was in the doctor's black bag – that the doctor had brought it in his black bag – it was the nurse, Mummy . . .'

Y.t.'s noddle rocked again by swinging slap and bed vibrating to rhythms of calypso-ing corrugated curtains. Jesus Christ, Mum – take it easy, for fuck's sake!

It was a nice little summer dress. Quite simple. Draw string, or rather draw ribbon, neck and long sleeves gathered to sort of ruched effect at the wrists with a well disguised, narrow strip of elastic. Mum was a dab hand with needles, be they knitting or sewing. Could manipulate them with just as much, if not more, expertise as she was applying to y.t.'s scraggy little arms.

Suddenly the hissing stopped. Poor bitch looked a fucking fright. Her voice as shagged-out as her phizog, she seemed to twig that it's a pair of arms and not knitting needles that she's levering back and forth.

'What is God's name is it that you're trying to do to me? If only I knew – if only . . . I told you – I told you and only because you asked me – no other reason – no other reason except you asked where the baby came from – I told you – I explained as best's I could – and now you say that the baby came in the doctor's black bag – why? In God's name, why?'

Huge, wide, dark peepers staring blankly up at the mad-woman.

Y.t. doesn't know why. Hasn't got a fucking clue. Forgot, most prob'ly. *Knew* the Alien'd come outta Mum's pod; had felt it dividing an' multiplying, for Chrissake. Too shit scared to say forgot. Brain cells nuked into meltdown by Hurricane Mum. For a few mos, the hissing spat about before giving way to a sort of wailing. Shell-likes ain't 'alf taking a bit o' flak here – can't handle the decibels, man. Lotta shit coming outta Mum's cake'ole. Big, heavy, clumsy, wailing shit stumbling all over the dying sparking an' fizzing of the hissing an' shrieking. Rock'n rollin' a fucking firework scene round and above and all the way over y.t.'s muddled noddle. Twistin' an' jivin' words, man. Fireflies flashing little sunbursts of rainbow sound in the dark.

The mouth gaped as if in supplication. Or a silent, frozen scream. The tears made an attempt in the way of offering solace as they interrupted their steady course towards neck and ears to briefly and unsuccessfully moisten the corners of her mouth.

The fat, metallic bodies of the sleepy, sated bluebottles highlighted the awful pallor of her skin as they shuffled lazily among the cold, glistening pearls of sweat. The eyes were half-closed, the lids unmoving but allowing a glint of flickering white to become visible every now and then.

Other than the occasional angry buzz of an irritated fly, disturbed by something of importance to a fly, there was no sound to be heard in the room. Nor in the squat. The fly-speak might elicit a response, of a different pitch, from a fellow fly. Then another. And another. Until the flurry of buzzes became a full-blown fly argument. There were a lot of flies in the room.

DAY TWO

August 18th

The light filtering through the bit of glass and the cracks in the metal sheeting was thin and watery, but an enterprising raylet managed to reach as far as the bed and its occupant. Seizing their moment, a throng of dust motes boogied frenziedly before being snatched back through both gaps and grime.

During that brief illumination, the ugly, creeping blackness of the crawling flies became a multi-hued iridescence emitting rapid, SOS flashes of momentary brilliance. Other than the extremities, which were a dull, bruised blue, the exposed areas of flesh were of a waxy-grey, bloodless pallor.

Almost imperceptibly, the head moved to one side. The wound looked sinister with its sinuous, living dressing. Heads down, they were feeding-defecating, feeding-defecating, but, in spite of their industry, there was still a quantity of mustardy pus oozing from the indented skull.

The house was quiet. It was very early in the morning.

Fluttering weakly, the lids opened slightly, but all that was visible of the eyes were the whites rolling gently in their sockets. Soon, as though exhausted by the effort of even such a partial opening, they closed once more.

Unconscious throughout the morning and early afternoon she was roused by the deafening blast of heavy metal coming from elsewhere in the squat.

Bunch of effing deadbeat wankers've surfaced at last – won't be long now – door'll open an' one o' scumbags 'll phone for Doc. Some o' arseholes might've been in an' left y.t. to finish kip. Might've. Fuck it all man – can't move. Not able to move. For Chrissake this pissing spas shit should be wearing off – should've worn off – not bleedin' funny – beyond poxy pale, man. Stay cool, babe. Stay cool. For fuck's sake stay cool. Noddle moving – noddle moved – just a tad but fucking move it fucking did! Work on it, bitch. Think positive. Stay cool. Y.t. dead bleedin' right about duration of pig-sicking spas shit – don't mind using poxy word now – spastic – spastic – spastic – paralysis – paralysis

– spastic . . . Wonder why can't even twitch any other part of bod? And why was the ice-cube brigade (cube? *cube*? – fucking great blocks more like) still out in force? Give it time, bitch. Give it time. Chill out some more – ha ha ha.

Please God or whatever, y.t.'ll cut out speed as well. Freaky, though. Thinking about it. Can't remember having that much more than the norm. Might've had a few more voddies. Seem to recollect more than the one bottle. Blowjob had forked out way over the odds. Had a snort or two. Y.t. not used to it. Maybe that was it. Fucked up y.t.'s neurons. Too late now, babe. Just have to sit tight an' wait ha ha ha.

Fucking reasons to be cheerful lark beginning to wear a tad thin. Sick to fucking gills of trying to be fucking cheerful. What the fuck was there to be fucking cheerful about? Being able to move poxy noddle an eighth of a millimetre? Wow! Thank you God! Have a wee try at flexing the old epiglottis – never know. If noddle able to shake it baby, then might be able to squeeze a squeak out of voice box.

Wouldn't you know it. Zilch. Zero. Just as spastic. Just as fucking dumb. Here comes old fearty, settling nice an' comfy, like a fucking unheard-of-tog duvet. Hey man, where in the fuck've these hot, wet little mamas sprung from? Itchy mothers! But Christ they were warm! Like weeny, diluted concentrations of sun-rays aimed through pinhole in lump of card. Practically burning holes in flesh, cheeky bastards!

Old fearty given karate chop, as Bright-side, grinning like a retard, did a wild boogie as noddle moved enough to let torrent of fucking toasty tears wash over neck an' shell-likes. Always look on the bright si-ide of life – de-doom, de-doom, de-doom de-doom de-doom. Good ol' Brian was one cool dude, man.

Reasons to be cheerful, one, two, three. Wanker mates had surfaced – deafening din meant that y.t.'d be on tod no longer. No more than a few mos. At most. Doc would have to be got. Chances were he/she'd refuse to come to squat. Happened before. Not y.t. Don't think it was. Clunie, wasn't it? What the fuck does it matter, bitch! Cross that bridge . . . Prob'ly have to go into hossy. Chance of a bit o' warmth an' a good hose down. Don't relish thought of being in fucking sterilisation unit. But anything – anything better than being stuck in poxy perma-frost.

C'mon dudes, get collective digits out an' come an' have a butchers at the heap o' shite ol' Blojo's up to neck in this time.

Mindless load of effing tossers. If they thought there was a chance of a bit o' dosh they'd be queuing six deep to be first through effing door. Fucking bastards.

Boat-race about to burst. Like a big fist pressing on inside on each cheek. Can see a mirror. Can see a small, painted clown. Its phizog a de Kooning dream of paintbox streaks and daubs. The cheeks, though. Some shit wrong with the cheeks. Bulging a lot. An' the bulges were on the move. A hand and part of an arm appeared in the mirror. The hand grabbed the back of the neck of the little, painted clown whilst a second hand, also attached to an arm, stuffed fistfuls of small, multi-coloured discs into the distorted little mush. Smarties. Fucking Smarties.

In spite of the melting and half-chewed clarts of chocolate slithering down chin, the wee gob kept opening to let more and more of the jolly comfits to be crammed into it. What an airhead! Stay cool, y.t. Whatever happens, gotta stay cool.

Paintbox clown was y.t. All this weird time-hopping shit beginning to do noddle right in, man. One mo y.t. lying like Tut's Mummy in the tomb, an' the next, catapulted in to the middle of the fucking Twilight Zone.

Leave it out Mum, for Chrissake – the old boat-race is hurting something chronic – please Mum – please stop – please – please . . .

Can't fucking believe it! Y.t. keeps opening poxy gob for more!

'Eat – eat – eat, damn you, if you want to eat them eat – eat – eat . . .!'

Mum's stuck in groove of hissing and spitting mode.

Wouldn't be so bad if y.t. could taste some of effing Smarties, man! Clown y.t. getting more than a tad pissed off with bloody Rowntree efforts being shoved non-stop into gob. Starting to snivel an' gurn at sheer weight of numbers of the bright, wee sods.

Here comes next stage. Mum trying to cuddle the little clown; clown having none of it. Fuck off, you sadistic old bitch! Keep shoulders stiff, an' plump wee bod at a distance from Mum's wrap-around arms. Plump? Plump? How far back has fucking Tardis come if y.t. still plump, for Chrissake?

Old fearty was back. An' this time he'd brought a pal. Another fearty. The pair of them grinning like sick fucks, struggling all over the little clown's rainbow phizog to try an' be the main man fearty. Fucking pair o' Sumos. Fearty 1 was to do with choking. Y.t. having a bit of a job getting breath in an' out o' gob. Throat blocked. Every time draw breath in, mashed Smarties falling all over gooey selves trying to find way down gullet, clarting Mr Epiglottis and even finding way up nasal orifices for Chrissake! Fearty 2 was of Mum going back into hissing spitting mode. With a vengeance. Happened sometimes. Especially if y.t. a tad too stand-offish when Mum moved modes.

Got away with it this time, kiddo. The bitch has gone straight into weeping mode. Black-fucking-heath. That's where they were. There's y.t. in the wee kitchen. Rummaging in the pedal bin. No sign of Smarties. What a headcase – never gives up quest for pickings.

Still fattish and bandy-pinned so can't be long after Smarties episode. Or can it? Could be before. Another fucking Tardis trip. Hopping in an' out of wormholes in the Blackheath universe of all these years ago. What's with Blackheath, you sick Twilight-Zone-y fuck?

There it is – what y.t.'s bin-raiding for – yum-yum-yum – ace move, kiddo, shove digit right in an' all around – c'mon – c'mon let's have a taste of that yummy cool frooty gunge before gob bursts into flames!

Mission in-fucking-complete. Here's Mum. Phizog like granite with lump o' semtex sticking up out of top of noddle. Hang on – hang on to it kid – finders keepers an' all that crap. No use. Mum's wrenching it outta y.t.'s clenched mitt an' flinging it back into pedal bin. Shoulder-shakin' time again, dudes! Steady on, Mum. Noddle hurting. Making y.t. mewl like kitten or little piggie. No need to get in such a bleedin' bate, bitch. Only an empty fucking yog carton. No big deal. Can feel rage boiling. Can feel sizzling heat. Enough to grill coupla waffles, man.

'If you wanted another yoghurt why in God's name didn't you just ask for one instead of rooting about in the rubbish bin like an animal for other people's leftovers you filthy disgusting little bitch.' All delivered in hissing mode with just a tad of spit. Didn't really want another yog, Mum. Wouldn't have said no but just wanted to see what the peachy one tasted like. Go on – tell her kid – tell her instead of standing there like a fucking mute! She ain't ever gonna wise up if you don't tell her, dildo!

Final vicious shake of shoulder – Jesus, careful of the kid's noddle, Mum!

No shouting this time. Stayed with the hiss. Wonder why?

Visitors. That's why. Some bitch pal of Gina's with a bratski about y.t.'s age (three-ish?). Looking at Mum as though she's some sorta lowlife. Mum's stammering some shit about old pal the pedal bin. Never saw the bitch again, did you Mum? And as for what she went an' told Gina . . . best forgotten. Ain't it.

Funny smell. Funny, earth, mushroomy, peaty sorta smell. Christ it's cold – fucking icy more like. Tight an' icy. Weird, man. No effing wonder! Snow on friggin' ground! Not deep, just a scattering, but friggin' snow all the same. Fucking great trees looming and leering as though they owned the fucking joint. Bastards trying to blot out the sky – fat chance – whatta sky – like an upturned porcelain blue plate some dopey giant's left lying around for his Mum to pick up.

Earthy smell mingling with pine tree pong. Lanky Dad an' titchy y.t. ambling along wide forest track. Y.t. not as plumpo and, thank Christ, not as bandy-pinned, but still a right little shortarse. Only a dress an' a cardy on in fucking Antarctica, man! What the fuck's Mum doing dragging along miles behind y.t. an' Dad? Trundling old pushchair ahead of her like a bleedin' bag lady with all the picnic gear piled on it. Blowing snitch. Blubbing a bit by the looks of it. Dabbing peepers. You an' Dad had another of your little misunderstandings, Mum?

Must be on one of their weekend walkies. No Ginnybitch. No bulge to be seen on Mum's gut. What time of the year for Chrissake? Looks an' feels like fucking winter but can't be. No one wearing winter woollies. Y.t. must be about four. Still at Blackheath then. *The Evening Standard* – the fucking *Evening Standard* – did a weekly map of a little walkie – all coming back, dudes! What they did was catch a choo-choo to the starting point, do the walkie then catch a choo-choo back home again. Fucking nutcases. All Mum's doing. Nice an' peaceful. Just y.t. an' Dad strolling along. His long, loping seven leaguers an' y.t.'s mincing little waddle. Hand in hand. Each knowing that they truly hated this fresh fucking air and communing with Nature crap. Fulfilled Mum's needs. Went some way to keeping marbles intacto. Sad.

Small hard hammers idly thumping their balls off inside skull. What the fuck's with the pain, man? Can't fucking see! Even if not much to see – seeing was seeing, man. Nothing. Fuckarse nothing. Only fucking darkness. Ol' pal panic grabbing chance to fill gob with hot sourness, burning already dried an' crusty flesh inside cake'ole. Please Jesus – please – anything but blind. Anything.

A voice. Low and urgent and full of concern. Mum's voice.

'Lou-Lou, Lou-Lou, come on, open your eyes. You'll be OK. What a silly girl! What on earth did you trip on? Nothing to trip on, only the stairs – was it the stairs? Did you trip on the stairs?'

The voice suddenly veers away.

'Perhaps we should call a doctor – leave her where she is – you're not supposed to move . . . why are the bloody stairs so narrow anyway?'

Dad's mumble joins the fray.

'She'll be all right. She didn't hit her head that hard. She's just not used to stairs. C'mon Lou-Lou, open your eyes and give your Dad a smile, there's a good girl.'

Mum's shoving her sodding oar in again.

'It's an omen – I knew it – there's something about this house – it's an omen . . .'

Dad: Mumble, mumble – rent cheap – mumble – get used to stairs – mumble – mumble – mumble . . .

Worcester effing Park. They were moving to Worcester effing Park. What a fucking downer! Couldn't afford the Blackheath rent since Mum had given up work. All fucking Alien Ginnybitch's fault, dudes! Even with Dad doing evening job as well as cheffing in canteen in Wapping Wall. Just couldn't make ends meet. Mum, the bitch, had earned a packet.

They were all in the front garden of the Worcester Park semi. Sun shining and shit hot. Ginnybitch a wriggling lump, glued to Mum's chest. As usual. Staying with this warp then, Jim? Mum and Dad wittering on about roses. Roses, for Chrissake! Get real! Dig the whole fucking lot over and lay concrete, more like.

Mum's thingy, the garden. Outdoor thingy, innit? Dad trying to look tuned-in. Mum off on a bleeding tangent. Y.t. about to vanish up own arse with boredom.

No one seemed to be muttering, but muttering could be heard. Low and insistent and coming from the direction of the pavement. All noddles turn to see, standing outside the garden gate, a short rake-thin, old bint. Hair as tightly knit as the narrow, stitched gob and thick, pebble-lensed specs giving all-over look of midget Nazi war-criminal in drag.

Daft bitch Mum smiling and going towards old turd thinking, it's a neighbour, come to say 'hello'.

Old Turd not even stopping for breath as she carried on with litany of mutterings.

'Pigs – nothing better than pigs – uncivilised pigs – not fit to live with decent people – pigs – pigs – pigs – only fit for trough – pigs – filthy pigs . . .' etc. etc. etc.

Neighbourly smile frozen into rictus of shock. Mum grabs y.t. by arm and scarpers back into Wate's semi with Ginnybitch bouncing off her chest like a freaky rubber baby. Good ol' Dad! After few mos of being gobsmacked, making way across to Old Turd. You tell the old Nazi, Dad! Tell her go buy a dildo and leave decent folks be – ha ha ha! Dad *was* telling the overpermed old bitch but fuck knows what he was telling her, 'cos he had that real nerdy grin spread all over his boat-race.

Mum trembling as though bones had dissolved, pale as a sheet and looking ready to puke, clutching Ginnybitch and y.t. as though life depended on hanging on to both.

Here comes nerdy Dad. Still wearing big, cheesy grin. Nice one, Dad. Really told her, did ya?

'Who is she? Who is that – that dreadful woman – is she the local loony? Is she, Desmond?'

'Nothing to worry about,' says Dad. 'Just a little misunderstanding. These paddy pads you've been putting down the loo, seems they've blocked the sewer and poor Mrs Crisp had a bit of an overflow in her back garden. It's OK though. I've told her you won't do it any more and she was all right about it. Quite nice, in fact.'

Ace performance, Dad. Y.t. couldn't have done better job of shoving both plates right in it. Mum says (after stunned silence). No. Mum *screams*, after stunned silence . . .

'Mrs Crisp – poor Mrs Crisp – poor bloody Mrs Crisp – who the bloody hell is poor Mrs bloody Crisp? Well? Well? Who is she? Who? Who is poor bloody Mrs Crisp, Desmond? Your new friend, poor bloody Mrs Crisp – why the hell didn't you tell poor bloody Mrs Crisp to go and screw herself instead of grovelling and creeping with that stupid bloody grin on your stupid bloody face,' (voice cracking in mid-shriek, so forced to come down an octave or so). 'I might have known it would turn out to be my bloody fault – how could it possibly have been otherwise? Why the hell shouldn't I put bloody shitty paddy pads down the bloody loo – it says so on the packet – flushable, it says – and even if they weren't and even if it was all my fault, that doesn't give Mrs bloody shitty Crisp the right to speak to *anyone* the way she did to me. She's the one who's uncivilised – what a thing to say to anyone – how could you be nice to her? How could you? How could you have said one nice word to her after that, never mind creeping all over her like a bed bug! It's always the same, Desmond – you're nothing but a prize toady – you always end up sucking up to people, making sure that they're all right – that their precious feelings aren't hurt. The last thing you're concerned about is your hysterical wife, the one who always over-reacts – who always makes a scene given half a chance according to you and my bloody mother. Why couldn't you have stuck up for me for once? And how the hell could the old bat be so sure it was me putting the blasted paddies down the loo? What about the couple the other side of the alley? *They* have a baby, don't they? Don't they? You never mentioned that to Mrs bloody Crisp, did you, Desmond? Did you? Why does it always have to be me? Always me – me – me!'

Some fucking soliloquy Mum! 'Specially when delivered at shell-like splitting volume! Sure as fuck succeeded nuking grin off Dad's mush into outer reaches of stratosphere! Brows beetling forward making noddle dangerously Neanderthal, Dad says:

'Well, it's not my fault. I didn't put the bloody things down the loo and if we're to live on good terms with our neighbours would you just make sure it doesn't happen again.'

Might as well have clocked her one, Dad! What a phizog – wait for it – plug ear'oles! Just opened gob and screamed. Really screamed. A real, someone's-trying-to-murder-me scream. Taking huge, gaspy sucks of air between long, ear-splitting screams.

Leave it out Mum, for Chrissake! You've made your effing point. Dad's a wanker. We all know that. Tell us something new. Ginnybitch starting to wail with fright, and no bleeding wonder. Y.t. starting usual whingeing snivel. Peepers darting about like dragonflies, though. Shit scared, both Ginnybitch and y.t. Who the fuck wouldn't be, Mum? Chill out and give everyone's shell-likes a bit of a rest, for fuck's sake.

Dad's doing a runner. Nice one, Dad. Can't cope with the family falling apart, so turn and run. All snivelling now. All three of them. Trying to outdo each other in the snivelling stakes.

Noddle fit to bust with all this effing din – what the fuck kinda mates are yous anyway? Squat coming down round ear'oles and none of yous can be arsed to even knock on Blojo's door. For

Chrissake shut off that fucking techno – can't stand it – put The Stones on, any ol' rock 'n roll better 'n that loada bollocks – fucking techno – like a thousand trains thundering through a thousand tunnels – SHUT IT OFF!

Someone loudmouthing. Sounds like coupla babes. Funny. Only Flo and Mo in squat and those babes too shit scared to even think about loudmouthing for fear of getting molars shoved down throat. Right in ear'ole this time. Not shouting. Just shooting gob off. Making minor tremor in shell-like. Mum. Who else but Mum. Not hissing, or spitting, or snarling. Just loud-mouthing. Who's she slagging off, then? And who's bad mouthing it back? Bit shakey, but determined. Factor successfully warped, Jim! We have visuals! Heeland Granny. It was Heeland fucking Granny. Mum and H.G. bad mouthing each other. Fancy H.G. turning up the volume – taking a chance aren't we, Granny? A member of the great unwashed might be on the ear'ole. Tut-tut – letting standards slip, Gran! Another weird smell wafting up snitch. What is it with these poxy pongs? Dry, dusty, yet sort of oily. Catching throat and elbowing way up noseholes. Jesus – need to cough! Can't. Throat feels like as though some bastard's wringing it out like a frigging dishcloth. Visuals gone. Where the fuck were they? They must all be there, Mum, y.t. and Ginnybitch. Unless rules had changed. And what the fuck was H.G. doing in the Twilight Zone?

Y.t. getting really shagged off with all this time-hopping shit. One fucking saga of fucking misery after another. Wasn't all like that. Why stuck in dim and distant, Jim? *The Enterprise* mislaid a gromit, has it? Pissed off with the whole effing peep show. Phizog and shell-likes itching like thousands of bugs creeping and crawling all over. There they all were. Mum, H.G. and yours truly. In a station. An underground station, for Chrissake. An' Ginnybitch, hanging onto Mum's tits in the slingy thingy. Must be soon after they'd moved to Behind the Net Curtain Land, a.k.a. Worcester fucking nightmare Park. Very soon. Everyone wearing summery gear so must still be August. Ginnybitch had been ten days old when they'd left Blackheath. She'd popped the pod on the sixth of August, they'd moved on the sixteenth and H.G. had come down for her hols and to help Mum settle in the new house with the recently emerged Alien.

Midwife had told Mum not to move house so soon after whelping. Had to. Lease up and couldn't afford rent. After few days all Mum's yummy milk fled the tit and Ginnybitch had to make do with Ostermilk. Broke Mum's heart. In seventh heaven with at least one tit shoved in Alien's gob.

What the fuck were they all doing standing in the middle of Charing X underground? (Could read sign, dudes.) Not far from the ticket office. Mum and H.G. having a right old slanging match within yards of the ticket office. Well, maybe not exactly having one, but on the bleeding verge. H.G. ready to nuke Mum at any mo. A wee Scots wifie, enough of a short arse to make Herr Crisp look like Long Tall Sally. Bit on the plump side; into beige and dull browns. Heart-shaped boat-race topped by usual middle-age-type perm. Skilled in the art of appearing both timid and friendly and hiding Cruella streak. Definitely a bit of a goer when threatened in any way, becoming uppity as shit when views and beliefs questioned, even moderately. Huge dislike and fear of the great unwashed rubber necking or ear'oling at private rituals. Y.t. most definitely not a fan of H.G. Mum clutching y.t. by the arm. Y.t. looking white and pinched round gob area and squeezing/unsqueezing scrawny thighs round mitt shoved up crotch.

Go on, kid! – let it run free! Nice to feel a bit o' warmth on the ice-lolly old pins! Can see thigh-squeezing getting on Mum's wick. Not exactly shouting, though up a few decibels, she says; 'For God's sake, child – I asked you if you wanted to go at Waterloo. Why do you always do this – how can you suddenly be so desperate? If you needed to go why didn't you go at Waterloo?'

Cue for H.G. to shove oar in.

'Now Margaret, there's no need for you to go on at the bairn in that way. No need at all. The same thing happens quite often to me. One minute I have no desire whatsoever to pay a call and the next I might be feeling quite desperate.'

Nice one, H.G.! Go on – shove yer tartan tootsie further into the heap o' shit you've dropped!

Mum's go. 'For God's sake, Mam, you have cystitis – you have to take pills – how on earth can you compare yourself with Laura?'

'I'm quite aware of that, Margaret, without you having to remind me. And there's no need for you to take that attitude. All I'm saying is that you should try and be a bit more patient with Laura. It's not the bairn's fault, you know.'

Go for it, Mum!

'No, no – of course it's not Laura's bloody fault. How could it be? How could it be anyone's bloody fault except mine? How could I be so stupid as to think otherwise? It's always my bloody fault, isn't it? Isn't it? It doesn't matter who or what, it's always my bloody sodding fault – everyone else as white as the driven snow – only me – me – me!'

H.G.'s snookered herself. Members of great unwashed turning and rubbernecking. Some with a bit of a grin; others with a look usually reserved for use of sightings of pile of steaming shit or vomit. Or both. H.G. white with shock, peepers writhing with cringe factor,

'For Heaven's sake, Margaret, will you please lower your voice – you're making a complete exhibition of yourself. I'm very sorry if what I said upset you – please try and calm yourself. All I meant was, and I'm very sorry indeed if you think I spoke out of turn, that it might be a good thing if you try and be a bit more understanding towards Laura. After all, she . . .'

(Funny little chook, H.G. Comes for hols every frigging year. Her and Mum always got bad scene going. Maybe that's why she keeps coming. Always sneaking sweeties to y.t. 'Don't tell your mother' shit. Seems to get her rocks off on it. Mum not keen on y.t. stuffing gob with neat sucrose but no need for H.G. to be so sneaky. Always shitting herself in case she's busted. Funny little twitch to the hooter; pinched and pleated round the gob; mince pies darting around like damsel flies on acid. Getting one over on Mum that turns the old bat on. Nothing to do with y.t. Didn't know that then, o' course.) Mum on the verge of blowing gasket. Go for it, Mum! Give it to the Heeland Cow!

Like the mother of all choo-choos, thundering and echoing through the tunnels, about to emerge and crush everything in its path before screeching to a hot and hissing halt, Mum bawls: 'You're a fine one to talk about understanding – who are you to pass judgement on me? If you'd shown me some bloody under-standing when I was a bairn perhaps none of this would be happening. Have you ever thought of that? Have you? Have you? No, of course you bloody haven't. That was all my fault as well, wasn't it? At least I've kept my bairn and not handed her over to someone else to look after. Three years old – how could you just turn your back on a three year old child – *your* three year old child? How could you? So who the hell are you to tell me how to be with Laura? All those bloody awful lies you told me – no room at the bloody inn. Not for me, there wasn't. But plenty room at the bloody inn for Gavin and Elspeth, though. Wasn't there? Wasn't there? Just no room for me. No bloody room for me.'

Nuked ain't the word for it. Poor ol' H.G. rooted to the spot with the onslaught.

'Please – please Margaret, will you please try and control yourself – think of the children . . .' Mum shoots off a few arrows of sarcastic cackling at this, but doesn't interrupt H.G. 'Think of yourself if not of them – I'm not asking you to think of me. What good is all this doing you – doing anyone? You really must try and get a grip of yourself – we can go and talk about it all over a nice cup of tea. You're just making a fool of yourself . . .'

Y.t.'s gone and pissed on the bleeding platform! Or ticket office area, or whatever. Just stood there and let it run down pipe-cleaner pins! No one's got peepers for y.t. Mum's still gotta missile to deliver.

'Then you shouldn't have left me with Granny – if you hadn't left me with Granny maybe I wouldn't be making a fool of myself now.'

No more nukeheads. Mum just looked shagged out.

H.G. white round gills but steely look in pale blue peepers. Voice quiet and shaky.

'Now Margaret, I don't know what reason you can have for saying such a thing. As far as your Dad and I knew you were always perfectly happy with Granny when you were a child. You certainly never gave any indication to the contrary. But perhaps now that you've calmed down we can go and discuss the matter somewhere less public.'

Poor Mum. She'd thought they'd have a nice day out, do a bit of window shopping in the West End. Knew it well. Used to work in Dickens & Jones. Had taken the wrong effing tube, all the same, and ended up at Waterloo.

They went for a cup of tea. Y.t. with soggy drawers rubbing skinny thighs red raw and dripping cold piss into socks.

Peepers darting around like flechs on heat, H.G. was asking Mum if there was anything in particular she'd like to discuss now that she'd calmed down.

No. Said Mum. And yes, she was quite sure. Said Mum.

The relief crumpled H.G.'s phizog like a manky old hanky.

Knock–knock–knock – some bastard knocking at door – at fucking last! One of selfish, dickhead mates has sobered up enough to remember poor ol' Blojo!

Try and call out – try, bitch, try. Try harder, harder – useless cunt – harder, for Chrissake! No fucking good. Can't even move noddle any more. Should be wearing off, man. Should be gone ta-ta by now. What is it with the sick fucking shit? Don't keep knocking, dickhead – just open effing door – for fuck's sake open the door and get y.t. out of effing strait-jacket.

Knock–knock–knock. H.G.'s Heeland poxy burr. Full of ruffled bloody feathers.

'Now look here, Margaret. It's time you learnt a thing or two.'

Knock–knock–knock. Muffled, ruffled feathers, then quick, Heeland chook pattering downstairs.

H.G., Dad, y.t., Mum and araldited Ginnybitch all draped round mess room in Wates Mansion. Still haven't fixed that gromit then, Jim? Can't even warp factor us out of Worcester fucking Park – too complicated a manoeuvre for that clapped out old tub, eh? Sick of the sight of Mum and Ginnybitch welded together like some weird, alien life form. Been out of the effing pod at least three weeks. Better if she'd never effing well come out. What's the difference between an internal and external growth? You can't fucking well see the internal growth, can you? Not as it is – not as a Ginnybitch. Only as a big lump. All there is now is Mum and Ginnybitch Mum and Ginnybitch Mum and Ginnybitch. Mum's having a bit of a go at Dad. About best mate Gina. Asking if he finds her dishy. Daft bitch. Should know better. Too late now.

Good heavens, no, lies Dad. Whatever gave you that idea? Why, he didn't even *like* Gina! Oh, she was a very nice person (bluster bluster bullshit bluster) very kind and all that. And a great friend. He'd say that for her, she was a very good friend to them both. But, as far as finding her physically attractive – why, he'd seen better sights down Wapping Wall!

Shit man, what a lying wanker – y.t. knows what Mum's going on about. Gina'd been in Canada with Oz artist for six months. Big reunion at Twickers pad. All well oiled. Mum had always known Dad had hots for Gina and was desperate to shove his dick anywhere at all on her big, brown bod. Seen the way he'd looked at her on first meeting. Fucking gobsmacked.

(Why don't you tell the big tosser what Big G had thought of *him* after that first close encounter, Mum? Tell him how gob-smacked *she'd* been when she found out that the eighteen year old lamp-post, wearing an elderly uncle-y mustard waistcoat over an even more elderly uncle-y pair of tweedy pants that had died several centimetres short of the bony ankles and huge dinner plates, was the gorgeous hunk as described in your letters?) Big G had suffered major cultural trauma when dearest buddy had actually married the callow, mustardy youth. It had been 1962, for Chrissake! Even Mum had been wearing the occasional bit of fringed ethnic and dried melon-seed.

But no, Mum said no such thing to Dad. Couldn't face it herself, s'pose. More than a tad on the beefy side now, Big G. Let herself go after the second whelping. Still with a phizog like Sophia Loren and a cunt like – well, a cunt. That was Big G's main feature. Made sure of that. At every possible opportunity, Big G would indulge in a spot of cunt-flashing. That was what was upsetting Mum. One flash too many. Not Big G's fault. Always been the same. Great pals with her cunt. Wanted everyone else to be as well. During reunion, everyone sprawled on various surfaces after huge nosh-up and crates of Big G's home-made poison. Gina had suddenly leapt up from floor by radiator, shrieking that her fucking legs were on fire. Flapping her sarong-y skirt wildly round her oak-tree thighs, she then hurled herself into an arm-chair announcing that she freely held herself responsible for any foul aromas that might waft in their direction as she hadn't washed her crotch for two days and wasn't wearing any knickers in case of immediate crotch-rot. Give her that. She was a fucking scream. The way she told it. A few mos later, apropos of zilch, Dad announced that he was feeling parky and was going to sit by the radiator. Mum took no notice until she realised that he was sitting directly opposite her dearest pal who was lying as though akip; peepers closed and pins akimbo. One outstretched at an angle and the other bent wide and high at the knee. Sarong-y thingy right up round the oak-trees. Poor Mum. Looked quite sick as she watched Dad take a peek, then another peek, then a longer peek, then shift his position to get an even better peek. Then get up and leave the room a tad sharpish.

When they'd got home, there'd been one hellova bad scene. Mum couldn't leave it alone. Like Dad and Big G's cunt. She couldn't stop herself from going back to it. Again and again. This time, Mum had made mistake of gobbing about it within ear'ole range of H.G. who, within a few mos, came cluck-clucking in from the kitchen, smiling her tight pursed smile and wringing the neck of a hapless tea-towel in her nervous claws. There's the shit, Granny. Just lift your tootsie a little and drop it right in it!

'You know Margaret, I hope you won't mind me saying this,' (smile trying to break through confines of anal-pursing; fails miserably), 'but you really don't know how lucky you are having such a good husband. There's a lot of women would,' cluck–cluck-cluck, 'give a great deal to have just some of the fuss that Desmond makes of you – ha ha ha.'

Mum loses cool straight off. No messing.

'Oh yes – oh yes – oh bloody sodding yes . . . ' (H.G.'s phizog wizens as though come across lemon hidden in gob – never could stand swear words) 'Oh yes – well everyone else might think she was sodding lucky but *she* didn't think she was so sodding lucky to be married to a bloody lackey who made cups of tea and did the bloody cooking – what was the cooking to him anyway? – he was a sodding cook, for Christ's sake! He enjoyed cooking! And what was so lucky about having a prize bloody creep for a husband – one who arse-licked his way all over the swine neighbours instead of sticking up for his wife and kids – why is it lucky to be married to a creep like that, Mam? Tell me? Married to a goddam creep and groveller and supposed to be lucky!'

Overdone it Mum. Too many swear words for starters. Doesn't matter that you're white and shaking like coming down from bad trip.

H.G.'s hooter twitching a few tads more violently; gob vanishing under a welter of neat, wee stitches. Peepers like chips of blue flint.

'Now look here, Margaret . . .'

Backed the wrong gee-gee, H.G.! No way is Mum hanging around to be 'look here'd' at! With Ginnybitch swinging and bumping across her chest, like some grotesque growth in the process of breaking free (again?), Mum fair sprints up the stairs. H.G. hot on heels, tea-towel slung over shoulder like ammunition belt.

Mum starting to wail and gibber. Can't blame poor bitch. Door slamming. Lock turning. H.G. knocking, knocking. Full of chest-puffing, pissed-offness.

'Now look here Margaret. It's high time you learnt a thing or two. Open the door, please. Stop behaving like a silly bairn and open the door. Margaret! Margaret! Will you please answer me! If you won't open the door, then at least answer me.'

Silence, except for muffled weeping. Then H.G. pattering back down stairs.

61

Come to the end of the rerun, O Twilight Zone-y One? Then what the fuck are we still hanging around Worcester fucking Park for? Y.t. snivelling. No one taking any notice. Hey Granny – your favourite granddaughter's starving to fucking death here. You know, the one you and Mum keep fighting over!

H.G. and Dad deep in cosy chat. Can't hear. H.G. always had soft spot for Dad. Ever since Mr H.G. and Dad had got legless one Hogmanay up in the Heelands. Dad had to be manhandled upstairs to bed. Puking all through the night. Mum and him married two days. Didn't matter. Dad has passed test. What test? Why, how much 80% proof needed to turn into drooling, vomiting heap o' shite. Mum had to drag him up and down the stairs all night for him to keep filling the lavvy with shite and vomit.

But Mr H.G. seemed to like Dad almost as much as he liked his wee drams. And that was more than enough for H.G. Dad could do no wrong in Heeland Granny's bluebell-blue peepers. That, as well as the sight and sound of Mum seeming to make the Heeland hairs on the back of her neck do a wee Heeland fling with their nerve-endings.

What's with the fucking hold-up, Jim? Can't you warp factor way out of this effing black hole? Seems different. Later. Getting dark outside. H.G. going across closing curtains. Why still here, Jim? Why still at poxy, effing Worcester Park?

No sign of Mum. Dad and H.G. still close-encountering. Bit of activity in kitchen and Dad going upstairs with cup of tea. Scrawny, half-starved y.t. follows. Bored shitless into bargain. Bedroom door opens to let in Big Cheesy Grin.

'How're you feeling, darling?' says Cheesy. 'Have you got one of your headaches?'

Yes, her mother was upset – what did she think she was going to be? Getting supper ready, though. A real trooper! And wanted Maggie to know that the last thing she wanted to do was upset her.

Mum laughing. Bit of a high-pitched cackle. Chill out, for Chrissake Mum.

'Don't you realise,' says Cheesy, 'what a strain you're putting on your mother? After all, Agnes had come for a holiday, hadn't she?'

Mum's words falling over each other trying to be first to reach top rung of screech.

'For God's sake, Desmond – I've not long had a baby – or have you forgotten? Ginny's hardly three weeks old. Can't you understand anything? Are you so bloody thick that you can't even understand that? And moving so soon – you know we shouldn't have – you're so bloody thick.'

Dad's all over Mum, patting and soothing. But she's pushing him off, shouting at him to bloody well leave her alone. Had to come down, though. Way past time for Ginnybitch's evening fix of Ostermilk.

H.G. well into the ruffled feathers routine. Bonce bobbing, chest puffed out, beady little mince pies darting on and off Mum when she thought no one was looking. Little bit of a chat between Dad and H.G. whilst grub going on table, before H.G. turns puffily to Mum.

'I'm very sorry indeed, Margaret, if anything I've said or done has in any way upset you. I've been trying my best to be helpful and I'm very sorry if that was the wrong thing to do on my part.'

Don't scream, Mum – please don't scream!

Phew. No screaming this time. Not this time. Poor bitch too shagged out. Peepers clenched and gob tight and white round edges of lips. Stay cool, Mum. Chill out, for Chrissake. Don't let the old Heeland Bat get to you.

Weird, though. When seeing H.G. off on train taking her back to the Heelands, Mum would be bawling bleeding peepers out. Happened every time. As plump, beige chook got ready to climb into Flying Scotsman, or whatever, Mum's phizog a frigging scream. Shitting herself from holding back the urge to grab and cuddle her Mum, H.G. Couldn't do it, though. H.G. most likely floor her with a couple of killer pecks if she as much as tried a clinch. Snitch twitching as though its little motor had slipped into a higher gear, she would find herself an empty seat with someone sitting opposite to ear'ole all her chooky chat. Once in train and settled in chosen seat, hooter would slip into lower gear and pursed gob would relax into a quirky smile. Lips still slightly pursed in middle, but corners of gob turning upwards. Broke Mum's bleeding heart, that smile did; could see it breaking. Could hear it cracking and splintering, prior to breaking. Mince pies no longer beady, but bluebell-blue-y with a hint of a twinkle. Heading home to the Heelands, aintcha, Granny?

If it's such a fuckawful drag, then why the fuck do you keep coming?

Hanging out of window until out of sight. Small beige noddle rapidly turning into tiny black dot and outstretched arm an antenna, searching and feeling its way into the future. Hours of blubbering would follow. From Mum. Fucking hours.

Most scrummy pong in the entire universe – some tosser's fagging, either in room or just outside door. What the fuck are these bastard so-called mates up to? Laughing – can hear poxy laughing! Jesus – could die for one drag on ciggy. Pong going right up hooter; wren-belly feathers of smoke tickling throat – need to cough – gotto cough – can't – oh God – like an army of bleeding ants setting up house inside hooter. Peepers prickling as though full of tiny thorns. Bunch of selfish fucking bastards! Just wait till y.t. out of poxy armour plating and back on pins. No more effing hand-outs – they could fuck themselves. Like they left y.t. to. Bastards. Fucking bastards the lot of them.

Some mother of a letter his holiness was going to get this time round! Funny. Still using that moniker. Nothing fucking holy about him these days. Looked much the same, though not such a cool dude as of old. Difficult to be cool whilst pleasuring Her Majesty, ha ha ha! Didn't bother any more with religious shite. Hadn't for a while. Full of crackpot plans for the future. Their future. Hadn't the bottle to tell old wanker what really thought of hair-brained ideas. Didn't want to make him give up hope altogether. As long as they kept the old tosser happy. No fun being stuck in the nick.

Jesus H. Christ, is there to be no effing peace? No effing foreplay either – straight into the mainframe this time. Y.t. taller and lankier. And wankier. Standing in front of table that was sagging under the weight of frigging tons of nosh of every sort. Just standing. And staring. For Chrissake grab something y.t. – anything!

Cakes, jellies, biccies, trifles, flans, gateaux, sides of beef, lumps of cheese – no end to effing spread. No chance. No effing chance. Airhead y.t. standing like zombie. Mum standing not far away, holding glass of booze – sherry by looks of glass. Wearing cool, denim Biba number. Ginnybitch sitting on floor playing with brat about same age but twice as fat. Must be summer time. Again. Ginnybitch wearing sleeveless, minty-green dress and wee red shoes. Birthday present! The red shoes were a birthday pressie! It was Ginnybitch's first birthday and they were up in the

Heelands for a week's hols. Y.t. wearing some sort of flowery thingy. Neat, though. Another one of Dork Manual (Mum's ol' pal *Cr. Dressmaking Made Easy*)'s successes? Dad standing next to old-oldish-red-faced jerk. Battle going on as to who was wearing most gormless grin. Mr H.G. – the whiskey man, who'd male-bonded so well with Dad during the Rite of Passage(s), both shite and vomitwise, on that post-wedding Hogmanay in 1962. Worked in a distillery, did Mr H.G., so no probs laying mitts on Usquebaugh in any and all stages of fermentation.

H.G. sitting on a stool nearly as big as herself over by window. Not only did she have a sherry clutched in one claw, she had a fag – and a lit one at that, in the other. Mum hasn't got a fag – stopped when Alien took root and never restarted. Gobsmacked to see H.G. with weed. And helping herself to a second sherry. Mum saying she never realised that she smoked. H.G. giggling – (giggling!) and blathering that she only partook on special occasions. Mum more gobsmacked that ever. And no effing wonder. How the fuck can anyone have a fag only on special occasions? Boozing only on special occasions was poxy enough. But having a fag? Typical wanking remark from H.G. Hadn't got a fucking clue what went on in real life. Fucking headcase. Glass of sherry held between fingertips as though glass writhing with bacteria. Fag held between fingertips of other mitt, as though about to hurl a dart. Clueless, or what? After each quick puff, she'd peer round chook-like to make sure no one was looking before surrounding herself with a weaving, spiralling ectoplasm of exhaled smoke. Bright red, peepers streaming, racked with fits of spluttering, she thus managed to have everyone in the room eyeballing her and her prowess with the fag. Who'd have believe it of ol' pucker-gobbed H.G.? On home ground, s'pose.

So it was the Heelands. On hols in the Heelands and having a bit of a do for Ginnybitch. The wee iced cake in the middle of the table of goodies, with its single candle, gave the game away. Ginnybitch's first birthday and this was her birthday party. Everyone starting to head for table and scrummy yummies when door opens and in sashays a plump, recently shagged chick. Could tell 'cos of red, sweaty phizog, tanglement of hair on back of noddle, satisfied–I've just had a good fuck-smirk, but most of all 'cos of smell of unwashed, sperm-filled cunt. Elspeth. Mum's Sis. The younger by five years or so. Looking good, babe! Better than last time. Last time in Twilight Zone-y land.

'Hi Laura, how're you kid!' she says, giving that funny, half-cocked grin. And, Hi, you lot, she says to the room at large. Not that long since she'd been staying in Blackheath. Wanted to see Bright Lights. Got job an' plenty o' shagging in some fleapit other side of ol' man river. In pup within few months. Weeks. Kid died during whelping. Just as well. Went home to the Heelands with shell-shocked H.G. and was in pup again within three months. Fat little git sitting grunting at Ginnybitch result of whelping. Funny chick, Elspeth. Secretive. Good to y.t. though. Stayed at Blackheath pad when in late stages of pup. Mum able to chill 'cos she didn't think Dad'd get his rocks off over such a gross cunt. Kid-minded when Mum was at work and couldn't get y.t. into decent nursery.

Nearly drove Mum witless having to clean bogies off lavvy wall. Knew it was sis. But couldn't bring herself to say anything. No bogies there before. No bogies there after. Fair do's. What the fuck could she have said to the dumb cunt?

'C'mon Gavin. Don't just sit there. Get me a cup of tea of something – I'm fair parched.'

Such a wee shortarse – hadn't even noticed him. Hi, Uncle Gav! Long time no see, ha ha. Getting up from chair at side of Rayburn and goes and switches kettle on.

'That bloody Craig, I think I've finished with him for good this time,' says Aunty Elspeth. 'You know what he's after, don't you? All you men are the bloody same.'

As Uncle Gav got back to his seat by the Rayburn, she boogied across and twirled her bulging arse onto his lap, twining her arms round his neck and all but shoving a tit into his gob. Steady on, Aunty! Ain't that little bruv you're coming on to? Not so poxy little if peek could be taken under Aunty's plump bum, eh?

'My God,' says Gav, 'you're putting on a bit of weight Elspeth – has no one told you?' And he settles her more comfortably on his lap.

Mum having a bit of a job keeping mince pies off them, as Elspeth fiddled with Gav's hair, squeezed zits, imaginary or not, from his mush, neck and ear'oles, while seeming to shove her tits as far into his phizog as was possible. After a few mos, H.G. said with a bit of a laugh, 'For heaven's sake, Elspeth, can't you give the poor boy a rest.' Took her a good few mos to slide off bruv's lap, adjusting her mini over creamy, cellulite thighs as she did so.

Nosh time – at long fucking last it's nosh time!

Mum uncool about display of sibling togetherness (euphemism

for shag factor – that's what pisses you off, ain't it?). She's got up and left room. Without as much as a word. What the fuck's happened to all the scrummy nosh? All gone. All fucking gone. How come? Not even any poxy thing to drink – gotto have summing to drink – gob filled with poxy glue. Pissed off with all this poxy time-hopping crap. Really pissed off.

Where the fuck are they now, for Chrissake? Sunshine – sunshine – don't need any more effing sunshine – fucking dried-up fucking fruit as it is – is it meant to look like a little prune, Maggie darling? Christalmighty what's with the feeble fucking funnies. They're going to the beach. The whole poxy lot of them. Still in the fucking Heelands. They're going to the effing beach – don't go to the beach – please don't go to the beach – all that fucking sand – can't stand any more of it – feels like fucking desert in gob – sand mixed with effing glue – please don't – please don't. Please don't go to the beach.

Must be in Marloch. Mum's home village. And this is the Front Shore. Never came here on her own. Not like the Back Shore. Only came to Front Shore sometimes, and always with pals. When they did, Mum and pals, men in raincoats would follow them at a bit of a distance. Until they reached the bathing huts. Then they'd close in. Like hyenas. Skulking round the sides of the huts. Never wasted any time on chat. What the fuck does a middle-aged pervert gink have to say to an eleven year old chick? Give's a fuck, then? Some might. But not these middle-aged pervs. Fathers of some of her school pals. Middle aged, middle-class pervs. Tried to get a mitt down her navy-blue school drawers. Wouldn't let them. Both eleven year old mitts clutching the desperate, forty-something year old fingers within the confines of the Granny-stitched elastic. As they writhed, moaned, rubbed and pleaded, she wondered why they didn't deem her good enough to play with their daughters, her schoolmates. All in the snivelling whinge she'd managed to pass off as a book.

Though Mum hated the Front Shore, it had lovely silvery sand. So was considered a better deal than the rocky, dune-covered Back Shore, for a family picnic. Gav had borrowed his Dad's car. Mr H.G. was working, so not able to accompany picnickers. Parked old banger at top of golf course. How the fuck had they all managed to cram into heap of scrap metal? All there – including brain-dead Afghan pup Mum had treated herself to few months ago. They had to walk across the golf course to get to the beach.

Aunty Elspeth and Uncle Gav quite a way ahead. Strolling arm in arm, heads close together. Whispering sweet nothings, no doubt – ha ha. Dad and H.G. walking together, each holding one of y.t.'s mitts. Mum dragging along behind with the daft mutt on a lead and Ginnybitch flopping about on a carrier on Mum's back. Since outgrowing sling, Ginnybitch travelled everywhere on Mum's back. Chill out Mum, for Chrissake! It's a picnic, not an effing wake! Know what the prob is. Y.t. starting thigh-squeezing lark again. H.G. bending down and muttering something, then turning round with knitted gob and, still whispering, though loudly, as Mum got nearer – why the fuck was the old bat whispering? – said that she thought that Laura needed to go to the toilet. Nice one, y.t.! Timing immaculate, as always! Puckers of pissed-offness crossing Mum's phizog as she catches hold of y.t.'s arm and gives it a bit of a shake. Not much of a shake. Just a little shake. And spitting gobs of grit, asks why hadn't y.t. gone to lavvy when Mummy had asked her in the village. H.G. in last throes of orgasm waiting to shove oar in, saying that perhaps the bairn hadn't wanted to go to the lav when they were in the village.

'For God's sake,' says Mum, 'it must have taken us all of five minutes to drive from the village and walk down the brae – how can she be so desperate in five minutes?'

Here we go again, dudes.

'Whatever the reason, Margaret,' says H.G. in best chook style, 'she needs to go now, and for Heaven's sake stop shouting and let go of the bairn's arm.'

'I'm not shouting,' shouts Mum, 'and I don't see what's wrong with being annoyed. According to you, every mother on the face of the earth, apart from me, is some sort of bloody angel in disguise.'

H.G. getting dangerously puffy-chested.

'There's no need for you to swear, Margaret. And will you please lower your voice. You're far too hard on Laura. That's your trouble, if you want to know."

'Thank you very bloody much,' shrieks Mum. 'Thank you for being so thoughtful and so helpful in giving your bloody opinion. I'm only sorry to have to tell you that you're wasting your bloody breath. I already know that I'm too bloody hard on bloody Laura and I'm seeing a bloody psychiatrist because of it, so why don't you keep your bloody mouth shut because every time you open it you put your bloody great foot right in it, don't you – don't you? Don't you Mam?'

Steady on Mum. H.G. about to fall arse over tit with shock of revelations. Phizog pasty sort of grey; gob a tight, livid sphincter; peepers trying to break loose. Voice clipped and Arctic-shot, H.G. says that she's very sorry, very sorry indeed to hear that Margaret is having treatment. She'd had no idea. Had she realised, then she would never have passed any comment on the way Margaret chose to treat Laura. All other tossers wandering on well ahead as drama unfolding. Elspeth, shaking long, ginger hair, glanced idly back, but registered zilch.

'The trouble is,' says Mum, all quiet and trembly, 'that you have not the slightest understanding whatsoever of the problem. You just see what you want to see and make spot judgements of something you know nothing about.'

Heigh-ho. Y.t.'s pissed drawers again. Piss running down pins into socks and StartRites. Weird look on Mum's phizog. Sort of tender. For a fleeting mo looked as though she was going to reach out and cuddle y.t.. But mo passed.

H.G. didn't ask any questions about Psychiatrist and what treatment Mum was having. Mum never said a word, so rest of walk to beach passed in total silence.

Mum and the shrink had first got together about three months after Ginnybitch's popping the pod. She'd had to tell GP about not being able to kip at night and wanting to top herself during the day. Touch of post-natal blues, m'dear, says he, giving her a script for Valium and old pal Seconal.

Went back couple of weeks later 'cos tabs not doing trick. Managed to blurt out about always getting shirty with y.t. Nice GP upped dosage, changed birth-pill and made appointment with shrink. On third visit to surgery, couldn't stop blubbering, so GP made urgent app. with Dr Blake Larsen.

French-looking chick, in early thirties. Thin, long, pale, bony phizog topped by dollop of sleek black hair clinging like shiny bat to her skull. Red gash instead of gob and long, blood-red Count Drac fingernails. Peepers a bit on the jumpy side. Had Larsen been a gee-gee, Mum wouldn't have gone as far as the paddock gate. Took a couple of months for Mum to find out how useless she was. And six months to get rid of her.

Bunch of tossers had stopped just past row of bathing huts and Uncle Gav was shouting, this be OK? Had to shout a few times before H.G. shouted back that yes, it was/would be, whatever. So they all ambled down on to the poxy silvery sand of the Front

Shore. As they began to catch up with the main party of tossers, H.G. started wittering on about how sorry she was, how truly sorry she was; that she'd been completely in the wrong and should have known better.

Mum taking no bleeding notice. Pale as bread dough and still trembling round the gob and chin. Busying herself with either Ginnybitch or Afghan mutt. Can't be let off lead 'cos he immediately scarpers until he finds another mutt, any old mutt, to follow to the ends of the earth. Mum standing, all fidgety, like a hermit crab mutation with Ginnybitch glued to her shoulders. Walking jerkily down to the edge of the sea. The greedy wavelets jerking each other off as they grabbed and sucked at her tootsies.

Come back an' have some nosh, Mum! Gav and Sis arsing about over bags of goodies, whispering and giggling like pair of retards. Tartan rugs being placed on sand. Placed. Then lifted and shaken. Then placed again. Nice one, dildo Aunty. Make sure every morsel shoved into gob'll have a generous coating of poxy sand sticking to every crumb, why don't you? Dad sitting very near to H.G., nodding and grinning like a sodding PG Tips chimp. Mum turning and slowly walking back to stand at Dad's side. Take that frigging growth off your back and sit down Mum, for Chrissake. No. Not going to sit down. Quietly saying to Dad that she wants to go home.

Mumbling through his sandy slice of flan, Dad asking whatcha say? Mum repeating it. Dad blustering that she couldn't expect people to turn round in the middle of a picnic and head home for no reason other than her whim.

Mum saying that she meant home home. Their own home. In Worcester Park. Bits of doughy bread and partly chewed filling flying out of Dad's gob as he tells Mum to be bloody reasonable and not start making a fool of herself in front of everyone. Mum starting to hiss. Funny. Never heard her hiss at other than y.t. Different sort of hiss though.

'I can't stand any more of this – you don't give a shit about me – in fact, I think you make the most of this sort of – sort of thing to have a go at me. Get your pathetic little own back in your two-faced, underhand way so that no one else will notice you, you big shit.'

Dad's peepers beginning to bulge as though invisible force squeezing them behind sockets.

'I'm not going to waste any time listening to such drivel,' in big, manly voice. 'You're not the only one to come on holiday and I, for one, am going to make sure I enjoy mine. It's entirely up to you what you decide to do with yours.'

What a prize dickhead! And he turns to share his smirk of self-importance between the amount of sand in his bit of flan and H.G. who appears to be equally concerned about the amount of sand contained in her scone – so much so, that she seems to be studiously counting and indexing each grain.

They let Mum scramble up the grassy bank and run, like a hunchback on acid, back the way they'd just come. Ginnybitch, bouncing around as though Mum desperately trying to free herself of the burden, seemed in danger of becoming unglued and the braindead Afghan kept leaping up and down like a hairy king-sized yo-yo, trying to grab the lead out her hand. Everyone could hear her blubbing. Even the grazing cows raised their noddles and cast a tad of sympathy from their vacant, limpid peepers. No one followed her. Or called out after her. Y.t. would have Mum, but H.G. in process of handing over plateful of gob-melting goodies. Sorry Mum. But there was nowhere for you to go, was there? What difference would y.t. have made?

What's with all the effing shouting? Dude's shouting. Real mad. What the fuck are these dickheads up to? Never lose cool when stoned. Bit of a straightening out of the pecking order now and then, but nothing as out of order as this shit. Stuff being thrown about, for Chrissake! Shouting – shouting – shouting – for fuck's sake give it a rest, you bunch of sick fucks! Why don't some of you try shouting your effing way into Blojo's room you useless load of arsehole wankers!

Jesus Christ. This is it. Fucking cardiac arrest time.

Except for Neanderthal forehead and e-enormous hooter, would barely know it was Dad. Peepers ready to catapult across the room at any mo; foam flecks flying from the ocean of spit spilling out of his gob. A Mr Hyde look-a-like, but Dad.

Jim/Spock/Dr fucking Who – whatever shithead's in charge of this pathetic apology of a Twilight Zone – this is the pits, man. The real pits. Mum and y.t. sitting on bottom step of stairs. Still at Wates Mansion then, you sick fucks? Mum clutching Ginnybitch to her chest; rocking back and forth. And sobbing. Y.t. snivelling between snorts of snot. And no fucking wonder! Dad standing by big bay window, kitchen chair held high, like flag of victory, in

71

one raised mitt. Looking as though about to commit murder. Put it down, Dad. For Chrissake put the fucking chair down and chill some!

Mum opening gob. Tootsie going to snuggle down further into shit, s'pect.

'You made sure of it – you did – it was you – you – you made sure I'd never have another baby – you bloody bastard you.'

Nice one, Mum. Couldn't have put it better.

This is about Dad having the snip-snip. Supposed to make Mum less frigid – not having to suffer so-called side effects of pill. Take her off the pill and she'll be a new chick. Been discussed at length, Mum. With GP and that well-known local loony, Dr Larsen. You wanted it as well as Dad. Even more than Dad. He had his poor balls cut out for both of you. Fair do's. So cool it, Mum, and try and get the mad bastard to put down the fucking chair. Too late. Dad's flung the chair right through the big, bay window. Wates'll be chuffed. Deafening crash of shattering glass. Shell-likes feel splintered into shards, like the glass. Slivers of glass in throat and gob and up nose, for fuck's sake. Stabbing, slicing and cutting into already burning flesh. Blood running down back of throat. Swallowing blood. Fucking pints of it. Thick blood. Won't go down easy. Mixed with poxy glass. That's why. Thick blood and glass.

To die, to sleep. To sleep: perchance to dream: Aye, there's the rub; For in that sleep of death what dreams may come . . .

Where the fuck's that pile o' shite sprung from? Effing Shakespeare for fuck's sake. Never seen any oiky bloody Shakespeare. Not true. Weird shit, this. Mum and Dad sneaking y.t. into Oxford Circus flicks. Olivier playing Hamlet. Bratskis not allowed in. Y.t. just over 2. Winter. Hidden under Mum's cape-y sort of thingy. Ipswich too. Saw it on stage. Much later. Wolsey Theatre, was it? Not Olivier, o' course. Ginnybitch there too. And Mum. Not Dad, though. Long time ago. At Ipswich. Funny. Music. Musical music. Piano. Some dude's tickling the ivories. No dickhead in squat able to play piano. No piano to play. Stop–start; stop–start – get on and play sodding tune, for Chrissake! Can't. Practising poxy scales. Nice sound, the piano. Even with effing gorilla mitts thumping keys. Whoever it was. Y.t. never liked it, though. Playing it. The piano. Obvious, innit? Scrawnier than ever, cranefly pins dangling. No StartRites. Purgatory. Rattling bloody scales up and down – up and down. Still at effing Wates Mansion, Jim? Gromit still unlocated, Scottie?

No wonder y.t. hated thumping keys. Never got further than poxy scales. Played cello later on. Much later. More at home pins akimbo and large, hard thing pressing on crotch ha ha. No. Really liked cello. Sat exams an' all. Much later.

Mum responsible for old joanna. Wanted to learn how to tickle ivories so's she could play Bartok. All she wanted. Nothing else. Bought Bartok for beginners, or whatever. Mikrokosmos. Could never forget that name.

Mum found piano teacher up the road from Wates Mansion. Another Oz shithead. This time with a limp and a Masters in total absence of Oral Hygiene. Wouldn't let Mum or y.t. play note 2 until note 1 had been played to his idea of perfection. Real shithead. Wouldn't let Mum near her little Bartok for Beginners booklet. Made her play scales all the fucking time. Whole point about Bartok, she kept telling him. Easy wee scale-type tunes. Wouldn't listen. Mum couldn't handle it. Especially when he started standing real close, nuking her with his dog-turd breath and placing one of his hairy Oz mitts on her shoulder then down her arm as she struggled to perfect note 1. Supposed to be relaxing. Instead, witless index shooting off end of graph. Stuck it longer 'cos Big G taking lessons as well. Advanced. Big G brill tickler of ivories. Had given it up after setting up shack with Old Man of Oz. Wouldn't let her do anything on her tod. Anything she got rocks off on. Unless shackled to sink. Or cooker, or whatever. Poor Big G. Had misunderstood Oz man's proposal. Thought the old fuck had said 'shack up' when, in fact, he'd said 'shackle up' – ha ha. O, never mind. Not that bloody funny, anyway. Started taking lessons on quiet when Mum got old joanna. Big G more laid back about oral hygiene disaster from Oz. Could afford to be. Far better at tickling ivories than he could ever be.

Fair do's. Mum asked y.t. did she want to give ivories up. And y.t. said 'no'. Dunno why. To wind Mum up, s'pose.

Knocking–knocking–knocking – endless bloody knocking. Poxy door not locked. No good. Effing bastards leaving Blojo to rot. Can't move noddle. Not even tiniest tad. Peepers starting to glue up. Not itching so much, though. Need a drink. Gotta have one. Any old piss'll do. If not, gob'll never come unstuck.

Sodding brass band practising – every sodding brass band in sodding universe – all together now: One, Two, Three. Thundering trumpets, deafening horns and tubas – have a bit o' mercy Jim – whaddya think this is, the bleeding Albert Hall or what?

This is hell. Must be. Y.t. popped clogs. Ended up in Hades.

Thundering brass of Berlioz bloody Requiem trying to out-din pounding and hammering on door. What door? Where's effing door? In Twilight-y Zone? Losing cool, babe. Mustn't do that. Mustn't lose cool.

Rog and Mum. Rog and Mum sitting at kitchen table in Wates Mansion, staring at each other like pair of fucking zombies. Not mates, then. Not mates wondering what had happened to ol' Blojo. For fuck's sake Rog, go and turn that wanky brassy row off and answer frigging door! Berlioz bloody Requiem – pair of arseholes would sit for hours and days on end listening to heap o' brassy shite, clutching each other and bawling and blubbering. Pair o' sick fucks. What brought them together in first place. Not the ear'ole nuking Frenchman, though, but ol' Ludwig. Mum had a thingy about Alfred Brendel's ivory-tickling of Ludwig's joanna sonatas and when Rog discovered this, he had the best come of his life. Right there and then. Ha ha ha. Spent most of their time getting records from library of different dudes playing the sonatas. Play a movement of one dude, whip off the record and put on Mum's hero playing same movement. Keep your Claudios and Vladimirs, Alf rules, OK?

Dad's fault. He'd been daft enough to let best mate Rog take Mum to concerts. Prob'ly wouldn't have come to much if it hadn't been that Mum at last-straw levels over Dad's shyster carryings on. Had good number going. Cushy not the word. Outsize plates resting on bottom rung of power ladder ha ha. Been made up to chef-manager in works canteen in Leatherhead. Had to go and fuck it all up. Being Dad, love of cooking included books as well as din-dins. Sacked on spot. Lucky not to have ended up in the nick. Not first time, though. Eh, Dad? Wherever you are, you daft wanker. History of wee misdeeds.

For fuck's sake, Rog. Stop doing your Lot's wife impersonation and go and answer the fucking door! Can't understand how the buggering thing's still standing. Dad's pet naughty had been fiddling the railways. After they'd moved to Blackheath, he'd travelled back to Hastings once a week to finish his HCI course. Fare not a prob. Mum working full-time. So Dad didn't do it 'cos of the dosh. Bought one ticket and kept flashing it until nobbled. Given a warning. Written. Promised never to do it again. Mum believed solemn vows of undying honesty.

Then letter came from BR saying Dad had to appear before beak on charge of fiddling fare. Poor stupid bitch Mum. Really believed he hadn't done it. Ma man ain't done me no wrong. Yeah. Thought some dead-beat had picked Dad's moniker at random out of phone book and used it when nobbled. Rang him at work. Shooting gob off about how pissed off she was with unknown wanker etc.

Dead Silence. Mum never got over it. Seems such a minor thing, she'd say to Gina, but I really, really trusted him. And he really promised. It was serious. That's why I can never forgive him. Never trust him ever again. Beginning of end of Mum and Dad? No. Had started long before that. When Mum in pup with y.t. Before then. But won't think about that shit. When Mum in pup with y.t., good enough. Dad working in hotel in good ol' Bexhill-on-Sea. Always short of the readies in those days. Mum not able to work 'cos of don't really know what. Didn't have morning sickness; had all-sodding-day-long sickness. Know that much. Doesn't fucking matter, anyway. Dad had a scooter. Real cool dude, ha ha ha. Well it was the sixties wasn't it? Reported to Old Bill that scooter had been half-inched. No probs with Old Bill. But insurance dudes smelt fish. Or rat. Or whatever. Dad charged with the Big One. Fraud. Denied it from start. Swore blind he'd had nought to do with vanishing Vespa. Went to Court. Mum sitting there, with seven month old y.t. doing butterfly stroke in her belly, believing every sodding word. Until he was asked by gob-smackingly eloquent and upper-crust prosecutor to describe dude he kept insisting he'd seen loitering with intent around the virgin Vespa on the night of the supposed theft. And whaddya think Dad, that real cool dude, had gone and been and done? Gave complete and detailed description of hisself o' course.

Mum's marbles rattling around for a good while after. Couldn't forget court filled with raucous laughter. Prosecutor wiped floor with Dad. The Fag lady would have gone down on bended knee to the True Master of Venom and Vitriol. Dad not in the least fazed. Big, daft, cheesy grin never faltered. Thought himself cool dude to bitter end. Hefty fine and two years probation. Why they couldn't leave Bexhill sooner. Why Mum had to put up with the Fag lady and . . . and – well, the Fag lady for another two whole years. All in her wee opus.

Thank Christ Rog has gone to answer door. What's with the Old frigging Bill, Rog? Two pigs. One of each. A he-pig. And a she-pig. She-pig doing all the mouthing. Figures. Phone call – reason to believe – bruises – ill treatment – concern – complaint – where children – fetch – examine . . . bla-bla . . .

Late at night. Very dark. Curtains drawn. Dad must have moved out. Mum supposed to be starting new life with Rog. Wanker Dad had been effing lodger, for fuck's sake, for a few weeks after Rog had laid claim to territory. Lodged in upstairs bedroom that used to be his and Mum's. Sick or what? Must have got rocks off ear'oling to Mum and Rog fucking the settee senseless. Which one biggest wanker? Lotta bad shit, though. Dad crashed van and said it had been stolen. Good try, Dad. Old Bill said they'd got lowdown on dude driving. Eye witness. Description fitted Mr FitzHugh. Nice one, Dad. Didn't work first time round, so let's have another go. Denied everything. As usual. All up to Mum. Her van. Could have had him shoved in the nick for half-inching. Didn't. Just wanted him out of her life. She-pig going over Ginnybitch's arms, pins and bod with a nit comb. Ginnybitch whingeing and stretching fat arms out to Mum. She-pig smiling. Aaah.

Mum grey with shock. Trying to find out who made phone call and why. Obvious innit, you daft bitch? Gotta good idea. Pigs sure as hell ain't telling. Finished with Ginnybitch. All peepers on y.t. Off with the nightie. Get yer effing peepers off, Rog! Stick-thin arms and pins. Never stop noshing – honest! Lifting arms up. Counting ribs and vertebrae. Seems like. Smiles all round 'cept Mum. Still shell-shocked. Murmurs of 'troublemaker'. Mum starting to blab. It's the relief, s'pose. Saying that she and Rog had recently shacked up together and that she know some people in the street were a bit jealous. Jealous! If we're talking about Psycho Jodie down the road then jealous is being a tad generous, Mum. Sick-fuck psychotic, more like.

What's happened to the bruises, then? They were there this a.m. piggy-wiggies. Mum had a wee bit of a go at y.t. for not cleaning toothie-pegs prop'ly. There had been a lot of the usual arm-gripping and pushing down onto knees. No tintawn to slice and chew into meagre bit o' meat covering pins. Only cold, hard tilles. Went a bit wild with the toothbrush Mum did. Shoving it round gnashers and gums; ramming it into sides of cheeks and bottom of gob. Watch the poor wee tongue, Mum. Like a wodge of dried old leather it is.

Next time it'll be a lavatory brush if you don't clean them properly. Do you hear? Shouldn't have done that, Mum. Gob in flames and phizog going to pop open like big, juicy fruit.

Mum and Rog sitting staring blankly at each other. Rog gets up and come back with hot drinkies for them all. Put paid to effing Berlioz, eh Rog?

Starting to relax and chat a bit when sudden noise at window. Big noise. Wet noise. Lot of water splashing violently on window. Not like rain. More like a waterfall. Shrieking and cackling and rushing water. Thuds of heavy things landing. A lot of dull, heavy things. One crashes through window and lands on floor near Mum's tootsies. A large, grey brick.

'Fucking child-batterers! If the fucking cops won't do anything about you pair of fucking child-beaters, then we fucking will! You fucking perverts – should be in jail!'

Everyone sitting as though related to Lot's missus. Even Ginnybitch. Not for long, though. Ginnybitch starts gurning with fear and y.t. the usual half-hearted snivelling. Both scared shitless by fucking monsters outside kitchen window. Mum and Rog haven't moved. Hardly breathing. Old Bill barging in bad enough. Never mind watery version of local Klu Klux Klan. 'It's Lisa and Jodie,' mutters Mum. Oh nice one, Mum. Full marks. 'That's Jodie's voice, so it's got to be Lisa with her.'

Give her credit, Mum sure knew how to pick friends and neighbours. Lisa was a genuine psycho. In and out of loony bin all the time. Though Wates lease said No Dogs, Lisa had a German Shepherd. Which was why Mum thought it OK to treat herself to imbecile Dookie. Within few weeks, Lisa had got rid of Prince and reported Mum to Wates for having a dog on premises.

It had been different with Jodie. Great pals at first. Jodie had made first move. Didn't take long to turn to shit. Jodie never outta Mum's hair. Mealtimes, bedtimes, any times at all. Took to buying same things as Mum. Wearing same clothes (borrowing Dork Manual and running little numbers up overnight). And buying same food. She'd ask Mum what she was making for din-dins then rush out and get the same. All fell completely apart when Rog moved in. Jodie palled up with Psycho and they both ganged up on Mum. Major crime committed. Jodie admitted it afterwards. Mum had turned fantasy of dishy young dude into reality. Also, admitted she'd been having 'therapy' for years. Y.t.'s fault that pigs came in dead of night. Well, not at dead of night.

That would have been Psycho. She'd noticed bruises that morning when y.t. out playing in garden and had asked about them. More red hand-prints than bruises, really. But y.t. had told Lisa about Mum and the lavvy brush threat. Only 'cos she'd asked what Mum had said to y.t. when squeezing her arms so hard.

Now look at what's come of it. Water pouring in window. Hosepipe. That's what they're using. No more bricks though. Water, water everywhere and not a drop to drink.

E.R. Y.t. must be in E.R. White walls and ceiling. Nose-clenching pong of Jeyes. At last! Y.t.'s been rescued!! Thank the good Christ! Bastards haven't forgotten Blojo after all! Lovely white, crispy sheets; nice, jolly, friendly, fatty nurse. Fucking ace, man! Hang on a mo. Not looking out from virginal bed. Looking *at* virginal fucking bed. So who the fuck is lying between the white, crispy sheets where y.t. should be? Effing Rog and y.t. sitting at side of bed. Rog being a hermit crab with Ginnybitch perched on his back.

WHO'S IN THE FUCKING BED THEN?

Why, it's Mum. Who the fuck else. Looking like effing death on parole. And no fucking wonder. OD'd hasn't she, the daft bitch. Won't talk to Rog. No fucking wonder again. Keeps asking her what happened.

'Please tell me, Margaret. Why did you go there? Your mother's worried sick. She had a terrible fright when she had the phone call from the hospital. Just tell me why you went to him, Margaret. After all you said.'

Mum won't answer. Choking to death on bullshit. Gave up his job so's he could be with Mum all the time. Biggest bullshit of all. All he wanted was to spend all his waking hours listening to the three B's. Berlioz, Beethoven and Brahms. Conducted with one of Mum's no.10 knitting needles.

Turned out he had a thingy about married chicks. Any married chick he fancied at work, he would wangle invites for the weekend and get his rocks off by being a worshipping-from-afar slave. Poor Mum, desperate for a decent shag, had called his bluff, so, after months of weekend worshipping, he had to either quit the comfy nest or take action. Though she hadn't known about the weekends with other married chicks, she'd known he was a wanker. Literally. Used to make her laugh, once she'd got over the shock, by telling how, if he got a hard-on over some babe at work, he'd rush off to the john and jerk off. Must have kept the bog cleaners on their toes. Did it several times a day, he said.

Listening to such puke made a change for Mum. After Dad, who denied ever touching his dick – ever – except when he needed a piss. Or when having a wash, o' course. Even when needing a piss, there was a suggestion that he had it zipper trained. Even when caught in mid-wank, Dad would remain in denial.

Rog didn't mind telling all. Admitted wanking over Aunty Elspeth when she'd stayed at Blackheath. In the flat, asks Mum. Yes indeedy, says Rog. But I never wanked over you, Margaret. Respect you too much. Ha ha ha. Mum knew it was a load of bullshit. Only reason she put up with it was 'cos, even though Rog had a totty dick, Mum had first ever come from simple shag. No hand work needed. No going down on her. Just a smallish come. And the first of regular smallish comes. But a come all the same. No money coming in. Mum had been doing job at home. Took over from Dad. Making charts for market research firm. Up most nights, all night, to meet deadline. Kipping all day. Wates Mansion like pigsty. Cooker top deep litter. Rog too busy conducting the three B's to do any housework. In desperation, Mum sent SOS to H.G. Came down for couple of weeks to help out. Had to put up with sound effect of Rog shagging Mum during day. Shags became boring. Comes stayed smallish then fizzled out. All Mum was left with was a big nerd with a small dick and no job, who seemed to get his rocks off more from waving a knitting needle (*her* knitting needle) in time to a bit of revolving vinyl than he did by having serious relationship. Serious meaning something other than shagging. Realises she's stepped sideways out of one pile of shit and landed up to her neck in another. One day (must have been yesterday in Twilighty Zone) when Rog supposedly job-searching and H.G. looking after y.t. and Ginnybitch to give Mum a bit of a kip, the daft bitch sneaks out and heads for Dad's bed-sit. Dad not in. Mum unable to keep marbles together. Doesn't know why. Takes handful of some pills or other, nothing lethal, and rings 999. And here she is. Stomach all nice and clean after its bit o' pumping.

Rog starting to blub. What a fucking sight. Give credit, good to y.t. and Ginnybitch. Bit sicky with it. Sicky. Not sicko. Yukky. Over the top in creepy-crawliness. Fair dos. Dude doing his best.

A pale and crumpled Mum appears from beneath the sheets. Reaches out for y.t. and asks Rog for Ginnybitch. Cuddles and squeezes all round. One last cuddle (not for Rog. No cuddles at all for the poor fuck) and it's ta-ta time. All turn to leave and almost have head-on smash with Herman Munster. Suddenly at foot of bed. Bonier and lankier than ever. Forehead more Neanderthal if that poss. Hooter sticking out like goblin's axe. Hair cut à la member of Inuit tribe. What a nerd! Why does Mum go for such prize wankers? Skin pulled dead tight. Yellow tinge round bony outlines. Mum takes one look at Herman and screams for him to fuck off out of her sight. Fuck off, you sick bastard. Fuck off!

In deep shit, Dad. Mum never uses the eff word. Never.

Dad spluttering and stammering that he thought she'd needed him – been looking for him – had come to his bed-sit – he hadn't been there so she'd taken an overdose . . .

'Get out of my fucking sight – get out of my fucking sight – I never want to set eyes on you ever again – I wish you were fucking dead if you want the truth so get out of my fucking sight, you bastard,' screeches Mum.

Dad's phizog turning livid. Like a huge bruise. Peepers on the bulge. Whites turning to yellows. No. Been yellows all the time. Try a spit of Persil why don't you, Dad? Ha ha.

'You know what you're saying – you know what you're saying – this is the end – this is the end of it – we're finished for good – you needn't come running to me again – d'you hear? D'you hear? This is the end of it – the end of it d'you hear?'

Entire effing hossy can hear, Dad. Flustered nursey comes trotting over and asks everyone to leave ward, please, as patient needs peace and quiet. Y.t. given up on snivelling and having good bawl. Ginnybitch on verge of joining in. Herman storms off without a backward peep. Hasn't said a dickybird to y.t. or Ginnybitch. Rog turning to leave as well. Picking y.t. up in scooping arms as he does. Mum sobbing heart out. Y.t. bawling like heifer. Ginnybitch on the gurn. What a load of miserable shitheads.

Why still shouting? Right in bleeding ear'ole again. Won't lose cool. Won't think of so-called pals. That have forgotten all about y.t. Consigned to scrap-heap. Would like to get gob round a voddie. Just a wee one. Enough to unglue tongue, is all. Odds are his holiness won't have missed y.t. either. Of course he won't, stupid cunt! Visiting's next week. Remember? Lotta visits. Every fortnight for past two years. Old tosser won't mind if y.t. misses the one poxy time, surely. Be the first time. Jesus H. Christ! How many fucking times? *Won't* miss a poxy visit, braindead bitch! Visit is next week, for Chrissake! Next week and every two weeks after that for eight fucking long years. Remission for good behaviour, mind. Five fucking long years then. Just as frigging bad. Good behaviour. Good, all right. Gave screws and Docs and Governor all they wanted. Real cool dude. He was whatever they wanted him to be. Played the religious card. Spiritual enlightenment. Ace, man. Always had wagon-loads of arseholes shit-hot to throw in lot and dosh with 'new' religion. Follow search for spiritual fucking enlightenment. Funny. Never talked to y.t. about it these days. Used to be nothing but. Can't remember name of it. Not like any other. Said he. And they believed him. All the believers. Y.t. believed. Believed that what they were doing was essential for their mutual spiritual growth and enlightenment. Ha ha ha.

Everything's dark. Can't see a poxy thing. Only Mum shouting gob off again. What and who this time, Mum? Chill out, babe. Might as well go along with it. No effing say in matter. Waste of breath trying to figure out. Must have had a bad E tab. Sort of hallucinations. Fucking punter must have slipped E tab somehow. Fucking coma from the one tab, man. People die, for Chrissake! That's not from the tab though, is it? Die from drinking too much fucking water. Chance would be a fine fucking thing, man! Y.t. prob'ly one of lucky bitches. Coupla days of mashed glass an' sand an' glue in gob, an' tad of lock-bod. That's all! Back on tootsies in no time. Just have to wait for bad shit to pass through system. Few more hours. That's all.

Middle of bleeding night and Mum's giving Rog Order of the Boot. Hanging out of bedroom window shrieking – Bastard – bloody sodding bastard – hope you rot in hell! Can't hear Rog's reply. If any.

Mum had woken him. Wanted a cuddle 'cos couldn't get to sleep. Rog had eagerly obliged. No probs there. Except that he muttered Daphna into Mum's shell-like. Name of married chick he'd used to work with and wank over. Prob'ly would have fucked Daphna instead of Mum if she'd given him the wink.

Shrieking like a personalised burglar alarm, Mum had kicked and pummelled Rog out of bed and carried on shrieking whilst he got dressed and legged it out of Wates mansion and down the road. Y.t. standing in doorway wearing thin, flowery nightie. Just standing. Pale and thin. Like bleeding Tiny Tim. Staring at Mum's arse. Seemed as though shrieking coming from between wobbling cheeks.

Over the next few days Rog never off doorstep. Knocking, knocking, knocking at door and pleading through letter-box. Please, Margaret – please – please – please Margaret. Mum wouldn't say as much as the one word to him.

Began to turn more and more to Valium – or was it Librium? and ol' pal Seconal. Or was it Nembutal? Told y.t. what to get for brekky. Y.t. bringing tray upstairs before going to school. Mum passing out till y.t. home from school. Must have got up to feed Ginnybitch, though.

No one to turn to. Doc Larsen been given the boot. Seems she spent most of their two hour sessions wanting to unburden her guilt onto Mum's strong, Mother-Earth shoulders. Nursing guilt 'cos she'd had an abortion in the dim and distant and was obsessed with getting Mum's approval. Didn't give a tinker's fuck about Mum. Said that she had the hots for Mum when, in theory, Mum should have had the hots for the Doc. Whoever he/she was. Transference, ain't it?

Came to Wates mansion on visits. Shouldn't have. Came once too often. Started ordering Mum around. Shifting furniture, re-arranging family heirlooms – ha ha. Mum told her to piss off and stay out of her life.

Crunch time (almost, for Ginnybitch – ha ha) came for Mum when she woke one afternoon and found Ginnybitch perched on outside ledge of bedroom window.

Threw all pills down loo. Dunno what day it was but somehow on a bus with y.t. and Ginnybitch. Went round and round same route all day. Past big loony bin. Near Epsom. Trouble was, shrink would be Dr Blake Larsen. No exit via that cul-de-sac, Mum.

Letter from Wates saying they'd had a snitch update and as Mrs FitzHugh hadn't got rid of mutt as requested, would she kindly fuck off out of Wates mansion within next two weeks. Mum at wits end. Nowhere to go. Rog still pestering the letter-box and doorstep. Would have zilch to do with him, but agreed to let him make room for Dookie among collection of knitting needles.

Couldn't go to Gina. Couldn't face her. Not after twat she'd made of herself during last visit to Twickers pad. Her and Rog gazing into each other's peepers like a pair of hypnotised rattlesnakes lusting to sink fangs into each other's throats. And Mum singing, no, *crooning*, 'It's all right no-ow baby, it's a-all ri-ight now, etc. etc.'

Old man of Oz looking at her like piece of female shit he'd always thought she was. She had to, though. She had to go see Gina. To find out that Dad's shacking up on a clapped-out pontoon in a derelict Kingston boatyard known locally as 'The Graveyard'. Nice one, Dad. Mum doesn't tell Gina much. Only that she and Rog having probs.

Goes and visits Dad in Graveyard. Eyeballs popping like giant, yellow gobstoppers, foam flecks flying like small, indoor flurry of snow, he does to Mum what she did to him. Tells her to fuck off out of it. Didn't even speak to y.t. and Ginnybitch. Scared almost shitless by eyeballs, snowstorm and arm-waving, Mum scarpers, sharpish-like. Old Bill not far from Graveyard. Mum seriously falling apart. Didn't expect Dad to welcome with open arms, but hadn't anticipated boot up arse. Nice, friendly female pig. Makes Mum a cup o' tea. Asks y.t. if she'd like a drink. Braindead twat shaking noddle! Mum seems as though suffering from Parkinson's. Weeping and hand-wringing and clutching at y.t. Ginnybitch fast asleep on Mum's back.

Tells nice pig that Dad won't take her and bratskis back. Pig says they can't interfere in domestic disputes, but why doesn't she go and have another try at persuading him? Chatted a bit more before Mum drags herself, whingeing y.t. and dead-weight Ginnybitch back to the Graveyard.

Inuit Dad's phizog like parchment covered skull. Cutting-tool hooter all shiny and newly sharpened. Gob funny brown-y colour. Peepers still seriously popping and snow flurries still on the go, but no arm-waving and doesn't tell Mum to eff off. Lotta game-playing. What about bratskis, Dad?

His terms. Take him as she finds him. No questions. Come and go as he pleases. New life. New friends. New job. North Sea Gas Convertor. Interesting new people. Meeting. All the time. Mum nodding. A bit vague. Either this. Or go under. Apart from clothes, books, toys and records and the tintawn, everything was left in Wates mansion. The-could've-been-naff-but-ain't-Habitat cane three piece, all the Crossley cords and all the rugs, cushions and wall-hangings she'd so lovingly knitted, woven or sewed. Psycho twins, a.k.a. Jodie and Lisa, swooped like vultures, vulture Jodie earnestly begging Mum to let her have all the stuff she'd hand-made. Mum couldn't have given a fuck. Nothing mattered any more.

Wasn't long before first big row erupted. Mum found out that The Inuit had been spending weekends down at the Fag lady's pile. Why not, Mum? She's his ma, for Chrissake! Fair do's, she wouldn't have minded 'cept for previous vigorous denials of ever – *ever* wanting any involvement with Fag lady. Trouble was, Mum didn't think it was the Fag lady that Dad had really wanted to see. Blazing row. Y.t. cowering under blankets. No dividing walls. Pontoon like big, wide, open floating caravan. Almost Exodus II when Mum found out about the doves. Don't know how dickhead Dad let it slip. Fag lady's pile had dove-cote. Proper stonebuilt skyscraper of a dove-cote. Lotta doves, natch. Beautiful, graceful, virginal, emblems of peace, white doves. Trouble was, kept multiplying. During one of Inuit's trips, Fag lady asked him to cull the doves with his airgun. And he had. He'd stood and shot them in their droves. Droves of bloody, murdered white and blood-red doves. Mum went nuclear. Never seen her so wild. Thought she might have gone for Dad with a knife. Screaming that he'd only done it to impress his effing mother and effing sister. Could see him there with his horrible little killing-machine, being goaded on by that pair of bloodthirsty harpies – just like he always used to – always doing whatever his bloody mother asked – how could he – how could he – how could he – bloody murderer – that's all he was – those beautiful beautiful doves . . . The Inuit left the pontoon and y.t. thought that was the end of The Homecoming. Mum and bratskis on ownio once again. Mum like mad creature all evening. Pacing up and down. When tide came in and pontoon rose off bed of sludge, everything – chairs, table, record-player – everything not fixed to surface, slid frantically across to other side. Fucking Titanic not in it, man. Out of one fucking madhouse into another.

Dad stayed out all night. Didn't come back till following evening. Greyish yellow mush and helluva jumpy peepers. Y.t. dreading Mum not keeping gob shut. She did. Crisis passed. Knife edge for a good few mos, though.

When Big G heard that she was back with Dad she said, 'Jesus, Maggie, you need your head seen to. You leave one wanker for another wanker then come back to the original wanker! Why not just dump the pair of them? You deserve a hell of a lot better.'

Mum couldn't answer. Didn't have an answer. Not then.

Noddle all light and floaty. Everything dipping and weaving and surging. Like poxy swing-boat. Faster–faster, falling–falling – don't let y.t. fall! Sick, feeling effing sick. Bit o' spew wouldn't be that bad. Might unglue gob a tad. Vertigo might be a good sign, eh? Part of recovery process – eh? Eh? Still can't move a fucking digit. Getting more than pissed off with shitty awful stink. Oily, rotten-fish-y sort of stink. Getting right up into brainbox, man.

Ginnybitch sitting on po on blue painted floor. Whole frigging floor moving up and down! Bloody heaving, more like! Daft mog winding itself round fat pins. Railings alongside floor. Floor coming to sharp point. Window boxes alongside railings. Full of scarlet, orange and yellow Tom Thumbs. No ceiling, no walls. Where the fuck are we, Jim? Ginnybitch and mog taking no notice of pitching and heaving. Trouble is, peepers seem a tad blinkered. Can only see pointy bit of floor and railings with Ginnybitch and mog. Can't see what's on either side. It's a boat. It's gotta be a frigging boat. It's *Rapid II*. The old hospital wreck they'd moved onto. Had to leave crap-heap pontoon. Leaking like a sodding sieve. Dad had to beg old cunt of Graveyard owner to let them rent rusting hulk. Only agreed after weeks of dildo-ing around. But only if they made it habitable, using their own dosh o' course, before moving in. Subject to his approval. Miserable old queen. Had two poxy mutts of his own but refused to allow Dookie in yard. Rog had moved bed-sit and new one wasn't big enough for Dookie and knitting needle collection. Mum traipsed round all of Surrey until she found a decent boarding kennel. Six guineas a week for that rotten hearthrug. There for nearly a year. Life of bleeding Riley. Bussed out to visit him every two or three weeks. Kennel girls spoiled him rotten.

Moored out in middle of fucking Father Thames. No wonder y.t. feeling as though losing moorings. Seasick. Bloody sodding seasick, for Chrissake! Awful pong must be Ol' Man River lying about in the bilges for too long.

Wonder why Dad became a North Sea Gas Converter? Last they'd heard from Gina, before Mum had decided to return to coop, was that he was planning on travelling globe and writing history of Art. Wonder what made him change his mind, ha ha ha.

Wind must be getting up. Whistling through corrugated sheets, rattling them like so many dried bones. Moaning and gurning like a baby with a bad colic. Whining through noddle like rusty pistons in need of good oiling.

Room swaying. Nausea lurching into throat. Gob of something – anything'll do – vomit, bile, anything, just to loosen wad of leather from roof of gob. And unglue teeth and gums from insides of lips.

Starting to rain. Big, solid drops splat-splatting on the corrugation. Like poxy nails being hammered in. How the fuck can rain be so hard, man?

Not rain. That's how. Mum sitting pounding away at old Remington. Really got started on opus on wreck of the old *Rapid II*. Jesus only knew how. Funny to see her there. Deadly serious. Did it all in longhand. In red biro. Only colour she had at the time.

Bunch of red roses on shelf. Loadsa cards. Ginnybitch's second birthday. Roses from dickhead Rog. Never gives up. Dad actually let him on to pontoon. Mum went apeshit. Ginnybitch must be at playgroup. Only there for three hours in morning. Mum does pathetic scribbling then. Big probs in afternoon and evening. Y.t. and Ginnybitch supposed to play in own cabin whilst Mum beavering away. But y.t. keeps sending Ginnybitch into Mum's wee space. Won't raise voice a third of an octave to Ginnybitch. Y.t. gets real buzz from watching Mum get worked up. So easy. Easiest thing in entire universe. Giggling is other cert for marble-tweaking. Y.t. giggling in cabin doorway. This time she's finished for the day. Covering old Remington and shoving it in cupboard. Must be having visitors. Always hides it. Can't bear anyone knowing. Paranoia triggered off by Big G calling on spec and catching her in mid-sentence. Blackheath. Mum tried to grab piece of paper back but Gina not letting go of ace chance to have a good sneer at Mum's expense. Begged Big G not to read it. Her very first scribblings. Bound to be a bit laughable. Gina pissing herself at purple prose before, with curled lip and sneering, falsetto voice, reading out loud all the most cringe-making bits. Mum had left the writing for a while after that. No Remington in those days.

Prob'ly Big G and bratskis coming for birthday tea. Still summertime, then. Hardly had any hair until she was over a year old, Ginnybitch. Now she's got a head of frigging golden curls. Rog won't have been invited. Taken to hanging around Gina's Twickers pad, of late. Wouldn't fuck her. Might want to. Good wanking material, s'pose. One thing for sure. No arsehole from Worcester fucking Park'll be coming. Wonder Psycho-Lisa hadn't been to boat already, axe in one mitt and shotgun in other. Hadn't moved onto *Rapid* more than a couple of weeks than her other half had turned up at half past eight in the morning. Asked Mum, in front of y.t. and Ginnybitch, if she'd ever thought of going in for modelling. Must have been hanging around outside the Grave-yard waiting for Dad to leave for work. Mum told him where to go, the effing creep. No wonder Lisa a fucking headcase!

Feel fucking knackered, man. Tide must be coming in. Boat rocking – rocking – rocking. Like a sodding big cradle – rocking – rocking. Like nerdy cradle with hearts cut out that Dad had made for Ginnybitch. Lovely movement. Say that for it. Laughing, laughing. Everyone's laughing. Happy birthday to you, happy birthday to you, happy birthday, dear Ginny(bitch), happy birthday to you. Can't see a frigging thing. Can hear. But can't see. Try and unglue tongue enough to poke it round corner of gob to catch some of peeper drippings. Tongue won't budge even a fucking millimetre. Stuck fast.

Tears coming nowhere near gob anyway. Running straight down poxy neck. Must've dozed. Feel as though shouting's shattered good kip. Dad's voice. No mistake. Know it straight away. Harsh and distanced. But no mistaking it.

'You never listen – you never bloody listen. That's your trouble – you never bloody well listen to what anyone else has to say. Fixed mind. Fixed mind – that's your trouble. I didn't do it – I didn't bloody well do it. Can't you understand plain English? Even the bloody judge said I didn't bloody well do it.'

Mum's voice wasn't angry. Just quiet and a bit sad. Very sad.

'The judge didn't say that you hadn't done it. He didn't say you were innocent. He said it was your word against hers. The girl's. Hardly the same thing, is it? Would you have got the sack if your boss had thought you hadn't done it? They wouldn't sack an innocent man, would they? Everyone knows you did it. Everyone. What are we going to do for the rent this week – there's no money coming in, and you know what Aggie's like . . .'

Dad does one of his flips.

'For Christ's sake can't you stop moaning woman! All you ever seem to do these days is moan–moan–moan. I'm bloody well going out and you can expect me when you bloody see me.'

Thunderclouds hanging over his eyebrows, peepers bulging like old, yellowing poached eggs, slammed his way out of *Rapid II*.

Weeping and wailing time again, Mum? Get it over and done with, for Chrissake. Can't really blame you. Think you've made a bit of a howler coming back to Daddy-O? Never done anything quite like this before, has the old tosser? Assuming that he did. Seems pretty cut and dried, Mum. No need to tell you that. Nasty business. Sexual assault in the nature of shoving his mitt up the kilt of a seventeen year old chick whilst she up a ladder painting wall of kitchen. Dad supposed to be converting to North Sea Gas. Bit pervy don't you think, Dad. Just shoving your mitt up her kilt? Out and out rape would have made you seem less of a perv in the view of some. Big G and the Old man of Oz, for starters. Gave them enough sneering material to last fucking months.

Ribs staging protest sit-in on lungs. Boa-constrictor practising crushing technique. New policy in Twilight-y Zone, is it? Scare poor, helpless, fucking Earthling shitless? Maybe y.t. providing entertainment for bunch of pervy effing aliens. Out there. Somewhere. Sort of peep-show. Sort of test, maybe. Waiting to see how y.t.'ll handle problem. Stick it out. Or lose cool. And marbles. Bunch of sick fucks!

It looked enormous. It *was* enormous. Its neck was stretched impossibly across the length of bed. Its muzzle within inches of y.t.'s phizog.

Slug-shiny black muzzle. Quivering with curiosity. Large bristles erectly twitching. Like fucking needles, for Chrissake! Long, white and stiff. Ready to pierce flesh at any mo. Huge, dark, liquidy peepers staring blankly. What the fuck is it? A cow? Was it/is it an effing cow? What the eff did a cow want in Twilight Zone-y land? Are we in the wrong warp factor, Jim? At least it wouldn't eat y.t. Cows were veg-heads, weren't there? Get outta here, you stupid effing grass eater – back off – back off!

Though no sound disturbed the silence, the animal, as though in response, began to draw back, languidly rolling its huge, pink tongue over its dripping muzzle as it did so.

Not an effing cow after all but a poxy Bambi! Who's a cool babe then? Must be a babe with all those cool dapples and sexy pins – could be wearing stilettos they're so effing long! C'mon ribs, scares over. You're safe now. *Relaxez-vous.* Come out of hidey hole in y.t.'s airbags. Sod off then, Bambi! What the fuck you standing there for, staring with those big, black, gormless peepers? Go on – piss off – vamoose, vermin! Thank Christ, braindead herbivore turning and strolling off into the wide blue yonder to become part of living mural. PR person's dream. Fucking holiday brochure, more like. Pigsicking blue sky with wanky little puffs of wanky cloud and acres of sodding greenery – fucking swathes of velvety, emeraldy grass, punctuated by frigging great trees all wearing pigging ball gowns of varying shades of pigging green. As if all that lot wasn't vomitously nerdy enough, plonked in the middle of this advertising copy spread, was a family. Or maybe two families, as there seemed to be two chicks and a swarm of frigging bratskis.

What the fuck is Bambi up to now? Typical braindead herbivore. Instead of hot-hoofing it into the undergrowth, it had sashayed itself bang between the two seated chicks. Christ – hang on to seatbelt, y.t.! In the true Twilight Zone-y fashion, part of mural had zoomed in close enough for y.t. to see that big, fat, foreign-looking bitch was Big G and she was gazing at Bambi with look of terror on swarthy boat-race. Daft bitch! Shuffling along on big, fat arse, thick pins scissoring like well, scissors, as she tried to distance her bod from the rubberneckin' Bambi. Pathetic! Now she was trying to shoo-shoo Bambi away, with wildly waving mitts. All of it wasted. Stand your ground, Bambi babe! Whites of peepers flashing, Big G lumbered up on to her size nines and the sheer, hulking bulk of her was enough to scare poor Bambi shitless. Flicking her saucy wee tail, she trotted away, leaving Big G to sprawl heavily back on to the grass.

No more than three years old. Tousled frigging golden curls. Wearing only a pair of knickers and wielding a long stick, she looked like an escapee from the set of *Lord of the Flies*. Ginnybitch. Who else. Funny how unalike in looks y.t. and Ginnybitch are. Bit like Dad and Unc. dickhead Simon. Ginnybitch all blonde curls and greeny-hazely peepers and y.t. with all of Dad's poxy tarbrush genes.

Even funnier, Dad and Big G could have been sis and bruv lookswise. *Ergo,* y.t. nothing like Mum's spawn and everything like Big G's. No hint of tarbrush in Big G's family tree. Just happened to resemble huge, Peruvian peasant. 'Specially with ethnic-y bits of cotton she wrapped round her bulk à la Dorothy Lamour. And the thonged sandals. Or bare plates. And the multiple rows of dried melon seeds wound round neck. All added to the image. Not contrived. Don't think so, anyway.

Here comes Big G's bratskis, Calvin and Rupert. Calvin same sort of age as y.t. Small, weedy and vicious. Especially to his little bruv. His fat, forever-eating little bruv. Same age as Ginnybitch.

More or less. A fat, jolly-looking Julius Caesar. Why Julius Caesar, for fuck's sake? Because of round, moon-like phizog and pile of thick beigy curls. No, it wasn't Julius Caesar. It was Peter Ustinov! Peter Ustinov. As a sprog. A sprog Peter Ustinov. He'd played Julius in a film, hadn't he? Or was it Charles Laughton? What the fuck – he looked like one or the other, or maybe both, of the mothers. Compared to Peter/Charles, Calvin's mush seemed almost elfin. Both had pale, indoor skin and beige hair. The elf had no curls. Neither looked as though they could have popped out of Big G's Peruvian pod. Perhaps P/C in his bulk and heavy-lidded peepers. The vicious elf took after the Old man of Oz. Both bullying arseholes.

Hi Mum! How's the granite industry doing these days? Christ, she always looked the poxy same. Mush devoid of any make-up. Not much of a tan yet. What the fuck month is it? Obviously summer. Skin not bad – acne in remission Mum? Looking quite Nordic. Bit of foreign blood there. Not Nordic. Canadian. Is Canadian foreign? Must be, for Chrissake. Half Canadian, was Mum. Dad had been a Canadian airman who had shagged H.G. back in 1941 before buggering off back to The Rockies and his wife and brats. Meant that y.t. must be a quarter Canadian. Never thought of it before. Weird, man. Christ, what a fucking mix! Orange Groves from Dad's side and Rocky Mountains from Mum's! Can tell from her frigging boat-race that she comes from somewhere like the bloody Rockies. Ha ha.

Ace spread. P/C, Ginnybitch and the Vicious Elf squabbling and grabbing at nosh like bunch of starving bloody rodents. Y.t. standing gormlessly at side of Big G. Long, skinny arms dangling, wearing a daft, too-short summer dress – or was it pins that were too long? Lanky not the bleeding word. Got that poxy gene from Dad as well. Pained sort of look on phizog. As though in process of doing dump in drawers (again). Wise up, twat-features – get a life, for Chrissake! Grab something – anything – a drink – grab a drink – squash, tea, home-made brew, water – water'll do – anything, anything to loosen dried-up slab of old leather from roof of gob. Nerdy, braindead bitch – peepers demurely down-cast but all the time scouring goodies and waiting. Just waiting. OK bitch. Just cut the crap and GRAB SOMETHING. Both here on poxy bed and there in fucking Twilighty Zone, y.t. FUCKING DESPERATE to shove something – anything – into gob. Even if vile enough to cause major puke, would be better than this chewed-up mess of blood and glass sitting in throat, unable to get down plug'ole and lump of leather on gob-roof.

Anything, as long's it could be stuffed into cakehole and fill and stretch mush to bursting point; push out and expand sides of gullet, thrusting blood 'n glass right down out of the way; strain muscles and tissues to limits of pain threshold, as whatever it was peristalsis-ed its slow, thick, comforting way into the welter of welcoming juices sloshing about in the poor ol' swoony gut.

'You are allowed to eat, Laura. You do know that, don't you? You don't have to wait for permission. It *is* a bloody picnic. Why on earth aren't you eating anything?'

Clipped, snipped ice-words spitting needle-y little darts all over bod. Didn't hurt. All bounced off and melted in a few mos. Made no difference to y.t. Still just sitting there. Nerd of the spread. For Chrissake kid, have a bleeding heart! How effing long is this going to last?

Good ol' Gina, handing y.t. plateful of yummies. And clucking – what the fuck is the fat bitch clucking? 'C'mon flower, get stuck into this little lot.' What a soppy cow! What an effing relief! Y.t. taking plate. Get on with it then, start cramming it in O Nerd of the Spread! Big chunk of Gina's home-made leftovers pie, wodge of home-made bread – nearly everything home-made – y.t. doing sod all with any of it – just sitting staring at bleeding ground! What a wanker! Could y.t. really have been such a total wanker of a brat? Nearly pissing drawers with thrill of getting big warm grin and plate of leftovers from fat, foreign-looking peasant and still sitting staring at tablecloth! Unless something's going into it, then for Chrissake don't open gob, kid! 'Cos, behind barriers of lips and toothy-pegs was shrieking, ravenous, clamouring mob, polyfilla-ing every pore and crevice of gob as they stampeded up from depths of sloshing gut. Clinging to sides of gullet; swinging and shrieking on uvula and running totally out of order under and over slab of leather and gums.

Can't it be given a miss? Just this once, y.t.? For Christ's bloody sake. Surely once won't make any sodding difference. No, y.t. unable to give it a miss. Now or ever. It was the sense of timing. That was what it was all about. That was where the artistry shit came into it. The timing. Y.t. had almost forgotten. Ace opportunity. Could see it now. Ace. Oh well. Lie back and enjoy. Let's see how good y.t. was in heyday.

Mo had arrived. With wodge of pie barely a centimetre from

drooling gob, y.t. slowly peeling back lids from peepers. Lashes tickling as they crawled upwards to piss off brows. Why do that? Where's the need of it? Sick, Twilight Zone-y fuck. No way can y.t. scratch lid – scratch any fucking thing, man. Could've put an itch somewhere y.t. wouldn't feel it – like anywhere on bod except frigging phizog. Wouldn't get your rocks off then would you pervy fuck?

Which most mind-blowingly far out, dudes? Knowing that, at any mo, Gina's old leftovers bit o' pie going to hit the spot in gasping gob – OR, cattle prod up arse jolt as Orange Grove peepers lock with Rockies Blue Flint Chips? Orange Grove v Rockies wins hands down every poxy time, man. Volcanic – another planer, another dimension – out of bod – out of brainbox . . . Truly (if you want the unvarnished) fucking orgasmic.

Always a real cliff-hanger, catching that microsecond flicker of bewildered hurt before Granite-features tuned in to 'Kill' mode. Then it was time for y.t. to catch up on a bit of sunbathing in the heat blasting out from the bottomless well of hatred. Waves of blistering range nuking across the gingham picnic cloth. The Blue Flint Chips had become Blue Lasers, man.

Christ, but y.t. had style! Which had caused the most sweat; keeping peepers fixed to floor until THE MO had arrived, or chilling out from the terrible urge to stuff the mangy bit o' pie, plate an' all, into desperate, shrieking cakehole?

What the fuck did it matter, dickhead? Mo had passed. Another kill for y.t. Now all that mattered was seeing how much scrummy nosh could be crammed into bod without busting gut. Gina opening bottle of home-made, stale-as-old-piss-nettle. Still sodding fermenting. Wonder it ever got as far as the bottle. Filled old, chipped tin mugs. Sloshing clear, snot-hued lemonade (also home-made) into yet more old mugs for bratskis. Christ, does the daft bitch want to finish everyone off or just turn them into family of slavering Hydes?

All grub and booze always made by Gina's less than fair mitts. That was the trouble. Great cook. Shame about the mitts. Never clean. Not only never clean; always effing dirty. Been known to divulge, whilst rat-arsed, her secret for turning stew into ragout, with a flick or two of menstrual flow. Honest. Brill chick tho'. Menstrual flow or no. Never had any dosh because of tying knot with Old man of Oz. Spent all his bread on state of the art Soho studio whilst P/C and the Vicious Elf ran around shoeless.

Mattered not that Gas and Electricity were always being cut off and the cupboards were often bare–bare–bare. He was an Artist, don't chano'! Big G had to run up huge credit at local corner shop. Wouldn't let her get a job. Wouldn't let her play the fucking joanna, for Chrissake! Not for a long time. While he was living all the time in the studio and shagging his tea-lady, or whatever. Thought himself a real cool dude, this short arse Old man of Oz. Wore denim bib 'n brace overalls, permed and dyed his few strands. Thought nobody knew. Old wanker. Considered inferior sorts, such as women, should spend all time chained to sink or cooker whilst wearing veil and/or sackcloth. And Big G took it all from the fucking old arsehole. No. Not as simple as that. Thought he was the main man, to start with. Loved him; looked up to him. But once he'd trodden her well into the ground, she found it impossible to scrape herself back together again. Not like Humpty. Not broken in pieces. Easy. Could just pick up pieces and glue. No. He ground her down like coffee grits and rubbed her round and down into the earth until she almost lost herself altogether. Didn't though. Good ol' Big G! Sort of thing he liked to do when in grinding mood was refuse to walk beside her (on rare occasion they ever went out *en famille*) so's no one would know they were together. Something to do with Big G being a six-footer and shortarse from Oz five foot six. What the fuck's that in metres? – one point six or something – but he married her for Chrissake!

Bowels doing a bit of a samba as Mum turns and hands y.t. mug of devilish brew. In mid-laugh, Mum was. Not for y.t. Something Big G had said. Phizog relaxed and frost free. Make the most of it why don't you, y.t.? Shove scrawny arms around her, 'cos no icicles to stab and prod and freeze nipples off. Didn't happen. Couldn't happen. Wouldn't happen. And the samba-ing turned into thick, varicose-y knots, looping and coiling sluggishly as Mum moved away. Taking the bit of a smile with her.

What the fuck's happened to the nosh? Mum and Big G clearing away debris; Vicious Elf kicking shit out of a prostrate, bellowing P/C; Big G tut-tutting at VE for constantly kicking, thumping, pinching, tweaking and generally making life hell for his little bruv. A tut or two's as far 's she'd go 'cos she and Old man of Oz were ardent groupies of Neill and his trendy Summerhill shit. Followed that bratskis, even if vicious elves, could do no wrong and good Mummies and Daddies must never ever even lightly smack their little botties. Or even the backs of their little mitts. Pure shite. Ginnybitch still doing bit part in *Lord of the Flies*: hadn't even sat down to eat. Had nosh on the hoof. What nosh? Where is effing nosh? Big G and Mum well into the stale piss. Nettle. Or was in Dandelion? All stale piss. Powerful, though. Hell of a kick to it. Hampton Court Park. That's where they were. Mum getting very red in mush. Booze never agreed with her. Should leave it alone, Mum.

Still living in Graveyard. Must be. Only there the one summer. No. Not so. There for bits of two summers. End of one summer, when Ginnybitch had second birthday on *Rapid II*. And part of following summer. Before they moved to Wimbledon. When did they move to Wimbledon? Where had Ginnybitch had third birthday? Was she three now? Had she had her third birthday? How the fuck old was braindead y.t.? Ginnybitch more than two. When did they move to Wimbledon? Why the fuck does it matter? Mum and Big G stuffing phizogs with poxy cake or whatever. Where is it, for Chrissake? Fucking nightmare this, man. Twilight-fucking-Zone bad enough. Why can't y.t. get anything into gob, for Chrissake?

Not on a diet then. Big G and Mum. The way they're shovelling it in. Always on diet of some sort. Before the summer. Once summer over, pile it on by sackload again. Big G was the worst. Sometimes she would hit the fifteen stone mark and scare the shit out of anyone and anything that came within spitting distance. Not fifteen stone now. Sorry. Not 90kg now. More like 77kg. Bad enough. Mum around the 63kg mark. Kept it fairly steady after Ginnybitch popped pod.

Big G around a lot during year spent on *Rapid*. Always trying to outdo each other in cheap nosh stakes. Mum got boiling chooks from Woolies for 1/6d per lb. (No kg in those days, man.) Then Big G found a butcher selling scrag end of mutton for 10d a lb. Bitches made vast pots of brill broths and stews that lasted at least a week. In winter, o' course. Bought stuff in bulk to save dosh. Coffee beans. Wheat. Ground both. Roasted coffee beans in little saucepan, stirring all the time with wooden spoon. Kenya peaberry. What a fucking thing to remember! Coarsely ground wholemeal flour (100% wholemeal, have you know) made bread like slabs of bleeding chipboard. Effing tasty, though. Got Wimbledon pad through pal o' Big G's. Became Mum's pal too. Big fall out after, 'cos Gina found out that pal was supporter of IRA.

Big G always going on about some dick or other. Always having crushes. Fantasies. Stayed faithful to the Old man of Oz until the day he popped clogs though.

Flushed and tousled from too much poison-piss and dirty talk, they shrieked and cackled the summer afternoon to death.

'Not that fat, little composer bloke, Gina,' screeches Mum. 'The one whose wife ran off with the postman! Not him any more? Who then? Not the new vicar, Gina – for Chrissake, not the new vicar!'

God, they could be boring. Drone–drone–cackle–cackle–drone–drone . . .

Hated each other at first sight, Mum and Big G. Queen Bee syndrome. Big G's patch. Mum cocky newcomer. Poor Mum. Dumped by solitary brain-celled fitter of something or other. Threw her over after first and only fuck. Said what they'd done was wicked and they should have waited until they were married. What a dickhead!

Mum's first fuck. Aged nineteen and too pissed to remember anything. Just a big, hard dick. Jabbing blindly and mindlessly. The fitter didn't live up to his trade and, in order to be successfully penetrated, Mum had to clutch the hot stump and insert it, as painlessly as poss, into her dry, virgin's hole. Much humping ensued, but all Mum had to show for her deflowering was badly bruised thighs and minge rubbed almost raw. Should've twigged he wasn't the one for you, Mum. When he threw a wobbly at sound of Ludwig's fifth and another (wobbly) when you penned him a poem.

All wedding pressies had to be sent back to H.G. to be returned to various senders. There had been none from dickhead's family. All eight sisters and a mother. No Da. Though Mum had felt like a piece of old shite, she hadn't been totally nuked 'cos she'd realised, after the Ludwig episode that her hunky fitter was Neanderthal Man hisself with Neanderthal breath to prove it. Had to move outta digs, 'cos N Man like member of family. One of them had to move out, so Mum moved in with Big G and Yvonne. Beginning of bad time. All in the opus.

What the fuck's going down, man? Nothing. That's what. Sweet FA.

VE still beating the shit outta P/C; overdoing the *Lord of the Flies* thingy Ginnybitch, aintcha? Mum and Big G whispering and cackling and throwing back the nettle piss as though dehydration was setting in with a vengeance.

Was? No 'was' about it, man. Is. Is setting in. *Has* set in. Well an' fucking truly. If y.t. minus a drop of whistle wetter for much longer they won't be any effing y.t. Even if some dude pissed in gob it'd be something. Effing lifesaver, in fact. Why the fuck doesn't scrawny y.t. swallow gubbins in poxy tin mug for Chrissake? Why such a wanker? What did it matter that it was home-made piss?

Stay cool, babe. Just stay cool. Maybe it'll be snack-time soon and nosh'll be dished out again. Grab some second time round, eh? Better make sure of it, dildo. Stay chilled out till then, babe. Feeling shagged – mother of a head – must be all that effing din coming from poxy so-called mates. Give anything for a bit o' kip. Peepers won't close. Buddies hadn't missed y.t. then. Bad news, man. No sign of life in pins yet. Funny. Noddle not moving. As much. At all. Should be. Should be more, not less for Chrissake.

Motherfuckers still there. Ginnybitch running around for ever-more, waving big stick; P/C grovelling and snivelling for all eternity as VE continued, for the rest of time, to beat the shit out of his fat little arse. Mum and Big G whispering and giggling into infinity, noddles close together, tin mugs sloshing and bobbing.

Faint distant humming of murmuring voices and muted laughter. All distant and lazy. Summer-distant hazy. Faraway sounds of a distant, dozing summer's day. Drifting, dozing, summer-hazy, distant dream. Disembodied sounds of summer. Like the sounds of the sea caught in the labyrinth of a seashell. Distant laughter; distant children; distant sounds of summer held fast in the curves of an unseen shell. The whole world of summer. Trapped forever. And y.t. all alone in the fucking Universe. On the outside. Holding sea shell summer world against ear'ole. Listening, listening.

Where the fuck are you – you motherfucking bastards?

Listening. Listening to sounds of happiness. Sounds of summer. Far, far away. Drifting. Shame about Mum an' the sixpences.

What the fuck made y.t. come up with that slab of ancient history for Chrissake? Seeing Mum an' Big G being such close buddies in the Twilight Zone-y time, p'rhaps. Wonder if they're such big buddies in the here an' now. Twenty frigging years on, man. Been outta touch for a tad, dudes. Don't get weepy, bitch! Fucking itching factory'll spring to life – so DON'T GET WEEPY, BITCH! Chill some, for Chrissake!

Get back to Mum an' the effing sixpences. What a poxy saga. Could've ended all this old pals right there an' then. Mum fleeing the coop with a carrier bag full of Yvonne's stash of saved-for-her-hols sixpences. Smashed jar. Nicked sixpences. Simple as that. Get real Mum. Should've put off sticking noddle in gas oven until evening when could've asked Yvonne for loan. OR – left a polite little explanatory note. Saying what, for Chrissake? Marbles flying about so much that she had to smash the jar an' nick the dosh in the first place but she's supposed to chill out enough to leave a wee note of apology and/or explanation! Weird, man. Yvonne never forgave Mum. Shame, 'cos she'd always been an OK babe to Mum in various times of need, both dosh-wise an' shoulder to lean on type scene. More than could've been said for Big G whose bonce was always full of who her next shag was likely to be. Couldn't give a fuck, one way or t'other, about Mum.

Yvonne helped Mum get a job in Dickens & Jones. Buyer's clerk. Bratskis' wear. Couldn't handle it. Not after spending her days on the hunting field and practice gallops round Newmarket. Stuck it for six weeks, though. Developed sicko tendencies. Phobias. Lifts. Stations. Trains. Telephones. People. Had a couple of weeks off. Yvonne spoke to Personnel babe. Went back. Stayed less than a week. Couldn't explain. Didn't know. Going to parties with Big G. Getting rat-arsed. Losing memory. Getting shagged. Weeping and wailing. Spending all day in beddy-byes. Falling down bottomless pits and getting lost in endless tunnels. Couldn't ask Yvonne for more dosh. Just couldn't. Felt like a giant sponge. Desperate for STs. Thighs and crotch raw and bleeding from wad of newspaper to soak up menstrual flood. Wrote H.G. asking for dosh. Letter contain ten bob note came return of post. Ran across common to chemist to get STs. Lost ten bob note. Scoured common. Couldn't find it. Thought she'd dreamt the bloody thing. Went back to flat. H.G.'s note – hardly a letter – sitting where she'd left it. Realised now or never. Gas oven or scarper. Tried to force gas meter. Couldn't. Only dosh available, Yvonne's jar of sixpences. Saving for hols. Broke jar. Half-inched sixpences. Made her way to only place of refuge. Dyke Bungalow. No memory of journey. Must have got some weird effing looks. Paying for tickets with pile of tanners. Train across London; coach from Victoria to good ol' Bexhill. Then bus from Bexhill to wherever it was.

A fucking cemetery – Ellesmere Cemetery? Something like that.

Undertakers opposite bus stop. Had to walk two or three miles in the pissing rain and blackness of a February night to get to safety of Dyke Bungalow. Her and her poxy mog in a poxy mog basket. Known thereafter in Dykelore as The Night of the Dripping Apparition.

Must be a dead dyke now. Ninety if she's a day. Been good to y.t. in dim and distant. Blotted copy book. As usual. Nothing serious. Not like with Big G. But serious enough for dyke to give y.t. the old thumbs down. No more riding hols. Must have nicked whatever. Or tried to shag someone shouldn't have. One of her pals, old men, or sons, or the gardener. The gardener, prob'ly. Hester would have been mortified at such a close encounter with the lower classes. Shame. Nice old bird. Little Prune, for fuck's sake!

The smell had returned. The oily, rotting-fish smell. And where the fuck was the wet coming from? Feels as though bucket of cold, oily water chucked over phizog. Raining. Can feel drops landing and trickling down scalp. Feels like little things creeping about in hair. Must be rain. Must be.

There they all were. Standing like a bunch of dickheads in the pissing rain. Mum clutching Ginnybitch close to her side, Dad and y.t. Far out Twilight Zone-y stuff this! Everything grainy shades of grey and dingy white. What the fuck are morons doing just standing? Looking at something. That's what. That's what they're doing. Not such bunch of dildos after all. Get peepers focused for Chrissake! What in the fuck are they staring at? Must be one helluva peeperful whatever it is.

Wreck. Total wreck. Wreck of what only just passes as boat. Makes *Rapid II* look like *QE2*. Covered in thick brown slime. Like plastered in shite. Bits of old carpet nailed along sides. Stinking–stinking–stinking. Awful stench of rot and ancient decay. Must sink with every tide, says Dad, in a hushed voice. We haven't any choice. Says Mum. All wrapped up but freezing fucking cold.

For Chrissake, Mum, move outta this poxy hell-hole. Nothing to see, in any direction, but swirls of pale, dank mist and curtains of poxy rain.

Going to vomit – guts heaving their way up into throat. Huge wave of heaving. Can't move noddle. Can't open cakehole. Will choke if stuff gets up into gob. Fucking stench not helping – what is it with this rotten-fish pong? Going to fall off the bed, for Chrissake! Pitched right off the bed and onto frigging floor! Floor's moving – how can effing floor be heaving as well? Coming up to meet vomit – floor heaving – guts heaving . . .

Sunlight glaring angrily, blinding peepers. Dad sitting by little gas fire called The Monster 'cos it chucked out such a massive heat. Holding a piece of almost-toast at the end of a long fork. Small saucepan on top of Monster, bubbling merrily.

Floor heaving, Dad heaving, saucepan heaving, toast on.end of fork heaving. All well on the way to being upside bloody down. Where the fuck is y.t.? On the ceiling? Like a fucking insect of some sort? A fly? Fly on the wall? Only not on the wall, on the frigging ceiling! Lift noddle, for Chrissake – have a look round – don't effing fall off whatever it is y.t. is hanging on to . . .

There's Mum! Holding on to a huge, wooden wheel and looking like effing Brunnhilde! All that's needed are the brass tit-covers and horny helmet, Ma! And there's Ginnybitch. Lying on a wide sort of shelf/bench behind Mum's wheel that joins on to a big, wide window. No wonder everything heaving – all that dark-green surging stuff with the prissy little lacy frills was the fucking ocean! Y.t.'s out in the middle of the fucking ocean! What ocean? Where ocean? Chill some, babe. For Chrissake. Chill.

Sick to fucking death of all this poxy weirdo shit. What the fuck is y.t. doing out in the middle of the fucking ocean, man? No fucker's gonna tell y.t. any fucking thing. Think, babe. Think. Think back. Why would FitzHugh family be out in middle of poxy sea? *Mikrokosmos*. Frigging *Mikrokosmos*. They were in the wheelhouse of the old lifeboat and they were taking it round the coast from Yarmouth to its new mooring in Sefton Boatyard. Not far from Woodbridge. Not under its own steam, so to speak. But towed by a fishing boat called *The Sunny Girl*.

What the fuck did Mum think she was doing with the effing wheel? Might need a tad of help with the steering. Keep it in a straight line behind *The Sunny Girl*. But . . .

Been having a kip by the looks of things. Ginnybitch wrapped up nice and cosy in woolly blanket. Y.t.'s seems to have fallen on to floor. No wonder y.t. hypothermia'd. Great gaps in side of wheelhouse. Pass up the blanket for Chrissake, Mum. Before y.t. freezes to bleeding death. No chance. Daft bitch bursting into song. Brunnhilde with sodding vengeance. Not 'Das Valkyrie' thank the Christ. Over the sea to fucking Skye – almost as bad as! Get real Mum, why don't you? Now dildo Dad's doing a Rog with the (toast-free) toasting fork and joining in the fucking chorus! Leave off, Dad! Voice like sick fog-horn. Mum's voice not at all bad. Don't often hear her warble. Usually after a few bevvies. Not the same then.

Wish this poxy heaving would stop. Old boat bucking and rearing like something out of rodeo. Mum getting off on it. Always been mad on boats. Fishing boats. Not just any old boats. Used to spend holidays in Wick as a kid. Stayed all day hanging round harbour with cousin Jimmy. Had crush on fisherman in thigh-high waders and oily jersey. Who wouldn't? Never knew Dad liked boats. Only went for the pontoon in the Graveyard 'cos nothing else going at the time.

Old boat called *The White Swan*, but Mum changed it to *Mikrokosmos* 'cos of Bartok and his poxy piano. Been up on blocks in Yarmouth dock all winter. Paid a hundred nicker for the old hulk. Could have got it for fifty. No one thought it would ever move from Broads backwater. Dad had come up on his ownio one weekend and got a dude with a motor on a dinghy to tow wreck round to Yarmouth harbour. Depended on how it settled during each ebbtide as to whether it took water during following incoming tide. All due to seams opening. Still took in a fair bit but not enough to sink it overnight. There it had bobbed, in Yarmouth harbour, like a dirty matchstick toy flung in the water by some pissed off brat, among the awesome tankers and container ships. Next day, they'd had it craned out and onto blocks on the dockside. Hairy few mos there, man. Dockmaster told them they were wasting his and their time as the bloody old wreck would fall apart the minute the sling went on. Cranedriver and mate sniffily said that hull would crumple like cardboard and they didn't want the job. Thanks. But no thanks. Mum and Dad in huddle. Whispering. What did we have to lose? If she did fall apart, a hundred smackers plus craning fee. But she couldn't be left in the harbour and they didn't have a mooring. Didn't realise then that she could have gone by sea. No one would have taken chance then, anyway. Didn't have mooring to be towed to anyway. Rubbernecking fisherman mumbling that she'd never make it and they should let her sink back under the water. Where she belonged. Vote of fucking confidence, eh Mum? As the huge crane swung the sad effort out across the quay and across to the blocks, they all heard the sickening creaks of yielding planks. All peepers glued on old hulk, swaying and groaning as though in death throes.

One of poxy dockers shouted, 'Look out! She's about to go!'

Mum and Dad about to go, too. Both looking fit to fall in or pass out. Phizogs grey with fear. Could be the fucking permafrost as well. If y.t.'d any bollocks, they'd be frozen solid by now, man.

Crane grinding to a halt, driver leaning out, shouting did they want him to carry on – if so, he refused to accept any responsibility.

Mum and Dad nodding and shouting, 'Yes – yes.'

Ginnybitch wrapped up like papoose, fast asleep in pushchair. Y.t. like Bosnian refugee. All this effing standing around! In all this sodding Norfolk mist and sodding Norfolk rain! Weeks and weeks they'd spent scouring yards and marinas for a cheap boat and not once seen a bit o' poxy sunshine! Seemed that way, man. Y.t. iced. Fucking iced. Phizog blue; peepers glittering with frost.

Sat in twenty-four foot open fishing boat once. Knees meeting across breadth. Mum trying to convince Dad that they could manage it for a while if he built a superstructure. Desperate wasn't the word.

As *Mikro* swung nearer, could see where creaks and groans coming from. Old, rotting planks held together by the strips of filthy carpet. Not part of the main hull. Added at some time to give extra height to bulwarks. Old girl not dying after all. Mum's already twigged and was tugging at Dad and pointing, all red-faced and sparkly. The rotten wood was bending like plasticine in the clutches of the cradle. But it didn't matter a tinker's dick. Give the bastards the finger, Mum!

They came up most weekends to clean out old *Mikro*. The only solid floor was one half of the wheelhouse. Every other cabin, four in all, was a mess of vile, thick, slimy foul-smelling mud and broken floorboards. In the small sea-loo, the lavvy seat was just visible above the layers of ancient ooze and, all along the port side, the slime covered the hull right up to the deckhead. Sometimes, other dudes came with them. One dude knew about plugging seams – caulking – and they found out that old girl's bod was solid teak. 'Cept for her ribs. Made of oak but only crumbly fragments left. Just enough to keep old bod from falling apart at seams. Literally. Mum getting wound up, going on about finding out history of old lifeboats in the area. Some fisherman dude had said he could remember a working lifeboat in the fifties. Called *The White Swan*. One of the old types, open below decks and with long benches for the rescued. Big wheelhouse would have been added much later on. Mum gabbing on about doing restoring job. Thinks old girl would have been under sail. Never seen her with such a buzz. 'Cept when Ginnybitch popped pod.

Before twigging that *they*'d have to move nearer to *Mikro* rather than bring the old girl down south, they'd paid a hundred smackers to have her transported to a mooring in Newhaven. Other end of the fucking country, man. Only mooring they could get for forty-eight footer. Seventy-five quid for hire of monster crane and twenty-five for month's mooring fees. Coulda done with Scottie doing a bit o' beaming up, Jim! Saved some dosh! Had to borrow from Unc dickhead Simon. Nearly finished Mum. Either that, or do without *Mikro*. Bastard humm-ed and haw-ed. Kept them hanging around for his bloody answer. Only a hundred, for Chrissake! Made Dad – his own bruv – sign IOU. Mum nearly went nuclear. Dad not too chuffed either.

Had been phoned and told, in warmth of Wimbledon semi, that transporter carrying *Mikro*, had left Yarmouth in wee small hours.

So all standing, freezing to frigging death, at Newhaven mooring. Waiting for *Mikro* to materialise. Ginnybitch always akip. No fucking wonder. Wrapped up like pupa in duvet of a sleeping bag while y.t. sick to gills of being dragged round country in either icy, pissing rain or freezing fog, in old, cold Post Office van.

Dad's phizog a weird mix of yellows and blues. Mum's mottled reds and blues and purples. Y.t.'s like piece of frozen cod on slab of grey marble.

Dad goes and phones fuzz to see if there'd been an accident or a breakdown. Fuzz say no such transporter reported on any of main roads out of Yarmouth and anyway, a thing that size would need a fuzz escort if allowed on the road at all. Sixteen foot beam? No way! Not allowed. Against the law. No transporter in the country big enough. Impossible. Dad phoned Yarmouth Dockmaster. *Mikro* still sitting serenely on blocks. All heap of shite lies. Lost all dosh paid for hire of crane and bastard, as well as craning one of his own boats into river, refused to pay back mooring fees. Couldn't have managed poxy mooring anyway. Thirty foot drop from jetty to deck when tide went out. How the fuck could Ginnybitch's fat pins clamber up and down a thirty foot metal ladder three or four times a day? Never mind Dookie and the mogs! And Mum – afraid of effing heights! Fucking desperate, or what? Just as well sodding shyster hadn't turned up. Mum and Dad had shit time getting dosh back from him – another hundred smackers. And then only some of it. So the traipsing starting all over again. But this time they used Yarmouth as a starting point and worked their way down the coast, calling at all marinas and boatyards until they found Woodbridge. And then Sefton.

Mum almost had spontaneous come when drove across single track railway into small, derelict yard. Nothing but river, trees and sky. And birds, birds and more poxy birds. Fat, round, orange chickens pattering around the old granary (working) and swans, ducks – loads of different ducks, herons and hundreds of funny, speckly, skittery things, fair seething all over the river bed. Not a house in sight. Except for the granary. And that didn't count. 'Cos it wasn't a house. Only three boats in small dock. And room for just the one more. Dream come true for Mum. Her and Dad hugging each other for ages.

No wonder the bitch was on such a high. Sea shanties now, for Chrissake! Dish up the brekky then, Dad. Coupla boiled eggies and few rounds o' toast'll see y.t. Sweet Jesus – all that heaving green lacy stuff *not* the fucking ocean – *Mikro* only coming up to mouth of river! All the surging and swelling making old girl act like deranged dodgem coming from wake of *Sunny Girl*! Sun well on way up now. Scary shapes of looming tankers and container ships getting smaller. Why did they seem so scary? Not all dark and sinister. Some bright and garish. All scary.

What the fuck's the sun up to? Like a poxy pumpkin splitting the sky with a grin as wide as the sea. All that vomitous turquoise and gold and cornflower blue. And the sulky-wanker sea only able to mirror the grinning antics of the pumpkin. Pathetic! Mum gazing, gobsmacked, as though she's just had a good snort. Been in frigging daze since night before.

Look at the sea for Chrissake! It's fucking huge. And it's alive! Flexing its pectorals and throwing its weight around like a bouncer in a strip joint! Mum laughing. Laughing out loud. Look – look at the waves – have you ever seen such waves? No, Mum. Like

103

being on a fucking giant roller coaster. A giant, out-of-control roller coaster. Pigging river a dawdle. This is serious shit, man.

Pass up the blanket, for pity's sake, Mum. Y.t.'s bloody freezing. All these ruddy great holes in the wheelhouse – draught making y.t. numb to the bone with cold.

And why the fuck so long with the eggies and toast, Dad? Why just sitting there? Why isn't toast burning, for Chrissake! Can't you turn gas fire over this way a tad, Dad? You can carry on sitting there with your Twilight Zone-y bit of toast. Why the fuck didn't you and Mum let y.t. and Ginnybitch go in *The Sunny Girl*? They said we could. Like last night. Needn't have even woken up. If we'd stayed on *Mikro* like Mum wanted, we'd all have popped clogs from hypothermia. Feels like that now, Dad. Frigging hypothermia. For Chrissake turn the fucking fire this way tosser! It had been so warm inside *The Sunny Girl*.

They'd arrived in time for *Mikro* to be craned back into the dock. No probs. Dockmaster well chuffed. For them and to see them go. And to see the old girl leave the quay. He'd had a bellyful of her sitting up on blocks for the past three months or whatever. The awesome tankers once more made her look like a toy dropped over the side of the dock. Thank Christ none of the monsters were berthed too close for comfort.

Bit of a fix. Being January, it got dark around 4.30. And one big heap shit colder. Choices: either sleep in freezing Post Office van or in even more freezing wheelhouse of old wreck. No sane chick would have given over-ventilated wheelhouse a second thought. Half a floor for Chrissake! But Mum, being Mum, decided they'd go down to see how things were. If too cold, they'd come back to the van. No prob. So they'd climbed down the long, narrow iron ladder attached to the harbour wall. Made Newhaven mooring seem piece of piss, man! Dad carried Ginnybitch down first. No mud down there. Only fuck knows how many metres of river. Only Dad and y.t. able to swim. Mum terrified of water. Unbelievable. Mum with peepers clenched shut following Dad who had hold of each of her pins in case she lost footing. Dad went back for gas fire, blankets, etc. etc. Still like depths of frigging Arctic. Mum desperate to spend night in the old boat. But worried about bratskis. As well as all the gaping cracks and roughly patched holes, there was no way of shutting out the staring emptiness of the other cabins. One on either side. Like mouths of separate gateways to hell. Blasting out an icy chill and stench of stagnant mud. Not a good scene.

104

Despair and hypothermia palling up nice and comfy for the night, when the skipper of *The Sunny Girl* shouted down that they were welcome to spend the night on *Sunny* as he and his crew were off home. They'd be ready to leave with the morning tide. About 6 am. 6 am, for Chrissake! Mum felt sick leaving the old girl. Would have stayed on her own if Dad'd let her. Frozen-pinned, they'd climbed up the long, narrow ladder, then climbed down another to the deck of *The Sunny Girl*. Didn't know which the most mind-blowing. The heat or the pong. The heat was blasting out from a small woodburner aspiring to furnace-hood and the pong was a mind-spinning mix of old-fish-stink from the holds, bitumastic and stale sea water from the bilges, diesel from the engines and fuck knows what else thrown in for good measure. Mum on real high. Childhood fantasy. Only one small cabin for living quarters. A fixed table with a small narrow bench on either side doubling as bunks. That was it, man. Y.t. and Ginnybitch out of it as soon as noddles touched down. The intense heat, the dizzying pongs, the rhythmic rocking and swaying, the sound of the river slapping and lapping against the hull; if poor old *Rapid II* had been a damp, dark cave, then *The Sunny Girl* was a womb.

And you took us away Mum! Wrenched y.t. and Ginnybitch outta the womb! Could easily have left us there. Sleeping. Why the fuck didn't you? The skipper had told you to leave bratskis finish snooze but oh no. You had to drag us out into the pitch fucking dark of a January dawn, up and down frigging icicle covered iron ladders, just because you wanted to get your rocks off playing fucking Happy Families. Pure shite. Pure effing shite. For Chrissake turn the frigging fire over here so's y.t. can feel a bit o' heat, you fucking dickhead! What's with the zombie thingy, man? Everyone staring. Dad just sitting and staring; toasting fork, with half-done bit of toast stuck on the end, clutched in one mitt.

Mum still gripping wheel, arms outstretched, gob open in mid-warble.

Another gromit fled the coop, Scottie? Christ, you're a useless bastard. Fuck knows why Jim hasn't booted you up the arse years ago the amount of balls up you make, ha ha. And all the time the poxy sea keeps leaping and heaving, leaping and heaving, leaping and heaving.

Lungs bursting out of chest and taking heart with them. Can't get breath – pain gripping throat and choking breath. Chest going to split open and let heart and lungs run free. Running along towpath – y.t. running along frigging towpath with Mum belting ahead. What the fuck are they running for? Mum haring across to the Granary.

For Chrissake – stop running y.t. – no need to keep up with the daft old bitch! Lungs and heart beginning to settle down again inside chest. Breathing returning to (almost) normal. Can see reason for Mum's loss of cool. Over by the Granary, looking more like a large, mutant rodent than an Afghan, was a sopping wet Dookie running round in circles trying to catch a chook. Chooks flying, squawking wildly, in all direction. One sod-awful din. Dudes from Granary trying to get hold of braindead mutt. One dude waving a shovel and cursing loudly. Mum shouting hysterically both at dudes and lunatic Dookie. Manages to get hold of collar. Trying to calm down dude with waving shovel; saying how valuable Dookie was etc. etc. Chooks still madly flying around, too fucking stupid to twig that danger had passed.

Turned out that incoming tide had lifted the old girl off the river bed at a half-arsed angle. Wheelhouse door had swung open allowing Dookie to make quick exit, though not before falling in drink.

Only been in yard a couple of weeks 'cos Dad hadn't fixed wheelhouse door. When tide went out, it jammed fast. When tide came in, it sometimes swung open. Never mattered before 'cos Dookie never left on his own in boat. But Mum and y.t. had taken Ginnybitch to new playgroup in Woodbridge. Why y.t. not at school, Mum?

Dad working in a mushroom farm. No dosh for first couple of weeks. No holiday money from Wimbledon job. All dosh spent on moving. Lived on bread made from gravel making out it was flour got on tick from Granary, and mushrooms. Mushrooms, mushrooms, mushrooms and even more effing mushrooms. Mushrooms fried, mushrooms stewed, mushrooms on gravel sannies, mushroom, on gravel toast . . . Not so bad for y.t. Got school din-dins.

Mum found an old, cast-iron stove along the tow path – down the bank, hidden in the undergrowth. A wee rusty corner bit sticking out among the brambles. Enough to set her nose twitching. Made Dad borrow dinghy and row down river to fetch old rust-bucket. Had to push and shove it up and over the bank and on to the dinghy. Nearly killed him. Cast iron well oxidised but not rotten. Called it 'The Dragon'. Ate a tree a day, but warmed every one of *Mikro*'s timbers.

One small cabin, the fo'c'sle, right in the bows. Bunk on either side. Y.t. and Ginnybitch as cosy as cockles. Like being in cradle when tide in. Rocked to bye-byes. Mum, Dad, Dookie and mogs slept in wheelhouse. Had to manage in one half whilst other half replaced with new floorboards. Then move across whilst ditto to other half. Tight frigging squeeze. Everything done in wheelhouse. Cooking, washing. Sea-bog working. Dad had fixed it up in a few mos. Working order. Flushed an' all.

Shouting's started up again. Can't be the granary dudes. Dookie only got out the once. Used to let him out at night. Just to have a last pee. Till he started coming home with pale-blood highlights on his long silky chest-hairs and stinking of raw flesh. Never found out what he'd murdered and devoured. Not chooks. Not granary chooks, anyway. Not rabbits. Too effing slow off mark to catch a rabbit. Blood not red enough for rabbit. Never let him out again. Spoiled it for himself, said Mum. Had to be tied up all the time. Who's doing all the bleeding shouting then? Bloke's dulcits. Dad, o' course. Who the fuck else? Standing in his knickers in middle of long room, looking like the Mummy risen from the Tomb. Peepers bulging, gob frothing – one sure as hell mad Dad.

Well and truly pulverised goggle-box lying dead at his big, bony plates. Mum standing few feet away, in her nightie. Y.t. cowering at bottom of stairs. Mum shaking and clutching at herself as though feeling cold all of a sudden.

'There was no need for that, Desmond.' Says Mum. 'What did you have to go and do that for?'

'It's settled now – it's bloody well settled,' shouts the Mummy. 'No more telly – are you happy now? Are you bloody well satisfied? Are you? No one can watch the sodding telly. Are you happy now? Are you?'

Thought SW 13 was going to be given the miss. All this warp factor shit really doing head in. Little grey cells falling arse over tit trying to get head together, man. Hope you're getting your rocks off on this, Jim. You and that deadbeat, Scottie. Pair of jerk-offs.

Huge living-room in Wimbledon semi. Mum did her scribbling at a table in the far corner looking out onto the back garden. The telly was – had been – at the opposite end of the room near the big, front window. Dad watched everything. Adverts an' all. Real slob. Daft grin on his gob. In a little world of his own. Drove Mum witless. Endless rows. Mum hated the way the box able to enslave. Y.t. and Ginnybitch severely restricted as to what allowed to watch. Only had it a few weeks. First ever telly. Black and white. Still rowing about it when they went to bed. Mum wouldn't let go. So, 'cos Dad unable to control peepers, goggle-box must die.

For fifteen or so of the eighteen months they'd lived in Wimbledon semi, Mum had hots for the landlord. Brother-in-law of Gina's pal. The one who'd put them on to the house. The one who was a fan of the IRA. Nothing to look at. The landlord. Small, slightly built, freckled, specs, gingery Afro, nice bum; few extra brain cells than Mum was used to, floating about under the Afro. Whatever it was, Mum fell for it. In a big way. Obsessed. 'Specially after she'd sent off the opus. Big hole needing filling. Two big holes. And Dad not able to insert even temporary filling in either. The one in her head or the one between her legs. Mummy going back upstairs to Tomb. Mum staring at telly carcass. Only cost a fiver. Won't know what's happened to 'The Prisoner' now, Mum. Should've kept your frigging gob shut. Mouthy bitch.

'What are you standing there for, child? Don't you know what time it is? Go back to bed – you've got school in the morning.'

Shaking like she's got the palsy. Frightened to go up to the Tomb where the Mummy lies waiting. Ha ha ha.

School had been a heap o' shite, but y.t. had all day to look forward to coming home in the afternoon. Ginnybitch always playing with cardboard boxes, making frigging houses out of them, for Chrissake. And, as if that wasn't sick enough, making frigging cardboard people to live inside the cardboard houses. And if *that* wasn't vomitous enough, sewing sets of little curtains, cushions, sheets, pillow cases and frigging clothes for the stiff little corrugated jerk-offs. Whole fucking family of cardboard cut-outs, for Chrissake, with smiley faces filled in with biro. Soon put a stop to all that shit, didn't we, Ginnybitch? Didn't take long to get Ginnybitch going. Mum at window, beavering away on old Remington. Hoping things might be different today? Soon giggle factor multiplying by the mo. Mum stops beavering. Lots of chatties about having to finish book, needing some peace and quiet – not asking for complete silence – bullshit, bullshit, bullshit.

Nods and smiles and 'sorry, Mum', before carrying on with more of the same. Bitch had only the two options. Either send y.t. and Ginnybitch upstairs (only option during dark evening or if weather bad) or into the garden. To play, ha ha ha. If sent upstairs, all that was needed was for y.t. to up volume of giggle factor with, maybe, the addition of a few regularly spaced heavy thumps. Like from jumping off the bed. Never failed. After a few shouts about a bit of peace – *please!* – and maybe a visit upstairs to deposit the remainder of the bullshit, the cover soon went on the Remington.

If sent out into the garden, all y.t. had to do was get Ginnybitch into full giggle mode outside Mum's work-window. Similar shit. She'd knock on window and ask for some peace, please. Or come to the kitchen door and issue a few bullshitty threats like, no supper; early to bed; no pocket money, etc. etc. She would never completely lose her cool because of Ginnybitch. So y.t. could wind up as far as poss.

Sometimes, if Ginnybitch got bored too soon with giggling, which she usually did, y.t. would resort to Method Two. Purely an outdoor thingy. The equivalent to the indoor thingy of jumping on and off the bed; ball-bouncing. Always worked. Never once failed. 'Specially with the added extra of a few well-timed peeks in Mum's direction as she got more and more pissed off. Sometimes, she would be able to put up with it longer, coming out and asking them to go and play further up into the remaining hundred or so foot of garden that stretched out the back. So off they'd wander. But only for a few mos. Long enough for Mum to have got settled at the keys again. If Ginnybitch bored, then y.t. would bounce ball on ownio. When Mum at end of tether and 'Why, why?'-ing witlessly, y.t. would deliver nuke head.

Slightly puzzled little shake of the noddle (as though emerging from a mild trance) added to following; lashes demurely shading downcast peepers; cunning smile/smirk – had to be just enough of a smirk to make it not a smile – and a softly murmured 'sorry'. Guaranteed. Every time. Straight into 'Kill' mode. Y.t. *had* to be sent upstairs then. Bitch couldn't trust herself to be in same room. Happened all the time. 'Specially at weekends. Made up for not having so much fun at nosh times. Big house. Big kitchen. Didn't look odd if Mum was a bit late coming for nosh. Used writing as excuse. Must just finish this bit. You all carry on without me. Good try, Mum.

When things got too heavy for Mum, she'd act as though the old Remington didn't exist. When y.t. was around. Then she'd give it another go. Never stopped putting herself through it. Chill out some, Mum. For Chrissake. She'd give it another go in the hope that y.t. had forgotten. Or was fed up. No chance. Even more fun after a bit of a breather. Ever so nervy. Nervier than ever. Desperate not to look, but peepers drawn by y.t.'s wee magnets. Keep 'em wide open, kid. And steady. Wide, steady and sort of gaze-y. Then, as soon as Mum's frantic little blues meet and click on, lower lashes and avert magnets. Next, position nosh on fork, or spoon, or whatever and raised slowly, slowly, ever so slowly to meet gob. Yummy, Mummy – it's so scrummy! Keep lashes hiding peepers until gob at dribbling stage then, at very same mo as nosh enters gob, raise lashes, aim peepers and spike Mum through the brain.

Bitch just couldn't stand it. Even if she managed to evade the magnets, she couldn't handle the fall-out. Sometimes she'd brush her hand across her mush as though trying to get rid of a creepy-crawly. Go on Mum – get up from the table. Warp factor into the living room with some excuse before putting your mitts round y.t.'s jugular and squeeze – squeeze – squeeze.

Mum had this weird idea of teaching y.t. to act like grown-up babe. Started with things like sewing badge on Brownie uniform. Make sure sewing gear put safely away after. Bo-o-oring, Mum! Much more fun to hand needles over to Ginnybitch. Bit of luck and she'd shove one in her gob, swallow it and stab herself to death from the inside, ha ha ha. Mum went apeshit. Serious session of arm-gripping and shoulder-pressing. As well as hissing, spitting and endless 'why-ing'. Shake of noddle, snidey smirk, muttered 'sorry' kept the bitch on the verge for hours.

Episodes of Mum in 'Kill' mode on the up. So much on the up that she had to start forking out three guineas a week to a shrink in Kew Gardens. Stuck him for six months. How? How did you manage it, Mum? It wasn't that he drew level with Blake Larsen in the useless stakes that got you down, was it? It was the farts. Each time you went into his consulting room, a great wave of both fresh and stale farts hit you straight between the peepers. The only things he showed a slight interest in were your dreams and your book being published. Sniffed as though he'd caught a whiff of his own methane when he heard the publisher's moniker. Couldn't handle it. 'Yes,' he sneered, 'they're precisely the sort of publisher I'd have expected to be interested in your sort of novel.' Fucking jealous screwed-up dickhead! Told Mum she ought to think herself lucky having a husband prepared to go on long walks with her and the children. At least they had something in common, hadn't they? Why the fuck are you paying three guineas to be told how lucky you are, Mum? H.G. been telling you that for years. For free!

Told her it was quite normal for there to be some rivalry between siblings. Don't leave them together for long periods, he said, after she'd told him about the needles. Don't make too much out of situations, either. He said. Ol' mountain out of molehill syndrome again Mum! All the same, these shrinks! Fucking worse than useless! When she told him that she wanted to beat y.t.'s smirk to a pulp, the old fart changed the subject mucho pronto. Couldn't handle that either, you disgusting old pervert. All perfectly natural – bla – bla – jealous – little sister – mother's attention – does it only way know how – stop over reacting m'dear.

Suffocating under weight of fart stench and bigger and bigger dollops of bullshit, couldn't tell old wanker that, when not wanting to crush life out of y.t., spent hours listening, over and over and over, to Shostakovitch string-y thing whilst blubbering and fantasising over freckly landlord.

Mad bitch arranged party. Invited him. Worked in Norwich or somewhere but came back to Wimbledon to see kid. Separated, but friends with bitch of a wife. Night before party, mother of all Herpes Simplex appeared spontaneously on lower lip. *Huge* mother. Had to cancel party. Big G hysterical. Called it your Instant Automatic Man-repellent. Christ, but you made a right twat of yourself, Mum! Drank a bottle of Special Vat, rang the dickhead at work and announced undying love. What a fucking dildo! Just as well he gave you the brush-off.

'It's not that I don't like you, Margaret. I think you're a very nice person. But . . .' Didn't make any effing difference. Months before you stopped lusting after him. And then only 'cos you found out what a total Afro-dickhead he was.

Arranged to meet him. In Dillons, was it? Some bookshop in London. After your little opus had come out. Came with his kid. Four years old. Spoiled rotten. Had coffee. Another dildo who turned a bit sniffy at the mention of the opus. But that didn't bother you. Used to that. Started wittering on about where to go. Kid wanted to do kid things; grown ups grown-up things. Kid whingeing and tugging at Landlord's sleeve. Landlord incapable of making decision. Turns to Mum. Says: 'You make the decision, Margaret.' Instant death of all lustful feelings towards Landlord. Fifteen months down the tubes. Never realised what he'd done.

Nor would you bring yourself to tell old Farting-Klaus about Dad's little habit of leaving sperm-filled florets of bog-roll on the floor by the side of the bed. For you to find. And pick up. Or how you'd wake in the middle of the night to find him silently jerking off, his buttocks clenching and unclenching as his arsehole tried to swallow itself.

Chest still hurting. Lungs trying to escape again. Bastard. Feel so fucking knackered, man. Just want to have a kip. Too much to ask for. A bit of kip for Chrissake. Don't need this effing shouting – going through skull like sledgehammer. Why the fuck is everyone always shouting? Sweet Jesus – leave off beating brains to pulp – noddle cracking – splitting – brains squeezing and oozing through peepers and ear'oles . . .

Y.t. on floor in corner of wheelhouse. Fist-sized hailstones landing on arms and mitts covering noddle.

'Bitch – bitch – bitch – evil little bitch – why did you do it – why–why–why? Thank God Mrs Black saw you and told us otherwise you'd have done it again and killed her, wouldn't you – wouldn't you, you evil, wicked, little bitch . . .'

Small matter of sending fuck-faced Ginnybitch across railway in front of train. Passed a few mos after she got to other side. Shame. Ha ha. Didn't really want to kill her. Just wanted to see if she'd get to boatyard gate in time. Silly Ginnybitch. Didn't know puff-puff was coming. Not till very last minute. Had to give her a bit of encouragement. Didn't want to cross without Big Sis. Trust that spying old bitch Black to be hanging around. Don't know what all the effing fuss is all about. Didn't come to any frigging harm, did she?

'For Christ's bloody sake, get the smirk off your face before I do something I'll regret – you simpering little bitch – don't you realise the seriousness of what you've done? Don't you realise if Ginny had tripped and fallen, she could have been run over and killed? Killed, do you hear? Bloody well killed!'

You don't half have a frigging mouth on you at times Mum.

'Why? Why did you do it, Laura? For God's sake tell me why. Do you really hate Ginny so much that you want to harm her? See her dead? That can't be true – it can't be – tell me.'

Go on, tell her kid. Get up from poxy floor – stopped hailing – ha ha. Get up off your scrawny arse and tell the bitch. Now's the time – grab the mo!

112

As usual, y.t. standing like dickhead of all time, with inane smirk plastered all over gob. Mum still loud-mouthing. Though volume decreasing.

'We trusted you. We felt that a ten-year old child would be responsible enough to cross the railway safely with her little sister. God knows, we've crossed enough times with you and made you use the telephone to ring through to Woodbridge in case there's a goods train on the way. The awful thing is that you knew what you were doing. Didn't you? You knew. That's why you stayed behind, you evil bitch. Why can't you say what's going on inside that bloody silent head of yours? Answer me, Laura. Answer me.'

Go on, airhead. She's given you another go. Tell her. Tell her. Tell her that you hate the fucking lot of them. Especially her. With butter-wouldn't-melt-in-her-fucking-gob Ginnybitch coming a very close second. Tell her, dickhead! For Chrissake tell her!

Thank Christ for a bit o' peace an' quiet. Sitting down in saloon with Dad. Oodles of patience, Dad. But only doing it 'cos Mum told him to. She'd tried. But within a few mos she'd be fast-tracking towards 'Kill' mode.

Couldn't do frigging sums. Couldn't do times fucking tables. Never mind poxy decimals. Mum in blind rage. Not with y.t. but with dick of a headmaster. All school reports said 'Satisfactory' this and 'Satisfactory' that. Mum found out somehow. Dad explained things over and over and over. No frigging good. Y.t. can't grasp shit. Mum rushing out of *Mikro* for fear of screaming or smashing something. Went to see Head dick. Mum had always hated him. Feeling seemed to be mutual. Mum all the kinds of chicks he hated and feared rolled into one big chick. Main thing he focused in on was that she was a veg head. Couldn't believe it. Might as well have said dropped in from Mars. Liked the area. Decided to stay. Dad was supposed to be a veg head too. But y.t. had caught him guzzling frankfurters outta the tin once. Must've been doing it all the time on the sly.

Head dick looked at Mum as though she'd just whipped her sanny towel out of her crotch and shoved it under his hooter, before telling her in real snooty verbals, that man was a hunter, always had been and always would be. Therefore, he needed meat in order to survive.

Mum went scarlet before stammering that y.t. and Ginnybitch weren't veg heads as he well knew, because they ate meat in school meals and she, in no way, tried to force her views and beliefs on to them. They were allowed to choose for themselves. Head dick almost outdid y.t. smirk-wise as he saw that Mum had twigged that she had, more or less, apologised for being a veg head. There was no going back for Mum after that. Now he was to be y.t.'s teacher as well as Headmaster.

Told Mum that kids didn't need to know times tables as, once they'd moved up to Middle School, they'd be using calculators all the time. Gobsmacked, Mum said she'd never heard such utter drivel.

'Calm down, Mrs FitzHugh. We've all got our own opinions, you know.'

Mum demanded to know why all y.t.'s reports said 'Satisfactory' when she could hardly do more than add two plus two. Head dick had to admit that he hadn't got an answer for that one but that Mrs FitzHugh should appreciate that the teacher concerned had to look after a bedridden husband as well as having to work and having other personal problems.

'In that case,' gritted Mum, 'she shouldn't be teaching – she should be at home looking after her bedridden husband full-time, shouldn't she?'

Dad never uttered a word until they left the Head dick's office. Then he told Mum that there was no need for her to fly off the handle like that.

Mum shouted that she wished she'd said a helluva lot more but nothing would have made a blind bit of difference to a low-life worm like Fiske. Didn't he realise that as far as the parochial little creep was concerned, they were the scum of the earth? Because they lived on the river in and old lifeboat instead of a nice, respectable little semi. Was he so thick that he couldn't see it? Too much arse-licking makes you blind, Desmond – as well as certain other activities.

Had to laugh at that. At least Mum had tried to stick up for y.t.

Breathing getting a tad iffy again. Lungs not trying to do a runner though. Grateful for small mercies. A bit of a smothery sort of feeling. Phizog being pressed against something soft and damp. Soft and damp and gulping and snivelling. Must be Mum. Can hear the frigging shelducks nagging and scolding. Bastards kept y.t. awake sometimes. If it wasn't the frigging shelducks, it was the oystercatchers twirping and peeping. Didn't mind the curlew. Liquid sadness pissing into river. Break frigging heart.

114

What the fuck are you wittering on about, Mum? On one of your 'I–love–you–really' trips? Right first time. Let's get it over with, Jim. For Chrissake hurry up with that gromit.

'I want to tell you how sorry I am for all the things I say and do – blubber – blubber – blubber – Sometimes Mummy's under a great strain and says things she doesn't really mean – blubber – blubber – blubber – I don't seem to be able to get through to you – sometimes I feel, I feel that you hate me, Laura. You don't, do you? I wouldn't, couldn't blame you if you did, but please tell me that you don't hate me. Please, Laura. Please!'

Squeeze, squeeze; blub, blub. Leave off Mum, for fuck's sake!

Wonder what's happened to send bitch into such fit of remorse? Must have had a real mother of a go at y.t. Prob'ly for leaving jetty gate open again. Not the only airhead. Dad leaves it open as well. Goes apeshit with him. Doesn't make any difference. Must be in the genes, man. So why do you keep doing it, Mum? Going apeshit?

Mustn't let braindead Dookie out 'cos he'll head straight for the chooks and the bad men'll be waiting at the ready with a shotgun in each grubby mitt. What a fucking shame! Not! Ha ha ha. Who gives a tinker's turd for the moth-eaten old mutt. Not y.t. That's for sure. Perhaps y.t. didn't do washing up properly. Again! A winner, that one. Guaranteed to get the marbles on the roll. Or not put dirty gear in laundry basket? Another winner. Always the simple little thingies that turned out to be the star turns. All this luvvy-duvvy shit ain't working, Mum. Didn't really think it'd be that easy, did you now? Feel how stiff y.t. is. Feel how the skinny arms are all stiff and bony round your neck. They may be round your neck but they're not holding you, are they Mum? Good job you can't see y.t.'s peepers. Good job it's dark in the fo'c'sle, 'cos the peepers are flatter and darker that any darkness could ever be. Scare the shit outta you, Mum. If you could see them. Nothing in them. Nothing at all. Better for you to run out of the boat and along the towpath, pulling at your hair and shrieking your uselessness to the friendly dark.

Shrieking – shrieking – shrill, piercing shriek of torture and torment too hideous to imagine. Unearthly, hellish, soul-spiking sound. Dad standing. Almost in middle of road. Mum a bit behind him. Nearer the grass verge. White and shaking.

'Do something Desmond – for God's sake do something – put

the bloody thing out of its misery – Jesus Christ – Jesus Christ –
call ourselves humans – sick bastards – sick sick don't just stand
there – do something . . . !'

A bunny rabbit. Or what was trying to pass itself off as a bunny
rabbit. Steady on. Don't get all carried away, y.t. Looks exactly like
a rabbit. Apart from the one minor fact that its peepers were
slowly dissolving and running, no, oozing, down its rabbity
cheeks. Blind and shrieking. But not in pain. Not according to
some dickhead scientific theory. Just shrieking for the hell of it,
Thumper aintcha? Myxomatosis o' course. Testament to Man's
superiority over lowly, soul-less, pain-free, emotionally dead
Animal Kingdom. Ha bloody ha. The sun glinted a brief salute on
the end of the wheelbrace as Dad brought it crunching down into
Thumper's melting noddle.

Mum well into overdrive. Looking totally deranged. Ginnybitch
snivelling and treading on the spot as though desperate for a piss.

'Don't leave it – don't just leave it – how can you – how can you
just leave it – how can you – how can you? Put it in the hedge –
cover it with leaves – don't leave it there – how could you – how
can you – put it anywhere – somewhere soft – cover it with grass,
with leaves – anything – how could you just leave it there – how
could you?' Blubber, blubber and more blubber.

No, don't leave it there, Dad! Get shovel from the Morris and
scrape what's left of Thumper into Tesco carrier. Apart from few
yukkie bits o' fur – practically ready for the pot, man! Ginnybitch
standing by van, as still and as white as the inside of the freezer
bit of a fridge. Y.t. not sure what supposed to be feeling. Shock?
Scared shitless by awful shrieking, that's for sure. Disgust? Melting
peepers made guts heave a tad. Pity? Sorrow? Hundreds of
fucking Thumpers around, man. That's their prob. Too much
fucking. If they didn't fuck as much, they wouldn't have to be
given a thingy like Myxomatosis. So it's their own bleedin' fault,
innit? Brought it on their bleedin' selves.

Shame? Does y.t. feel shame? What the fuck for, man? Heap o'
shite. Y.t. feels none o' these mealy-mouthed nerdy things. Just
thinking how much Dad looks like Freddie. Leaning up against
the Morris, blood-splatted tyre lever dangling; phizog a dark
yellow mask with 3-D gobstopper peepers straining to plop outta
sockets. Eat your heart out Frankenstein!

On way to Riding School. Mum's got it into noddle that, 'cos
she gets rocks off whenever within sniffing range of a gee-gee,

so should everyone else – even Dad, for Chrissake! Sitting atop Dobbin. Plodding along, smoking his poxy Briar. Dad, not Dobbin. What a dork! Ginnybitch loves gee-gees. She would, wouldn't she? Y.t. likes gee-gees too. Likes rub–a–rub rub for best part of hour on snatch – ha ha ha. Not much can be done in the way of winding Mum up. Can't get close enough. Wouldn't notice, anyway. In a poxy little world of her own. Make up for it after, though. Drop reins on floor in hope that scurvy nag'll shove tootsie in and fall arse over tit. Or forget to loosen girth after getting off. Don't run up stirrups – don't give smelly brute a thank-you pat – loadsa options, man. All guaranteed to get Mum sniping and snapping and well into 'Why' mode on way home. Why this, why that, why the frigging other. Do ya really want to know, Mum?

BECAUSE Y.T. DOESN'T GIVE A SHIT, MUM. THAT'S WHY. Y.T. DOESN'T GIVE A FUCKING SHIT.

Bag o' cement plonked in middle of chest. Two bags o' cement. Pain dull and throbbing. As if heart getting too big for chest. Lungs being flattened. Like fat, flat bits of tapeworm. Long, wide stretch of road. Evening. Summer-y sort of evening; getting late. Languid lapis lazuli and old rose painted saucer of a sky. Just visible sliver of camembert moon. Turn yer silver over y.t.! Bring ya luck if moon's just popped pod! Might be day old bit o' camembert. No turning silver over. What fucking silver? What's with these fucking chest pains, man?

Y.t. striding along road as though in marathon. Slow down y.t. for Chrissake! Long and gangly. Tits making nice debut. Thumbing lift. Phizog carved out of granite hard enough to make Mum's Aberdeen look like plasticine. What the fuck's up with y.t.? Car stopping. Pair of old farts peering out through window. Open the effing window then, you pair of dildos!

'Hello dear. Where on earth are you going at this time of night?'

Can't be that bloody late, surely. Ten? Half past ten? Late for a pair of old farts, s'pose.

'Missed last bus – been staying with Aunty . . .' Nice one, y.t.!

Laughing farts. 'Easily done – where do you want to go, dear?'

Twickenham. That's where. Twickenham. Twickenham and Big G. Big, soft flabby, brown, smelly Big G. Fags. Booze. Nosh. Safe.

Disappointed farts. 'Oh dear, I'm afraid we're only going as far as Ipswich. Will that do? We could drop you off at the station, if you like.'

Hadn't a clue where Twickenham was. Could've said Timbuc-fucking-too. Might be able to tell Big G about dream. Must have been a dream. Must have. Couldn't have happened. Not really happened. Must've been a dream. Big G'd know if y.t. had screw loose. Or missing. Can't tell Mum. Even if wanted to. Last person. Couldn't stand sight of y.t. Couldn't speak. Couldn't look, even. Tells Dad to ask y.t. whatever. Everything through Dad. Y.t.'s fault. Shouldn't wind the bitch up so much. Went way over top. Can't help it. Can't stop. Need buzz. So easy. One little flick and she's off. Shouldn't've written letter. Bad move. Shouldn't've gone swanning off with that new bitch, should she? Shouldn't've dumped y.t. for new bitch. Never thought cunt would show letter to Head dick. Deep shit, man.

Always the frigging same. Y.t. flavour of the month to start with, then off like a shot with some other bitch. Why haven't you got any friends? Says Mum. Why don't you go out and play for God's sake? Says Mum. Instead of sitting around the bloody boat all the time.

What? You mean do a Ginnybitch? Make camps and dens out of bracken and bundles of fucking twigs. You mean run around wearing a coat hanging from neck like a cape, pretending to be the effing Nazgul? With a poxy corgi called Frodo? Leave it out, Mum. Much more fun to sit with you in the boat. Reading when you're reading. Knit when you're knitting. Put down knitting, pick up book. Put down book, pick up knitting.

Why don't you show y.t. how to make bread? Again. Then grind gnashers and tear hair 'cos too much, or too little, or none at all, salt and/or yeast. So-orry, Mum. Forgot. Or too much/too little oven heat. Whatever it takes, and it don't take much! – to make a complete fuck-up. Wouldn't matter if y.t. too thick to get hang of poxy bread-making, and had made shit loaves from the start. Would it, Mum? But y.t.'s first few batches had been dream-loaves; a melt-in-the-gob fluffy dough all hot an' bothered inside a crust you could die for.

Follow you down to the saloon; follow you back up again (allowing a few mos in between just to get your hopes up), into the wheelhouse. Watch as you get nearer and nearer edge. Not long before Overture of Swinging Fists and Wielding Inanimate Objects begins. It must be shit to feel so feeble, Mum. So feeble and useless and desperate. Desperate to nuke smile/smirk off y.t.'s mush. Bit of a prob. there, Mum. 'Cos you know if you do start clocking y.t. you might not be able to stop. Sometimes, didn't even have to bother with smile/smirk. The thought of it enough to activate programme.

Send y.t. for a walk with braindead Dookie. Soon manages to slip his lead, ha ha. So-o-orry, Mum. Didn't mean for you to come haring out of wheelhouse and run demented along the towpath, shrieking, 'Dookie–Dookie–Dookie . . .' Fat lot of good that'll do. Daft mutt won't even twitch an ear'ole. You know you won't see him until he's shagged himself out. It's a shame, Mum. So many things could happen to him, couldn't they? Could be run over by a train. Or a car. Or a lorry. Could sink gnashers into bratski. Wouldn't be the first time. Got away with it before. Might not again. Might have to be put down this time. Parents mightn't be so understanding. Or he could savage someone's pet mog, bunny, or doggie. Find himself some fat red chooks to massacre. Or even find some sheep to worry shite out of. You know how he likes a bit o' mutton. After hols in the Heelands. Definite shotgun job. Can quite understand you being so uncool about it. Send y.t. out to play in summer sunshine. Freak out and yell 'For God's bloody sake go outside and find something – anything – to do'.

Something to do all right. Walk up and down towpath dead opposite *Mikro*. Kicking aimlessly at anything and nothing and glancing glancing glancing across at Mum sitting at typewriter in wheelhouse. Wouldn't, couldn't write if anyone there. Lot of work to be done on opus. Lot of revision before final 'yes'.

Overdid things once or twice. Mum'd really blow tubes. Running up and down towpath, running in and out of boat. Over and over. Happened after the Dookie thingy. Couldn't find the poxy mutt. Went all the way to Woodbridge. Searched the town and walked back along the main road. Not a fucking sign of the deadbeat. Didn't come home until after dark, covered in mud and tangled thorns and bits of twigs and branches. Stinking of blood and recently eaten flesh. Blood all over his teeth and jaws, matted into his long blonde coat-chest, ear'oles and all down front legs. Whatever he'd murdered, nothing was ever heard. Weeks before Mum stopped shitting herself with fear of a knock at the wheel-house door. Y.t. quite hefty babe but Mum stayed true to arm-pressing outlet. Never hit y.t. but, whilst pressing into floorboards, would hiss and spit at wordless snivelling crouching heap on floor. Bit hazy, but could see phizog reflected in wheelhouse window. Red and shit-ugly, with big, wide rubbery gob.

119

Letting go of arms; flailing air with fists and making quick lunges towards y.t. Had to stop. Nothing else left but to beat y.t. to pulp. Crush and flatten to pulp, just like Dad did to Thumper, then tread and mash pulp into the ground. So no more y.t. Mum sobbing and gibbering and running down to one of the lower cabins.

'It's me – it's me – I'm not fit to live – I should be locked away – monster–monster–monster – mother from hell – nothing but a monster . . .' Etc. etc. *Ad infinitum.*

Wondered why Dad didn't shove his oar in. Just a tad. Could have tried to stop things going so far. Could have grabbed Mum. Smacked her one. Or tried to calm her down. Made a cuppa. Instead of always agreeing with everything she hissed, spat and shrieked about y.t. Yes, Laura was sly; she was cunning; she was evil. She knew exactly what she was doing. All she wanted was to cause as much trouble as possible in as little time as possible. Something definitely needed to be done about her. He couldn't agree more.

Sent Mum even more apeshit. Knew what she was feeling and saying and doing was all wrong, yet Dad was telling her it was all OK. Mum afraid of topping either self or y.t. Went to GP in Woodbridge. Bared all. Again. Gave her a few Valium to be going on with and made emergency appointment with Institute of Family Psychiatry in Ipswich. Nice Doc. Young-ish. With kids of his own.

Old farts asking would y.t. like a drinkie or something to eat before going to station? Should've realised. Lemonade and crisps no sooner plonked on table than one of old farts goes and phones Fuzz for advice on possible runaway. Comes back all smiley and relieved. 'Think it's time we had a little chat, dear.'

Nice young pig runs y.t. back to *Mikro*. Don't do anything like this again, will you? All sorts of things can happen to a young girl out alone at night. Yes, sir. No, sir. Mum's phizog all streaked and blotchy from gnashing and wailing. Dad's just more yellow and tight round the gob and peepers. Y.t.'s mush all tight and yellow round the gills as well. Peepers darting around as though attached to bits of elastic behind scenes. Will have to tell Mum about dream. Can't. Don't know how. Too late, anyway.

'Why, Laura? Why? Is it because of me? It must be – it's got to be – Jesus Christ, that it should come to this . . . Can you ever

120

forgive me? I'll get help – there's an appointment coming through – I'll go and see Dr Knowles tomorrow morning and tell him . . . Why, Laura?'

Lie, y.t. Lie. So fucking good at it. School. Say it's because of school. Hate school. Dread school. Fiske's got it in for y.t. (All true. All bloody true. But not reason.) Swallowed it all no prob. Nice move, y.t. Not long since Head dick paid Mum a visit. Dad asleep after night shift. So Mum had to cope on ownio with the hated HD. Not that Dad being there would have made any frigging difference.

Stood at end of gang plank; mitts in tweed pockets jingling loose change.

'It's not the bananas I'm concerned about, Mrs FitzHugh. Laura has said that she's sorry and Mrs Bovis has accepted her apology. No. It's the other things I'm worried about. I'm sure you'll understand. It's the money, the books, the little personal things. But, most of all, the money. It's not that I'm accusing Laura of stealing but, under the circumstances . . . Then there's the business of the letter Laura's written to another girl at school. Do you know about that, Mrs FitzHugh? Do you know that Laura has written a dreadful letter, full of the most appalling language – using terms I've never heard of in spite of all my years in the Army – and all because the girl refused to go around with her? You really ought to have a long talk with your daughter, Mrs FitzHugh, and try to find out what it is that's troubling her before something of a more serious nature occurs. Amazing how the younger daughter – Ginny, isn't it? – is such a different child. Frank, outspoken – almost too outspoken at times – ha ha ha! Infinitely preferable to lies and deceit though. Wouldn't you agree? Oh, and by the by, Mrs FitzHugh, just in passing – neither I, not any of my staff, have ever come across a child with such an enormous appetite as Laura has. She eats like a horse – all she needs is a horse collar, ha ha ha!' He knew y.t. was in the wheelhouse. He could see y.t. through the window. He knew that y.t. could hear every frigging word.

'The amount of meat she puts away during school meals is quite astonishing – if I hadn't witnessed it with my own eyes, I wouldn't have believed the reports from various members of staff. My point being, Mrs FitzHugh, that if Laura was getting enough meat in her diet at home, she wouldn't want so much of it at school. Not that I'm begrudging it in any way. On the contrary, I'm only too pleased that she's getting enough to eat.' Smile, smile. Jingle, jingle.

121

Mum had her killer mush on, but it was for Fiske, not y.t. Too gobsmacked to say much. Only stammer, red with cringe-factor, that she'd talk to y.t. about the missing gear. As Head dick went back up the gangplank and started walking along the towpath, he turned and called, 'I'm not so bothered about the books and other things Mrs FitzHugh. But I'll be very grateful to have the money returned. Thank you.'

Mum apeshit on two counts: 1) 'cos of Head dick accusing y.t. of nicking dosh: 2) 'cos of y.t. eating meat. No. Not for eating it. For pretending at home that dead animals were a no-no. Ginnybitch ate flesh. Mum never tried to stop them. Wasn't forbidden. Just tried to put them off. Told them what was likely to be in pies, bangers, etc. Wouldn't buy chickens or chunks of dead flesh like legs and shoulder.

So why did y.t. pretend? Fuck only knows. To get one over, s'pose. Why did Dad pretend? Fuck knows even less, man. Mum didn't know whether to believe that y.t. hadn't half-inched dosh from school but gave benefit of doubt. Too fucking right, man. Hadn't frigging seen it, never mind nicked it. Turned up a few days later. Mum went and demanded apology from Head dick. In front of y.t. How come he didn't turn to dust in withering blast from Mum's peepers? Never mind Siberian syllables! Made sure y.t. had a good report at end of term.

Quote: 'It has been a long time but Laura is now making an effort. Her work has much improved and she is showing much more interest in her practical work. Good progress!' Unquote. Under the heading, 'Application and Conduct,' he had written: 'Well-behaved in class and certainly a much happier pupil.'

Changed his fucking tune not long after the hols were over.

Wrote Mum asking her to 'kindly refrain from giving Laura so much pocket money to take to school as she was squandering it on sweets, most of which she was giving to other children and creating a bad impression on the younger kiddies. He'd had a word with her and explained that that it was no use trying to buy friendship. It has to be earned. Like everything else.'

Mum knew that Fiske had twigged that y.t. had nicked dosh but after cock-up he'd made before, he daren't mention words like 'steal' or 'stolen' or anything like it. Might have done – would have done, if he'd thought y.t. nicking from anyone at school. Knew it was coming from home. The old fuck. Y.t. been doing it for quite a while. On and off. Not too regular, or Mum'd suspect.

Got a bit carried away, though. Overdid it. Letter was final straw. Mum and Dad rowing more and more over lack of readies. Mum thought Dad was digging into purse for baccy and petrol dosh. Budget so tight she kept a housekeeping book. All purchases and expenses entered. Shit scared to ask y.t. about missing loot in case she freaked out. Fiske's frigging letter changed all that. If it hadn't been for letter, could have carried on without any prob.

Didn't accuse y.t. of half-inching. Just asked for explanation. And y.t. blew it. Went way out of order. Started as big wind-up. Y.t. had not taken money from Mum's purse – the very idea! Had found notes lying on towpath on way to school. In spite of building up head of steam, Mum chilled enough to ask few more times. Giving y.t. chance to come clean. Y.t. kept repeating towpath shit. Getting one helluva buzz from Mum's crumbling phizog. One sneaky smile/smirk too many, babe. Mum suddenly hurling herself at y.t. Hitting, with clenched fists, on noddle and shoulders and arms. And screaming at the top of her voice.

'You bitch – you bitch – you filthy lying bitch – you miserable rotten lying bitch – I hate you – I hate you – do you hear? – do you bloody well hear? – I bloody well hate you – I wish you were dead – I wish you were six feet under – I hate you – I hate you – I hate you . . .'

Dad pulling Mum off y.t. Big mistake this time, Dad. Should've left well alone.

'You useless bloody wanker – you never do anything – do you – do you – except wank – that's all you're good at – wanking – once a wanker always a wanker – why in God's name do you let it get to this? Why do you always stand there like a bloody dummy? You're her father for Christ's sake, why don't you ever take responsibility? How long is it going to go on like this? Is it going to be like this for the rest of our bloody lives? Is it? Oh God, what's the use of bloody asking you – you just stand there – saying nothing – doing nothing – except want – wank – wank – useless – useless – useless wanker.'

Mum told the Doc at The Institute of Family Psychiatry that, for a few mos, she had felt herself capable of killing y.t. Couldn't keep effing gob shut. Bawling and mitt-wringing for frigging hours. Y.t. and Ginnybitch in play area. Listening to Mum in stereo. Seemed that way. Whole fucking Institute nuked with her catapulted marbles. When safe to put riot gear back in cupboard, Doc said had she/they ever thought of sending Laura to a boarding school. Mum gobsmacked, totally, at first. Then phizog slowly lit up as though a great truth had dawned.

In extreme cases, said the Doc, it was considered to be a possibility. To ease the pressure building up within the family.

Been attending The Institute quite a few months. Funny. Didn't even see Mum and y.t. together until after two months of separate weekly visits. And then only the once. Until the end. Mum and Dad had weekly session together; Dad not keen. Hated it. Y.t. put in with bunch of other no-hopers. To socialise. And to be observed, discreetly, to be socialising. Load o' effing bullshit. No probs there, Doc. Mum the one with the bad attitude. But all you could do was give her anti-depressants and advise her to try and chill out more. Accept things as they were, instead of always trying to change everything and everybody. In other words, same shite that every other Doc had dished out to her. This Doc well-meaning, though. Nice, middle-aged bitch. Nervous tic. Bit like H.G.'s. But round peepers.

Many parents, both male and female, felt the same way as Mrs FitzHugh, says the Doc. Too ashamed to come forward and admit to behaviour. No fucking wonder, Doc! Great help if more would do as she was – come out in the open, so to speak – bla–bla–bla. Go on Mum – feel better why don't you?

Educational Psychologist. Pipe-puffing, tweedy nerd name of Humphries. Took all of five mos to wind him nice and tight round pinky. Whole family had to go before tweed and twinset committee-from-hell, to explain why wanted to get rid of y.t. Mum into mitt-wringing and snivelling straight off. Like it all the time these days. More or less. Funny. They don't want to know about Mum's urge to do for y.t. Keep wittering on about age difference and personality clash between siblings. Siblings? First mention of probs between y.t. and Ginnybitch. Can't handle the real thingy, cowardly fucks. Didn't make any difference anyway. Old buggers gave thumbs up to boarding school idea. Ol' Humpy'll be link between Institute and school, wherever it is. Will have to apply to several. It'll depend on whether there's any vacancies. Would Mr and Mrs FitzHugh object to a Quaker school? No. Mr and Mrs FitzHugh would not object to a Quaker school.

Dad and Humpy having a smoke signalling contest. Dad furrowing slopey forehead in effort to get one over Hump. Funny looking peeper brows Dad's got. Never noticed before. A bit like the Fag lady's but a lot more bulgy. And not pencilled in. Not a lot of hair, though. Quaker school came good. Mum shitting herself in case y.t. can't have the place at start of Autumn term. Term starts September. Y.t. not eleven till end of October. If it's not one thing, it's a bleeding other Mum, ain't it?

Dad hated going to the weekly sessions 'cos, as well as wittering endlessly on about her killer instincts, Mum blabbed all about Dad's love of wanking and constant need to appear before beak at regular intervals. All the hard graft and TLC put into tarting up old *Mikro*. New decks (second-hand timbers) and catwalks, hull scraped, where poss, filled and painted. All down the tubes when bit in local paper about Dad being nicked for half-inching a tyre – a single tyre for Chrissake! hit the big time at last, Dad! – from local scrappie. Dad completely lost his cool when Mum told the Doc. Shouted that she had no right to make him look such a bloody fool. Awful slanging match on way home.

What drove a stake through Mum, far more than Dad's tea-leafing was the terrible knowledge that an arse-wipe like Fiske was proved right. They were scum. They were low-life scum. They lived on an old derelict boat, they didn't let their kids eat dead animals, one of their kids was already a suspected tea-leaf. Now everyone – everyone – locally, knew that Dad *was* a fucking tea-leaf, and a fucking useless one at that. What chance had the kids got?

The thought of the Head dick lobbing such pellets of shit across the staff room to the bovine Bovis did Mum's head right in. Funny. Them thinking of the FitzHughs as being the low-lives and Mum thinking of *them* as the real scumbags.

Much worse for Mum, though Fiske and Bovis didn't know about it – don't think they did – was what happened after and because of Dad nicking the tyre.

Mum on way to hang washing out on the other side of towpath. Had twirly thingy down bottom of the bank. Bunch of plainclothes fuzz came swarming on to *Mikro*. Mum had stopped and turned to look as the cars screeched into the yard. All flapping macs and flashing ID's they pummelled and knuckled the wheelhouse door until a dishevelled Dad emerged. Then they strip-searched the old girl. Lotta gear being half-inched from boats all along river. Big stuff. Outboard motors, radar, etc. Dad at top of list of suspects 'cos of tyre nicking. Not involved. Mum would have known. Nowhere to put stash on *Mikro*. Bit too big-time for Daddy-O!

Mum standing on towpath. Watching. Motionless.

All the more scary 'cos she wasn't losing cool. Just standing. White and silent and unmoving. With a basket of washing under one arm.

Phizog dripping wet and ice-cubed. Funny – top of noddle feels warm. Hot, almost. Bobbing and floating. Floaty and icy and swimmy and splashy. Floating a bit then turning and having a splash. Y.t. in middle of soap-suddy sea for Chrissake! Currant bun burning back of noddle something chronic. Ginnybitch splashing wildly with stupid orange puffballs on arms. Scared shitless. Just like Mum. Dad thrashing around like he was going to go under for the last time. Good swimmer, Dad. Donno why he had to churn up sea bed all the time. Mum wallowing in the shallows. Daft bitch can't swim. Never picked it up even though she spent a lot of time, as a bratski, in the sea. Pretending she was swimming by hanging on to collar of paddling mutt.

Where is it now, Jim? Not Bexhill that's for sure. Bexhill long ago and faraway. Y.t. wearing navy-blue school swimsuit. Gotta cleavage, would ya believe! Still in *Mikro* warp, Scottie? Is y.t. at new school yet – can't be. Would be a whole year later – a whole summer, and y.t.'s tits no bigger. Must be summer before going to boarding school. Gotta deliver a monthly report, O Twilight Zone-y One?

Felixstowe. Result of one of Mum's poxy hikes. Worst one ever. Way over top. Followed frigging river from Sefton to Felixstowe. On fucking pins. Carrying picnic gear. Not legging it back Mum. No fucking way. Knackered ain't the word.

Mum had to learn to swim 'cos terrified of Ginnybitch pitching off *Mikro* and not being able to save her. Visions of both ending up in watery grave, 'cos she'd jump in after her. Both sink like stones. Nice one, Mum! Why not give it a try?

Tried lessons in pool. Couldn't handle being hassled by bunch of splashing dickheads. Dad would try to get her feet off the bottom by holding her round the middle. She freaked out if anyone watching. 'Specially y.t. So y.t. would move away a few metres, have a bit of a half-arsed splash, then come back and tread water within a couple of metres of struggling Mum and semi-hard-on Dad. Within seconds, Mum shouting at y.t. to piss off, for Christ's sake, and do some swimming – what in God's name had we come all this way for? After a few more goes Mum would lose her cool and angrily splash away to a bit of shallows where she could flounder about on her own.

Y.t. can't be arsed swimming. Much more fun to horse around with Dad. Soon got Mum wound up again. The giggling that did it, plus Ginnybitch getting freaked out by water being chucked about. Not long before Mum gives up the ghost and stomps back to bags and blankets on the sand. After a few mos, y.t. would follow and lie as near as possible. She'd try and stay cool. Try and ignore y.t. Phizog changing shape like playdough with struggle going on. Bit of added interest guessing how long it would take her to blow gasket.

'For God's sake, Laura – will you go and *do* something – anything – if you don't want to go in the water, then go and play with Ginny. What in the name of God have we come all this way for? For you to carry on exactly the way you do at home – go away – just go away.'

Ginnybitch making poxy sand castles, houses and frigging villages. All tarted up with shells and bits of seaweed. When bored with the building trade, she'd draw huge, fancy pictures in the sand. Also tarted up with shells and bits of flotsam. Never took more than a few mos to start Ginnybitch bawling because y.t. had 'accidentally' knocked over house/castle and/or trodden all over pictures which weren't all that noticeable, ha ha ha. Usual half smile/smirk and murmured 'so-orry' and Mum was into overdrive.

Mum told the Doc all about this sort of thingy. When they had their one and only session together. Y.t. and Mum. Pathetic not the word. Should have heard yourself, Mum. Blabbing on about wanting things to be better. Saying how sorry – how *very* sorry you were that you didn't feel the same for y.t. that you did for Ginnybitch. No use pretending, you said. Pretending? Who the fuck would ever accuse you of pretending? Didn't mean you loved y.t. any the less. Only in a different way. Bla bla bla and bla. Nothing more you could do about it other than what doing now.

Yes Mum. Letting Doc Medhill take rap. All that shite about understanding.

All that shit about thinking y.t. might have learning difficulties. Just 'cos of lighting fucking candles in fo'c'sle so's could see to read? Fire hazard – fire hazard – forever going on about a fucking fire hazard. And putting wet gear on top o' oil heater. How the fuck is y.t. to get jeans dry? How can one pair of Levi's block

127

fucking air vents, bitch? Never give up on the nagging, do you Mum?

Didn't get you fuck all, did it?

Doc asked how Dad was with bratskis. Didn't like it when Mum told about him being nothing but a big bully with Ginnybitch. Always making her blub. Starting off teasing and horsing around but soon blubbing as knocked on to floor.

Dad said he thought the world of Ginnybitch and it upset him that she was more Mum's child that she was his. Steady on, Dad. Getting a tad deep here, aren't we? Why don't you ever talk to Laura, says Mum. Why don't you act more like a father? No answer. The Silent Treatment. Dad was brill at the Big Silence shit. Y.t. not bad at it, but a helluva long way to go to ever be as shit-hot as Dad.

Sometimes, Mum would shriek at y.t. – 'For God's sake speak your mind, child! Just say what's going on in your mind – it doesn't matter what it comes out like – just say it!' Sometimes, y.t. would shout back that she couldn't. Because she didn't know how. 'Then write it down!' she'd scream. But y.t. not able to do that either. As Dad's silences went forth and multiplied, with y.t.'s not far behind, so Mum's craving for answers grew.

Some people, said the Doc, were more verbal than others.

Must've been in wheelhouse. Y.t. supposed to be akip, but awake and ear'oling. Couldn't have been when with Doc. Wouldn't have said it in front of y.t. Mum asking Dad why didn't he make more of an effort to communicate with y.t. Y.t. often helped Dad with jobs round the yard. Just to get out of Mum's hair. Couldn't he talk to y.t. then?

Dad said that he tried, but they didn't have anything to say to each other. Mum said didn't he care what the child must be going through? If he'd played more of a role in the past then maybe things wouldn't have got so bad. He'd never tried to help, had he? He'd always agreed with whatever she said and done whatever she thought was the best thing to do.

After one of his silences, Dad said that y.t. meant nothing to him. He didn't even like the child. You knew that was a big porkie, didn't you Mum? Dad always said that he didn't like chicks when the opposite was true. Always. Never learnt. Thought it would stop Mum being jealous. Could not get it into his Neanderthal skull that it only made things worse. An awful lot worse.

128

I don't believe you, you lying bastard. Mum said.

It's true, said Dad. Never felt anything for Laura. Right from the start.

Did that happen before the dream? Or after the dream?

The cold is biting. Fangs of ice. Ice in gob and throat and gullet. Cold and hard on phizog and skull but hard, hot and dry in throat and gob. Packed in sizzling slabs in middle of chest. Not melting. Pressing harder and tighter together. Can't get breath. Can't breathe. Everything grey and blurry and snowy. Like telly when aerial pulled out. Huge albatross of a sky looming and lowering nearer and nearer by the mo.

Ginnybitch and y.t. standing on bank along towpath. Can see *Mikro*. About 400 metres away. All wrapped up. Hats, scarves, gloves, boots, thick coats. It *is* snowing! A mixture of snow and sort of hail. What the fuck are the dickheads up to? Not enough snow for a snowman – and why are they just standing? Mum and Dad appearing over top of bank. Can't see phizogs 'cos of hats an' scarves. Have they gone off their trolleys? Together? Ginnybitch and y.t. rolling hard-boiled eggs down bank for Chrissake! Hard-boiled eggs with painted phizogs! Another of Mum's little efforts at prolonging her infancy at the expense of frostbitten digits. Not hers, though. Nanook of the Fucking North. Y.t.'s orange-grove tootsies already swollen and stinging with sudden crop of frigging chilblains. Big, translucent drop dancing on end of Dad's 'ooter. Ain't going to fall on it's ownio, Dad! In process of turning into icicle!

Hedges covered in network of greyish, crystal-splattered lace – must be wincey wonderland – ha ha ha. Where are the fuckers – might be all getting ready to leap out of hidey-holes in hedge and grab poxy eggs!

Mum's happy. Phizog a mess of blue-red mottles, breath almost solidifying into small cloud of tiny pearls, she's telling y.t. and Ginnybitch to crack open the eggs. Crack them open! That means eat them – eat them out here in the permafrost! The mad bitch has brought a flask – at least that'll mean a tad of warmth. And *Mikro* only a few mos walk away! Have you remembered to bring the bin bags, you mad bitch? Might as well carry on as far as Woodbridge and do the usual. Won't be able to see 'cos of the covering of snow. Wouldn't put it past her, otherwise. Weekly chore. Clearing litter from towpath. OK Mum. You've made your frigging point. Fulfilled childhood fantasy (happens every effing year without fail) relived childhood whatever. For Chrissake will you get us out of the effing cold before Jack Frost gets serious.

No sign of poxy ocean, but still have swimmy feeling. Bit worse. Feel pukey with it. Christ – could do with a kip! Give a lot for a nice long kip.

Someone at the old joanna again. Very faint. Gina used to play. Real cool, man. Had crush on fat little composer living coupla roads along. Gave her lessons in Composition when all Big G wanted to know was what sort of music his little dick would make inside her big snatch – ha ha. Famous dude now. Sir somebody.

Not a piano. Too thin. And reedy. A recorder. Another recorder. Two recorders. A frigging duet. A descant and a treble. Sounds cool. Mum and y.t. sitting in saloon. In front of blazing and belching rescued Dragon. Mum playing treble and y.t. descant. Music propped up on stand. Like something out of frigging magazine illustrating Perfect Family. Carols. Christmas effing carols. Going back a warp too far, Scottie? Last Christmas before going to boarding school. Last Christmas before dream. Don't need this. Don't want this. Can't you change the warp, for Chrissake? Sick to fucking death of all this fucking crap. Way outta line. *Mikro* tarted up like old babe on the game. Coloured chains and flouncy silver and gold efforts, all cut out and pasted together by poxy clever-clogs of a Ginnybitch. Y.t. supposed to help, but had managed to cock matters up p.d.q. Banished to cabin till Mum chilled out. Ginnybitch left to get on with effing little paper factory she'd put into production.

Mum's phizog a picture. To help chilling out process, she had started going to Yoga classes and had joined a bunch of losers who liked playing Early English Music on a variety of reeds. Y.t. learning recorder at school. No bleeding choice. Worse luck. Mum not at all bad for a rank beginner.

Glowing in the Dragon's gaze and glowing even more 'cos her and y.t. doing something together, man. Ginnybitch learning recorder at school as well but managing to produce no more that stuttering effort. Just the two of them. Y.t. and Mum. Until Dad, of all naff things, starts to sing! Couldn't string two notes together in the right order! Trying to make his crackly, croaky voice sound deep and manly for Chrissake! Everybody laughing. Proper laughing. Including y.t.

Mum's stopped playing and started singing with Dad. Putting him on right course. Funny. Their phizogs in the flickering Dragonlight. Mum's all red-rosy and excited, full of the fire and passion of the Dragon. Dad's a dull, deep yellow, seeming to take on the yellow of the leaping flames.

Ginnybitch flushed and blonde and rosy. Losing poxy curls. Never noticed. Getting lanky. Going to be tall. Like Dad. Only resemblance.

Y.t. also in glow-mode. Phizog like burnished Cox's Pippin. Helluva scrawny. Long Tall Sally ain't in it, man. Dad's smaller clone. Apart from 'ooter. Y.t. has small, button-mushroom of a snitch. Dad has big, hooked beak. Mum's just a hooter. Nice one. But just a hooter. So's Ginnybitch's. Y.t.'s peepers glittering like jet.

Whole fucking scene looks like living, breathing Christmas card. Was it Christmas Day? Had they scoffed their Christmas nosh? It seemed very dark outside. Almost black. Dad had connected *Mikro* to mains electricity, but Mum liked using old oil lamps. Lovely and cosy. Give the bitch that. Frodo and Dookie stretched out on settee. Dragon's light dancing everywhere. Thinks it owns the fucking joint.

Mum's on a roll with this poxy family shit. Can't get through to her. Haven't really set mind on it. Half-hearted efforts. Few bum notes, few shakes of noddle along with bit of a smile/smirk, say 'so-o-rry' after bum notes. All a frigging waste of space. Bitch not even looking most of time! Laughing when y.t. plays bum notes!

Cool enough at the time. But soon wears thin. How about a game o' cards, Mum? So's y.t. can take half a century to decide which frigging card to play. 'Cheat' was great. Best wind-up of all. Meant to be fast and funny. Not with y.t. man. Most boring game ever invented. Never played it any more. Shame. Or how about a game of Scrabble? Ginnybitch had been known to doze off whilst waiting for y.t. to make a word. Or a bit of reading out loud. So's y.t. can stumble and pause over shit-easy words. Only Mum could come up with naff idea of them all taking turns to read out loud. Used to with Dad. Put the poor fuck through most of Dickens and Dusty-effsky and Gawd knows what other crap. Y.t. used to lie awake in bed listening to droning. Now she was punishing bratskis with it as well. Finished *Lord of the* fucking

Rings and just started on weirdo *Gormenghast*. Ginnybitch didn't make balls-up. She wouldn't, would she? Come to think, y.t. had to make real effort to cock things up with the reading.

After Christmas, Mum wanted to carry on with cosy duets. No chance, bitch. Y.t. didn't have to bugger it up. Couldn't. Mum thought she was on to an 'Answer'. All y.t. had to do was show no interest. Shrugged shoulders. Turned away. Really did her head in. Tried telling y.t. to take up Clarinet 'cos played recorder so well. Might have done, Mum. If you hadn't been daft enough to let out secret desire to play cello when elderly bint. Soon put mockers on that, didn't we Mum?

Lights have gone out. How can lights have gone out? Frigging oil lamps. No light from Dragon. No Dragon. Everything pitch black. Like a deep, black pit. A deep, black, empty pit. *Mikro* a vast, gutted upturned pod. Dripping slime and ooze. Y.t. stranded in middle of rising tide of thick, puddingy, swampy mud. Pins nailed to floor. Arms frozen to sides of rigid bod. Y.t. trapped in creeping, clutching, lapping, sucking, fudge-y mud! Trapped in rising gurgling surge of choking, stinking sludge! A huge cavern filled up with sludge and filthy ooze! A tomb! *Mikro* a fucking tomb!

Flies and bluebottles crawled fatly and lazily over face and neck and in the corners of eyes and mouth, nuzzling their proboscises into the various goodies. Tasty moisture on the exposed areas of flesh; a mixture of dried and semi-dried tears and sweat; and clusters of crusty, flaking skin — all made a bit of a change from the dipteral gorging at the main feast lying, viscidly ominous, up the escarpment and round the corner. Still enjoying a fairly brisk trade from the couch potatoes of the fly world. In one or two places, small clumps of very pale grains of pudding rice had appeared. And were continuing to appear. But they weren't pudding rice. They just looked that way.

Someone was knocking at the door. Someone was calling her by name. They didn't open the unlocked door. They didn't even try the handle. Music of all sorts swelled and pulsated throughout the squat. There were sounds of raucous laughter. People were enjoying themselves. Having a good time.

The light bulb, hanging naked and dirty from the ceiling, had sprung to life again and its stark glare angrily surveyed the room and its occupant. There were a lot more flies than there had been before.

The person knocking at the door, assuming it was the same one, knocked a few more times. The sound of voices, both male and female, came closer to the door. But only for a few moments. Then the knocking ceased. And the voices went away.

DAY THREE

August 19th

It was very early. The remains of the night sky, blushingly yielding to a bit of a macho morning, was forced to allow a few weak, pale orange slivers to filter, via cracks and corrugations, into the room, irradiating the bed and its occupant.

As though in response to the quivering, tentative touch of the feeble rays, the eyelids, after several attempts, lifted heavily. The whites looked like small, bluish eggs and the irises were dull and vacant. The skin, where exposed, was both waxy and mottled, with a sinister, bluish tinge. Where the mouth hung slackly and gaping, there was a reservoir of dark liquid resting in the slight well, formed by the cup-like position of the lower lip. Some of the liquid had dribbled down the chin, leaving a dried and crusty trail.

There was no movement other than the silent undulating of the flies, as they concentrated on the morning's business.

Shouting – shouting, do these sick fucks never give up on the shouting? Different sorts of poxy shouting. Some high and drawn-out, some sharp an' staccato and some half-groany. What the fuck are the dickheads up to? Too early for any of them to be on the go. Frigging light bulb's been given kiss o' life during wee small hours! Gotta be good omen, man. Can't make out poxy smell. No fishing boats on horizon. Just as well. Couldn't stand sight of all that frigging water when gob crammed full of dried-up bit of old shoe leather. Christ – y.t.'s decks could do with good scrub down – noddle needs wire-brushing – feels fucking alive, man!

Must be early. Very early. Thin, watery-gruel light barely managing to squeeze through window slats – ha ha ha. Slats. That's a good one! Always look on the bright side of life dee-da dee-da . . . Wonder if it's bleeding Giro day. Hope to Christ it is. Mates'll be banging on door before long. Always surface a tad earlier on Giro day. Someone'll have to cash Giro for y.t. How the fuck'll y.t. sign bloody thing?

Be rushed into hossy by then. E.R. No messing. Priority case, man. Medico dudes'll know all about effect of bad E. Allergies and all that sort of shit. Prob'ly seen loads o' dudes with same bad scene going on. Y.t.'ll be outta there in no time and able to sign own poxy Giro. No probs. Just case of waiting for useless effing mates to come. What a turn up – that effing Blojo! One shit hot babe, man.

Some dude in the room. Sitting in a fucking chair – slumped forward, having a kip, the lazy mother! Wake up, arsehole! So they hadn't forgotten y.t.! Yo! Which one of you mothers is doing a Flo Nightingale on Blojo?

Noddle lifts just a tad on one helluva floppy neck. Jesus, what a wanker. Too far outta it for land of nod; must be having a bad trip. Wake up, for Chrissake!

Hair all wild and spiky. Phizog a blank. Foamy spit bubbling through flabby lips and meandering down chin. Peepers flat and empty. It was y.t. And not all that long ago. A few years. But not a lifetime. No need to wonder what the fuck was going on. Knew only too well. Tad unfair, Scottie. Bit of a leap in the old warp factor. Nothing inside the noddle. Nothing to get hold of. No thoughts. No feelings. Might as well be a frigging zombie. Bad scene, man. Who are the dildos creeping along behind y.t.? Bedraggled line of hunched, mud-coloured weirdos straight out of *Thriller* shuffling slowly past to flop into chairs and slump across table.

The ECT brigade let loose after having a few volts shot through their skulls. All of them. Including y.t. Electro-Convulsive-fucking-Therapy. Not real people any more. Just sucked-dry husks.

Fucked up well and truly this time y.t. Jumped head first into shit.

Uniformed dudes dishing out steaming mugs of whatever and plates of biccies to rag dolls. Rag dolls staring vacantly at nothing at all. Like all well-behaved loonies do. All babes. All wearing drab, droopy cardies over shapeless sack efforts. No bitch here with a copy of *Creative Dressmaking*, man! Dun-coloured stockings, or, just as hideous but a helluva lot more degrading, pop socks.

Pop socks, for Chrissake! And why the fuck did they all have the same hair job? Either been chopped by some freaked-out acid head or hadn't seen a comb for months. Short and spiky and sticking out at all angles. Y.t.'s always been like that. Still is, most prob'ly – ha ha ha.

Y.t. had freaked out, flipped lid, scattered marbles. All together and altogether. Combo of mother of all bad trips, finding out four month old Alien in pod and Ellen coming home unexpectedly and catching y.t. and his holiness in mid-fuck. Doggie style. Nearly went into terminal shock, poor bitch. Thought it had ended years ago. Tell the truth, y.t. hadn't felt too cool about it. Being regularly fucked since moving in. During the day. When Ellen out at work. Lots of deep, meaningful chats about y.t. and his holiness. What's to be done. Sorted itself out when Alien made its presence felt. Then followed worst trip of y.t.'s natural born. Should've kept away from acid. Ended up in loony bin.

Hey, chill out, Ellen babe! Its not fucking – not *really* fucking. You *know* it's not! Just freeing bods of last few lingering little demons of lust and covetousness. Surely you wouldn't have denied his holiness the chance to cleanse and purify his tortured psyche? If so denied, he would, in turn, be denying countless others (as well as y.t. o' course) of the God-given labour of love needed to transform them and, most of all, his holiness, into truly enlightened and spiritually free exalted levels of human beings. And being Humans. Still weak, Babe. Weak and flawed. Full of human weakness and human flaws. But spiritually unshackled. Thereby allowing him the freedom to fulfil his God-given obligation to help and advise and guide, spiritually, those more lost and needy than himself.

This was the gist of the dude's Spiel. Real cool. Pure shite, more like.

And Ellen believed every putrid word. And y.t. did. At first. And for a long time after. Nearly ended up on slab. OD'd. And where had his effing holiness been then? Only Ellen had visited. Only Ellen talked about the Termination. Told y.t. that Marcus had done a runner. Just as well. Didn't want a kid to have pimp for Dad. Didn't want kid. Not pimp to start with. Not y.t.'s anyway. Christ – what a total fuck-up!

Why doesn't zombie y.t. grab mug o' tea for Chrissake? Gob so clogged that hot, luke-warm piss would do trick. No chance. Zombie not even turning peepers to look at tea and biccies. Been in bin a coupla months. And what had his holiness done towards restoring equilibrium of y.t.'s marbles? Written to Mum. That's all the poxy arsehole could bring himself to do. Suggested it would be more inducive to y.t.'s recovery if she was looked after, in her own country, with her own family.

Un-fucking-believable. Airhead Ellen told all. Bastard wanted to get rid of y.t. 'cos he couldn't afford to pay medical bills and couldn't even have a hand-job, never mind a fuck, with all the nursing staff that were hanging about the ward. Not that the bastard hadn't tried. Shoved mitt under sheets on one and only visit. Y.t. couldn't be arsed and told him to eff off. Wrong move. Crack in spiritual veneer. Selfish cunt. Didn't come within spitting distance of y.t. for ages afterwards. He'd told Ellen it was all over between him and y.t. because y.t.'s breakdown had accomplished more in the way of spiritual cleansing and healing than he was ever capable of. And, thanks be to the Good Lord, the shock of it all had thoroughly cleansed his own troubled psyche. Dumb cunt had swallowed the lot.

Strong sunlight streaming through huge, floor-to-ceiling windows. Go and stand in it dickhead! Get some bleeding warmth into frozen bones for Chrissake! Zombie just sitting. With other zombies. One of a bunch of gleaming, gold-plated zombies created by Midas touch of macho sun.

Y.t. moving, dudes! Bending and picking something up from floor. Hope it's a poxy biccy, man. Tangled tangerine. Tangled fucking tangerine knitting. Some mistake, surely? Y.t. had never knitted as much as a stitch in effing life. Mum had tried teaching in dim and distant, but had ended up hissing and spitting and breaking the wooden pins over her knee. Fucking knitting! And what a poxy colour! Surely not tangerine dishcloths! That's what loonies usually did, wasn't it? Knitted dishcloths? Not orange ones, but effing dishcloths. Y.t. not knitting a dishcloth. Part of a little dress. A baby's dress. A dress for a baby. Why the fuck was y.t. knitting a dress for a baby? The baby wasn't a baby any more. It was a Termination. Or an Abortion. Wasn't it? It couldn't still be wallowing around inside y.t.'s belly could it? 'Course it couldn't. The main reason Y.t.'d OD'd was because of the Termination/Abortion. So why the fuck the tangerine fucking dress? Why any dress? The stupid cunt was laughing. Couldn't reach out and get a cup of effing tea but splitting gob into big, gormless grin. Holding up tiny dress and showing it to the other loonies. One of sleeves smaller than other. All loonies having hysterics for fuck's sake!

Major cock-up in number of stitches. Going to have to run whole sleeve back. So why all laughing so much? 'Cos bunch of dickhead loonies, s'pose. Effing drag having to run sleeve back.

Loonies suddenly galvanised. Some jumping and/or gyrating on spot as though in throes of come. Others just standing. Pointing and/or staring fixedly. Slack gobs hanging gormlessly open. Y.t.'s just as bad. A few rodent-y screeches and squeals.

A tea trolley. A fucking tea trolley. Wheeled into ward by phalanx of uniformed bods. Like seagulls round a tip, gaggle of gibbering half-brains surround trolley. Another chance for airhead y.t. to get mitts on nice, warm, wet cuppa! Never mind the nosh – just grab a cuppa, dickhead. Have to wait a few mos. Wait for a space to clear round trolley. Loudmouthing bitch coming into ward. Tightly gripped by nurse on either side. Speaking English, for fuck's sake! Load o' shite, but English. Well-spoken English. Rabbiting on about bloody disgrace – father a Euro MP – place should be burnt to the ground along with scum dregs – useless fucking scum rotting useless lives away in fucking rat hole – bla–bla–bla . . . Nurses sitting her on empty bed and starting to undress her. Nice gear. Expensive. Can smell Chanel something or other.

'What the fuck are you staring at, you ignorant fucking cow? You're fucking pregnant, you fucking cow – a pregnant cow – you should be fucking well ashamed of your fucking self – fancy coming to the nuthouse to drop your brat – you should be sterilised – all your sort should – my father would soon do something about your type – he's a Euro MP you know – fucking dregs – this isn't a fucking nursery, you know – some of us come here for a bit of peace and quiet – pay our fucking way as well – not slum-bred scrounging scum like you and your scum sort – my God, I wouldn't be seen dead in a shithole nuthouse if I was going to drop a brat – what sort of fucking scumbag are you anyway?'

Y.t. gobsmacked. Totally. Brought back shit memories of the Fag lady. Well enunciated verbal vomit. How the fuck did the loud-mouthing bitch know that y.t. was pregnant? (Not pregnant. Couldn't be. Had it sucked, vacuumed out.)

Can't see belly. Can't see if bulge still there. Not much of a bulge. But a bulge. Leave off y.t. for Chrissake! Can't be a bulge. Been well and truly nuked. Popped tiny clogs in Vax dustbag. Ellen knows. Ellen was there. Not there. But waiting outside after. Gotta get out of this shithole. Doing noddle right in, man.

Y.t. leaping out of chair and doing runner out of ward. English bitch letting out earsplitting shriek. Staff not even raising peepers. Out of ward, down couple of corridors, through big, glass doors and eating asphalt down gravelly drive.

Lungs bursting out of chest. Guts packed with jiggling pebbly things. Can't breathe. Knives slicing through chest – chopping up lungs. Breath winnowing through holes in chest. Almost through main gates before arsehole white coats turn up. Stupid effing bitch – what the fuck was the point in doing a runner from bin? No idea what to do with a nice hot cuppa but it takes it into noddle to do Big Escape. Four white coats – two big dickheads and a coupla Myra Hindleys. Dragging y.t. Arms flailing like bleeding windmills, tootsies scraping along gravel back to glass-fronted bin.

Loudmouthing bitch cackling like madwoman she was an' clapping poxy mitts whilst bouncing up an' down on bed. Y.t. dumped an' turned on side. Sack/dress hauled up and needle shoved in butt. Noddle filled with sudden rush of noises. Jabbering, shrieking, clapping, squeaking. Tinny sounds. Sounds of marching feet. More jabbering. More shrieking. Shrieking. Shrieking. Endless shrieking.

Must think of the baby. The baby comes first. If the mother keeps freaking out then the baby will be born doolally. Can't get it out of my head. Can't stop thinking about it. Over and over. All the time. Day and night. Knows what he's doing, the bastard. Wanted wifey out of the way so's he could go back to the bloody Beeches and shag his little sister. No. Not so little. And no. Not into shagging. Only into staring up akimbo-d crotch and jerking off. That was then, though. And only because she was afraid of becoming pregnant. Different now. Bitch probably on the pill.

What the fuck's going on, man? Who the fuck's inside y.t.'s noddle? Feel sick – want to spew – can't – can't move. Needle in bum doing its jobbies.

Had to get away. Nowhere to go. Wasn't serious about Seconal. Felt like it at the time. Looked like it too. Scared the shit out of the bastard. Desperate. Knew he wanted to go. Understandable. Big brother's twenty-first and all that crap. Knew he wouldn't go without his eight and a half months pregnant wifey. Not because of any concern for the fat, mad bitch but because it wouldn't look good in eyes of Mafia Boss Ma McPhee. Called his bluff. Shouldn't have. He went. But that was what he wanted all along.

Did she have any hairs on her pubes this time round? Eleven years old would have been asking a bit much first time round. No. Eleven years old wasn't first time round. Four years old was. Eleven was when it had stopped. Because she'd started her periods and was afraid of falling pregnant. Even though it was simulated sex with no actual penetration. That was her again. Not you. You'd have shoved it in regardless. But she, she was doing Biology at school so had a bit more savvy.

What do you mean an obsession? What do you mean it only stopped a few months ago before meeting me? If she wasn't your sister would you have wanted to marry her?

Must have been terrible for you wanting to have sex with her so much and not even being able to pretend-screw her any more. She still charged the same, didn't she? For the spread legs job. You had to be found out sooner or later. If Ma McPhee hadn't noticed the light under Debbie's door late one night during her search for a hidden bottle, then Pa McPhee would have started missing the notes from his wallet, wouldn't he? Poor Ma McPhee. Almost felt sorry for her. Had a hell of a job stopping Pa from sending for the cops there and then. Somehow, she got him to agree to accept you seeing a psychiatrist as long as his beloved Deb hadn't been penetrated by her half-brother.

Get outta my skull you sick bitch – you an' your fucking shite book – never read the poxy crap – not prop'ly – who wants to know about a loada shite lies – no-one believes it – only you, you sad psycho bitch – fuck off an' take your poxy lies with you.

Knew you hadn't got over it. Otherwise, why keep buying her little presents for no reason other than you wanted to please her? To see the scaffolding glitter with gratitude as she smiled her salivating smile. Why did you ever tell me? Because if you hadn't, Ma McPhee would have. You'd have thought she'd have been pleased that you were forming an apparently normal relationship, wouldn't you? Instead of calling us dirty filthy animals when she found us in a sleeping bag in the café basement. Even though we hadn't even had as much as simulated sex. You shouldn't have pinched her bum in the café that time. Red, shirred-elastic, swimsuited twelve year old bum. Meant it that time. With the aspirin. Mixing them with milk screwed everything up. Didn't mean it with the Seconal in the lavvy. Had to get away. Had to see if you really wanted to go to the party. And you did. Couldn't get away quick enough. Wifey safely shut up in loony bin; hubby hot-cocking it to try and get a glimpse of Sis's crotch just for old time's sake.

Saw the party photos afterwards. You'd been so miserable, you'd said, without your little wifey. If it hadn't been for sense of duty . . . And *there you were. Clowning about under the table. Having the time of your life. Whilst darling little wifey and soon-to-emerge foetus were safely ensconced in loony bin. Did you get a look at her hole? Plenty of hairs, black hairs, there now, I'll bet. Does she have scaffolding there as well. Like she had on her other mouth?*

Please – please – Jesus – please get her outta y.t.'s skull – please – none of it's true – none of it. What's wrong with bratskis playing doctors an' nurses anyway – only a sick bitch would see something wrong with it – a sick mad bitch who belongs in a bleeding loony bin. Her and her fucking poxy lying book. Leave y.t. alone for Christ's pity's sake.

The tangerine knitting was sticking out of the locker at the side of the bed. Marley's bleedin' ghost done a runner then. Thank Christ for that. Y.t. got enough on friggin' plate without that sorta spooky shit. Funny. Outta the glare of the old currant bun the frigging orange knitting had an almost pinkish tinge. Nice.

Did y.t. still have something growing in belly after all?

Why the fuck hadn't the stupid bitch grabbed a cuppa – even a cold cuppa would've been better than no cuppa at all.

*   *   *

In swingboat. Or cradle. Gently rocking. All cosy and coochy. Water shushing and softly slapping. Friggin' ace man, if it wasn't for poxy quacking and jabbering in ear'ole. Endless bickering of bastard shelducks. What the fuck do ducks find to bicker about? Why can't they be more like curlews? 'Cos curlews are too effing sad, that's why. Hear a coupla the sods an' innards nearly ripped out. Funny. Y.t. lying in bunk in fo'c'sle. Two dinky little portholes. Shove bod up on elbow an' can see shelducks grabbing last few gobfuls of grub before the tide comes in too far. *Mikro* beginning to creak and shift as timbers come alive under force of incoming water. Awesome when she suddenly lifts herself free from the river bed and swings across to the length of the mooring ropes before swinging back an' doing a coupla little shimmies before settling into an even, dreamy float. Y.t. not feeling all that brill. What going on *Mikro*? Where's Ginnybitch? Must've moved into larger cabin. Dad had been planning on fitting new bunks etc.

Christ – feel as weak as gnat's piss. Hangover? Not on *Mikro*. Someone knocking on cabin door. Mum's dulcits.

142

'Are you awake, Laura?'

'Yes, Mummy.'

In she comes with a tray of goodies. Smiling, but tense round the peepers. Always tense round peepers.

'Feeling any better this morning? Did you have a good sleep?'

What the fuck's the matter with y.t.? Never been ill on *Mikro*. How old? Difficult to tell. Twelve? Thirteen? Tits sticking out a tad. Could be a trick of the duvet. Hell of a colour. Phizog pale primrose. Big shadows circling peepers. Looks knackered. Glandular fever. Had glandular fever. In school San. For a month or so. Sent home to convalesce for another month. Or so. Not even twelve. Only eleven and a half. Trick of duvet after all. Beginning of summer term. No wonder Mum's looking so shifty. Feeling pig-sicking guilty 'cos thinks y.t.'s spent last few months building up to Big Illness. Prob'ly ever since starting boarding school. So said school Doc. Explains it all, thinks Mum. Stupid bitch.

Thought most of probs would vanish once y.t. tucked neatly out of the way at boarding school. Almost flunked entrance test. Needed to do well to make up for being year younger that the rest of first-year dunderheads. Did shit. Didn't mean to. Thought school brill. Old, ivy-covered stone. Polished wood floors. Friendly dudes. Seemed cool. Headmaster shit hot. Couldn't mess with him. Peepers like electric-blue ice picks. Hair so fair almost white. Y.t. told him what he wanted to hear. Funny, though. Kinda meant it all.

Y.t.'s math non-existent. Surprise! Spelling dodgy, but English good. Ol' Ice-pick thought y.t. intelligent, mature for age and very self-possessed and – and! – deserved a chance. If prepared to work really hard, stood as much hope of success as any of pupils in school. Mum pissing herself with relief. Almost kissed Ice-pick. He knew all about probs between y.t. and Mum. Had to. He and Ol' Hump had long chatties 'cos y.t. would have fees paid by Council. Mum and Dad would pay some. But not a lot. School only took about half a dozen y.t.'s. Do-gooders, the Quakers. For real. Didn't shove poxy religion down throat either. Mum convinced y.t. would develop own personality away from her. Once out from under jackboot. Another New Beginning. Had to get through summer hols first. Big G came to rescue. Had y.t. to stay with P/C and VE in Taff Cottage.

Special shop in Cambridge for uniform etc. Bottle-y green gear; skirt, cardy, cape. Neat. Got complete new kit. Nighties, underwear, socks, dressing-gown – three of each. Except the dressing-gown, o' course. Mum took photo of y.t. all in green among poxy flowers she'd planted along bank of towpath.

Everyone acting like dopeheads on way to Saffron Walden. Dad started telling story about old witch called Mrs Grimble. All had to take turns in adding bit to story. Ginnybitch never able to finish more that a poxy sentence. Y.t. boo-ed by everyone for taking so long to even open gob. Mum dead embarrassed but almost coming 'cos of sudden outbreak of family atmosphere. Everyone yelling at Dad to carry on with the incredible adventures of the amazing Mrs Grimble. Mum gobsmacked at Dad's sudden use of original thought.

Managed to get a bit of giggling in. Just so's not to get rusty. Always worked ace in the back of the car. Mum trying to chill out and keep gob shut so's not to cast shadow on 'family' thingy but, after a lot of crack about scenery, the new school, trying to get them to play I-fucking-boring-Spy, just had to ask y.t. to please stop that stupid senseless giggling. Went all quiet after. Couldn't even control yourself on the day chucking y.t. out of family home, Mum. You sad fuck!

Big hugs and kisses after carrying trunk and bags etc. up to dorm. Managed to keep bod fairly stiff and distant. Upset Mum. Tried to pull y.t. closer. Y.t. having none of that shit. What do you expect, for Chrissake?

Y.t.'s recovery time passed OK 'cos of Mum being rattled with guilt. Convinced all probs of previous year due to incubation of virus. Thought y.t. ailing and well under par 'cos of it. Poor Mum. Visits to San had started after first month. Genuine chilblains. Not funny. Fucking crippling. Had always had the bastard things. Got a lot worse. Central heating prob'ly. Always shoving tootsies up against radiator. On mitts as well. Jolly, fat nursy. Just what y.t. needed. Lotta fuss and TLC. Started going regular. Sometimes for real. Sometimes if pissed off and feeling a tad mizzy. Worked out brill. Beyond wildest. School Sec had to send Mum and Dad a letter each time y.t. in San. Just to keep informed. Long, white envelopes taking up semi-permanent residence in post box came to fill Mum with as much dread as y.t.'s visits home. 'Cos of envelopes, they had to make special visits. Several times. Lotsa chatting with Old Hump. Homesickness, Mrs F, he says.

Mum's head being done right in. Can't dig that. Knew that no sane bitch would pine for life with Mum. Or for life after the dream. Mum didn't know about that, though. Don't know exactly when y.t. sussed there were a coupla ace scams begging to be worked over. 1) Visits to San any time felt like a doss/a cop-out/a bit of TLC. 2) Effect of slender white arrows winging way, via courtesy of Royal Mail, to softly plop into wooden letter-box Dad had made and nailed to big old damson tree in boatyard. Serendipity. Great word. As well as regular fortnightly visits, at least three extra per term. Said that already y.t. Plus killer buzz of totally winding Mum up – from frigging miles away! No need for poxy smile/smirk etc. All y.t. had to do was pop down the San and let everything follow of own bleeding accord! Ace, or what? Took y.t. a whole term to really suss scam. Don't know if Mum ever twigged, 'cos of all other shit that happened. After.

In meantime, y.t. told Mum what the bitch wanted to hear. That y.t. had been naughty for wasting everybody's time. Been a bloody nuisance (said y.t. ha ha) always running to the San on the slightest pretext. But now was determined to make up for all hassle caused by selfishness and thoughtlessness. Would have to work hard on History, Geography and French. No use pretending anything other than useless at Maths. Always would be. Brainbox went blank. Wouldn't need to worry too much about English and Art. Naturals. A bit too cocky there. Overdid things, babe. Swallowed it all. Stupid bitch.

Lotta other things going on to keep Mum wound up. Number of houseboats increasing along stretch of river from Woodbridge to Sefton. Local council shits began to take interest. Cluster of grey-coated clones carrying clipboards appeared, like creeping alien fungi, around the yard and up and down the towpath.

Mum totally nuked to see hideous photo of *Mikro* – taken before any work had been done on her, staring out of a local rag. Accompanied by shit editorial using shit words like health hazard – floating slum – river polluted – planning permission – what might be acceptable to residents of Hong Kong not accept-able to residents of Sefton and Woodbridge etc. etc. Mortified Mum had penned an impassioned reply, citing reasons for and advantages of living on river. Usual Mum bilge. Wide open spaces; peace and quiet; beauty of birds and river wildlife etc. etc. Long letter. Made good copy. Gave another viewpoint. Even if total shite. Shame, 'cos a few weeks later, another piece appeared in the same rag, reporting on the small matter of a Mr Desmond FitzHugh, resident of *Mikrokosmos*, Sefton Boatyard, being fined the sum of twenty-five pounds for stealing a tyre from a local scrapyard. Great timing, Dad! Y.t. couldn't have done better! Getting back into the swing o' things, Daddy-O? All you managed in Wimbledon was a fine for speeding and another for no road tax. True, there was an air of mystery about the sudden appearance of an expensive camera which seemed to be the result of spontaneous generation in the back of the Morris. Nothing ever came of it. Still using it. Mum took pics of y.t. in green gear.

Sharp, stabbings through back of noddle. Shooting pains. Arrows of burning, throbbing pain. Want to throw up. Innards heaving up through lava of pain.

Shouting, shouting, shouting. It's a wonder the bitch has any fucking voice left with the amount of effing shouting she does. What the fuck has y.t. done this time, man? Brainbox being used as frigging punchball. Got the knack, over the years, of folding arms up and over, so when Mum lashes out, she hurts own mitts more than y.t.'s noddle. A few landing on target. Bitch. Trumpeting in ear'ole, frigging drum ringing with it.

'Is there nothing you can do right – nothing? Nothing? Why are you always doing the things you're told not to and never, ever the things you're asked to – why – why – why? You must be trying to drive me mad – is that it? Is it? Is that your aim in life? To drive your mother mad? Answer me, damn you – answer – answer!'

Y.t. snivelling which, along with lack of answer, freaked Mum out all the more.

'Don't you understand anything? Is there anything you're capable of understanding? You're so bloody stupid – I've never come across anyone as stupid as you – as thick and mind-bogglingly stupid – you're an idiot – do you hear? A sodding stupid thick pig of an idiot! Do you hear? Do you? Do you?'

Turns and hurls herself into chair, slumps head in hands and begins usual whinge.

'Why does it have to be like this? Why – why? What have I done for this to keep happening? What have any of us done? Why won't she do as she's told? It's always the same – always little things – always ordinary, little things – things that a bloody three-year old could understand – why does she do it – why – why – why does she keep on doing it?'

Dad trying to chill her some. Putting arm round shoulders.

Steady on, Dad! Don't overdo understanding hubby shit – injured babe's over here on the poxy floor, for Chrissake! Peering through digits, can see Dad all yellow-flushed and furrowed. Y.t. crouched in corner of wheelhouse like a frigging great insect that's been knocked off its perch, limbs all folded up into its bod for protection.

'Why the hell can't you manage to do what your mother asks you to?' snaps Dad, turning on y.t. with his economy-size, discoloured gnashers ya-booing in his sulphurous mush. Y.t. gave him a mouthful. Just shot out. Called him an effing ignorant bastard. Well, who the fuck does he think he is, man?

Big mistake. Mum freaked out on different tack. Turned like a she-wolf, or some bitch or other. Always sticking up for him, Mum. Can't blame you s'pose.

How dare y.t. speak to her father like that! The way he worked – and who did he work for? Who? Who? He worked for them all, that's who – for their home, their clothes, their car and all the extras. Like horse-riding and y.t.'s holidays with Gina and with Hester. (Forgot about that. Old bat had told Mum that y.t. didn't give a hoot about gee-gees. Just liked sitting on top looking good. Hit the spot there, miserable old dyke.) Did y.t. think Daddy enjoyed the work he had to do? Did she? Well, if she did, she was wrong, because he hated every minute of every day of it. (What *was* the wanker doing workwise at the mo? Apart from boosting local crime figures, ha ha.)

Mum totally freaked out. Shaking with rage. Dad standing with hangdog scowl on yellow mush. Mum still sounding off. For Chrissake, give it a rest you stupid bitch. Too busy being a good husband and father bla bla. (Do you really believe that, Mum?) Working himself to ground, day and night so's they could all be comfortable and secure. For Chrissake cut the fucking crap, Mum.

Gazing gobsmacked at y.t. Trying to fathom out expression on phizog. Contempt, Mum. That's what. Thought it best to do as told, so muttered barely audible 'sorry' in general direction of doormat Dad. What a fucking sight y.t. was! Slitty peepers in red, swollen phizog. Funny, all this shit happening, 'cos school hols, up until last day hadn't been a bad scene. Until y.t. had fucked up.

Didn't mean to. Don't think so. Mum had asked y.t. to pack trunk for school and let her know if anything missing or needed. Y.t. said everything OK. No probs. In the morning Mum had said check, just to make sure. Nothing missing, warbled y.t. Always a big deal 'cos everything checked and ticked off on arrival at school. Mum about to leave it at that. Then decided to recheck. At last mo before leaving. At least half a dozen poxy things not packed. All necessary.

No idea how it happened, Mum. Would prob'ly have been OK if y.t. hadn't overplayed hand and resorted to smile/smirk and 'so-orry'. Shame. Everything had been cool over Christmas hols. Don't know why things got fucked. Who wants to be arsed checking poxy trunk, man? Know it has to be done. Look right twat if not when Mrs Jenkins checking. Why did you have to be so fucking super-perfect, Mum? Another few mos and we'd've been well on the way to Suffering Boredom.

Lotta things could have freaked you out over the hols, but you'd managed to stay chilled. Dad losing his job, for starters. Sacked for sleeping on duty. Can't blame poor sod. All he was needed for was to change dud light bulb if and when. Well-paid number. And cushy. Too cushy. Swore he'd never work in canteen again after Leatherhead scam but only job going, after light bulb disaster, was night-cook in sugar factory. Effing beggars can't be effing choosers, eh Dad? Always seemed to lose his job just before Christmas. Can't believe how chilled out you were, Mum. Also unfazed by y.t.'s first report from new school. Fair do's. Not that frigging bad. Usual shite negativities.

'Talkative in class', 'Inability to concentrate', 'Capable of more effort'.

Quite a few on the plus side, though. Surprise! 'Pleasant, friendly manner', 'Co-operative and well-mannered', 'Willing to please'.

Comment at end saying that all dickheads were willing to make generous allowances due to Laura's being disadvantaged by several months age difference and the fact that it was the end of the first term. Ta very much arseholes.

First few days of hols stretched Mum's cool. Y.t. finished school a week before Ginnybitch; Dad asleep in saloon 'cos of night duty; so Mum and y.t. stuck in wheelhouse on ownio. When Mum unable to stand creeping claustrophobia any longer and grabbed Dookie to go for walkies, y.t. tagged along behind. After few times, over few days, Mum forced to blurt that if y.t. didn't mind, she'd rather go walkies on her own with braindead mutt. Nice buzz from seeing phizog tying itself in knots 'cos of guilt *v* need to breathe. When not at school, Ginnybitch always out playing with poxy pals and poxy Frodo. What the fuck would y.t. find to do with a bunch of frigging six year olds for Chrissake.

Over actual Christmas, Mum wanted to do recorder thingy again. Y.t. can't be arsed. Bo-oring, man. Then Ginnybitch started tweetering away on pathetic descant, so y.t. had bit of a go on the treble. Wouldn't play duet with Mum. Give us a break.

Everyone said how good y.t. was. Why on earth didn't she take up the clarinet? And what, for heaven's sake, had decided her on the cello? Think Mum had an idea on that. Had to go along with effing carols. Mum sang a few and Ginnybitch read poems from poxy *Lord of the Rings*. Voice reminded y.t. of frigging curlew. Bitch. Mum taped all the pathetic efforts. What a loada wankers.

Yes, y.t. liked school. And yes, she was settling down nicely, thank you. No, there were no problems. Mr Hump said he'd see what he could do about arranging music lessons for free. Like a music grant. Mum thrilled. Almost pissing herself. Pathetic bitch. Yes, y.t. intended getting down to some serious work next term. Had it all planned. Soon after Christmas, y.t. started getting seriously pissed off. Hols too long. Nearly a fucking month. Bored witless with all the family walkies and piccies and poxy theatre. Not so much the theatre. Only went the once over the hols. Went a lot in Cambridge. Every time they visited. Matinee performance on Saturday afternoons. Majorly pissed off with having to go to bed same time as Ginnybitch. Half-past seven, for Chrissake! Always been the same. No way can Mum put up with y.t. fucking around in evenings as well. Dad at work. Not even a frigging telly, man. After what happened at Wimbledon, Mum refused to give boat room to a goggle-box. Didn't do anything too way out. Kept Ginnybitch awake. Start off talking. Then giggling. Mum OK with that for a while. Stayed cool. Working on poxy book. Or home-work. Started a frigging full-time college thing. Only got rattled when Ginnybitch shouting at y.t. to shut gob. Mum would call down and tell y.t. to let bratski Ginnybitch get to sleep. Silence would fall. But only for a few mos. Soon, murmuring and giggling would start up again followed by Ginnybitch shouting even more at y.t. and beginning to whinge and blubber a bit. Mum would have to come down to cabin and tell y.t. to leave off pestering little sis. Why couldn't y.t. wait for said sis to fall asleep, then put light on and read for a while?

After a few nights of same, Mum would lose cool. Not totally. Just normal. And threaten to punish naughty y.t. No good smirking in dark. So y.t. would wait till morning. And when Mum asked why y.t. kept doing something (irritating Ginnybitch, she meant) when repeatedly told not to, y.t. used smile/smirk trick to full effect, with slight shake of noddle and shoulder, as if walking from trance and softly 'so-orry'-ing. Expected her to blow gasket. Didn't. Stayed cool. Deserved fucking medal. Y.t. not all that fazed. Thinking about getting back to school. New pals. Things to do. People to see, ha ha ha. Then all the shite with the effing trunk happened.

No Mrs Grimble on journey to Saffron Boredom. Silence reigned. Y.t. too shit scared to wind up Ginnybitch. Mum all stiff and pale. Saying good-byes. Had to force herself to peck y.t.'s cheek. Ain't got the frigging pox Mum! Y.t. stood and waved as Morris drove off. Usually, all waved back. Not this time. Only Ginnybitch. Stupid phizog pulling faces, starfish mitts spread out on back window.

Two weeks into the Spring term, the long smooth, white arrow plopped into the postbox. Laura was, wrote the Secretary, in the School Sanatorium suffering from an attack of chilblains. There is no need for them to worry. Or to visit the school. Yours sincerely. Got you going a treat, Mum. It was then y.t. realised nuking potential of long, white arrows.

Belly about to burst. Explode. No. Lower than belly. Bladder? Bowels? Some fucking organ thingy about to splatter itself all over walls. Can feel frigging gut swelling by the mo. Being pumped full o' something. Not air. Pumped full o' fucking pain, man. Splitting, funny, burny sorts o' pain. Feeling burny. Like being pumped full of smouldering polystyrene bubbles. Weird. Nice bit o' currant bun, though. Can feel toastiness on noddle and phizog. Je-e-esus! – y.t. going to do a dump, for Chrissake! A *huge* dump! 'Mummy – Mummy – need the lavvy – need the lavvy – need – need it now . . . Mummy . . .' Back to reedy pip-squeak time again. Sick of these sick fucking sick jokes, man.

'Mummy, Mummy . . .'

Everything is shifting – moving – heaving. All this effing heaving and swaying. Bowels feel as though breaking through belly wall – pushing up into abdomen and gullet. Shit peristalsising fucking backwards, man! Don't let shit go to gullet – please don't – gotta do a dump – gotta do a dump – don't let y.t. puke shit for Chrissake!

'Please Mummy – please . . .'

Laughter. Warm sun and laughter.

'Just hang your bum over the edge or squat in the bilges – Daddy'll turn the other way.'

Not a wee, Mummy. A dump, Mummy.

'I can't believe it – I just can't bloody well believe it! Only Laura could do this – What'll we do, Desmond? You'll have to find somewhere to moor – there's nowhere – it's all reeds – I can't understand you, Laura – if it was a wee, fair enough. We've been on the river about an hour. But a crap! You could have tried before we left. You're beyond anything. Do you know that? Beyond anything.'

Out in a rowboat in the middle of the effing river. One of Mum's little weekend-outing ideas. Row down to Felixstowe. Have picnic on way. In boat. Better than shank's effing pony, s'pose. But trapped, for Chrissake.

Dad getting narked. No buildings or jetties or even bits of sand or shingle on which to haul up dinghy. Reeds reeds and more effing reeds.

Y.t. can't help it, Mum. Didn't ask to need a dump.

Not getting any lighter in room. Seems frigging darker, man! Pathetic, anorexic streaks o' greyness faltering through cracks seem to be getting weaker and fade-y grey. And where's the effing currant bun? Should be bursting through, swinging left hook at effing light bulb on its way.

Noddle hurting. And phizog. This shit is getting serious. Not getting. Is. Pig-sicking lockjaw should be easing off more than a tad. Instead of zilch. No effing difference. Worse. That's the difference. Getting fucking worse. Gob stuck together. Tongue stuck fast to roof of gob and gob sealed across whole fucking shebang. Can only breathe through hooter. Painful rattle. Have to take short rapid breaths. Trying to move noddle. Try, bitch. Try. Feels wrong. Wrong way round. Feel as though lying on belly. Trying to raise noddle off floor. Can't. Effing can't. Effing pinned to effing floor. Like upturned turtle. Or beetle. Only other way round. Y.t. trapped on front. Can't turn over on to back. Want to get digits into gob – must – must get digits into gob!

Fat baby, wearing pale yellow summery dress thing; lying on carpeted floor. Bare, fat arms and legs waving and jerking in futile effort to right fat bod. Just like big, fat, yellow beetle. Yummy, yummy, summery Mum sitting on settee with plain, beige-grey bitch. Ugly bratski, paddi holder hanging like a carapace, staggering about on skinny, bandy pins. Why does fat 'n bandy look cool(ish)? But skinny and bandy look yukky? As though suffering bad case of rickets. Snot hanging thickly and greenly, just resting on upper lip, waiting for tongue to emerge and lap it into gob. Discoloured sixpences for peepers. Blank. Flat. Depthless.

Selena. The mutant spawn called Selena. Y.t. and Selena nine months old. Fuck-face Selena. Empty fuck-face Selena. First ever flat. Sea Road. Bexhill-on-Sea.

Overweight beige-grey bitch sitting on settee with Mum is Grace. Been in hospital at same time. Stayed sort of pals. Grace giving Mum lowdown on how to get y.t. to move around. Y.t. hadn't even started to crawl, never mind stand up, or walk – for Chrissake! Mutant fuck-face Selena staggering all round room. Picking stuff up, climbing on and off chairs. Falling off. Looked real weird man. Unnatural. Doing all this shit whilst y.t. sat fatly all the time, wherever put, sucking endlessly and deliciously on digits.

Nothing got y.t. going. The mutant would tack across from other end of room, give y.t. long, mouldy-sixpence stare, before leaning forward and delivering shove to shoulder. Over y.t. would topple. And stay where fell. In same position. On side, with neck twisted. Didn't matter. If uncomfortable, would start gurning. Mum would prop up again and watch with screaming peepers as digits flew back into y.t.'s gob. Didn't matter how many times the Mutant knocked y.t. over. Would never try and defend or hit back. Or anything, but restore digits to rightful nesting place. Beige-grey bitch kept telling Mum to let them get on with it. Y.t., or Laura, as she said, would have to learn how to stick up for herself. But Mum knew it would have gone on all day. Mutant knocking y.t. over; y.t. gurning; Mum righting y.t.; Mutant knocking y.t. over . . .

Y.t., as a result of grey-beige bitch's gobshitting, been deliberately placed on belly. Idea being that t'would encourage lazy, digit-sucking little turd to use arms to push bod off floor, and thus crawl. Mum not at all sure. Knew that the way the Mutant was scuttling around at nine months was just as weird as y.t. being a fat slob. Could see Mutant must have a ganglion at some part of lower spine, behind Paddi carapace. Directing all development to advancement of limb function and leaving sod all for the brain. What brain, for Chrissake? Look at the bleached sixpences –

152

connected to zilch! Nothing to log into! Y.t. snivelling and gurning and looking right pissed off. No frigging wonder, man. Neck feels broken, chest gotta bloody great weight on it, pins hurting, peepers shrieking 'cos can only see grubby green carpet – phizog an' gob hurting – gob sobbing for fat, comfy, sucky digits. Straining and stretching to get digits near gob. Try and move arms y.t. – try – try harder – bring them up – up and across – up to sides of noddle first, then across to gob – go on, go on, try harder, babe! No good. Can't twitch a fucking muscle. Bad scene, man.

Sit y.t. up, Mum – for Chrissake! Not ready to start effing press-ups yet! Poxy carpet fluff getting up hooter an' crawling up/ down tubes into throat. Tickling an' itching over uvula and trying to creep up and over slab of araldited leather. Need to sneeze, man. Stinging prickles swarming up hooter and into peepers, bringing midget watering can brigade out in force. Relief or what, man – Mum taking pity on yellow beetle! Wish you hadn't, Mum, when you see fat digits dive-bomb into desperate gob.

Don't think much of the decor, Mum. Carpet OK but green a mistake, wouldn't you agree, with black/red/gold bamboo patterned wall paper and black gloss window frames and door. Not your fault. Not a lot of say in choice of carpet, had you? Wedding pressy from the Fag lady an' the Butcher. Second-hand carpet that'd been stashed in the garage for years an' Dad's train fare (single) up to Scottish nuptials. Made sure they pushed the boat out. Pair o' fucking wankers. Bit of a downer having to accept loan o' rest o' shite from garage depths. No choice. No dosh to get own gear.

Y.t. had started to sprout after first honeymoon fuck – maybe sooner. Didn't you an' Dad have a pre-nuptial fuck on the rug in front of the fire in Heeland Granny's living-room? Or had it, the fuck, been aborted 'cos of Mr H.G. shoving hooter round the door in pretext of whatever? Can't remember. Y.t.'ll have to have another browse through the opus when outta lockjaw land. Never did read the bloody thing prop'ly. Either of them. Don't think got as far as opening no two. Kept meaning to. Never seemed to get round to it. Don't even know if still got effing things. Lying around somewhere, s'pose.

Short 'n sweet effing relief – Mutant staggering across on rickety pins, stopping for a mo to fix witless sixpences on y.t. before tipping bod over like one of those round-bottomed toys that always rocked back into an upright position. Not y.t. Stayed where shoved. Fluff up the 'ooter time again. Dad had been in middle of laying down the green carpet when Mum and y.t. came out of hossy almost a week early. Mum freaking out with Matron shrieking every time she passed. Pull yourself together Mrs FitzHugh – comb your hair at least, for goodness sake – you're a disgrace to the ward!

Stood at the top of stairs, clutching y.t., bawling peepers out at sight of roll upon roll of the Fag lady's old, unwanted carpet. Fag lady running fucking shop. Knew about y.t. popping pod before Dad. No visit. Not one. But rang hossy then rang Dad at work to tell him he'd got an 8lb 12oz daughter.

Stupid prick needn't have told you. Never could stop blabbing gob off.

Belly straining – gut stretching and ballooning as though pump attached to belly button. Iffy smell. No. Wet smell. Stench. Like worst ever shite. The runs. Skitters. Worse even than that. Belly going to burst. Must have shat the bed. Shitting the bed, for Chrissake. Someone knocking. Ever so softly. One of effing mates at last! No. Wouldn't knock softly. Knock bleeding door down and barge straight in. Ignorant fuckers. Could've been air-lifted by frigging aliens, f'rall they care. Bastards. Bad E should've worn off, man. Still feel like pure shite. Like whatever's been dumped in the bed. Just want to kip. Get outta this effing ice-box and have a good, long kip.

What's with the effing knocking, dudes? Just give door a good shove and come in. Y.t. more than ready for the off. Get the hossy on the blower, loada scumbags. Y.t. in deep shit here. More ways than one, ha ha ha.

Door opening, but at bottom of bed. Give it a frigging rest, why don't ya! Who the fuck's opening the door, man? Real cool chick. Sleek and glossy, hair gleaming like polished plumage, phizog glowing so much, in need of a geiger counter, peepers glittering jet, vivid red slash of a gob, equally red long, dragon's fingernails. Huge belly. Huge, proud belly straining out of cool little Laura Ashley number.

Y.t. ready to whelp at any mo. Y.t. opening door to Mum/Mags/Maggie/Margaret.

Definitely Margaret. Original uncut slab of Aberdeen granite. Followed by toffee-nosed Ginnybitch. Tits beginning to put in an appearance. His holiness'll approve – ha ha ha. And a still podgy P/C. Not Charles Laughton. Nothing to do with Charles Laughton. Definitely Peter Ustinov. Still call him P/C, though. What the fuck's he doing with Ginnybitch and the Founder of the Granite Industry? Still pissing the bed, Rupe? No one else would have him. Big G used to have y.t. for hols and Mum P/C. Him and Ginnybitch great buddies, even though first time Mum let Ginnybitch spend the day at Twickers, Rupe shoved her off the top of a chest-of-drawers, splitting her top lip. Bleeding like a stuck pig. Scared shit out of Big G. Still got scar above lip. Doesn't spoil effing looks, though. Bitch.

An' here's good ol' Uncle Gav, sloping along in the rear. How're tricks, Unc? Is that a Kalashnikov in your pocket, or are you just pleased to see y.t.? Ha ha ha. Fair do's. Mustn't be nasty to Unc. Been a cool dude to y.t. Always ready with the readies. No questions. Bit of a tit-man, aintcha Unc? Make sure plenty on show when he calls round. No harm done. Bit o' innocent. Made lotsa visits 'cos he worked in the Big City and Tadworth only a short train ride away. Like being involved, dontcha Unc?

Aberdeen Granite too gobsmacked to manage more than a mutter, and no frigging wonder. Last heard from y.t. three weeks ago asking for a tenner to buy grooming kit (a.k.a. fags and voddie). Then, few days ago, phone call from Heeland Granny passing on info that y.t. due to whelp in very near. And who'd spilled beans to H.G.? Who else but his effing holiness, o' course. That's real reason for Aberdeen Granite and flint peepers.

Why you freaking out, Mum? Not as though it's his sprog. Wait till you hear that y.t.'s been booted out of poxy riding school – months ago. Not 'cos of being with pup – didn't even suspect, thought extra pounds due to more-than-usual bingeing. No. Given order of boot 'cos wouldn't obey house rules. House rules! Like being back in effing boarding school, man! Bunch of wankers strutting around in Barbours and green wellies thinking they could tell y.t. what to do and when to do it. No way, José. Some of the arsehole inmates were paying, for Chrissake! One bitch had come all the way from the US of A and was forking out a hundred and fifty smackers a week, would you believe! Didn't have to do any of the dirty work, the bitch. Just swanned around the yard looking like an advert from *Horse and* fucking *Hound.* Had her own room. Didn't have to share the dorm with the low life. The working pupil low-life.

Here comes creepy Evelyn. Popping beige boat-race round door to make sure no-one giving any aggro to precious-s-s-s y.t. ha ha ha. Social Services did brilliant finding a sucker like Evelyn. Pat on the back all round, guys.

A. Granite looking as though about to be Semtex-ed as Evelyn, after giving cursory nod to bunch of dickheads, asks y.t. if 'everything's all right' and wouldn't it be better if Evie stayed – just to make sure? All delivered in loud stage whisper. Nice one, Evie. Still, in view of lurid details y.t. had filled that Tupperware brain with . . .

Y.t. shakes glossy, black noddle and moues, 'It'll be all right, darling – really', before nuking A. Granite with rapid delivery of ace eyelash curve and dive, then sweeping up and over to allow locking of peepers. Hairy few mos, man! Thought y.t. going to *be* nuked instead of doing the nuking! Sparks o' rage and aggro bouncing and flashing from Mum's bits o' flint. Oh – the scrum-miness of the meeting of the mincepies, man! Be nice to stroke pussy at same time, ha ha ha. Don't have to bother with smile/smirk. Bitch is well into overdrive already.

'Just give a shout if you need me, dear, coo-coo, coo-coo . . .'

And the permed and twinsetted dork simpers beigely out of the G-plan living room.

Whom would you most like to throttle, Mum? Not much to choose between y.t. and Evie, eh? But the one you'd really like to see six feet under is his holiness, ain't it? Mustn't forget, though. 'Twas y.t. who made first move.

Couldn't believe peepers when dickhead Uncle Simon appeared on goggle-box. Only a crap kid's programme; but there he was. As large as an elephant dump and twice as thick. Only wanted to touch miserable tight-arse for a few notes. Should've realised he'd still be as narrow as a chook's sphincter. Suddenly popped into noddle to ask about his holiness. No prob, says Unc, only too relieved to pass buck. Hiding out in Amsterdam. Jammy bastard. Popped wee scrawl through post box – hardly expecting a reply, never mind him turning up within matter of days. Y.t. still at poxy Riding School then.

Let's face it, Mum. Y.t. could not be fucked with iceberg moralising from you and Taff toyboy. OK? You did your duty by y.t. Or so you liked to think. Found a decent Riding School. (Did you really think that y.t. didn't twig that you found one as far away as poss? None good enough in Wales – had to be Surrey. Ha bloody – ha.) Did all the right things. Came down. Vetted place, etc. Yeah, yeah – more that H.G. ever did for you when you left the Heelands to come down to the Great Unknown of Harlow frigging New Town. So fucking what? Bought all gear; helped y.t. move in. Bottom line, you just couldn't wait to get rid of y.t. Been waiting sixteen fucking years, hadn't you?

Didn't need an A level in logic to work out that you'd prob'ly feel the same about y.t.'s bratski. Your idea of Hell Mk.11. Another little y.t. shoving oar in. Not that what you might feel enters into pic. 'Cos y.t. doesn't want bratski either. Adoption papers all at the ready. Middle-class pair of wankers waiting in the wings. Gawd only knows how she manages, but through ice-enamelled gnashers, A. Granite grinds.

'Why did you feel it was necessary to get in touch with him? After all that happened? How could you do it?'

Haven't you just been told, you stupid fucking bitch? No. No, you haven't. Only in thoughts. Not a word's been uttered by y.t. Mum might be clever, but she sure as hell ain't a mind-reader. Demure glance downwards allowing impossibly thick lashes to brush cheeks. Few murmured arsehole lies about being all alone in the world; having no-one to turn to; seeing dickhead Simon on telly, bla bla bla.

A. Granite still in shock. White round the gills with it. For fuck's sake – now she was asking y.t. was she sure about having spawn adopted! Had y.t. really thought it through. Christ almighty – there was nothing to think – zilch, man! The last thing y.t. wants is to be stuck with an effing bratski! Seen nothing – done nothing. Want to see some action. Travel. Not tied to snivelling sprog for rest of natural! (Didn't say any of that; not a poxy word. Just kept olive brow prettily furrowed and shook gleaming bonce a few times as though in deep shit with torment etc.)

Now Uncle Gav shoving his oar in! Not the only thing you'd like to shove in, given half a chance. Eh, Unc? What the fuck was he gibbering on about? He'd be willing to do all he could to help, financially and otherwise, if y.t. decided to keep sprog. Christalfuckingmighty – were they all ganging up, or what? Time to put effing cards on G-plan coffee table. Not because of money worries or any other worries, thank you all very much. Just don't want effing bratski. See? Boat-races drop in unison. Thank Christ – creepy Evie undulating across Axminster with offer of refreshments – refreshments for Chrissake! Shows in a word kind of super-shit y.t. having to put up with! Fair do's, the bitch had been cool enough to offer y.t. and bratski a permanent gaff after whelping. Christ – the thought of being stuck in Ercol Lodge with the cashmered and pearled Evie acting out frustrated maternal urges was too much, man! Wonder if it had been Mr Evelyn's idea? Stupid fucking bitch. If it wasn't for the dosh she was so eager to dish out, y.t. would like nothing better than to watch her boat-race as she observed the little titbits concerning her old man and what he liked doing to y.t. A suck or two (or three or four) of a milky tit and a fumble of a preggy cunt for a tenner; fifteen if he just *had* to stick a finger or two up. And twenty for bumhole and cunt at same time. Nice little earner, when all's said.

You'd love his holiness's new wife, A. Granite. Sweet, gentle, understanding, tolerant – oh so tolerant! In short, a complete wankress. A total effing walkover. This one believes anything and everything. But 'specially, she believes that the entire solar system shines out of his holiness's arse.

Frigging hard to credit that the prissy-faced little cunt sitting between A. Granite and P/C is anything to do with y.t. Never mind full-blown sis. Mummy's fucking little pet. Funny. She's got a good look of Unc dickhead Simon. Greeny, hazely peepers and same colour, or similar, hair. No. The bitch had got tawny hair. Long, thick, tawny hair. Tawny! It's light brown, for Chrissake! What's with fucking tawny, man? Ginnybitch the bitch is a looker. A thirteen year old bitch looker. Wonder if she's had anything shoved up her cunt yet? Should've done. If she remembers any of info y.t. obliged her with on cunts and how to get the best out of them, ha ha ha. Short of demonstration, she should know almost as much as y.t. Doesn't like y.t. Peepers tell all. Her and fat Rupe make a right pair of Mummy's arsehole-licking pets. Keep sneaking glances at y.t. when they think they're not seen.

Not Unc Gav. His glowing peepers are, and have been, since he sat down, araldited to y.t.'s tits. Ginnybitch casting quick little under-lash flicks of curiosity and – could it be? – admiration across at Big Sis. Y.t. looks and feels like a fucking goddess, man. Sleek and shining. Purring with self-love and pride. Pride in enormous belly, mesmerising tits, vivid scarlet gob gleaming as though lipstick living part of flesh. The fucking power of it all! Queen y.t. surrounded by slaves and adoring minions! All noshing out of whatever part of bod they found most scrummy!

All accept A. Granite, o' course. Nanouk of the frozen fucking North.

What about the father? Says fucking frozen-faced Nanouk?

What about the father? What about the fucking father? What fucking father? Want the unvarnished, do ya? Could have been one of a dozen. Thirty notes a fuck. Satisfied? They sure as hell were – ha ha ha. Y.t. didn't say any of that. Not a bleeding syllable. Said that didn't want father to know 'cos he already had family commitments. That sure as hell made A. Granite, a.k.a. Nanouk of the frozen-to-the-power-of-ten-North shut the fuck up.

Terrible weight on chest. Can't breathe. Weight lifting then pressing. Pressing up and down. Like sacks of fucking cement, man. Crushing poxy airways. Can't get frigging breath. Not in hossy, then. Still not in hossy. Pals not come to rescue. Some fucking pals!

Door open. Just stroll through. Lazy bunch of useless wankers. Can't even manage that. Noddle at bursting point with all this effing pumping and pressing and great surging throbs of blood slamming against skull trying to find means of escape through peepers and ear'oles. Christ man, what an effing smell – no, not smell. Stench. Like worst ever dog's breath come from years of noshing other dog's shit. Wafts of rotting gnashers cradled loosely in bed of pyorrhoea'd gums. Geroff for Chrissake! Y.t. on verge of major throw-up – hot stench-breath on neck; something gripping, squeezing, pressing.

Fucking chest about to burst – eager-beaver flames licking and curling round lungs – stench-breath gusting faster and faster. Weight on poor, crushed chest thumping up and down, up and down, faster and faster and faster. Trying to keep up with racing rancid breath. Y.t.'s being fucked, for Chrissake! And not by only the one punter, but a whole queue of the bastards! As one sweaty, spermy carcass prised itself out and off, another, clutching unzipped denim round dripping, curtseying cock, took over pumping and thumping. Gang-bang, man! Y.t. being gang-banged! Boarding school. Third form. Stoned out of skull. Wanted it. Enjoyed it. Six dudes. Including 'steady' Dunc. All pissed out of skulls. No one ever knew about it. Until. Put bit in diary. Big mistake. Mum found it. Found out about The Dream, too. No. No. No.

Pain everywhere. Molten rods, bars, pokers, knives searing up cunt into guts, ribs and gullet.

Tongues of psycho flame leaping and flicking through every

venous and arterial alley; lava pouring out of cunthole and running thickly down pins. Choking, acrid stench of bursting mattress. Fucking bed's on fire, man! Y.t.'s done for! Joan of fucking Arc'd by a killer bed! Pins raised and spread wide. Then narrowing and clenching to keep hold of thing that was eating cunt. Keep thighs clamped like vice – don't let it get away – keep in place – don't stop – don't stop . . . Lapping and sucking; stapling clit and sucking long and hard before zip-zap lapping both cunt and arsehole with huge, slapping tongue and vacuuming gob. Farts creating carefree staccato explosions at y.t.'s bod bucking and arching over brown boat-race welded to snatch.

Holy shit – was that a come, or was that a come, man! Best ever! Best ever, on y.t.'s scale – and that's saying one helluva lot, dudes. Camel's frigging tongue still lapping and sucking, lapping and sucking – leave off dildo! It's over – how was it for you – ha ha ha!

Not a frigging joke, man. Cunt shrieking for araldited, lapping flap of lifetime – guaranteed rubber to get the fuck off and get a life, for Chrissake! Cunt hurting for real, man. Bod writhing and corkscrewing to get free from burning armoury being shoved up holes – slicing and chopping as they're sucked slowly into bowels.

Rubber, camel's tongue and gob suddenly dislodged with drawn out slurping like rubber suction thingy for unblocking drains. What the fuck's the matter with you, you sick fuck? Trying to scream. Can't. Sick joke. Huge, naked noddle, thick, sausagey lips stretching wall to wall, phizog a huge, cheesy, glistening pizza, dripping red and gelatinous with cunt-juice and blood, emerging from between y.t.'s screaming pins.

Eaten! For Jesus effing Chrissake – y.t.'s being eaten alive, man!

Skull splitting open. Gunge oozing out. Spilling slowly onto mattress and lying lumpily, a thick broth, before creeping to edge of bed and sliding heavily over to form pool of reddish-grey jelly on the floor. For Chrissake stop. Please stop. Please, please stop. Emptying areas of skull filling up with deranged shrieking.

'You pig – you pig – you filthy rotten little pig – you pig pig pig – you stinking rotten pig . . .'

Sweet Jesus – Mum is really going to do for y.t. this time! In the back seat of the Morris. Y.t. and Ginnybitch. Mad bitch leaning across in front of Ginnybitch to reach cowering y.t. Battering skull to pulp. Ginnybitch crying Mummy, Mummy, Mummy and trying to put skinny arms round the crazed bitch. Y.t. doing utmost to fuse bod into back seat. Words struggling to squeeze through butterfly's wingbeat gaps in barrage of blows.

'It's only Mrs Jenkins – no one else knows – it's only Mrs Jenkins – why don't you listen . . .?'

Thank Christ, the bitch has left off pulping brainbox. How the fuck is y.t. supposed to get goo back into skull? All over the effing place, man.

No end to the shrieking. Voice hoarse and beginning to crack a tad though.

'You can't seriously think she's going to keep something like that to herself, do you? Do you? You pig of a fool. The first thing she'll do is tell the Headmaster – she'll have to. She couldn't accept the responsibility on her own. And he'll have to tell the other staff because he'll think it might have something to do with your bloody anti-social behaviour – you pig of a fool. And all to get out of being caught with a bloody fag in your hand. For what? The hundred-thousandth time, is it? Not a scrap of concern for anyone else. Just save your own stinking skin. You really had me fooled, Laura. I fell completely for your lying slimy spiel. Congratulations, you pig-faced little bitch. I hope you're satisfied with what you've done.'

Chill out Mum, for Chrissake! In effing car park in middle of Cambridge – dudes stopping and rubbernecking 'cos of your bleeding fog-horn.

What a pile o' shite – really blown it this time, y.t. If Mum not in front seat of Morris, y.t. could have ended up hossy case. Bitch meant business; OK, so y.t. had fucked up. What's new? So fucking what? What's done's done. No need to beat frigging brains out. Shit-boring business with ciggies had been going on since beginning of second year. Poxy staff had got wise to y.t.'s frequent trips to the San. Overdid things there, babe. Fat jolly nurse jolly no longer. Hardly spoke. Bitch. Y.t. couldn't bear to deprive Mum of regular supply of long, slender, white arrows. No. Not real reason.

Lots of freedom at school. Prats believed in letting kids discover potential through becoming part of community. School community, o' course. Learn moral values and such shit through constructive and co-operative involvement with others. Total heap o' shite. No dosh for ciggies. Borrowed from feeble first-formers. Bratskis with seriously loaded family. Loadsa pocket money. Never missed a few notes. Y.t. bought ciggies with borrowed dosh. Sold them back to bottom-of-the-heap first-formers. One ciggie per sell. Dead easy. Too easy. No big deal when nobbled. Lotsa serious chatties. Anything worrying you, dear? Bla bla bla. Ol' Ice-pick peepers only dude not wearing y.t.'s soft-soap. Didn't do anything much. Other than stop privileges; confine to dorm for afternoon. After repeat offences, suspension. Sent home for whole week. Big fucking drama.

Visits to Doc Medhill and putty-in-mitt Hump. Mum and Dad had to have meet with Ice-pick. Y.t. smiling and nodding and smirking. Bunch of wanking bastards. Started finding out how far staff prepared to let y.t. go before turning heavy. Left school grounds without permission. And out of school uniform. Oooh, how awful! 'Borrowing' wanking first-former's clothes. Without their permission. 'Borrowing' dosh and not paying it back. Then nicking the odd note or two. Suspected. But not caught. Smiling. Endlessly smiling. Told Mum once that H.G. had sent dosh. Bitch afraid to check, 'cos if a porkie then it was straight into 'Kill' mode.

Yes, y.t. was happy at school. No, y.t. didn't want to leave. (Who would – frigging walkover!) Got king-sized buzz ear'oling to all the shite spewing outa all the waffling gobs. Y.t. was this – y.t. was that – y.t. was the other – ha ha ha. Had them all disappearing up each other's anal sphincters at the end of it all. Loada useless effing wankers.

Towards end of second year y.t., an' a few pals, caught boozing in French student's gaff in centre of town. Suspended and sent home for couple o' weeks. Bad scene. Long, white arrows arriving even though y.t. not at school! See how Royal Mail concerned about your welfare, Mum? This one's from Ol' Ice-pick, requesting a meet. Mum so shit-scared almost throwing up. Convinced he's going to ask for y.t. to be removed from his poxy, ivy-covered red-brick heap.

Not Ol' Ice-pick. No way. Too much of a Mother Theresa. Concerned only with welfare of y.t. Why wasn't y.t. settling down? Why not responding to school environment? Community spirit – bla bla bla. Where had he and his staff gone wrong? Subject of school with more disciplinary ethos raised. Y.t. soon steered him back onto straight and narrow. Convinced him of sincerity of urgent desire to make amends and stay on at school as worthwhile and worthy participant in communal activities. Took a lot, but got there. Perhaps they, as parents, could try and find out the depth and extent of y.t.'s true feelings, says Ice-pick. Difficult, he knew. Under the circs. But they were all united in their concern for y.t.'s well-being and future, weren't they. Ha ha bleeding ha.

Big change in Mum. Shit scared of losing it. Nothing to say. All been said. Over and over and over. Could see each time she went to open gob. Small, silvery needle rising and coming to rest on matt black revolving disc. Surely not spooked by y.t., Mum?

Hell of a thingy, ain't it? To keep repeating the litany of contrition and ardent promises to change destructive into constructive (ha ha ha) and then when no more than a few days back at Ice-pick Manor achieve, with gobsmacking finesse, the exact opposite! Blow your mind or what? Like telling Mum that y.t. hardly ever sucked on a ciggie but was just unlucky to be fall guy when having occasional puff. When that one wore a tad threadbare, tried swearing blind not going to give into temptation. If some dude offered drag on evil weed, y.t. would simply refuse. Wasn't worth getting into all this hassle for something that y.t. didn't even enjoy. Bitch took it all in at the time, would you believe? Long, white arrows kept winging their elegant way across the Suffolk fields of Mustardseed and, last time, suspension for a whole week was punishment for being caught with lit weed in mitt.

Only a few days into summer term when most recent rectangle arrived. Follows that Mum's noddle done in a tad to read bald statement informing Mr & Mrs F that y.t. had been caught smoking, yet again, on the school premises. No mention of any punishment. No mention of meet with Ol' Ice-pick. Mum didn't contact school as fortnightly visit due on following Saturday. She'd got tickets for matinee performance of 'Private Lives'. Managed to keep gob shut all the way to Cambridge. Until the car park. Could see the bitch getting wound up. Reaching 'First Strike' mode.

'Cos she wasn't mouthing off, no other wanker uttering a syllable. Meaning Dad. Can't count Ginnybitch. Playing some weird game of her own. Prob'ly zapping the Nazgul. Mum sussed that y.t. couldn't/wouldn't lock peepers. Usually so shit hot to spike the bitch. Couldn't keep it in any longer. Couldn't face two hours of Noel surrounded by such a smog. Says, casual-like, that she and Daddy had been surprised to get a letter from the school saying that y.t. had been caught smoking yet again.

Stay cool, y.t. Stay cool.

We're even more surprised, she goes on, to see that you've not been given any punishment. After all, last time you were sent home for an entire week. For the very same offence. Keep peepers down and lip well buttoned for Chrissake. Still cool, Mum asks what reason was for no punishment. (Hoping, poor bitch, that y.t. might have suffered minor lapse that Ol' Ice-pick was willing to overlook just this once.)

Silence frigging electric, man. Let it go, bitch. Just let it go.

She's turning and asking why y.t. doesn't answer.

Can see phizog in car mirror. Dark red. Funny brown-y colour round peepers. Gob all tight and stitched. Doesn't look like y.t. Peepers wide, flat and staring. Can't handle it, man.

'Laura,' says Mum in a scarily calm voice, 'will you please answer me. And for God's sake look at me when I'm talking to you. Will you please tell me what's going on? Why are you looking at me like that? What on earth is the matter with you? This is bloody stupid . . .'

Turns to Dad for a bit o' moral. Big, dark, silent Dad.

As if key turned in back, y.t. galvanised into speech. Phizog deep crimson. Peepers like Herman Munster on a bad day. In clockwork-doll voice, blurts out that had to tell Mrs Jenkins about being worried and depressed over what had happened and not being able to sleep 'cos of thinking about it all the time.

Mum gazing bewildered-like at y.t. Worried and depressed about what? she says.

About the dream, Mummy. And y.t. cowers as far back as poss into the corner of the seat. For a few mos, the poor bitch looked as though she'd had a stroke. Deadly silence, before inside of Morris filled with horrible, sick-y crackling, like small brittle bones being snapped. Could almost see the spurts and flashes of juice firing out of her bod. The longer the silence. The greater the build up. Say something Mum, for Chrissake!

'You told Mrs Jenkins – you told Mrs Jenkins – you told her about a dream you'd had over three years ago – you told her that? You told her you'd been worried and depressed, after telling me only weeks ago that you never ever thought about it? That you'd forgotten all about it? How come, then, that you're so worried and depressed after three years of forgetting? How could you? How could you tell anyone? How could you do such a dreadful thing? Answer, damn you – answer – answer – answer!'

Totally uncool y.t., in quaky, clockwork-dolly squeak, stutters that it would have meant suspension again, but for a longer time – maybe a month – so said first thing that come into noddle. Thus began splitting open of y.t.'s brainbox by totally freaked out Mum. Could understand bitch losing cool.

Discovered y.t.'s diary when y.t. in France for fortnight. Mum had got job in local loony bin and used first month's salary to pay for student exchange trip. Not only reason for getting job. Bored shitless with Dad getting order of boot from job after job after job and forever whingeing about need to express himself as An Artist. Got right on Mum's tits, that did. Always wittering on about hidden Artistic Talent. Couldn't nail anything specific. Just knew it was there. Waiting to be unleashed. Ha ha ha. When she'd left him for Rog, he'd gone round loudmouthing about travelling world collecting shit to write book on History of Art. Fact that he never got further than local Magistrate's Courts fazed Dad nota jot. Now it seemed (at time of French trip) that wood was to be his true *métier*. What he'd been searching for all of his natural.

Last thing he ever expected was Mum to get her act together and call his bluff. Went out. Got job. And told him to use the saloon as a workshop. Gobsmacked weren't the word. Took him a week to get over the shock. Told Mum she'd never stick the job. Dream on, Dad! What he didn't know was that Mum had made up her mind to leave him as soon as Ginnybitch old enough to move up to Middle School. Another two years. Mum reckoned that by working, having first opus published and second on the way, she could get her noddle together enough to stand on own tootsies.

One of final straws was Dad losing job just before Christmas. Job that Mum had pleaded with him not to take. Couldn't even get any money from DHSS. Not till after Christmas. Y.t. had gone to stay with Big G for entire hols, thank Christ.

Second of final straws was, during Mum's last trip to Dykeland, Dad and a pal had nicked a Council van and – in attempt to fulfil frustrated attraction to wood as rightful Artistic Medium, ha ha ha – had loaded lorry with planks half-inched from local sawmill. When parking lorry full of purloined planks, in secluded spot at end of towpath, it had slid up to its sills into the ditch. Unable to free it, they had abandoned both lorry and wood. Theft never been linked to Dad and pal, but Mum had twigged 'cos of remark he'd let slip. Blown gaskets flying all over shop. Mum had it up to whatever with never-ending flow of bullshit.

Whilst y.t. in France, Big G had brought P/C to boat for Easter hols. Mum desperate to tell someone about second opus being accepted but could sooner have described a majorly brill crap than bring subject up with Big G. Never told anyone. Apart from Dad.

If it hadn't been for P/C, diary would have remained unread. Mum rooting around for dry jammies for him one evening and came across small book. Not hidden. Not in drawer. Didn't look in it straight off. Didn't even pick it up. Just let her mitt sort of rest on it. Then let it fall open. By itself. At random.

At a later time, she told Big G how her mind had cleanly split in two. With the one half hell bent on reading some of the entries whilst the other half crawled, gibbering, into the furthermost dark corner it could find. The gibbering lost the toss and she let her digits flick aimlessly through pages whilst robot peepers carried out the scanning process. Had no intention of reading entire diary. Let pages come to a rest at will. Only a small diary. Bit bigger than pocket size. First few entries mundane accounts of outings into town. Didn't say whether legit or not. Carried on flicking. Still unable to overcome distaste at actually picking up diary. Run of mill refs to staff and other inmates. Almost dizzy with relief, she told Big G, she was about to let the thing close (having no intention of deliberately searching for info) when small short word leapt out and smacked her right between peepers. Small, short word was 'hymen'. Mind fused back into one unit again. No part of it wanted to read what was in diary. Had to force peepers onto page. Force them to read rest of entry. Entry being operative word, ha ha ha. Spelling out how Dunc had used coupla digits to stretch and then break y.t.'s hymen. After which y.t. had gratefully jerked him off. Mum stayed cool over that little lot. Y.t. almost fourteen – thirteen and a half. But what the fuck.

Mum now compelled to turn pages and snoop for real. Wished to Christ she hadn't. Read about y.t. and gang-bang. Didn't believe it. Couldn't believe it. Fantasy. Had to be. How could such a thing happen at such a school? At any school? Remembered that Ol' Ice-pick had once said that not all pupils responded to general philosophy and lack of orthodox discipline. Some had been asked to leave, or were expelled, as a result of repeated anti-social behaviour. Some just didn't respond and were removed by parents.

In spite of these titbits of recalled info, Mum put diary entries down to y.t.'s fantasising. Reference to boozing and borrowing were OK. In the sense that she could believe. On the same page as one of the bits about booze and borrowing, was one short entry. Only the one line. Had to go over it a few times, didn't you Mum? And then some. Stayed down in cabin for much longer than intended. Deaf to bickering and squabbling of Ginnybitch and P/C. Stayed until Dad called you up into wheelhouse.

Had to stay sane through entire fortnight until y.t. came back from France. Poor bitch. Shouldn't have been such an effing snitch, shouldya? Pandora's and all that shit. Managed, somehow, to spills beans to Dad. Agreed with bits about booze and borrowing, but pooh-poohed the rest. Wanted so much to believe, didn't you Mum? More than anything else in the world, you wanted to believe. Dad said Dunc probably losing interest, so y.t. telling few porkies to try and wind him up. Grabbed at that one, Mum. Fair enough s'pose. Adolescent bitches well known to be fantasy prone. Done it yourself, so could understand. Nuked serious shit going on between older pal and straight dude by telling loadsa big fat porkies, didn't ya? All in poxy book. As if that made it OK. What mattered was that you would accept that y.t. was hanging out in Fantasyland.

After lotsa long, serious chatties, you and Dad agreed to see Ol' Ice-pick and tell him, or show him, what you'd found in y.t.'s little black book. For all he knew his school could be a regular frigging vice ring. Talked about seeing dickhead Hump and discussing possibility of y.t. going to more discipline-conscious school, where perimeters of what was considered to be acceptable/unacceptable behaviour more clear cut. Felt a lot better after that, didn't you Mum?

Could see it in your peepers when you and Dad came to meet y.t. at Victoria station. Full house o' fear bustling about. Fear of something going wrong. Desperate that nothing should go wrong. Desperation arm-wrestling fear. All in peepers. More than that this time, though. Something larger and darker. More serious. Made y.t. detached and cagey. Straight into defence mode. Monosyllabic answers to all questions about hols. Trying to sniff and feel way round effing minefield, man.

Situation saved/helped by Ginnybitch and P/C farting around like pair of juvenile dildos. Funny. Ginnybitch seemed pleased to see y.t.

Apart from stream of infantile drivel spewing from their gobs, conversation nil during endless drive home. Atmosphere as thick as shit. Didn't know what. But knew, whatever it was, would be a real bad scene. But it all ended up ace, didn't it? Didn't it? 'Cos it was only a dream wasn't it? Everyone agreed that it had been only a dream. Needed to be talked about. Brought out into the open. Aired. Well aired. But a dream. A bad dream. Maybe even a nightmare. But it hadn't really happened. Whatever it was.

Went walkies along towpath next morning. You and y.t. Early. Before leaving for Saffron Boredom and start of summer term. Right out of it, you were. Like a serious acid-head. Only your fix was hope. Not acid. Shouldn't have let it happen, Mum. All that pathetic shite about loving y.t. as much as Ginnybitch. Only differently. Repeat that one *ad infinitum*. Always good for a giggle.

Twittering like a demented tit in the warm, spring sunshine about regaining lost ground and phoenixes rising from effing ashes. Clutching y.t.'s arm and laughing like small drain. If only they'd (you and y.t. s'pose) been able to understand and accept this simple fact instead of behaving like each other's worst enemy! Constantly trying to make things different! Instead of working on and nurturing what they already had! It was all so simple! Watching you slowly burn crimson as you forced yourself to sandwich in a bit about y.t. not needing to mention dream to anyone at school. Even though little, black book had said that y.t. had told Dunc. Or was going to tell Dunc? No. Told Dunc.

Managed to get you to swallow shit about where got dosh for booze. Said y.t. and some fifth-formers put some pocket money into kitty each week to buy few bottles of cider. Cider being all they ever drunk – ha ha ha. Wanted so desperately to believe. Couldn't face thought that y.t. was nicking to further booze habit. Even though knew that y.t. had been banned from certain areas of school unless specific authority given. Like staff rooms and fifth and sixth-form dorms. All poxy pads that had anything worth half-inching, in fact.

Had to ask about gang-bang. Duty as responsible parent. Thought you'd chicken out. Managed, at last mo, to plaster suitable wide-peepered look of astonishment/hurt/disbelief on phizog before sounding off.

'That was written as a laugh, Mummy! Surely you didn't think – you didn't really think – honestly! How could you think – we all do it – write things in diaries – everyone in dorm – put things in to shock each other – even have competition at end of every week. Everyone reads everyone else's diary, you see . . . to see who's been able to shock the most! You should read some of the things some of the other girls put in – you'd never believe it. That anyone could write such things – when you see them. Who they are, and all that.'

Y.t. in complete command. Your phizog like naked sensor. Receiving, collating and interpreting all info on surface. Once satisfactorily computed, relaxed into flabby mask of relief. Could see where you were at. Thought it was The Dream that had made y.t. fuck up at boarding school. So you made it, The Dream, the focus for all the bad shit that had happened since. Couldn't stop you. Even if wanted to. Off you went, on self-propelled little roller coaster. Didn't want to stop you. Wanted to see where you were headed. How far you'd go. Didn't take long to find out, did it? Led you by the hooter all the way round the block and back again. Didn't mean to. Don't think so, anyway. Just went along with flow. And you sure as fuck were in full flow! Fucking flood warning should've been issued, man!

At least no more shit's been beaten outta poor old brainbox. Some dude musta come into room. Don't want to be caught in act. No. Not true. Not like that. Never like that. Once started, couldn't stop. Didn't matter how many dudes in room. Not in room. In poxy car park. In car, in car park. In Cambridge. Whatever happened to Noel? Did 'Private Lives' have four stiff, cardboard cut-outs perched in stalls? Silently shuffling wooden thoughts, like jigsaw pieces, behind plywood phizogs? Can't bleeding remember.

Something packed its bags and did a runner in you after that. Or died a death. Had to go and see Ol' Ice-pick. All on your ownio. Never got over it. All stuffing aqua-vacced right out. Never did get reupholstery job.

Gotta get a few scrawls off to his holiness. If one of effing deadbeats would come get them to do it. 'Cept most of them can't string two syllables together. Phone. That'd be better. Phone nick. Leave message. Saying y.t. totally freaked out after bad trip. That'd get his holiness on the move! Might even get whatsit leave for twenty four hours. No. No chance. Wind the old tosser up a bit, though.

Frigging lightbulb gone supernova – can feel heat blasting

down on phizog for Chrissake! Blazing through centre of noddle – burning hole through frigging lot – peepers sizzling like fried mushrooms. Can't turn away. Cast-iron strait-jacket. What the fuck's the matter with the poxy thing – covered in shit – how can it be nuking so much effing fall-out? Sizzling getting louder – peepers screaming in puddles of hot oil – close lids for Chrissake. Can't. Can't close peepers. Gotta keep staring at A-bomb poxy lightbulb. Sizzling and hissing. Y.t. frying. Frying alive. Fried peepers on toast coming up.

Not frying. Poxy sea hissing in ear'ole. Y.t. and his holiness lying on rug on beach. Side by frigging side. But not touching. Arms down at sides. Stiff. Like pair of fucking stiffs. Only peepers moving. Swivelling round and back again like brown castors. Y.t. wearing bikini. His holiness swimming shorts. Hairless. Forgot how hairless he was. Is. Poxy sun doing the frying. Why the fuck doesn't y.t. move? Get up and move bod out of nuclear blast. Casters fixed on something. Followed it around. Swivel. Swivel. Mum. Phizog like ghost. Stretched and grey and hollow.

I think I'll just take Dookie for a walk. Walks away. Turns and looks back at pair of wooden clothespeg dolls lying side by side on tartan frigging rug. Look of – what? What? What's y.t. supposed to say? What sort of words supposed to use? Ones like anguish? Pain? Bewilderment? Howzat for starters? Bollocks! What the fuck do words like that mean anyway. Fuck all. That's what. Convenience words. That's all.

Who the fuck's come into room? Can't effing see. Lightbulb still nuclear. Never did get a forty watt. Bod standing near side of bed. Not close. Fuzzy and foggy. Ring for Doc, for Chrissake man! Y.t. in some serious shit here. Some effing pal. Prize dickhead. All y.t. needs is a quick jab to take care of this effing allergy. Just a prick in the bum – ha ha ha, and it's business as usual! Heard that same sort of shit happens with peanuts. Peanuts! For Chrissake! Some guys have only gotto touch the poisonous little effers and they're in serious shit. Thank Christ – dude moving outta glare. Not looking at y.t. Looking to one side. Holy shit, man. It's Ricky. Can't be. How the fuck would Ricky suddenly turn up? How the fuck did you find y.t., sweet babe? Sweet Jesus – it must be five or six years since . . . It can't be. It isn't. What the fuck are you looking at babe? Why not delivering some action? Y.t.'s in deep shit, babe. Be cool, y.t. Stay cool. Don't let fuckers get one over. Stay cool. It's still Twilight-fucking-Zone-y time. Just chill out and wait till sicko time-hoppers gets rocks off again and leave y.t. alone.

Can't you bear to look at y.t. babe? What the fuck are your peepers araldited to, for Chrissake? Giving y.t. frigging heebies, man. Can't we talk, babe? About what happened? What's with freezing fucking ice-cubes all of a sudden? Fucking Arctic shifted half a hemisphere or what? Armies of creeping ice-insects carrying sackload of ice-cubes inching frozen all over bod. Dry, cold, husk-like crawling things. No. Not insects. Some punter's mitts creepy-crawling all over. Dry and fleshless and deathly.

Like cold, dead bones. For fuck's sake man – what's happened to the voddie? Can't take this sorta shit without a few swigs of old pal. Cold, wet, sucking thing. Cold spit dribbling and sliming way into gob. Get the voddie for Chrissake – can't take this – can't do this – can't do it without few more voddies – two or three voddies – one voddie!

Hard, dry rubbery thing forcing into cunt. Cunt as dry as a nun's. What the fuck is the sick bastard using? A truncheon? A baseball bat? A cricket bat? Getting harder and bigger. Searing its dry hunger along inner cunt sides. Ripping and peeling off layers of flesh. Lunging and gouging. Skinning y.t. alive from the inside, for Chrissake! Tits being clutched and kneaded like lumps of unwilling dough by dry reptilian claws. A tortoise, for Chrissake! A giant, desiccated, ancient-beyond-belief tortoise was fucking and rubbing its scaly, leathery carcass all over y.t.'s bod. No wonder Ricky standing gobsmacked and araldited to spot!

Only it wasn't a tortoise. Giant, or ancient, or otherwise. It wasn't an animated truncheon. Nor was it a scaly thingy from outer space that was skinning lining of y.t.'s cunt. It was his holiness. Y.t. was being fucked by his holiness. After being oiled and primed by liberal amounts of voddies. Bastards! Fucking sicko bastards! And Ricky standing. *Rigormortis*-ed. Staring, staring, staring.

Should never have let his holiness into flat. Big mistake. Biggest ever.

Been given order of boot by Ellen. Bitch too clean. Not into heavy shit.

Thought he would change ways. Seeing as he married her. Stupid dumb bitch.

Never saw Ricky again. Wouldn't even talk. Just packed gear and left forever. Had cool scene going. Had flat. Had job. Had dog. Had Norton. Had parents. Met parents. Liked them. Had asked y.t. to marry. Ricky had. Ricky babe.

Shouldn't have let his holiness in. Bottle of voddie and few joints. Last quickie. For old time's sake. Ricky home early. No more Ricky. Ever again. No Big G. No Ginnybitch. No H.G. No Mum. Not even A. Granite. Only his holiness. Y.t. and his holiness.

Darkness. Everywhere darkness. Maybe blind at last. Any fucking shit could happen. Not getting better. Y.t. not on mend. No fucker bothered if alive or snuffed it. Something wrong. Can't see; awful din. Terrible smell. Everything moving all of a sudden, for Chrissake! Lights whizzing past. String of shiny oranges on high, thin poles. Like Chinese lanterns – halloween pumpkins – or turnips – or oranges – what the fuck, man. Whizzing–whizzing. Could be out in fucking space. Maybe Twilight Zone-y dudes have taken y.t. on board! In space capsule. Out in frigging space!

All darkness again. Silent, except for rumbling drone of engine and vibration of wheels. On road. Not in space, then. Not with Twilight Zone dudes. Not in space capsule. In car. Poxy fucking car. Going at one mother of a speed, man. Who the fuck's at the wheel? Ginnybitch asleep. Noddle leaning on y.t.'s shoulder. Y.t. sitting stiff and straight as though coat-hanger between blades. Dark shapes in front seats. Dad at the wheel. Driving like fucking braindead dickhead. As usual. Mum not in tears. Makes a change. Not begging him to slow down. But stiff and silent as y.t.

Going to Twickers to stay with Big G. Mum taking y.t. away from his holiness. Shame. Y.t. big girl now. Can easily handle dudes like his holiness. No probs. Fourteen and a half. Tits shaping up nicely, thank you. Short, glossy hair. Bit of a fringe. Cheeky. Good-looking babe. Jailbait.

Business of y.t. and his holiness had come out in the wash that weekend, ha ha ha. Gotta laugh. Mum twigged whilst y.t. loud-mouthing in laundrette. All out in open. Well, not all. Nowhere near all. Hardly any, really. But enough to wind bitch right up own arse.

Bastards shouting again. No beat. No rap. No rock. Not even shite techno. Not mates, then. What effing mates? Y.t. all on effing ownio. No mates. None at all. All gone.

Mum shouting. Who the fuck else – goes without saying dinnit? Not shouting at y.t. Who then? Awful sound. Like animal in trap. Eating own pin to get free. Lightning bolts streaking into ceiling, shattering against walls. Sunbursts of pain falling in shards; small neons of agony scattering round room.

Hurling phone to floor as though cause of torment; screaming; then slumping onto knees. Scream demoting to croaky screeches. Then weeping. Kneeling, noddle on floor in front of knees. Weeping. Shaking as though palsied. Rocking. Clutching at arms, hair, pins – whatever. Like newly qualified loony showing off. Perhaps she's really crossed great divide? Finally made it, Mum?

Y.t. standing at top of stairs. Open plan effort. Twickers, then. Still at Big G's pad. Too shit scared to move. Darting sidelong peeks. Must have wound bitch right up. Didn't mean to. Force of effing habit, man.

'Where do you think you're going?'

Gnashing and wailing over. Cold dead voice.

'T-t-to the t-t-toilet, Mummy.' (For fuck's sake y.t. – is that squeak human or what?)

'For Jesus Christ's sake, child – can't you even come down to the toilet without behaving as though I'm going to sink an axe between your shoulder-blades – launch myself through the air and sink teeth into your neck – or maybe just cast an evil spell as you pass?'

Words belching an' steaming out of gob. Not like Mum's voice. In any mode. Harsh, grating, low-key screeching. Like no screech she'd ever screeched before.

Y.t. standing as though cryogen-ated. Looking good, babe. Gotta be said. Wearing virginal pinky, house-coat-y thingy. Not y.t.'s. Whose then?

The screechy grate, or gratey screech – yes, gratey screech, suddenly dropped a few octaves. Well, one or two, at least. Flat and lifeless. Dull monotone.

'Is there anything bothering you, Laura? Something you haven't told me about? Why don't you come down the stairs? Why are you standing there as though you're too frightened to move?' (Because y.t. *is* too frightened to move, you sick bitch.) 'I know there's things you haven't told me. And, whether they're bothering you or not, you'd better come down and tell Mummy what they are. For once and for all.'

Y.t. as red and pink and squirmy as lobster about to be dropped in pot. Actually squirming, for Chrissake! Don't want this shit. Don't need it. Had it up to here with this sick-fuck Twilighty Zone shite. Beam y.t. up Scottie! Ha ha ha. Sick of making funnies.

Sick of it. Sick of it all. Bunch of sick fucking weirdo bastards fucking about with y.t. Just want to go to kip. Nice, long kip. Wake up and all this bad shit'll be thingy of past. All y.t. needs. Nice, long kip. And no more of this sick Twilight Zone shit. Don't need this. Don't want to see it. Or hear it.

Y.t. still standing. Scarlet lobster mush and pink-y lobster shell squirming at top of stairs. Don't keep saying there's nothing more to tell, for fuck's sake! What a moron! All she needs – grist to mill – can see roots sprouting – 'me thinks the lady doth . . . bla bla.'

Screaming that she hadn't been born yesterday thank you very much – knew there was bloody well something else to come out of the can of worms – that y.t. didn't want her to know – could see it in stinking, lying, rotten, smirking face – hear it in stinking, lying, rotten voice.

Never seen y.t. look so mother-fucking ugly. Gob all twisted – peepers bulging – looking more like Dad by the bleeding mo, babe! Could at least have stayed cool enough just to *say* it. But no. Had to deliver it in sort of half-shout, half-spit. What a retard, man.

Blurt–blurt – 'He asked me to make him come!' – splurt–splurt – ha ha ha!

Peepers threatening to catapult over to radiator. Say something, Mum. For fuck's sake. Y.t. near enough pissing on stairs. Looking for mo as though wanting to reach out and touch y.t. Wanted to, but couldn't. 'Cos y.t. as red and distant and alien as Mars. Mo passed. As mos do.

'And did you? Did you?'

Trust bitch to come right out with it. Can feel peepers sliding and slithering trying to find way out. Shouting. (Wrong move, babe. Wrong move.) Cauldron of seething, boiling, bubbling H_2O coming closer and closer to lobster y.t.

'Of course not – of course not! How on earth could you even think such a thing, Mummy?'

'I haven't got a fucking clue, Laura,' (the F-word from Mum. Worst shit ever.) 'other than I know damn well that you're nowhere near as innocent as you're trying so very hard to make out – you *have* done it to him, haven't you? Haven't you? Answer me – answer me damn you – damn you to hell you filthy little bitch – you jerked him off – you jerked him off and you enjoyed it – didn't you – didn't you – didn't you – answer me – answer

174

me – his prick was a hell of a lot bigger than that stupid little twerp Duncan's, wasn't it? Wasn't it? Wasn't it, you filthy dirty little fucking bitch! Fucking – fucking filthy bitch!'

Lobster blubbering at top of stairs. Phizog awash with downpour. What a total nerd. Shouting again. Do no good, babe. Never change the bitch's mind now. If ever.

'It's all lies – it's all lies – didn't do it – hadn't done it – he asked – he kept asking – that's all – knew it was wrong – didn't do it – felt sick . . .'

'Get out of my sight, you filthy lying bitch – I hate you – I hate you – I hate you . . .'

No point in lobster going to loo. Pissed all over stairs. Just as well. Too fucking scared to pass the bitch. Good job stairs open plan. Noddle in hands; in weeping mode again.

Seems it's over for now, thank the fuck. Definitely can't handle this, Jim. Feeling tad sorry for the poor bitch. Had started off not too bad. Been Mum's birthday, day after they'd got to Big G's. Big G and bratskis off to Taff cottage for Easter hols. Told Mum that she and sprogs could stay there, Taff cottage, as long as they wanted after hols.

Brill first evening. Mum and Big G huddled under duvet up against radiator. After few jars of Elderflower, Mum all over y.t. like fungi. Big G on high. Huge peepers brimming with excess of elderflower and thrill at seeing y.t.'s new-found togetherness with Mum. Only wish in life that they'd be the same when she got back from Taffland. Gold outta dross, gold outta dross, she kept muttering into elderflower dregs.

Next day Mum's birthday. Y.t. and Ginnybitch spent whole morning baking, even though cupboards, as usual, practically empty, thanks to Old man of Oz. Y.t. made cake like square slab of rock. Rock as in stone. Texture as well as appearance. All of them laughing like drains as y.t. trying to cut into slices. Y.t. also made custardy sort of tarty thing. Edible, thank Christ. Ginnybitch made some biscuits. Supposed to be biscuits, but more like pebbly babies of y.t.'s effing stone-cake! Hell of a thing.

Best birthday ever. Big G and bratskis came back in middle of it all. Didn't get as far as Taff cottage as car broke down on motorway. Old man of Oz gone back to nice, warm state-of-art studio. Natch. Second evening spent huddled under duvet, cuddling each other and radiator, watching daft weepy on goggle-box. Sniffling into duvet like pair of over-sized retards.

Turned to mindless giggling as they caught bratskis giving sidelongs. Stupid bitches couldn't stop shrieking. Tears streaming. Paralytic. Never seen anything like it. Mum and old Dyke used to be the same. Couldn't understand it.

Later on, Mum rat-arsed on elderflower, nettle, dandelion and any other old piss that happened to by lying around. Frightened shit out of bratskis. Smashed glasses and bottles. Verbally abused Big G's pals that had turned up and totally pissed off Big G. After driving everyone away, beating table with fists and noddle. Screaming at Big G to tell her why y.t. hated her so much; that she was useless as a mother, a woman and a person. Bottom of the barrel. Deserved to die – bla bla bla. No-one loved her. *Ergo*, no-one cared if she lived or died. Even her own mother hated her. And if *she* hated her, how in God's name could anyone else care? There must be something really rotten in her if her own mother hadn't wanted her, mustn't there? Three years old – three bloody years old – could Gina imagine it? Yes – but could she *really* imagine it? Leaving a three year old child – she must have been the most vile and hideous three year old in the entire universe for her mother to want to – no, to *have* to leave her. Mustn't she? Mustn't she. Shouting, bawling, weeping, banging, thumping . . .

For Chrissake, Mum. All those hairy old chestnuts. Repeating same boring old shit over and over and over again – banging table until legs looking decidedly dodgy. No wonder Big G suddenly got up saying she'd bloody well had enough shit for one frigging night. Scraped chair back so hard it fell on floor. Slammed out of house. Phizog like thunderous cloud. Happy now, Mum? Not content with pissing everyone else off, you've managed to piss off the unpissable Big G. If she can't be fucked with your self-pitying whingeing, then who the fuck can? Nothing for it but to give the Samaritans a tinkle. That's what the fuckers are there for. To lend an ear to deadbeat, end of the road, no-hopers like you spilling their pathetic guts into a lump of coloured plastic.

Phizog tight and sort of prickly. Job opening peepers. Ice-cold and gritty. Like thinly covered with layer of frost. Breathing hurts. Nose and throat burning. Sucking in hot ash. Tearing lining from nasal passages and gullet. Tongue glued to roof of gob for so long. Got used to it. Forgotten ever had tongue. Swallowing bit of an effort. Lava running down back of throat. Sizzling round small daggers of hot steel bristling in gob and gullet. Sleep. Just want to sleep. More than anything ever. Be all right after decent kip. Lot of the trouble. Reason for deep shit. No proper kip. What the fuck's point of it all? Hadda bit of a giggle. Hadda bit of a blub. OK. So y.t.'s done a lot of uncool shit.

Shame about Big G. Real downer. 'Nough's enough, all the same. Keeping y.t. from having decent bit o' shuteye. 'S all that's needed. Good long kip. Chest burning too. All way down. Lava pouring down back of nose into throat, down gullet and filling lungs. Should be going straight into gut. But stopping at chest instead. Filling up poxy chest.

It's snowing. Big soft, huge soap flakes making thick, creamy foam on ground. Not foam. Crisp. How can foam be crisp, dickhead? Meringue. Meringue is. Crispy on top and foamy underneath. Meringues drifting slowly down from seagull sky. Not meringues. Not whole meringues. Meringue flakes. Ha ha ha. Ginnybitch and retard Frodo running around in yummy meringue. Some dickhead sawing logs. Bloody great branch sticking outta side of makeshift sawhorse. Sawing away as though no frigging tomorrow. Stopping for breather.

What a dickhead! Y.t. Dickhead is y.t. Y.t. sawing fucking great trees. Branches, anyway. Where? Where the fuck are they? Middle of fucking winter. Still as death. Silent as death. Except for distant bleating of poxy sheep. A lot of sheep. Taffland. Where else? They'd left Twickers and come to Taff cottage. Ginnybitch carrying logs inside. No wonder throat and chest on frigging fire! All this sawing graft knee-deep in effing meringue.

Y.t. not used to pulling digit out. So frigging cold – icicles hanging from roof. April – for Chrissake! More like midwinter! So they'd made it to Taff cottage. Big G had driven the mini. Dad had left it – Mum's car anyway, bought it with proceeds from Opus – and had hitched back to Suffolk. Not long passed test. Too shit scared to drive on ownio. Too shit scared to drive at all. Wanted to be independent. Whole reason for learning to drive in first place. Couldn't get it together to do it alone.

Big G nightmare fucking driver. Crashed gears all the time. Kept losing cool. Cursed. Swore. Took Heathrow turning. Wouldn't listen to Mum. On verge of turning back to Twickers. Mum started snivelling. Journey to Carmarthen in dead silence. Except for Big G cursing at Dookie and Frodo. 'Specially Frodo. 'Cos he bit her on the ankle. Didn't matter that she'd almost

177

flattened the poor sod with her ruddy great plates and he thought he was fighting for his pathetic Corgi life.

Two mogs. Ashpit Anna and Baby. Sack o' wheat an' frigging grinder for fuck's sake! Nearly left without Baby. No wonder Big G in such shit mood. P/C had let Baby out in wee small hours. Mum refused to leave without witless tabby. Everyone creeping around neighbours' back gardens at four o'clock in the morning whispering, 'Baby, Baby'. Found her in the end. Big G already in foul mood. Didn't get any better. She and Mum not speaking by time reached Taff cottage. Took huge, scrummy brunch and couple of bottles of vino before Big G returned to normal. Fair do's. She hated driving too.

Stayed the night. Then Mum had to drive to Carmarthen the following morning for Big G to catch coach back to London. Then drive alone back to Taff cottage. First time. Two weeks later, drove to London. Then to Saffron Walden. Then all the way back to Taffland. Never looked back after. Never liked driving, though. Hated every mo.

Y.t. stacking cut logs. Like scene from effing Christmas card, man. Filigreed trees swathed in spun candy and dusted with icing sugar. Snap off a twig or two and have a good suck! Sky a pig-sicking peach and rassy sorbet with smudged slivers of vanilla, angelica and orange peel pasted on horizon. Pig-sicking ain't the word for it. Meringue-covered earth glittering and winking responses to flashing of secret messages from cold, metallic gee-gaws pulsing in smoothness of china/turning to cornflower/turning to violet/turning to indigo blue sky. Could be stars. Could be UFOs. Each meringue flake drifting down to join others on earth's surface could be a miniature UFO. Like swarm of bees. Each one useless on its own unless acting on behalf of its community. But taken all together . . . Different scene, man. Possible that Earth being taken over by layer of meringue – ha ha ha.

Strange buzzing in centre of chest. Phizog glowing like effing beacon. Chieftain apples for cheeks; large rose-hip for hooter. Could be a small crimson, crab-apple. Hard to tell. Peepers gleaming as though just been Mr Sheened. O, sallow, milksop moon, keep your custardy mush turned well away, else risk a nuking, total eclipse by radiant supernova of y.t.'s phizog! Y.t. was happy, for Chrissake! Buzzing, throbbing, pulsing, vibrating 'cos of being so motherfucking happy! Burst into effing song any mo if not careful! Can't remember ever feeling such a buzz without a tad o' substance assistance!

Want it to last forever. Keep throbby buzz inside chest. Tether it – wrap it up – put it in box – carrier bag – anything. Just keep hold of it. Only thing that matters. Only thing that exists. That and the sunset. And the meringue snow. And the sawhorse and logs. And Taff cottage. All bundled up with y.t.'s happiness buzz. No more bad. All wiped out. No more his holiness. Especially his holiness. Nuked, eclipsed, wiped out. Like flabby, cheesy, paper-thin, secondary moon. Y.t. picking up sawn logs and carrying them into cottage. Blazing fire in funny old range. Hurricane lamps. Big black kettle hissing steam.

Mum sitting in armchair by fire. Not moving. Not reading. Not anything. Just staring. Cup o' tea, Mum? Looks up slowly. Nods slowly. Doesn't smile. Peepers flat and dull. Dull, red-veined pebbles. Lids pink and puffy. Phizog a right mess. Hair ditto. Been in stupor ever since Big G left. Came back from Carmarthen and caved in. Or under. Or whatever. Being snowed in didn't help. Maybe. Maybe not. Couldn't get Mini up steep hill on either side of cottage. Trapped in valley. Trapped in heaven. Old, damp, smelly Taff cottage like warm, musty nest. Cocoon. Hidey-hole. Never wanted to leave. Stay in nest forever. Just Mum, Ginnybitch and y.t. And mogs and stupid, braindead mutts, o' course.

Didn't last. Couldn't. Y.t. back to Saffron Walden after Easter hols. Only for half a term. Mum shit scared that his holiness would get hold of y.t. Ice-pick knew all about everything. Arranged meet with Mum after Easter.

Y.t. and Ginnybitch played housies in cottage. No electricity. No water. Tap on wall over by old vicarage. Y.t. fetched big cans full. Boiled it on range. Wanted to wave wand. Stop time dead in tracks. No more school. No more his holiness. Happy never to set peeper on him every again. Then.

Read out loud to Mum to try and break the spell. Y.t. and Ginnybitch took turns, though Ginnybitch bored with few efforts Big G had left in cottage for sake of visitors. Found a coupla Agatha Christie's. Thought they might create spark of interest. Non-starter. Made up stories to try and get a reaction. Brushed her hair. Started getting shit scared. Thought would have to get Doc in. Started coming round after eight whole days. Knew she was going to be OK when she started brushing dickhead Dookie.

Ice-pick not at all chuffed at Mum taking y.t. away from school. Even though living in faraway Taffland. Even after business with his holiness. Said he could handle it, as could rest of his staff. Been playing it cool after contents of little black book had become part of fucking syllabus. Major meet after y.t. had loud-mouthed to Ma Jenkins. Mum had been right about that. Old bitch had told Ice-pick within few mos. About everything. But mostly about the Dream.

Didn't cut much ice with ol' Ice-pick. Wiped floor with y.t. in front of Mum. Said he and rest of staff totally pissed off with y.t. winding everyone, pupils and staff, round pinky. Didn't put it like that, o' course. Said y.t. manipulated everyone who came within range. Didn't respond to any attempts to understand aberrant behaviour. Offers of help, friendship, kindness, sympathy – other than what she managed to inveigle for Sanatorium – all thrown back in donor's faces. She lied blatantly and unnecessarily.

Had stood in front of him, aware that he could see the nicotine stains on her finger, stared him straight in the eye and denied ever having smoked a cigarette. Impervious to any type of punishment as meted out by the school. Loss of privilege; loss of pocket-money; fines; having to carry out tasks and chores; being confined to her room; being denied access to the common room; deprived of company of other pupils during free time; being sent home under suspension. Nothing worked. Absolutely nothing. Y.t. was, he said, socially and sexually promiscuous and he felt, as did the other staff involved, that he was completely wasting his time. Y.t. did not, in any way, wish to be part of the school community and he felt that, after her departure, there would be no impression left on her of the three years she'd spent at this school. Poor ol' Ice-pick! Believed in y.t. didn't you, you daft old tosser. Mum asked did he want her to remove y.t. from school. Gobsmacked when he said No. Why, says Mum. Because she's only got two years to go and we'll probably be able to scrape her through with a few passes at CSE.

Not because she's not capable of O levels but because she simply refuses to do any work. Turns up for lessons minus text-books or equipment, thus ensuring that she'd have to sit out during the lesson. Mum asked him, if y.t. was so awful, why did he want her in his school? Because, said Ice-pick, he and his staff knew her well, were able to cope because they knew exactly what to expect and were well prepared. Should she go to another school, the staff would have to start from scratch, just as he and his colleagues had three years ago. Completely in the dark. In his opinion, it wouldn't be fair on either y.t. or the staff at another school, to inflict such a fate. At least here, she was known fairly

180

well. Though it had taken three years to reach such a stage. But they were quite at liberty to try Laura at another school if they so wished.

No way, said Mum. And what did Dad say? No frigging idea. Agreed with Mum, most like. All he ever did. All that shit had happened a few weeks after the outing of the Dream. Didn't make any difference to Ice-pick. The Dream. Almost as if he'd known about it all along.

After Easter hols, Mum dropped Ginnybitch off at Twickers and drove y.t. back to school. Told Ice-pick she wanted y.t. to be with her and Ginnybitch. Chance for a new start. Might just surprise them all. Ice-pick told her she was making a big mistake. But big. Y.t. would never change. Incapable of it. Would end up manipulating her in the same way she'd manipulated, and was still manipulating, everyone who came within her sights. Shrewd old fucker, Ice-pick. Didn't budge Mum, though. Laura deserves the chance, she kept repeating. So what happened to it? What happened to the chance, y.t.? What had y.t. done with it? Would have been all right if could have stayed trapped in Taff cottage. Fetching, dragging wood across snowy fields and sawing, sawing to fill bottomless pit of greedy old range. Walking three miles to local shop for goodies. Bus to Carmarthen once a week. Couldn't be like that. Only for the few days. No more than a few days. Dosh a bit of a major prob. Only had family allowance. Dad told DHSS that Mum had income from writing. Lying bastard. Sat in office of Friday afternoon refusing to shift until given some dosh for weekend. Penniless. Ended up giving Mum £3. Enough for bread, spuds, baked beans, dog and mog food, etc. Only for the weekend. Had to go back and sort it all out on Monday. Could understand Dad wanting to shit on Mum, but why take it out on bratskis?

Would have been better never to have had two weeks trapped in Taff cottage. Like tasting a dream. A proper dream. A beautiful dream. The nearest lick, suck, gob-wetting taste of how things could/should/might/ought to be, before having it snatched away. Makes sense. 'Cos it could never be more than a dream. Could never be the truth. But it *had* been the truth! Only for a few weeks. No. Not even a few. Only until Mum took y.t. back to Saffron Walden. A few days, then. Ten, at most.

Would've got bored shitless before long anyway. Stupid bitch couldn't lift digit to help herself. Wanted pair of effing handmaidens. Tears in peepers 'cos y.t. and Ginnybitch best of mates. Working together. Playing together. In perfect ha-a-r-mo-ny. Ha ha. Already bored, tell the truth. Glad to get back to poxy Suffering Boredom. Bored shitless, but different sort of pissed-offness. Plenty booze and fags and fucking to keep grey matter off crucifyingly boring shitlessness. Funny. Never wanted a fag, never mind a fuck, at Taff cottage. Never gave either as much as a passing thought.

Will have to get one of mates to drop few scrawls to his holiness. Said that already. Saying it again. Don't want old tosser losing his cool. How effing long has y.t. been out of it, man? Hours? Days? Can't even tell what time of day. Fucking lightbulb nuked again. All dark. Nothing seeping through 'blinds' ha ha. Blinds being word of the mo. Hiccup, 's all. One of short-term effects of dirty E.

What to say to his holiness? Never much to say on effing visits never mind a poxy script. Put a loada dirty stuff in, s'pose. Keep the old bastard happy. Get pissed off. Putting it bleeding mildly. Well tanked up before going to nick. Same old story. Y.t.'s mush split by big grin. Feel it splitting – splitting. Gob falling apart in two pieces. Top piece ready to fall off and bounce along floor. Couldn't face it without tankful of voddie. Never admitted it before. All y.t.'s got. Throw everything away for his effing holiness. Not true. Didn't chuck Ricky in. Ricky threw y.t. over. Over and out. Shouldn't 've done it. Shouldn't 've fucked his holiness one more time. Voddies again, see? Got a lot to answer for, have voddies. Ricky knew all about his holiness. Had told him the lot. Ellen and his holiness and Amsterdam. Mum and Ginnybitch. And Liane. Ghost dragging sackful of ice walking across bed.

Don't want this – don't want it. Can't handle it. Take it away – for Chrissake take it away.

Wonder if she looks like y.t.? Had dark, fuzzy down covering tiny scalp when born. 7lb 6oz. Grizzling, frizzled little scrap. Prune II. Eh, Hester? You'd have fallen, you daft old dyke. Wanted her but didn't want her. Didn't want her more than wanted. How old now, Liane? Must be getting on for twelve. Twelve sometime in September. Next frigging month innit? When in September? Can't effing remember. Been shagged yet, babe? ha ha ha. Not funny. Didn't mean it. Why say it? Won't have been. Not Liane. Y.t. sure could have shown her how! Not much cop if anything like po-arsed Ginnybitch. Far better off without y.t. Would never have got it together. Even if helped. H.G. would have done her bit. As would Nanouk of the North. And Uncle Gav would have got his rocks off on a regular basis watching y.t. shove tit in sprog's gob. Small price to pay, eh? Never would've worked. Never would've got it together. Knew from the start. Knew it when clutching warm, squirming, toasty little bod and feeling hungry, toothless, limpet gob vacuum milk out of swollen, groaning, feast of a tit. Amazing sensation. Like brill come. Only deep, deep, deeper, as though attached to some secret, special place. The Sleeping Beauty of the nervous system; woken, not by a prince's kiss, but by the vacuuming gob of a new-born sprog!

Kid would have been a non-starter if stayed with y.t. Why? Wanted life. Wanted freedom. That's why. And got? What did y.t. get? His holiness, that's what. His fucking holiness. All that's left. Out of everything. His holiness and y.t. No one and nothing else.

Can't face it. Can't face visit. Not another visit. Not any more. Never too late to mend fences – bridges – whatever shit needs mending. Got plenty time. Go about it the right way, man. Not like last time. BIG MISTAKE. Should've written proper letter. Not sent whingeing arsewipe. Could understand why no reply. Then phoned. Got hold of Taff Toyboy. BIG MISTAKE No 2. Told y.t. stop pestering Mum. Leave to live own life. Didn't know then – y.t. didn't know that his holiness had not long since turned up on Taff doorstep, blubbering about y.t. being in hossy in Amsterdam and needing Mum to mop fevered brow, ha ha ha. Bastard only wanted shot of hassle and having to pay hossy bills. Tried passing buck. Give wanker credit – hell of a fucking nerve. Suitcase 'n all. Thought he'd be asked to stay the night. T. Toyboy sent him off with flea in ear'ole. Told him y.t. had made choice and there was no way they were going to clean up shit.

Could see why Taff T. losing cool. Y.t. had promised never to give address. Should've known better, Mum. Should've known never to trust y.t. Been told often enough. Didn't mean to. Just slipped out after few voddies. This time though, thingies could really be different. Y.t.'s had one big shite of a fright, man. No more dope. That's for sure. Promise. Maybe the odd joint – no harm in that for Chrissake. But strictly no shit. Absolute promise.

Will even consider taking pledge on voddies. See how it goes, eh? No need to go all the frigging way. Not all at once. Never too late to turn over new leaf, Mum. Even put it in writing. Draw up contract, ha ha ha. Couldn't tell his holiness where you are now. Even if wanted to. 'Cos don't fucking know. Dudes in old house gave phone number but wouldn't give address. Said you'd made them promise not to. Even to own daughter. Especially to own daughter. Did you know that his holiness had hired a gumshoe? Bet you never. Not for long. Couldn't afford the dosh. All gone on y.t.'s hossy bills.

Will have to stop seeing his holiness before coming within hundred miles – not only seeing. Any contact at all. Not on. Y.t. knows that. How will *you* know, Mum? How will y.t. be able to prove it? Few more years in nick for old tosser. Must be more to effing life than these poxy never-ending visits, man. Can't stand any more. Won't go. Let bastard stew. Like he let y.t. stew. In loony bin. Things're different now though. Nothing left. Nothing fucking left. Only his holiness. Needs y.t. Always needed y.t. Always said so. Over and over. Right from start. Can't let the old wanker down. Not after everything – too much lost. Only thing to show. His holiness. Can miss a couple of visits. Need a break. Can't face it. Same old shite. Over and over.

Few gobs of bullshite hover for a few mos in cancerous air before peepers begin agitating like flat, dark buttons tap-tapping on glass door of washing machine begging to be let out. We're not supposed to be in here – we just happened to be attached to trousers/cardie/jersey – let us out – please let us out!

Sick or what? For Chrissake – let's get it over and done with.

Mitt down inside jeans. Hope cunt not too dry. Depends what's happened on way to nick. Can hardly ferry fingerful o' spit in case one of screws rubbernecking. If lucky, might work up to real come. Small. Very small. But real. If not, just act out usual dance of the peepers, fast-breathing shit. Old fuck can never tell the difference.

If desperate, mitt starts jiggling around in pocket before y.t. done. If not, pass warm sticky (hopefully) digits across table. Good long sniff – maybe crafty lick if screws having a quick kip. Good job old tosser doesn't know where else y.t.'s mitts might've been on way to nick! Let's face it – wouldn't make any effing difference. Then he's on the off. Got it down to a fine art. The silent art of wanking. The art of silent wanking. Kleenex bunched at the ready to transfer mitts at last mo. Only reason for y.t.'s visit. Like poxy religion. Had to pretend to believe. Hated what they were doing. Hated it. Hated the things he said. Got y.t. to say. Rub by rub account of what was going on as poor old clit was tweaked and kneaded half to death whilst back of mitt almost gouged in half by bleeding zipper. Describe being shagged. In detail. Down to every ooze and drip. Hadn't been too bad at first. Bit of a laugh and, gotta admit, bit of a turn-on. Doing it under peepers of dozy screws and moron visitors. Stopped being a laugh, after a while. Turned into duty. Always the same. Didn't matter what was happening to y.t. Outside. Or inside. All he wanted was sniff of cunt-rubbed digits and plenty o' Kleenex. Only reason for wanting y.t. to visit. Talking about it. Talking about doing it. What he wanted to do. What he'd do when he got out. To y.t. Knew it was tough doing porridge. Must be something else in life, though. Perhaps should come clean with old wanker. The come bit, yeah. The clean bit – no way. Too effing tanked-up to do anything other than the necessary. What else was there, anyway. All gone. All gone 'cos of his holiness. All y.t.'s fault. Almost all. Voddies as well. Voddies had a lot to answer for.

Wish to Christ noddle would stop feeling like fucking ice-box. Pains in chest again. No. Not again. Never went away. Just eased up a tad. Cold and burny right through to marrow. How? Molten ice. That's how. Hurts to breathe. Don't breath. Don't breathe then. Dickhead. Only taking little ones. Doesn't hurt so much. Nose on fire. Can almost see flames licking out of nostrils. Funny word, nostrils. Why not noseholes? Both shit moron words.

Peepers burning as well. Little dude with flame gun jumping around behind each peeper. One in throat and up behind nose. Ambush job. Whole effing army of mannikin flame throwers. Slurpy, bubbly feeling in chest. Rattling. Things rattling in chest. Some sort of guerrilla warfare. Poxy mannikins chucking hand grenades, as well as flame throwers. Mannikin-sized grenades making small explosions in chest. Inside chest. Explosions creating volcanoes; into each bronchia and bronchiole to lie, seething, in pools of moltenness.

Lungs, gullet, ribs – everything encased in chest cavity (Heart? Heart, too?) melting and dissolving to meld with simmering lava. Chest becoming a container, an urn, a pot, a saucepan, for gallons and gallons and gallons of bubbling, lapping lava.

Hairy, dark, thick pillars jostling each other to flounce the weird, tiered, green gear swaying about on their noddles. Trees, man.

185

Fucking great forest of them! Blasted space in front. Looks like place's been nuked. Trunks and branches scattered all over. Some charred and blackened. Like the earth. Couldn't really have been bombed – could it? Guerrilla-type dude standing on edge of outcrop. Where the fuck is this, Jim? No time marks to give y.t. a clue. Too effing nippy for Nicaragua, ha ha ha. Dude looks like poxy IRA – maybe did the nuking! Practise range or whatever. Wearing combat green gear. Boots and black beret. Not IRA. Balaclavas, not berets. Would have shooter if IRA.

What the fuck is dude doing. Bending and lifting. Chucking great cabers from top of outcrop to nuked land below. Tits bouncing under army-type jersey. Mother of all dykes, for Chrissake! Surely not y.t.! Can't be – looks like a bloke! Eat your heart out, Hester!

No wonder frigging chest rattling and bubbling – y.t. hurling effing tree trunks off bank! Can hear voices – laughter. Can't see poxy thing other than y.t. doing an Arnie. Have a gander round then, daft bitch. There's the old Bedford van – what a frigging wreck! Ginnybitch bumbling around at the back of it. Knew it was Ginnybitch 'cos of the hair. Tawny. Long, thick, tawny fucking hair. Grown up. Must be sixteen or seventeen. Last time y.t. saw either Mum or Ginnybitch. Christmas. Eight years ago. Or was it nine? Nine. It was nine. Major fuck-up there, babe. Only came 'cos nowhere else to go. Kicked out of frigging Ibiza – Ibiza, for fuck's sake! Fucking dregs, man! Some trumped up shit about vagrancy or something. Only trying to turn a trick or two. Fucking tourists.

Went straight to his holiness, natch. In Amsterdam. And what did y.t. get? Order of the effing boot, that's what. New effing rules, according to Her Royal Ellen. Visitors not allowed to stay longer than a frigging week – pair of snot-rags. All Ellen, o' course. His holiness desperate to get his dick in where it felt nice an' cosy. Couldn't blame the poor bitch. Never been the same since finding his holiness and y.t. playing at doggies. So y.t. had no choice but to head for fastnesses of North frigging Wales. Had to do knee-trembler to get dosh for coach fare from Victoria. Christmas Eve and both bitches nursing serious hangovers after bingeing on home-made barley wine the night before. Only supposed to be 4%. Turned out more like 14. No nosh in house. Other than basics. By the time they dragged themselves upright and into Caernarfon all the pissing shops were closed. Christmas fucking Eve, wasn't it? Didn't seem fazed. If hadn't known otherwise, would've had them down as serious acid-heads. Idea of a wild time was to spend day in forest logging great fucking trees. Still the same as ever, Mum was. Bent on getting rocks off on Great Outdoors. All that poxy crisp Christmas air. Endless frigging vistas of frigging forests and frigging mountains. Main-man Yr Wyddfa no more than a glowering half-mile away, looming and leering like a dirty old man desperate for a wank.

Really doing noddle in. Doing everything in. Every poxy breath drawing in gobfuls of ice-needles, splintering and jagging bastard way into throat and up hooter. Like ice-armoured sperm, viciously thrashing up into peepers, slicing and slashing at everything in the frantic need to reach goal. Not womb, but brainbox. Not to fertilise, but to kill. Prick, puncture and destroy every little brain cell. Thousands, millions, zillions of icy little terminators swarming their murderous way through y.t.'s phizog and skull. Dissolving though, before delivering death jab. Dissolving in pool of lava and wafting back into Antarctica as poofta puffs of carbon dioxide.

Y.t. had to split logs to get a bit o' warmth flowing through tubes. Split logs, man! Their idea of life in the fast lane? Rice 'n lentil burger thingies cooked on a primus in the back of the Bedford. Serious head cases. All three of them. T. Toyboy paid for rights to fallen and damaged trees in bit of forest. OK. So their fuel bill for entire winter was about a tenner. But at what other cost, for Chrissake! Endless weekends spent in the vast blue yonder of the Great Outdoors! Wouldn't have gone within a mile of the mad bastards if hadn't been on downers. Hadn't meant to do such a major dump on doorstep though. Had gone into pub in Caernarfon after getting off coach and asked hillbillies for spliff. Or whereabouts of. Christ, only a joint. Not effing coke, man.

Shouldn't 've, though. Not in such a one-horse dump. Shit didn't hit fan until Ginnybitch back at school after Christmas hols; called into Head's office. Said someone calling herself Ginnybitch's sister (he said Ginny, o' course) had been asking for drugs in a pub in Caernarfon and did she, Ginnybitch, know anything about it? In other words, did she have any involvement in drugs. Bad news, man. Smack (ha ha ha) in the gob for the holier-than-thou snotty little bitch. Hadn't meant to make such total fuck-up, though.

How fucking long do these airheads mean to hang around in this rump of Antarctica! No other fuckers around. Not even a rambler or two – and they're mad enough for it. Only bunch of loonies in entire universe and y.t. stuck with them! Even the frigging sun's beginning to chicken out for Chrissake. Red with rage – hurling bolts of blood-soaked turquoise, gold, aquamarine, asparagus, avocado, lapis lazuli, saffron, spinach – no beetroot, hadn't got as far as beetroot yet, ha ha ha. Acid head's dream, man. Real cool. Not doing much for frigging fir trees. Looking right pissed off. Glowering black, mile-long beetle brows hanging on to their bit of the horizon. Closing in on sulky, piney selves.

Forest suddenly like massive black hole, sucking and swallowing all the light out of the sky. Fucking scary, man! Knackered old sun, pissed off with bollocking the sky, leaving vacuumed vault to anaemic, nail-paring moon. Who the fuck needs acid, man? Could go with a joint, though. Long-haired pseud-dude living next door. Asked for roll-up. Hoping he'd deliver. No chance. Gave y.t. couple of ciggies. Did Mum's head in. How was y.t. to know she couldn't stand the sight of pseudo-dude and his missus? 'Specially the missus. Thought T. Toyboy fancied her – ha ha. Not when y.t.'s around, Mum. Only fanciable chick in the universe. You know that, Mum. Don't you? Can't blame you for feeling a tad unsure of self. Not looking good this Yuletide. Neither's y.t. Put on a helluva lot of flab. Phizog pasty and puffy. Puff pastry phizog ha ha ha. And full of zits.

Do ya think y.t. might have inherited zit gene, Mum? Didn't want to mention that. Didn't want to totally spoil your Christmas. Wouldn't be so cruel, ha ha ha. Not like arsehole P/C who asked you if it was true that you were an Avon lady. Didn't blame P/C 'cos you knew he'd overheard Big G telling it to some wanker. Showing off her bitingly original wit (so she thought). Only way she could get one over you. Through your Acne Rosea. Or Vulgaris. Whatever. Some pal, eh? Never mind best pal.

No dope. But plenty home-brewed rotgut. Didn't half deliver some shite, Mum. Got a neat buzz watching you swallow it all. And ask for more. Donno about T. Toyboy. Kept out of scene. That screwed you up nicely. Didn't know if it was 'cos he couldn't keep peepers off y.t. or 'cos he was pissed off with endless streams o' shite pouring outta gob. Gotta tad carried away. Gotta admit it. Went too far with the shit about the Art Exhibition. Rattled you straight off. Shame. You'd nicely swallowed everything about the dog. Even gave y.t. dog's lead and brush. Donno how managed to keep phizog from splitting. Should've left it there. Well-played sympathy card. Had you eating outta mitt. *Had* to go over the frigging top. You consider yourself to be a natural artist, says you. No need to go to Art School, to train, to learn techniques, such as perspective, says you. Yes. No. No. Yes, Yes, says shithead y.t. tongue tripping all over twat self. Should've buttoned lip there and then. Might have been OK. But carried on shooting gob off. Great Christmas nosh. Weird. What else? But ace. Gazpacho with home-made bread straight out of oven. Better than that macrobiotic shite you used to go in for on old *Mikro*. Christmas cake and pud that had been fermenting since previous Christmas an' a huge trifle that no one else seemed interested in. So y.t. ate the lot. And lashings of rotgut. Really thought it was all going to be OK. Even after gobbing off about Art. Then blew it. Nuked it. Cruising along. Beginning to chill. Few pockets of air turbulence – ha ha ha – all that rotgut! Nothing too heavy. Any irritation nicely lubricated by parsnip and willpower. Chilling good. Maybe that was it. Shouldn't 've let your guard down, Mum. Only needed a mo for y.t. to blow it. Blew it. Nuked it right out of the big blue yonder.

Said, casual-like, had been to Amsterdam and been turned away by his holiness and Ellen. Hundreds of years old Beddgelert forest might be, but you could sure teach it a thing or two about sucking all the light into a vacuum of darkness, about slaying the slavering, blood-red sun and allowing the thin, grey, slice of cold porridge moon to sidle in and take over the sky. Y.t. might have pressed the nuke button, but you finished the job by laying waste with a blast of murderous cold that killed off any remaining signs of life. Not shocked. Not even surprised. 'Cos you know that y.t. had stayed with Ellen and his holiness in Amsterdam after handing over Liana to Mr & Mrs Can't-Have-a-Kid-of-Our-Own. You knew 'cos he'd turned up and told you. 'Cos he wanted to palm y.t. on to you. No. What bothered you, what stripped all your wires, was the knowledge that you were second choice. Second best. Second rate. Didn't have the nerve to tell you that you weren't even that. Hadn't even made it as far as second anything. You were third. Third on the list. And if H.G. didn't hang out in the frigging Heelands, youdda been fourth. Y.t.'d gone straight to Big G's after getting off ferry. Hitched all the frigging way. Big G no longer at Twickers, and no forwarding address. Didn't have Uncle Gav's address or phone number, so did knee trembler in alley for dosh and hopped on coach headed for North Wales.

Bottom of heap, Mum. You were bottom of the heap.

Tried to salvage something of Christmas. Hadn't been so bad. Known a lot worse. Far better than could've hoped. Turn on tap. Blub for a bit. Couldn't stay there anyway, blub-blub-blub – couldn't take it – always wanting to fuck y.t. when Ellen not there – blub-blub-blub – sometimes even when she was in next room – blub-blub – wouldn't leave y.t. alone – blub-blub.

Why didn't you just say 'No', says you. You're a grown woman. You're not a child.

Christ, but you're a hard nut to crack on times, Mum.

Blub–blub – says we've got special relationship – blub-blub.

Didn't like what you said then. Didn't like it at all. Not one little bit. Wasn't first poxy time. You get these fucking bees in your fucking head and there's no stopping you. No fucking wonder you nearly drove Dad off his trolley. 'Specially as he only needed the slightest nudge, ha ha ha. But you – you go on and on and on. Y.t. didn't want to hear – don't want to hear – won't hear – won't listen – fuck off and shut your trap you mad jealous bitch – only reason you got rid of y.t. 'cos you knew T. Toyboy had a job keeping peepers off. D'you think y.t. an' Ginnybitch never ear'oled on you and him rowing in bed? All y.t. had to do when having to suffer boring fucking Scrabble or even more boring Pontoon or Brag, was to raise peepers, let them rest for a few mos on his hairy Taff phizog and you were set up for a bleeding week. That's the trouble with being such a jealous bitch, Mum. Could never accept that y.t. and his holiness had a special thingy on the go. Still have. Always have, still have and always will have.

Somehow, all ended up cool. Scared the shit out of the lot of yous by talking about hanging out for a few weeks – might even look for a job, ha ha ha! Ginnybitch's lip curled as though about to launch itself from the top of her gob and land y.t. one in peeper. Could teach her a thing or two. Probably don't need to. Told her more than enough already. Won't give out though. Bitch. Snotty little bitch. Bet she's had a few dicks shoved all the way up her prissy cunt. Good-looking bitch. More than good-looking. Bitch. Give his holiness detailed info when next see him.

Talked y.t. into going back to London. Didn't take much talking. Gave Big G's new address. Handed over mortgage dosh for fare and grub. Saw off on coach. Give T. Toyboy big smacker on hairy gob. Didn't like that did you, Mum? Bet you rowed about it for days. Should be grateful, not jealous. Only 'cos of y.t. playing silly buggers that you and the Taff got together in the first place. Like to think things would've worked out if only y.t., Mum and Ginnybitch. Know they wouldn't. Knew it then. Bored witless. Summer job in Carmarthen after saying ta-ta to Ice-pick Manor. In poxy rundown cafe. No chance of extra dosh. Had to catch bus there and back. Couldn't get out at night 'cos of no effing transport. Living in frigging clapped out old caravan you'd got for thirty nicker.

'It's ours, girls,' you kept warbling, 'it's something of our own – our own home.'

Divorce came through in the August. Decree Nisi or whatever. Irretrievable breakdown or whatever. Shacking up with the Taff by the September. Waiting for divorce to be finalised or would have had him park his bike sooner. No. That's not right. Didn't go out with him till middle of September. Divorce had already gone through. Didn't waste any fucking time Mum, didya? Could say that was why y.t. started going off rails. Yet again. Wouldn't be true. Started before Taff ever on scene. Like said, reason you and Taff got together was 'cos of y.t. arsing around. Not home on last bus one night. Waited. Then went to ask neighbour to run you to Carmarthen to look for y.t.

Taff there. Had already met him in Carmarthen car park. Couldn't start Mini. Taff came over, gave one of wheels bloody Welsh kick and way to go. Not a total stranger, then. Got his frigging Welsh oar in that night, didn't he? Drove round all pubs and clubs. Y.t. long gone. Met punter. Made a tenner (don't ask how). Thumbed lift home. There by time you an' Taff got back. Dished out heap o' shite. You knew. You knew it had started again. There'd been one or two wee warning signs, but you'd let them pass. Hoping they'd go no further. Stay happy being little warning signs. Shoulda known better, Mum. Taff had asked you for a date on the way home. And that was it. One frigging date an' he'd moved in. For good. Gotto admit was wrong about him. Big G an' y.t. like couple of Bastille babes, cackling and jeering and prodding fragile embryo of relationship. Big G at Taff cottage for most of summer hols. Tried like fuck to trample it to death. Hadn't reckoned on Welsh fucking grit. Welsh grit and Aberdeen frigging granite – what a combination!

Another major nail in coffin of mateyness with Big G. Lotta nails flying around. All banging down lid on coffin. In spite of later abject grovelling by Big G, best-palness lying groaning on floor, bloody and battered.

191

Wouldn't mind staying on for a bit. Sign on dole. Make a few contacts. Could put up with the Great Outdoors. On a temporary basis. Might do y.t. bit o' good. Digits all a-tingle. Could help Taff T. with the logging. Mum'd never allow that. Who don't you trust, Mum? Different from last time y.t. here. Lot done to house. Extension-kitchen-bathroom-stone exposed, cleaned and pointed. Taff's job, innit. Bleeding stonemason. Looks cool. Wood floors, tilled floors, wood panelling, big, open fireplace – gouged that out before poxy contract had been signed hadn't you, you mad bitch!

Mum likes a bit o' rough, especially a twenty-five year old bit o' rough, ha ha ha. Shouldn'ta told Big G such porkies. Just wanted sympathy vote. Said y.t.'s been chucked out. Penniless. Nowhere to go. Big G shoulda known better. Always ready to condemn. All Mum's fault. Everything. Changed tack later. Much, much later. Never told her about meeting Uncle Gav (got work phone no from Mum). Therefore, didn't tell her about him offering to put y.t. up for couple nights or find decent bed and brekky. Took dosh from silly old wanker, but found disco sort o' place, turned a few tricks, smoked a couple spliffs before heading for Big G's Islington pad in the wee small hours.

Just like old times. Big, warm, smelly, truffle-y G. No dope to be had but unlimited supplies of homebrewed rotgut. Not y.t.'s fault that Big G wrote arsehole letter. Didn't help that y.t. put own stoned effort in with it. Both had skinful at time of writing. Drooling all over y.t. My daughter that never was, bla bla bla. If didn't know better, would swear she was a big dyke. Said how shocked she was at poor, homeless little waif y.t. turning up in middle of winter night, freezing cold, starving hungry and boracic. (And y.t. built like a medium-sized brick shithouse at the time!) Gotta admit, y.t. egged the old twat on.

Mad as hell 'cos no answer to last couple letters. After all you said. Gave y.t. copy of books. Wrote in them. Keep in touch – 'we mustn't leave things so long' or whatever. Then never answered letter. Sent photos of y.t. an' Ricky an' Norton an' Dawg. Only the one letter. 'S all you could be arsed with.

Wouldn't speak to Big G for how many years, Mum? And all for zilch. A year, two years or whatever, and y.t. no longer part of Big G's scene. Shouldn't 've shut y.t. out. Y.t. dope head an' all that. Wrong. But shouldn't've locked door. Y.t. already freaked out. Locked door sent hurtling over edge. Should've understood,

Big G. All those far-out fucking ideas about being saviour of misunderstood bratskis. What happened to y.t. then? What happened to the daughter you never had and always wanted and saw every time you looked at y.t.? Loada fucking bullshit, Big G. Like everything else about big, frigging, bloated carcass. Fucking bullshit.

Bad enough doing dump and smearing all over walls. Shouldn'ta set fire to P/C's gear. Never put a match to anything before or since. Funny. His holiness had been into the firebug scene for a while. When he was fifteen or sixteen. Set fire to gorse bushes on heath and round school. Big blaze. Serious. Did it a few times. Never caught. Said he got his rocks off seeing everyone running around witless. Offered to help. Y.t. not like that. Just totally pissed off 'cos door locked.

Trapped. Trapped in stark, silent forest. Apoplectic sun done a bunk. Dead 'n gone. Feeble sliver of toenail moon flittering between dark feathers of gull-wing sky. Trapped in circle of darkness, stillness and bitter cold. Where the fuck's the Bedford? Glow-worm flicker of primus stove, scrummy pong of sizzling rice and lentil burgers; Ginnybitch wittering on about getting back in time for Bond movie on box. Mum wittering back that no way is she going to be governed by the bloody telly and if that's how things're going to be, then they'll have to get rid of it for once and for all.

Who was the one to give in and get a telly, Mum? Rented one at first, 'cos of Bartok's frigging Centenary. Videoed everything, then succumbed to lure of Elizabeth R. Still same old bickering. Cool though. Cosy, somehow. Like slipping into warm, old jacket. Where the fuck's Taff T. and his jerk-off chainsaw? Christ, how many frigging times did it break down on this one day! Got a brill load, though. Bedford chassis scraping along ground. Gotta drive real slow 'n careful. Singing on way home. Carols, natch. Taff a tone-deaf Taff. Unusual. For a Taff! Ha ha ha. Phizogs glowing like lanterns. Not T. Toyboy. Mush too hairy to glow. Him and Ginnybitch get on real well. Like he was her Dad. Even looked a bit like him. Bitch. Bastard.

Why all dark? And cold? And lonely? Terrible loneliness. Stillness, darkness and loneliness. Trying to move. Can't. Want to shove digits in gob. Must. Got to. Nothing in universe matters except

193

shoving digits in gob and suck-suck-sucking. Can't move arms. Trying – pulling. Something holding back. Fucking strait-jacket, man! Someone fumbling around mitts. Orgasmic or what? Can get digits up to gob! What the fuck's wrapped round juicy little fingers? Rough, stringy stuff. Covering mitts. Mitts. Mitts on y.t.'s mitts! Poor mad bitch had put mitts on y.t. to try an' stop finger-sucking. Must've tied handies to sides of cot for a few mos. Wouldn't do it for long. Not Mum. That's why bitch is blubbering. Wants to. Wants to more than anything. Can't. Wool not so bad once soggy. Nothing like naked digits o' course. Filling gob nicely, though. Driving Mum even more witless. Not nice sound. Must admit. Sort of wet, slurp-y, sponge-y guzzle. Steady on, Mum! Mitts being ripped off – arms being flip-flopped back an' forth . . . aaaaah. Digits back in rightful nesting place. Mum weeping. Why in same room as y.t.? Can't see a frigging thing. Must be one of homeless thingies. Had to live in boxroom of flat of some cook Dad worked with. Beat his pale, Irish wife until peepers looked like cartoon character's. Only there for a few weeks. Long enough. Bexhill. Still in Bexhill. Y.t. still a baby buddha. Stuff sheet in ear'oles why don't ya, Mum? Silly bitch. How can a wee thing like sucking keep you awake and make you blub–blub – all fucking night? Beats y.t.

Everything's white an' pongy an' swimmy. Can put up with the white an' the pongy, but for Chrissake leave out the swimmy! Is y.t. in hossy at last? Dudes come to rescue? Hossy pong an' hossy whiteness. Blurry bods an' phizogs swimming around in swim-miness. Close peepers for a few mos an' wait for world to stop so's y.t. can geroff.

Definitely in hossy, but another of Scottie's effing time warps.

Mum. Ginnybitch – tall an' skinny Ginnybitch with long, thick, tawny hair – tawny – tawny – what the fuck's with tawny all the time? Light-brown – mid-brown, for Chrissake! It's mid-brown! – an' Taff Toyboy. All looking totally pissed off.

In hossy. In Taffland. Living in Taffland; going to frigging school in Taffland; got rat arsed in Taffland. After school. Went to dude's pad with other dudes from school. Parents out. All but cleared out drinks cabinet. Drinks cabinet! Shade of Ercol Evie! Shagged by some of dudes. Others couldn't get it up. Even with helping handie. Scared shitless when y.t. passed out. Dragged outta house an' left on pavement. In snow. End of term party, ha ha ha. Just before Christmas. First Christmas of y.t., Ginnybitch, Mum an' T. Toyboy. Still in poxy caravan. Fucking mog pissed on all pressies under Christmas tree. Kitten. No. Young cat. Looked like frigging rabbit so called it Bunny.

Passing chick saw y.t. being dumped on pavement. Phoned 999.

Gotta get a bit of sympathy on the go. Mum's gob set in stone. Taff T. not even looking. Say something. Anything. Something that'll set the Aaaaaah juices flowing. And melt that fucking stone carving that's trying to look like Mum.

Coming closer to bed. Reach out y.t. Reach out an' try an' catch hold of arm. Set sob-factory into operation. (No probs there; feel like a dollop of mouldy old dog turd.)

'It's him – it's him,' (sob, sob) 'can't stop thinking – seeing – him,' (sob) 'every time eyes close – he's there,' (sob) 'big and black – long coat and black cap – standing. Standing and staring.'

Who? Who? Mum says. Coming even closer.

Sob–sob. His holiness. Sob–sob.

Loada bollocks, mutters T. Toyboy.

Who asked you, you Welsh fuck?

Mum's phizog darker. Definitely not melting. Not even softening.

Hasn't panned out, y.t. Hasn't panned.

Funny, that. 'Cos it's more or less the fucking truth, man.

Snow makes for sleep. Hear about dudes caught in drifts. Get out of cars and start hoofing it, get knackered, fall akip in snow. Never wake up. Don't know that they're freezing to fucking death, man. Not that much snow in forest. More of a heavy frost. Is this still the forest, Scottie? Don't feel cold when they pop their clogs. Just drift off. In a drift. Sounds cool – ha ha ha. Wonder if y.t.'s caught in a drift. No drifts in forest. No snow. Feels like a drift. Ice duvet. Wrapped in cold crystals. Can't keep peepers open. Wonder if y.t.'ll ever see Mum an' Ginnybitch ever again? Not all that bothered by Ginnybitch. Not true. Better looking than y.t. (Now. Not then, though. Not then.) Cleverer than y.t. Don't mind that. Not important. Loved more by Mum. Boo-hoo. More important. A lot. All that shit about different kinds of love. Did the bitch really believe it? Hated y.t. Couldn't stand sight or sound.

Told Big G that y.t. refused tit in hossy. Can't be true, man! Thought of y.t. saying no to something being shoved in gob! Tits like boulders. Had to have them strapped up. Agony. Baby y.t.

couldn't get hold of ginormous nipple. Nurse milked Mum's boulders twice a day, then fed y.t. on bottled goodies.

Sick-fuck nurse said she'd never seen such a messy birth. Mum'd had two enemas but still managed to produce a huge dump as well as eight and a half pounds of y.t. Started off well an' truly in the shit, didn't you, Mum? Wouldn't let you keep y.t. Two in the morning. Gave you a cuppa and sent you back to bed. Only had a short, wee cuddle of Little Prune. Whisked away. Wouldn't even give you painkillers for guts-ache. Myra Hindley lookalike said it was only a bit of the afterbirth anyway.

Feel a tad sad about the bitch. At times. Can't stop winding her up, though. Shouldn't make it so fucking easy, Mum. Doesn't matter now. Nothing matters. Thrown in lot with his holiness. Mum won't know. Maybe she does. She will. Big G knows. Big G knows 'cos y.t. wrote saying that his holiness had been sent down for ten years for pushing dope. Big G tried to get y.t. to make break. Let the bastard rot, she said. Fucking arsehole. Never forgave him for getting shot of Ricky. But y.t. couldn't desert poor old wanker. Ricky long gone. No fucker left. Too late to start over. Too much water. Too many bridges. What for, anyway? He'll only find y.t. Come an' fetch. Wherever run to. Wherever hid. His holiness would ferret out hidey hole. Special relationship, see? That's what it means. Meant for each other. Two against the rest of the fucking world. Can't have one without the other. That's what a special relationship's all about.

Noddle lurching backward like hammer being swung before the heavy, numbing thud as contact made with whatever surface. Repeated over and over. Jesus effing Christ – great, blinding flashes before and behind peepers. With each thud, a searing rod shoved up hooter and a lightening flash to follow. Only, y.t.'s noddle not the hammer. Mum's frigging arm the hammer and y.t.'s bonce the point of contact.

Where the fuck now, Jim? Y.t. dwarfing Mum, but bending like reed under storm of blows from both clenched fists and open palms. First one, then the other. Makes a change, s'pose. What in the name of fuck had y.t. done this time? Outside, whatever it is. Randy sun fucking everything in sight with its massive heat. Must be summertime. Siop Newydd. That's where it's at. September. Indian summer. Or is that if it's October? Wouldn't be so frigging hot, though. Moved here at end of August. Sure know how to pick scene from 'Come to Wales' brochure, Mum. Fucking breathtaking.

At wit's end when came across cottage. Sat in car at gate and bawled peepers out.

'If we don't get this we're finished – I can't go on any more.' And you meant it.

Moved up to North Wales sometime in June. Taff T. had got a job in Port Dinorwic and arranged with friendly farmer to park caravan for few weeks. Big council estate round corner. Kids' sole entertainment coming after school and chucking dollops of sheep shit at caravan. Only when the Saeson were in it, o' course. Usually when Taff T. at work. So bad had to go and fetch him. Shouted at them in Taff. Frightened shit outta little bastards. Only about eight or nine years old. All you needed, Mum. To round off the paranoia. Driving around knocking on doors asking for info re empty cottages. Found Siop Newydd just by driving aimlessly from village to village. Empty. Found owners by asking neighbours. Talked them into letting it. Said you needed peace and quiet to write. First time you ever used it – said it, to a stranger. Only 'cos you felt it would add weight. It did.

Fucking awesome scenery, as already said. Vast tracts of heather covered moor and mountain with old man Yr Wyddfa hisself only a few miles away and hugely visible form the big heap o' rock known as Y Graig directly behind the cottage. Sit at the top of Y Graig and on one side the entire Snowdon range was at tootsies; turn the other way and Criccieth, Porthmadog, the whole of the Lleyn Peninsula if a really clear day – Tremadog Bay, Harlech – it was like being in the middle of a fucking fairy-tale land. Y.t. spent a few hours up Y Graig. Never anyone there. Couldn't understand it. No ramblers or climbers or birdwatchers. Only sheep. And heather. And y.t. Mum went up a lot, too. Not with y.t. Not with Ginnybitch, either. Not so bad, then. Sometimes, felt coulda stayed there forever. Feeling of vastness – step off edge and in deep space, man – no, not deep; deep is black. Outta the earth's atmosphere, anyway – mystery, tranquillity, yet feeling of being cradled. Lying on top of crag, as though cupped, contained, held safely in limitless hugeness of arching sky – can see the earth's curve on horizon, for fuck's sake! – and sheltering, watchful gaze of Yr Wyddfa. Weird, or what, man?

Mogs. It was about mogs. Two of the bastards. Bruvs. Prune and Lychee. Sad, really. Prune blind as a bat. Peepers like mutant pearls. Total drop-outs. Taff T. brought them home. Conned by blonde with big tits. Sucker for big tits. Most blokes are. Funny, innit? Mum blew gasket. Thick snot result of ulcerated nasal tubes.

Y.t. told over and over not to leave gate open in case dildo Prune escaped. Daft mog had a habit of following at heels like mutt. Y.t. couldn't see any harm in letting him come for walkie with mutts. Wouldn't let anything happen to the basket case. It's not 'cos of the mog Mum, is it? It's 'cos y.t. will *not* do as told. Guess we all knew by then that zilch was going to change. Never saw Y Graig again. Must have been one of most awesome places in entire universe. Beautiful place; poisonous people. Literally. Poisoned favourite moggie, Gabriella, the small tortoiseshella. Just over a year old. Broke your frigging heart. Some sick fuck had got hold of her and dipped her – dipped, for Chrissake! into a bucket of oil with whatever shit killed her. Vet unable to identify poison. Oil was cooking oil. So's she'd lick it off and be deliverer of own death.

Poisoned other moggies too. Only English ones, though. Ones belonging to the English. Or what was perceived as The English. Newcomers. Didn't realise Gwynedd hotbed of Welsh Nationalism. Sons of Owen Glyndŵr an' all that. Mightn't 've been anything to do with them, o' course. Just a sick xenophobic fuck who hated moggies.

Y.t. only under spell of Yr Wyddfa and Y Graig for about six months. Left poxy school at Easter. Had to stay till then 'cos not sixteen till previous October. No O levels. Not even a GCSE. As it was then. Couldn't be arsed. No idea what wanted to do. Except get mitts on lotsa dosh p.d.q. Said wanted to work with gee-gees. Only 'cos couldn't think of anything else; could ride; and saying it brought a smile to your gob. Didn't want to please you. Don't get that idea. Just like pressing button. Always worked. Bought house in Nantlle. Different view, just as awesome, of Yr Wyddfa. And a big frigging lake right outside the back door. Only reason you could accept a mid-terrace. Lotsa space, space, space once outside four walls. Moved end of May. P/C came and helped. Christened beds – ha ha ha. Not fair. Not nice, either. Not nice to piss beds. Is it? Visited y.t. Give you that. You an' Ginnybitch. Had job grasping that y.t. wanted to come home for week's hol in October. 17th birthday an' all that, Mum. Gotta spend birthday with family, man. Got through. Somehow. Then y.t. announced coming home for Christmas. Couldn't handle it, could you? Asked H.G. to make room for y.t. in Granny's Heeland Home. What a heap o' effing shite that hol turned out! Bored witless, shitless or what? Shame, 'cos took a lot for you to ask favour of H.G. Not exactly favourite bitch after what happened during divorce. H.G. came down to lend hand, give moral support etc. Some frigging moral support, man! Trying to grab photos of Dad as you were ripping them to shreds. Could've tried sneaking one instead of doing it under your hooter. Typical H.G. Always sided with Dad. Blamed you for everything. Including divorce. Married too young, she said. Dad. Not you. You married him. Therefore, your fault.

Y.t. nearly put final nail in coffin of that little lot as well. Would it've mattered? Had to do *something* to liven up proceedings for Chrissake! Woulda gone completely hairless if not. Peepers lit on best-looking dude in pub. Not pub. No pubs in the Heelands. Hotels. Best-looking dude in hotel bar. Didn't find out till too far gone that tosser was engaged – ring an' all – to fluffy little local chick. Had wanker eating outta mitt within few mos. Could tell what he *really* wanted to eat . . . dragged it out all evening and into wee small hours. Couldn't take peepers off y.t. Mesmerised. One far gone dude. How was y.t. to know that fluffy chick would throw major epi and that her Ma and Pa would be knocking at H.G.'s door at three in the frigging morning? All tanked up to the mince pies o' course. Hogmanay. Any bleeding excuse. Shouldn'ta put poor ol' H.G. through such shit though. Even though deserved it. Fluffy chick threw ring at tosser. Floodsa tears. Y.t. played ace. Told about THE DREAM. Been so worried and depressed ha ha – had to talk to someone – dude really friendly and good listener. Told y.t. about his problems – felt a helluva lot better after. (Sure did, man. Ate pussy all night long for a measly tenner! Gave good head. Hope the fluffy chick'll appreciate it.) H.G. only too grateful to swallow shite y.t. ladling out.

It *was* true. What y.t. said on way back from station. In back of Bedford. She *did* say it. Don't care how much the old bag goes into denial.

Y.t. blubbering on about being misunderstood bla-bla-bla . . . H.G. said that you (that's you, Mum) had always neglected y.t. and that, if you hadn't, things might have been very different. Didn't realise that you'd take it into your noddle to write Elspeth saying that if H.G. had said these things, then you were through having anything whatsoever to do with her. Natch, Aunty stood up for H.G. and had to tell all about y.t.'s little escapade. Hairy few mos. Didn't believe what Elspeth said about H.G. didya?

Zilch you could do about it. H.G. never the same to y.t. after that. Blabbermouth. Couldn't be trusted. Never expected Mum to know what she'd said. Auld bitch. Burned boats, though.

Back in cradle. Gently rocking. Can't be; y.t. never had rocking cradle. How know? 'Cos Dad wouldn't 've had to make one for Ginnybitch. Kept everything else. Little, brown Tansad pram. Carry-cot on base. Cheap and cheerful, but Mum liked it. What she wanted. If not in cradle – what in? Must be ol' *Mikro*. Like big, comfy, cushioned swing-boat. No gibbering shelducks. Bastards. Curlew, though. Even more bastard. Turn innards to jelly. Not curlew. Deeper. Much deeper. Totally different, bitch. Still turning innards to jelly. Frigging cello, innit? Who the fuck's playing? Playing Bach. Bach's Cello suites. Must be Tortelier. One o' Mum's few favourites other than bleeding Bartok. Which suite? How the fuck does y.t. know?

Mum very private about music. Sad she never had a chance to learn to play whatever when bratski. Only dudes on similar wavelength, Rog and Big G. Never went to a concert with Big G. Funny. Went to Festival Hall with Wimbledon landlord's missus once. How the fuck had that come about, Mum? Musta said liked Bach. Or Tortelier. Played all the Cello Suites. Five encores. Mum up on tootsies clapping and shouting 'Encore, encore' as was most of the other dudes. O Christ. Not again. Said landlord's missus. Mum totally freaked out. Could hardly speak to the ignorant bitch on the way home. Could've understood – no, accepted it if Bartok. But Johann Sebastian! And the Cello Suites! And Tortelier! Experience of a fucking lifetime, man. Mum kept her gob well shut after that.

Y.t. walking along towpath. No, not walking. Drifting. Floating. Drifting/floating through heavy muslin layers of mist. River and banks hiding behind swathes of loosed bolts of the stuff. Small hanky sized piece o' rainbow flashing in front o' peepers. Perching on mooring rope. No more than metre away. Preening, fussing and fluttering; iridescent noddle held swiftly to one side for a mo as glittering little beady peepers fixed on y.t. Frigging chest as neon-orange as y.t.'s tangled-tangerine effort, ha ha ha!

What a long beak you've got – an' a wee, fat, scrummy-yummy bod. Could reach out an' give you a big smacker right in the middle of your tangerine tit. Flash-flash an' the little arsehole's gone. Turn noddle a tad an' can see old *Mikro*. Looking good babe! Sitting straight and proud in the wide bed Dad had dug out of the mud for her. Funny how she settled every time the tide went out. Give or take a few centimetres. Post-box red hull. Guess who? Better than Dad's choice. Thunder fucking cloud grey. Looks like a poxy painting in the rising mist. Every detail etched clear and bright. Like a Vermeer. Didn't do boats. Did he? Who Vermeer anyway?

Muslin being drawn off both land and river by Mad Max of rising sun. Pulling armfuls of it up to form a pale, fragile, fairy-cloth mist bow. Tide just beginning to come in. Surface of water glittering as though handfuls of diamonds've been scattered at random. Diamonds'd sink, wouldn't they? Sequins, then. Like handfuls of sequins. No. Too flash. Ain't a flash sort of glittering. An expensive sort of glittering. A diamond glittering kinda glittering. Leave off y.t., for Chrissake. What's with the poxy glittering thingy? Mist bow there only for a few seconds before the rest of the muslin swirled eerily and thinly. Higher and higher, until trees and riverbanks became visible.

Gorse and bramble woven with hundreds of small, lacy cobwebs shimmering with the pearls of early dew. What's with pearls, y.t.? Diamonds a few mos ago. Now pearls for Chrissake! Turning a tad precious, eh?

Air suddenly twanging with the clamour of bird calls. Not river birds. Lot of movement in hazel, willow and hawthorn. Tiny, plump, walnut-wren whizzing across path at knee level. Usual white-trash of the bird world – sparrows, starlings, thrushes – where all the frigging warblers, buntings an' long-tailed tits then?

Rub peepers for Chrissake – there's the frigging Tintawn wafting through the atmosphere like a poxy magic carpet! Dipping and soaring, twisting and arcing – flashing a richly creamy underside when edges sweeping up into wide, scooping curve. Rustic weave remaining intact until fluidly draping along water's edge to become instantly transmogrified into a flock of small, fat clockwork birds. Scurrying and rummaging in the watery ooze for whatever their bird brains thought of as a scrummy bit o' nosh.

Why so frigging cold, man? Rambo sun snatched all the muslin mist up, up, up into the wide, Wedgwood bowl to be washed and hung out, way outta sight, ready for next time Heavy Muslin Mist on Morning Schedule – ha ha ha. Reasons to be cheerful – one-two-three . . .

Shouldn't be so effing parky. Should be roasting on spit under Dragon-sun. All birdies gone. Tide too far in. Tintawn regrouped and magic-carpeted away. Water like blue glass. Blue mirror. Porcelain swan silently gliding through blue mirror accompanied by its one-dimensional doppelgänger mimicking its every move – every slight variation in the degree of arching and flexing of the gobsmackingly long and slender neck. How're they joined together, the Siamese swans? What happens to the in-the-water swan when the on-the-water one heaves itself out on to land? Does it lie, the in-the-water swan, unseen and waiting, under the blue mirror's shining face for the return of its twin? Or does it become disembodied, separated into individual atoms and molecules, like Jim an' Spock in the Transporter room – ha ha ha? Then when the earthly twin returns, do all the dispersed molecules fuse once again to form the flawless mirror-image? Or is the mirror-image the real swan? In a parallel universe it would be, wouldn't it? And the earthbound creature, so achingly elegant in the water, so embarrassingly awkward on the land, the unreal? The true mirror image? In a parallel universe, man. Only in a parallel universe.

> Far over the misty mountains cold
> To dungeons deep and caverns old
> We must away ere break of day
> To seek the pale enchanted gold.

Rising and falling, the voice was tremulous but strong and full of music. What a curlew might sound like if it opened its gob an' started talking instead of burbling like a frigging waterfall. Getting a tad carried away, y.t.? Twisting ribcage a mite, agreed – but curlew with human voice? Get real, for Chrissake!

> On silver necklaces they strung
> The flowery stars, on crowns they hung
> The dragon-fire, in twisted wire
> They meshed the light of moon and sun.

Shut your fucking gob Ginnybitch – shut it – shut it d'ya hear! Sick to fucking death of hearing the effing Hobbit – can never give it a frigging rest, can you – you stupid effing infant moron.

Christ – it's freezing – might as well be in a frigging morgue, man. Bod been hollowed out, warm innards scooped out and thrown to bastard shelducks, cavity packed with solid blocks of ice. So cold it's dissolving flesh from bone.

In the caravan. Mum's old, thirty-nicker caravan. Nantgaredig. Still parked in sodding field. No water. No juice. No lav. Indoor or outdoor. Only a whadyacallit – what the fuck is it called – bucket thingy you shit in then pour blue stuff in to dissolve the crap or something – definitely the crap, but either dissolve it or make it smell edible – an Elsan, for Chrissake. A frigging Elsan. Taff T. built a corrugated shed an' put an Elsan in it. Had to keep digging big holes at the far end of the field every coupla days an' bury four lotsa bladder an' bowel emptyings. Poor sod! Mum begged y.t. an' Ginnybitch to try an' do craps in school lavvies. Ginnybitch did, but y.t. hung on to dump just to listen to it increasing volume level of Elsan with every plop.

Small coke fire in caravan. So why feel as though in Antarctica, man? Ginnybitch doesn't look parky. Sitting at table with frigging Hobbit. Closing book, thank the Christ. Couldn't take much more of the puerile shite. Wee Christmas tree in corner. Small but perfectly formed, ha ha ha. Must be the year that braindead Bunny pissed on all the pressies. Didn't find out till started opening them. Dripping and reeking. Nothing spoiled though. Huge bastard trifle sitting on table. Mum really into trifles. Plate o' mince pies. Christmas cake. All home-made. How'd she manage to cook? Oh yeah – big gas cooker – part o' Taff T.'s dowry. Where is Mum an' Taff? Only y.t. an' Ginnybitch an' table o' goodies in caravan. Can't see y.t. As though Ginnybitch on her own. Sitting alone with The Hobbit. Opening the bloody thing again. Starting to read aloud. Don't. Don't Ginnybitch. For Chrissake don't.

> It cannot be seen, cannot be felt,
> Cannot be heard, cannot be smelt,
> It lies behind stars and under hills
> And empty holes it fills.
> It comes first and follows after
> Ends life, kills laughter.

Ginnybitch laughing. Lifting phizog up from book, looking straight at y.t. and laughing. Nice laughing. Happy laughing.

Christmas laughing. Bright, autumn-y coloured peepers, with a funny little dark dot at the top of one radiant green orb. Really radiant, man, like little hair-fine spokes webbing across from dark, central disc to almost fill all of peeper. Frigging lashes as long as y.t.'s – bitch! Gap between front teeth. Never noticed it before. Fucking hair *is* tawny. Thick, long and fucking tawny. Bitch, bitch, bitch. Going to be a real looker one day. Is now. Smiling up at y.t. Laughing and pointing at page of poxy Hobbit. Laughing. Laughing. Don't really hate you, Ginnybitch. Never really hated you. Wanted to get rid of you – get you the fuck out of it – but never hated you. Not really.

Ginnybitch must be laughing up at y.t. Y.t. must be laughing too. Where is y.t.? Must be there. Must be. Must be laughing – laughing with Ginnybitch. Remember the poppadums an' jam, Ginnybitch? Donno why Mum an' Taff T. were so broke. All there was to eat, one weekend. Poppadums an' jam. All of us sick as pigs after.

Didn't mean to make you steal the strawberries, Ginnybitch. From Miss Jones. Did at the time, o' course. Big buzz from seeing scared-shitless look on Mum's phizog. Scared you were going to go along same road as y.t. Been great if you had. Can't say didn't try. Too much of a poxy Mummy's brat.

> It cannot be seen, cannot be felt,
> Cannot be heard, cannot be smelt,
> It lies behind stars and under hills
> And empty holes it fills.
> It comes first and follows after
> Ends life, kills laughter.

Ginnybitch – Ginnybitch – y.t. knows the answer – knows the answer to Gollum's riddle! Y.t. remembers. Not difficult to remember. Only the one word.

Dark. That's all. Dark.

Prickling needles in skull. Creeping, prickling needles. As though brainbox being crocheted. Little skullcap being stitched into scalp. Noddle not being stitched, thank Christ. Dirty great rollers being shoved in hair. Big G spiking poxy pins through flesh of scalp into brain goo. Take it easy, Big G for Chrissake! No need to dig frigging holes in skull! Big G – Big G – Big – Big – Big – Big G! Built not like a brick shithouse but a bloody great Gingerbread house. All dark and sweet and warm. Skin like softened Demerara. Large, moist, muscatel raisins for peepers. Big, chocolatey, truffley bod. Y.t. like a stick o' friggin' rock in a too-small summer dress with skinny pins like pair o' knitting needles Rog'd be prepared to die for – ha ha ha! Big G laughing – frighten the shit outta the local fauna with those great flashing gnashers. Y.t.'s phizog all glowy – Christ but they looked alike. How was it possible that y.t. wasn't Big G's bratski?

The sudden pain sizzling pokers – chainsaws – knives and swords. Why only y.t. an' Big G? Where were the rest of the bratskis? Why this pain, man? This awful, burning, tearing pain?

Sitting in the sunshine of a garden. No. Not a garden. A small yard. Don't recognise it straight off. Twickers or Taffland? Dirty. Old carrier bags spewing their innards out on the filthy, patchily and anciently concrete, floor. A large, new, cedarwood/redwood/ stained deal(?) shed took up almost a quarter of the 'garden' area. Twickers. Could remember Old man of Oz getting posh shed to use as a studio. What a frigging joke. Poxy sun doing an Arnie again. Blasting heat down from meticulously ironed blue sky. Careful! Gingerbread Gina might melt in awesome furnace – muscat peepers oozing down syrup softness of buttery flesh.

Don't just sit there y.t. – stupid, mindless grin plastered all over stupid, mindless gob. Say something – anything – before Arnie gets to Gingerbread Gina. Anything – tell her anything – sorry would be good – sorry would do – just say sorry – anything – anything – just say something – please – please – please . . . Guts being kneaded into doughy gunge of loss and emptiness. Despair gnawing and muzzling at pathetic, silent screams for forgiveness. And all y.t. could do was sit in the summer sun and grin like a retard.

TELL HER SORRY? FOR CHRISSAKE TELL HER SORRY!

Would sorry do? Would sorry be enough? How could sorry make up for smearing shite all over walls of P/C's flat? How could sorry wipe out memory of piling gear in middle of floor and friggin' well setting fire to it? Whole poxy block o' flats coulda gone up. Sorry not enough. Door slammed on y.t. forever. Big G had begged his holiness to leave y.t. alone. After Ellen kicked him out. Told him all about y.t.'s New Life. Ricky and Dawg and Norton. Gave him address, though. Too rat-arsed not to give address. Too rat-arsed even to remember if she'd let him fuck her. So what's an address?

Christ, they looked like Ma and Daughter! Like Ma and Daughter out of a friggin' advert. Advert for olive oil or sun-dried tomatoes or whatever. And y.t. had turned it all into a heap o' shite. Helluva bad scene, man.

A huge, dark Groke of sadness shuffled hopelessly in and around, settling nice and comfy. Knowing it had found the right nesting place. Like the final stages of cancer.

Phizog all stiff. Frozen. Rictus splitting gob. Stretching from ear'ole to ear'ole. Peepers hurting. Haven't stopped, man. Phizog frozen and stiff but peepers burning coals. Pissholes in the snow. Faceache. Funny word. Never thought to use it. Bit o' light – just a glimmer – in the middle of the black forest thank Christ. Everything on the poxy move – swaying and spinning – light swinging back and fore, back and fore. In wheelhouse. In fucking wheelhouse of fucking *Mikrokosmos*. Oil lamp swinging from deckhead. High tide. Must be rough. Old girl surging as though on open sea. Whizzing to ends of mooring ropes and back again. Over and over. Wind howling. Can't see too good. Shapes in wheelhouse. Fuzzy. Someone standing in entrance to saloon. At top of steps. Skinny. Wearing dressing gown. Y.t.'s dressing gown. Y.t. then. Must be y.t. Phizog trying to outdo Bacon's Bishop in yawning maw stakes.

No. No–no–no–no–no. Won't listen. Won't look. Shut peepers – shut them tight – keep peepers shut tight – as tight as poss. Gob still hideous maw. Peepers flooding – can't – can't – can't say no – special – special – special relationship – can't say no – can't – can't . . . Voice from depths of hell. Harsh, hollow, empty, but filled with poison; dripping; slavering with every filth dredged from pits of hell. Naked and leering, wagged semi-tumescent dick in mock wank. Contempt spits in peepers.

'What special relationship you pathetic deluded idiot – the same special relationship he had with his little sister? That sort of special relationship? Where he paid her to lie with her legs spread so's he could jerk off whilst staring up her crotch? That's the sort of special relationship you mean is it? Where his little sister blackmailed him so's he had to steal money from his stepfather's pockets to pay her off? That's the sort of thing is it – the sort of special relationship you mean? Well, eat your heart out, you sad twat. How can he have a special relationship with you when he already had it with her? Long before you ever arrived on the scene. Second best, that's what you are, you stupid, pathetic cow.'

Shut the fuck up – shut up – you sick bitch – you're mad – you're sick – you've always been unhinged – everyone's always said so – who the fuck's going to listen – take any notice you sick mad bitch – you don't know the first thing about y.t. and his holiness – it *is* a special relationship – it is it is it is – you could never understand – there's only ever been y.t. – it was different with his sister – they were only kids messing about – it was a kid's thing – playing kid's games – not a proper – not a proper – proper . . .

'Proper what? Proper what, you bloody freak? Proper love affair? Is that what you mean? Is it? Is it? What did he tell you, then? What did he tell you? Did he tell you that he was obsessed with her? With his little sister? That he was seventeen years old when they stopped playing their little games? That they only stopped because he was caught in mid-wank staring up his sister's cunt in the middle of the night? That they'd have been shagging instead of just going through the motions – oh yes, they did that too – if she hadn't recently started her period and been wised up enough to realise that she could become pregnant? Wised up enough to know that just going through the motions was dangerous enough. That if they hadn't been found out it would still be going on? The special relationship – the real, one and only special relationship? You poor cow. You poor, sad cow. Don't you realise that you're only a substitute for the real thing?

'YOU REMIND HIM OF HIS SISTER. EVERY TIME HE FUCKED YOU, HE THOUGHT, HE IMAGINED, THAT HE WAS FUCKING HER. *HER*, HER – NOT YOU!'

Every word a sharp thing scything flesh to the bone.

'You look like her, you bloody fool. You're a clone – a doppelgänger – a mirror image. It's not you – it's not because it's you – it never has been. It's because you look like her.'

Bring back the darkness. Please God. The blackness, the darkness. The snowdrift. The duvet of ice. Snow and ice like a warm, fluffy muffler wrapped round noddle and neck and stuffed in ear'oles. Blocking out hated noise of sick, jealous bitch's hammer-drill rant. What the fuck does she know about any of it?

In the wheelhouse. Sunshine arcing and nuking through windows. Going through pockets. Finding letter.

Bla-bla-bla – am very sorry, can only send a fiver. Otherwise she'll suspect. Your mother will suspect. You know what she's like. Love you and miss you. Longing to see you.

'You stupid, stupid fool. Don't you understand? Can't you understand? He's paying you like he paid his little sister. Paying you to keep your idiot mouth shut. He's living it all over again. Reliving the best time of his sick, pathetic loser's life. Only this time it's not pretend fucking, is it? He really is getting to shove his dick up, isn't he? Isn't he? Isn't he?'

It's not true – none of it's true – you're mad with jealousy – you always have been – it's *you* that's second best – you, not y.t. and you can't frigging handle it – you never could . . .

Blubbering in Morris on way back to school. That's when it started. You wouldn't talk to y.t. Wouldn't sit in same room. Wouldn't stay in boat. All 'cos of y.t. telling Ma Jenkins about the Dream. Extra visits to Doc Medhill. Extra visits and chatties from old Hump. Sick to fucking death of whole bunch of useless wankers. Wanted good time. Why too much to ask? Fags, booze an' fucking. Sex an' drugs an' Rock 'n Roll, yeah! Not necessarily in that order, ha ha ha.

Stopped Morris. Put arm round shoulders. Gave a bit of a squeeze. Seemed cool at first. Then tried to kiss y.t. Said you wanted y.t. dead. Said only wanted to be friendly, but stuck tongue in gob. Y.t. not happy. But went along. Tried to find angle, after. Easy. Had him by the balls. Meant to be. You never came on visits any more. Bit of a turn-on. Had him on his knees. Begging. One thing you'd sure as fuck sussed. Nothing but a wanker. Happy as a pig in shit just beating meat. Did it for the dosh, after. Good, regular source of readies. Not long though, before he began getting out o' order. Be when he knew you were serious about leaving. When you started going out looking for places. Thought he'd never see y.t. again. That was it. That's what he was afraid of.

What the fuck do you know? You know fuck all about it. He wanted to look after y.t. Only started as a kiss an' a cuddle. Nothing wrong with that, is there? Told y.t. all about his childhood; how unhappy he'd been – no friends, bruv getting all the attention – cleverer, talented – no expense spared . . .

'Did he tell you how he use to jerk off dogs as one of his hobbies? Did he? Did he tell how he let himself be fucked by his

208

'friends', did he? How he loved lying face down and having his arsehole stretched – did he tell you that? Did he? Did he? Did he?'

SHUT UP – SHUT UP – SHUT THE FUCK UP – NONE OF IT'S TRUE? NONE OF IT? YOU'LL SAY ANY FUCKING THING – ANY FUCKING SHIT – JUST TO TRY AND SPOIL IT ALL – CAN'T STAND THE THOUGHT OF Y.T. AND HIS HOLINESS –

'Did he tell you it had been going on since she was four years old? Little games with his little sister in a little tent in the garden.

'Did he tell you that someone tried to top herself because she didn't know how to handle it? Took three-quarters of a bottle of aspirins mashed in and washed down with milk before lying on a cold floor in an empty building and waiting to die? Waiting, waiting, waiting. It was the milk that saved her. Did he tell you that he was stealing money from his stepfather when she was – that someone – in hospital? Buying her flowers and chocolates with money stolen from one of her workmates? She'd gone as far away as possible, that someone. Back to where she was hated and unwanted. Anything to get away from him. But he'd followed her. He'd followed her to Scotland. His need was greater. The need to prove that he was normal. That he would do normal things, like his brother. Normal things like getting married. Don't you see? He needed to do it to prove to his mother that he was normal. Do you know why that pathetic someone wanted so much to die? Of course you don't. How could you? Well, I'll tell you. Because she'd read somewhere that, due to the time it takes for the light from earth to reach distant planets, any intelligent life on any planet in any galaxy, would be seeing events on earth as they happened x number of years before. So, if certain planets were situated in certain positions and had intelligent life forms capable of seeing what was happening on Earth, a permanently running film of your father, my husband, jerking off whilst staring up his sister's hole would be going on, at every stage, through all eternity, till the end of time. It's been happening ever since he first did it; it's happening now; it'll be happening everywhere in the Universe, forever.'

YOU'LL SAY ANY SHIT – ANY SHIT THAT COMES INTO YOUR SICK HEAD – 'COS YOU CAN'T STAND THAT THERE'S ONLY THE TWO OF US LEFT. JUST THE TWO OF US. Y.T. AND HIS HOLINESS.

Wheelhouse a space capsule. Whirling through space. Black all around. No stars. No anything. Nothingness. Black nothingness. Silent, dark figure in shadows. Light reflecting feebly from windows. Where's the light coming from? Dark, hunched, silent, unmoving figure. The Nazgul! Ginnybitch – Ginnybitch – come an' see – come an' help – come an' help y.t. – it's the fucking Nazgul! For real, man! Cloaked in the darkness. No. The darkness itself. The essence of darkness and blackness in the shape of the Nazgul. Fear bubbling an' gurgling. Filling throat with bile. Trickling into ear'oles. Burning. Sizzling. Steam rising. Black, cloaked noddle slowly lifting. Don't look y.t. – whatever frigging happens, don't look! Must never look at the Nazgul – Ginnybitch – Ginnybitch – what happens if anyone looks – if anyone looks at the Nazgul, they're a goner, aren't they? That's what it says – that's what Gandalf warned – didn't he? Was it him? Why the fuck didn't y.t. listen? No one must ever look at the Nazgul. Unless they want to die. Don't look y.t. – for Chrissake – don't look!

Saved by Mum – saved by Mum's warble echoing and trilling through the stratosphere like acid drops.

'And I suppose you put in the bit about what Daddy did to you in Scotland for a laugh as well did you?'

Slow, loud and sonorous, as though heard through immeasurable fathoms of bottomless oceans and/or thousands of light years of endless space, y.t.'s answer boomed through the space capsule and bounced off the murky glass of the windows.

Oh that. It wasn't in Scotland it happened. It was here. On the boat.

Please, please, O God of the Twilight Zone – Ruler of the Great Unknown. Please go away. Please, please have mercy. Please go away and leave y.t. alone. Don't do this. Please don't.

It was a dream. It was The Dream. A dream can't be broken. And it can't be turned into anything but a dream. Please don't. Please, please don't.

Peepers so huge that phizog seemed nothing but one huge, gleaming orb. Gob hanging open. Waiting. Suspended in space capsule. In space. Waiting. Waiting for something to happen; some natural disaster, an earthquake, an exploding jet overhead with a cargo of bombs. They were meant for plebs, weren't they? The bombs. It was always plebs they hit and slaughtered and maimed. What matter a few over here instead of over there. Wherever over there was at the moment. Just want us all to die. To be exterminated. Terminated. No. Exterminated.

Wind blowing a frigging gale. Phizog tight and tingly. Can almost feel sparks leaping off. Rough underfoot. Tootsies feel unsure of landing. Walking backwards for Chrissake! Y.t. walking backwards. Mum and Dad about ten metres ahead of y.t. Not walking backwards. Not together. Dad big, black and broody. Long, black coat. Black leathery sort of cap on bonce. Not cool. Not cool. Dworky. Big space between them. Ginnybitch running around with braindead mutts. On Dunwich frigging beach. Freezing tits off. Come to say ta-ta to favourite place, Mum? Godforsaken hole. Loved it so much you rented a poxy run-down cottage to get away to scribble your frigging efforts.

Look at the phizog of Mistress of the Universe! Peepers like effing lasers, man! Zap-Zap, big Daddy-o on his knees. Begging, man. Begging. Just a look, Lou-Lou – promise not to touch – just a look Lou-Lou – please – please – Daddy'll do anything – anything . . .

Go on then. Have a gander, Dad. Who's stopping you. Oh – you mean a proper gander! In the flesh, so to speak. Cost you, Dad. Arm an' a bleeding leg.

Y.t. smirking Mistress of Universe smirk.

Come on then, Dad. Come an' get it. On yer knees first, though. You bastard. Then start begging. If you want it, then you gotta beg for it, ha ha ha. An' then start paying for it.

Mum looking a tad in the doldrums. Bit of a long phizog on the bitch. Doesn't know how to handle the Great Dawning that's descended on her all of a sudden. Descended earlier on in the old girl when y.t. dropped goolie about coming to spend summer hols with Dad on *Mikro*. Poor sad bitch welded to deck with shock.

'You c-can't do that – after what he tried – what he did – what he said – it's impossible – how can you even think such a thought – how can you possible *want* to stay with him . . .'

No probs, y.t. had warbled. Can easily handle him and anything he might try on. Not that he's likely to. Into major guilt scene – only wants to please y.t. Make up for everything. Shock waves increased by y.t.'s response. Overdid the icing. Phizog as grey and muddy as the pockmarked silt of the river bed. You'd started to gob off about Dad, hadn't you? About his fucking nerve, maybe. Or his tipping over the edge into psycho-land. You *did* say that.

At some point. But then you saw flash of pissed-offness dart across y.t.'s phizog. Fleeting though it was, it was enough. You knew. You knew that y.t. and Dad were in cahoots. And you were afraid. Sweet Jesus, were you afraid! Aura of shimmering, pulsating naked fear. Had a wee glimpse of what was going on in the abyss. Started talking about Doc Medhill and the Social Services. Knew it was a dead duck.

Always gotta put the effing mockers on, haven't you Mum? And to think that none of the shit would have hit the fan if y.t. hadn't let slip in laundrette about being sorry to hear that Mummy and Daddy had decided to separate. Why the fuck had y.t. done it, man? Said it? So fucking quick off the mark, weren't you? Would you have been if you'd realised what lovely, juicy can o' worms you'd just prised the lid off? You'd made him promise not to say anything to y.t. or Ginnybitch about separation until you'd found a place. Thought at first he was just trying to do a bit o' creeping – get y.t. on his side. Once the frigging Inquisition had started y.t. sussed it was high time to think about swapping sides again. No way was y.t. gonna hang out with a loser, man. So spilled all – well, about half to three-quarters – beans.

Never cottoned on the real nature of it. Could see by peepers. Started off being cool. Oh. He mentioned that, did he?

Yes, y.t. had trilled. He told me today on the way home from school. He said that not to worry, some of school hols could be spent on *Mikro*, with him.

'And what did you say to that, Laura?' so quiet and steady, your voice.

Didn't mind – said it was up to you, really. Looking dead shifty, y.t. For Chrissake, keep peepers flat an' smooth. Don't let the bitch get under skin. Christ, ol' Ice-pick could take a few lessons from you with these effing steel-tipped blue stilettos you're stabbing y.t. with!

Still cool, you said that you were very sorry but you could never allow such a thing and surely y.t. understood why?

Y.t. unable to prevent flicker of pissed-offness flitting across phizog and sniffer-bitch supremo that you are of identifying and kebabbing the nanosecond nuance, you speared and spit-roasted the innuendo imperceptibly (to any normal dude) lurking round the edges of the otherwise healthy phrase.

Long time since you had to resort to a bit o' arm-squeezing, Mum? Haven't lost the knack. Give you that. Like riding a horse, s'pose. In your case. 'Cos you can't ride a bike. Ha ha ha.

212

'What else did your father say to you, Laura?'

Seem chilled. But can feel tremors running through your gripping arm.

N-n-nothing, Mummy, n-nothing.

Bones moving under steel fingers. Phizog pushed up close to y.t.'s. Sparks flashing off peepers and gnashers, for Chrissake! Hissing–hissing. Right in y.t.'s shell-like.

'What else did he say, damn you – what else?'

Thought your fingers had gone right through to the poxy bone. Cried out from the pain. Nothing, Mummy. He just put his arm round shoulders and tried to get a kiss. But y.t. wouldn't let him, Mummy. Honest. It's God's honest truth – swear it is, Mummy.

Started blubbering. Well, what the fuck else. The bitch knows now, so y.t.'s gotta play the old sympathy card. Get on her side, for Chrissake. Dad's the loser now. Miserable bitch in beige nylon overall glancing across all the time. Mum couldn't give a fuck who's looking. Few other plebs fidgeting around the dryers. In own universe. Tinny little sounds emerging now and then from tinny little people. Ginnybitch's noddle into probs of unwrapping socks from determined embrace of towels etc. Y.t.'s phizog reflected in dryer door. Sheer fucking terror, man. Who's got the worst palsy? Can't speak properly 'cos of terrible shaking-gnashers, pins, noddle – the lot, man. Slowly and disjointedly now, the words laboured out of her gob.

'What you've just described. Did it happen today. On the way home from school?'

If you're gonna be a winner – be a winner. Sorry Dad. You're on your own.

'Yes. But it's not the first time it happened.'

Can't stop shaking, man. Can't stop.

Mum's asking, in a dead voice, about the other occasions. Y.t. can't keep peepers still. Got the fucking palsy as well. Peeper palsy, for Chrissake!

'Well, the first time was when Daddy visited on his own at half-term. You didn't come 'cos things were so bad between us. Knew you were angry. Dreaded coming home; had a few tears. So Daddy stopped the Morris in a lay-by and put his arms round shoulders. He started off being nice and friendly. But then he asked if he could have a kiss and he wasn't being nice and friendly any more.'

This must be what it's like to have Parkinson's Disease. Both heads, Mum's and y.t.'s spinning slowly off shoulders and carouselling a few feet above bloodless necks. Noise in skull like noddle-sized fairground. Mum's peepers like dead person's. Y.t.'s like black insects on acid. Flat dead words coming out of dead woman's dead gob.

'What did you do, Laura?'

Y.t. gibbering. 'Said No, Mummy, and pushed him away because it was wrong. But he said he only wanted to give a bit of comfort and there was nothing wrong with a kiss and a cuddle.'

Chilling out some. Palsy almost gone. Noddle back in place on shoulders. Dead woman still dead. Yet speaks again.

'Was that all?'

Y.t. on a roll now. 'On that occasion, yes. But it happened again on the way back to school. He talked a lot about his childhood. He also said that he'd always felt a sexual attraction, even way back at the beginning and wanted to have a meaningful relationship. He said you felt only hate and loathing and wanted y.t. dead.'

'Have you had sexual intercourse with your father?'

For Chrissake – why won't effing peepers stay still? Shake noddle, y.t. – put some frigging effort into it and maybe bitch won't notice return of palsy to peepers. Seems cool. Vigorous denial by the way of noddle-shaking and look of outrage and disbelief seems to have done trick. Thank Christ – Ginnybitch finishing folding up washing and coming across. Really thought things might have panned out. Gotta hand it to you, Mum – you were one helluva cool chick. Especially as you thought Dad had gone seriously off his trolley. Sent y.t. an' Ginnybitch off to get sweeties and told him a heap o' shite about being worried 'cos y.t. tripping in Fantasyland. Have to make an emergency app. to see Doc Medhill first thing Monday morning as y.t. obviously disturbed. Wily wanker didn't believe a word of it. Asked you what y.t. had said and how acted when said it. Never skated on such thin ice in all of your natural born, did you Mum?

When y.t. and Ginnybitch came back to car with sweeties, the thing inside him that was about to break loose at any mo, was grinning and peeper-popping like Marty Feldman on a good day. Must say, didn't think he'd fall apart at the seams quite so easily. Like a lovesick third-former when back at *Mikro*, y.t. giggling in galley making beans on toast. Even when in deep shock, still able to organise things to appear normal, Mum. Dad unable to take mince pies off y.t.

'Got enough beans Lou-Lou – here, have some of Daddy's. Pass Lou-Lou the salt and pepper, Ginny. Got enough toast – would you like Daddy to make you another piece?'

Should have seen your phizog, Mum. Looked about to throw up. And no fucking wonder. His cover blown, all he could do was retreat down to the saloon on the pretext of being whacked out and needing a coupla hours kip.

That's when you found the letter. He'd asked y.t. for it back that morning in case anyone at school came across it. Running close to the wind. Living on the edge, ha ha ha. All that shit about not being able to send more than a fiver. When y.t. knew he was making a frigging bomb at the pallet packing. Apart from all his sleazy sidelines. That's when you twigged that he was reliving the business with his sister. Y.t. didn't take it all in at the time. Couldn't give a fuck, to tell unvarnished. Too much else zooming around in noddle. Working out survival strategy, man.

Almost went over top at Dunwich. Shouldn't 've been such a prick-teaser. Awesome feeling. Almost coming with wave after wave of sheer power. Him crawling like a low-life grateful for any mouldy old cunt hair that might get stuck in his gnashers.

And you – you unable to say or do a thing that might threaten the nail varnish thin veneer of normality that you'd managed, Christ knew how, to lacquer over everything. For sake of Ginnybitch, s'pose. Mainly. Though if he'd flipped, he might have done a Waco. After you rang Big G, he went out and got drunk. Ginnybitch in bed. Hardly knew anything amiss. Used to all the awful scenes between y.t. an' Mum, s'pose.

Sat very still. Just staring at you. Said how interesting it was watching someone watching him and his every move. Said he knew you were shit scared of him. Deserve a medal for handling that one, Mum. Really thought he was about to go nuclear. Y.t. scarpered off to beddy-byes.

Had to go through with phoning Doc Medhill for sake of appearances. Had to keep him believing you thought y.t. was going schizoid or whatever and needed help. Appointment made for eleven that morning. Couldn't face going all the way back to *Mikro*. Called in to see GP. Nice enough as Docs go. Walkover as far as y.t. Wished to Christ we hadn't. Nearly threw a wobbly when told about Dad. Prob'ly 'cos he'd made such a cock-up. Always looked on Mr FitzHugh as being a stable partner in the marriage – gabble – gabble – always so good-humoured and easy-going . . . Then he turned to y.t. and launched into benevolent-uncle friendly chat. Poor Mum, keeping peepers turned away from y.t. whilst having to listen to shite about how natural it was for fathers to find their daughters sexually attractive, but that most fathers were in possession of invisible line which they knew, instinctively, that they must never cross. Unfortunately, Mr FitzHugh did not appear to have such a line. Or, if he did, he chose to ignore all the moral and cultural barriers . . . bla bla bla . . .

He asked Mum if she wanted to have the fuzz sent over to the boat – he could authorise such an action. But it would be with the likelihood of Mr FitzHugh turning extremely violent. However, if Mrs FitzHugh felt that it was necessary, he would be more than willing to do so. Mum said she just wanted to get herself and the children away as soon as possible. She told him about Daddy wanting to drive them to Big G's. Not a very happy Doc but he agreed that what she was doing was the right thing. Keeping everything as normal seeming as poss. By far the best course of action. If she felt she was capable of carrying it off. Thanks Mum. For not wising him up to the less than pure involvement of y.t. Didn't ask for y.t. to be examined. No point. Knew Dunc had been in there long before Dad. Don't know why the fuck we bothered with Doc Medhill. Oh yeah – keeping up appearances. Didn't have to actually go, surely? S'pose you needed to talk to someone about all that had happened. Doc Medhill had known all there was to know whereas poor Doc GP hadn't even known about The Dream.

After hearing basics of recent events, Doc M saw y.t. alone. Bit late, don't ya think? Second time in over three years of weekly sessions at Institute of Family Psychiatry. Good going Doc! Didn't give an inch to the old bat. What the fuck had she ever done for y.t.? Saw Mum again after, and said that there was definitely a degree of collusion between Dad and y.t., but she was unable to determine how much as Laura was being totally uncooperative – ha ha ha – and refused to admit to such a consideration, though it was more than apparent from her demeanour that there was a lot to be uncovered. Poor old bat clearly gobsmacked by speed and nature of events. All she kept repeating, after original little burst of spiel, was that 'therapy had been going well, hadn't it? Mr FitzHugh had given the impression of responding very well, but, probably because of Mrs FitzHugh's decision to leave the family home . . .'

Glaringly pissed off with all this half-baked analytical shite, Mum demanded to know what the Doc thought was going on in y.t.'s noddle. Why had she behaved and responded to her father in such a way? Especially after her reaction to his advances of four years ago. All the poor, useless wanker of a Doc could do was shake her beige noddle and keep repeating, like an addled parrot, how sorry she was that things had turned out so badly.

Waiting, suspended, in the space capsule of wheelhouse. Waiting for an earthquake. For a bomb to fall. To be exterminated. Wiped out.

Then, through the awful stillness, Dad's voice.

'I told you it was all a fantasy. Or else she just wants to cause trouble between you and me. I see no point in carrying on any further with this ludicrous conversation and I suggest you go back to bed, Laura, and forget all about these silly, dangerous fantasies. You're nothing but an attention-seeking troublemaker – can't you see how much you're upsetting your mother? Go to bed – go on – go to bed with your lies and your fantasies.'

Time hanging motionless about their noddles. In the spinning space capsule. Mum, in that horrible, quiet voice, ignoring Dad and asking y.t. to tell her exactly what had happened. And when.

A bad scene. The worst scene ever. Y.t. wants out of here. Make it go away, for Chrissake make it go away. No. It ain't gonna go. Y.t. starting to open gob. Look out y.t. – peepers about to explode like rotten, soft-boiled eggs! Voice cracking and quavering, but still cool. Tells Mum it happened in the saloon one morning when Daddy had gone to bed.

How long ago? Mum says. It's a long time since we slept in the saloon . . .

Why can't you clever-dick Twilight Zone-y fuckers pull your digits out and move on to another time warp? Twisted bastards getting your rocks off on all this sicko stuff! Leave it alone why can't you – what the fuck's the point of dragging it all out. It's a frigging long-dead corpse, for Chrissake! Long dead. Long dead an' gone. Excepting it's not frigging gone. It's right here. In front of y.t.'s peepers. Y.t. watching y.t. squirm like a worm with embarrassment. And hurt. Y.t. listening to y.t.'s voice cracking under weight of three years of fear and shame. Says can't remember exactly when it was, but before y.t. went to Suffering Boredom. Don't know where Mum and Ginnybitch were. Y.t. tidying cabin. Mum prob'ly taken Dookie for walkies.

Dad's harsh croak. 'I don't know why you're wasting your time listening to such drivel.'

Mum ignoring him. Continuing to gaze at y.t. as though a creature that had spontaneously generated before her peepers. A creature from another universe, speaking a strange and dreadful language that, somehow, she understood.

'What exactly happened, Laura? Take your time. There's no need to hurry.'

How can you be so cool, Mum? So chilled? Y.t. wanting earth to split asunder and swallow the lot of them. Phizog crimson, squirming as though desperate for a piss. Saying that Daddy had called y.t. over to bed settee in saloon where he was supposed to be kipping. Asked if wanted to play a little game with him. A game that usually only grown-ups played.

'For Christ's sake, Maggie – how much more of this rubbish do you intend listening to? Well, you can listen for as long as you like as you obviously get some weird kind of thrill out of listening to a pack of lies and fantasies, but I've had enough. I'm going to bed.'

Pulling himself up from chair, with an abrupt jerkiness. Mush dark and sort of twisted. Especially round the gob.

'I think you'd better stay where you are, Desmond. If Laura *is* telling lies, then it's your responsibility as much as mine to find out why.'

The chill factor is awesome, man. Awesome. Turning back to y.t. Saying to continue. Y.t. writhing as though being bitten all over by ants.

'Do you have to know, Mummy?' Christ, y.t. – what a frigging mess your phizog's in. Looking like a dude about to fire the last chamber in Russian Roulette, Mum nods briefly. Y.t. opens floodgate. What the fuck.

Blubbering and bawling, says had forgotten about it for most of the time since it happened. Sometimes unsure if it *had* happened – if it had been a dream or not. Casting desperate peepers in direction of Dad. Slumped in chair. Staring at floor. Taking no notice of y.t.

'What else did he say, Laura?' Gentle. Ever so gentle. Made y.t. bawl and blubber all the more. Feels as though choking, strangling on The Dream. As it emerges into atmosphere. Takes over all oxygen in the space capsule. Y.t. giving birth for Chrissake! – giving birth through gob – huge, grotesque thing struggling out after three years of gestation, shrieking and

218

clamouring with the thrill of freedom unthought of. Gob stretching; becoming as large as phizog – taking over phizog – phizog no longer phizog but a vast hole. A vast cakehole. As dream metamorphoses into reality. No going back, y.t. Once it's out, it can never go back in again!

The words seemed to explode with a sharp, staccato force that seemed capable of puncturing the space capsule thereby ensuring they'd all expire slowly in a vacuum. Please God – let it happen – please. Y.t.'ll believe – believe anything – anything if it'll stop now.

'He pulled my knickers down and touched my privates.' Now the capsule must surely explode. Shouting – y.t. shouting. Shouting in the middle of horrible great shuddering gulps. Why not? Let them know – these sick-fuck Twilight Zone-y bastards – Dr Who – Jim and Scottie – let the whole fucking universe know – the entire crew of *The Enterprise*! Are you well pleased, you bunch of frigging perverts? Are you happy now – got your rocks off now it's been dragged outta y.t.?

Choking, y.t. choking. Fucking tears flooding down phizog, mixing with thick trails of snot and channelling way into Bacon's Bishop's gob.

'Started to cry, Mummy. And asked him to stop. Then he did. And he said not to say anything to you about what happened as he could go to prison for a very long time. Then he said that he would explain everything when Lou-Lou was sixteen.'

Weeping, weeping. Never has there been such weeping.

'She's mad. You do realise that, don't you? Stark, raving mad. Why would I need to do such an unspeakably vile act? When I can have any number of women I want? My God, I would never have believed this of you, Laura. What lengths are you prepared to go to? You want to break up Mummy and Daddy's marriage, is that it? Words fail me, except to say that I'm bitterly disappointed and ashamed of you as a daughter. What kind of daughter are you, anyway? Well? To tell such terrible, evil lies . . .'

'It's not lies – it's not lies – you know it's not lies!'

Bubbling through the placenta of tears and snot. Phizog ugly as a phizog could ever be. Remoulded yellowy, dirty rubber. Covered in The Dream's placental slime.

'How could you have forgotten? How could you?'

Huge valve opening inside y.t. Innards dissolving, welling up and spilling over. Burning liquid surging through bowels, stomach, lungs and gullet and up into throat. Melting, bubbling, burning. Bowels melting and coming up through oesophagus. Terrible stench. Coming through gob, out of ear'oles and peepers. Running down phizog. Molten lava running down from peepers. Meeting up with molten lava spurting up from bowels, through gob and spilling all over lower phizog and neck.

Arm round shoulders. Squeezing gently. Mum's voice all soft and trembly.

'There's no need to say any more, Laura. Just go on down to bed now. I'll bring you a hot drink in a few minutes. I don't expect you'll get much sleep, but try. We can have a long talk together in the morning. Just you and I. What would you like to drink?'

And y.t. blew it. Less than two weeks later, y.t. nuked it out of the earth's atmosphere. By being caught with a frigging ciggie and telling Ma Jenkins it was 'cos of what Daddy'd done. All the nightmares (made up, o' course) an' all. 'Cos of what Daddy'd done. Worked a fucking treat. Never gave the fucking thingy a fucking thought. Other than getting out of hole. Lost them. Mum and Dad. Lost them both. No. Had never found Mum. Until that night. For a few days after. Then lost her forever. Never found her ever again. Never came anywhere near. Lost Dad that day in the saloon. Dads don't put their huge brown calloused mitts right down inside navy-blue school knickers to knead and finger hairless pubes. Lost the Dad who'd made the wooden, kidney-shaped dressing table one Christmas and said that Santa's elves had to work overtime to finish it especially for Lou-Lou. The Dad who, one summer, had made a papier-mâché ladybird shell in a wire frame and exquisitely painted, for Lou-Lou to wear in the school fancy dress competition. Wimbledon that was. Y.t.'s fault. All y.t.'s fault.

Y.t. standing on open plan stairs in pink thingy. Mum on telephone. Shrieking.

'You mad bastard – I'm not coming back and I never want to set eyes on you again as long as I live. I've started divorce proceedings so you would be well advised not to try and contact either me or the children again – do you hear – you fucking pervert bastard! Nothing needs to be explained,' (screaming). 'Nothing – nothing – nothing! Laura explained it all – everything – all of it – you're nothing but a bastard child molester – do you hear? Pervert bastard child molester!'

You told Big G that he'd had the unbelievable nerve to ring to ask if you were coming home for your birthday as he had a few nice surprises ready. Then he said he'd pop down and give you the pressies at Gina's. Some really nice surprises that you'd really like. After you told him that divorce proceedings were on the go, he'd suggested you wait until things calmed down and then talk matters over as there was a great deal needing to be explained. After you'd screamed that he was nothing but a bastard child molester, he had replied, 'Yes. You're probably right.'

Then you made y.t. tell that he had wanted to be jerked off. You made y.t. tell. Need never have known but for that insatiable blind worm of questioning, lurking and trawling the depths without rest, tiny light attached to snout to enable it to search out most inaccessible corners where Truth might be desperately trying to find concealment.

For a few days, if that, y.t. thought that a bit of Mum, at least, might be found at Taff cottage. Might have been possible if Earth had stopped revolving, sun gone on blink and stars pulled down shutter. But Mum not really Mum then. Only half alive. So all lost. Dad never Dad again. Never mind Daddy. His holiness. Only his holiness. Don't know why that moniker. Spiritual shit didn't start till y.t. went to Amsterdam after handing Liane over to Mr & Mrs Infertile. Y.t.'s baby. Y.t.'s little girl. Wonder if she'll ever try and find out who her real Mum is? Hope to Christ not. Please, God, no. Don't let that happen. If there is a God in the Universe, please, please don't let y.t.'s baby find out. If she finds y.t. then she'll find his holiness. He'll be well away then. Second, no third, fucking childhood. With the accent on fucking, man. He'll think it's all his birthdays rolled into one ginormous, dream-come-true pressie. Imagine the sick thrill of fucking your granddaughter as well as your daughter! Christ – if only there was some way y.t. could warn her – warn her baby! Pray, y.t., pray – pray – pray that she'll get to Mum first. If she ever starts looking for y.t. Which she might. Or mightn't.

You told y.t. that his holiness only saw y.t. as a mirror image of Debbie. Was that what you saw too? Another little Debbie? You told Big G all about it. And it's in one of your poxy books. How you'd never heard of the word 'incest'. How you thought Dad was in love with her. How you'd asked him, if she wasn't his sister, would he have wanted to marry her. He set you off. By using the word 'obsession'. You couldn't get it, could you Mum? It was a commodity. Debbie had it. Y.t. had it. Y.t. knows now.

'Spect y.t.'s always known. Dunno. Don't fucking matter any more, do it? He wanted it. You thought it was love. With Debbie anyway. You thought he was madly in love with his sister. All throughout your pathetic marriage that's what you truly believed. Every time he fucked you, you couldn't stop yourself from being tormented by the thought that he was pretending that Debbie's cunt was receiving his thick cock. You were never to escape from that hideous maze. Round and round you went. Like a blind hamster on a wheel, with the nightmare thought stuck on a rung a few centimetres from your reach. Meeting it; turning and running; trying to hide; then digging it up again to have another quick decko. Did you see y.t. as another little sister for Dad? The looks were there. The orange-grove, light choccy skin, black hair etc. Too late now ever to find out. Too late for anything. Except to have a good, long kip. No fucker's going to stop y.t. from having a kip, man. Deserve it after all this poxy time-hopping shite. Knackered ain't the word. Mates'll be round any mo. Didn't want to disturb y.t. Respecting privacy. Like decent mates. Wake up in morning between nice, clean sheets in nice, clean hossy. Just stay cool, babe. Tha's all.

Throat closing up a tad sharpish. No. Something closing it. Filling it up. Something big. Something solid. Gagging – retching – try an' get rid of fucking monster. Hurting roof of gob and stabbing back of throat. Hurting one pig-sicking heap o' shit, man! Can't swallow – can't breathe – can take smidgen of breath in, but can't let any out 'cos of hard, prodding thing. Gob seriously hurting, man. Splitting, for Chrissake. Lips wrenching apart. Thick, hard, pulsating thing thrusting and jabbing. Can't take breath. Can't get breath. Take it out for Chrissake – whatever the fuck it is – take it out of y.t.'s gob! Choking – choking – can't see properly – peepers all foggy . . . Looks like sprog sitting on floor. Liane? Liane – is that you baby? Liane – Liane – come to Mummy, come to Mummy – Liane, Liane!

Fat baby. Fat, little buddha baby. Wearing buttercup-yellow summery – shift thingy. One of Mum's *Creative Dressmaking* efforts – ha ha ha. It's y.t. for Chrissake. Not looking at all chuffed. Bit of a gurn on the go. Fat little git! About eighteen months old. Must be Sea Road flat. Y.t.'s second summer.

So tired, Jim. Don't need any more warp factors shit. Just want to go to kip.

Gob all pulled down and lower lip sticking out. Peepers like frightened Thumper's. Giant Dad standing in front of baby buddha. Naked Dad, except for funny, T-shirt-y effort. Swinging what looks like swimming trunks in the one mitt whilst holding short, fat club in the other. Short, fat club with fat strawberry stuck on end. Well past sell-by date strawberry. All browny pink and oozy. Bending over and bringing it close to baby buddha's gurning wee gob. No Daddy – no – for Chrissake have mercy – you can't shove a bloody great thing like that into the baby buddha's wee gob. Y.t.'s wee gob!

Being lifted up from the floor. Big gorilla paw under each small armpit. Daddy's only playing, after all! How could y.t. have thought . . . peepers beginning to give up ghost – so fucking knackered, man . . . thought for a mo . . . looked almost as though . . .

Flames shooting up through roof of gob into centre of brain. Shooting down throat, meeting river of lava on way up. Each stab a zillion volts. Fireworks shooting into nasal cavities, up into peepers and Catherine-wheeling out through every orifice and pore. Tongue wrenched out by force of thrusting club and shoved straight down throat, blocking oesophagus for once and for all. Thick flap of dried-up leather making seal across Mr Epiglottis. Gob filling up with hot slime. A paste, a glue to ensure permanency of seal across tonsils. Horrible, guttural gurgling. Drain blocked. Y.t.'s drain well an' truly blocked. Please don't Daddy. Please don't. Heaving, bucking, y.t.'s little, buddha-bod concertina-ing like a rag doll. Pinioned. Impaled. His holiness – Daddy – Dad skewering y.t. on the end of his big, brown dick. Darkness. Blackness. Daddy – Daddy – don't worry Daddy. Lou-Lou won't tell. Won't tell anyone. Won't tell Mummy. Especially Mummy. Promise – promise – promise. Hot, rancid slime spilling out from nose and gob. Hard, stabbing thrusts eased. Turning into long, slow strokes. Slime oozing out of peepers an' ear'oles. Shutting out last bit of light.

EPILOGUE

Gaggle of voices outside the bedroom door. Much in the way of jostling and mock arguing. A lot of 'you go's and 'no, you go's, before a large, dishevelled woman pushed open the door, shouting as she did so, 'Blojo – are you in there, you lazy heap o' shite?' before shambling into the room followed by the noisy, straggling bunch of misfits that shared the rest of the squat.

Giro day had arrived. But not for Laura.

ABOUT HONNO

Honno Welsh Women's Press was set up in 1986 by a group of women who felt strongly that women in Wales needed wider opportunities to see their writing in print and to become involved in the publishing process. Our aim is to publish books by, and for, women from Wales, and our brief encompasses fiction, poetry, children's books, autobiographical writing and reprints of classic titles in English and Welsh.

Honno is registered as a community co-operative and so far we have raised capital by selling shares at £5 a time to over 350 interested women all over the world. Any profit we make goes towards the cost of future publications. We hope that many more women will be able to help us in this way. Shareholders' liability is limited to the amount invested, and each shareholder, regardless of the number of shares held, will have her say in the company and a vote at the AGM. To buy shares or to receive further information about forthcoming publications, please write to:

Honno, 'Ailsa Craig', Heol y Cawl, Dinas Powys,
Bro Morgannwg CF64 4AH.